Hell hath no Ambition

Ashuan Lust 2

Janna Ruth

First published in New Zealand in 2024

www.janna-ruth.com

ISBN-13: 978-1-0670001-1-0

also available in ebook: 978-1-0670001-0-3

ASHUAN LUST BOOK 2

HELL HATH NO AMBITION

JANNA RUTH

A note about sensitive topics

There is a lot of magic and fantastical creatures in this series, but the teenagers at the heart of the story are just that: teenagers. As such, they deal with a number of very real issues alongside their magical ones.

If you don't like spoilers and you're cool with everything, skip this note and start the book. If you want to be prepared, read on. I'm writing this because reading should be fun, not a nasty surprise.

While this series started out as YA fantasy, all the main characters are now eighteen or older, and over the legal drinking age in Germany. As this trilogy is about the Archdemon of Lust, there will be various sexual encounters, although there will be no explicit or overall graphic scenes.

This series deals a lot with demons, Hell, and the seven deadly sins. Demons have no morals to speak of and engage in incestuous relationships, most of which are only implied. If the idea of this makes you uncomfortable, this isn't the book for you.

In this book in particular there are a number of potentially triggering events woven into the plot. There is a lift malfunction in Part 1, magical experimentation on small animals in Part 2, and domestic violence in Part 5, plus mentions of burnout, financial stress, and family conflict throughout the book.

There is also an attempted murder, which is cloaked as a suicide attempt. It's mentioned and there's a brief scene in Part 4 (Lucille 3), but nothing too graphic. All goes well.

As usual, hunting monsters may be fun, but it is also dangerous. People get hurt, sometimes even killed.

The characters live in a dangerous world, but it's also a beautiful one. For every dark place there is light and humour. And, of course, magic. Lots and lots of magic.

Enjoy it!

Love, Janna

Part 1
Storms & Regrets

Balthasar

It wasn't easy to find a deserted spot in the Residence of Lust. The sprawling caves that surrounded the Council of Seven allowed for many nooks and crannies, but in Melaney's realm, most of them saw constant use. Not that the demons needed to hide when they satisfied their urges. One was just as likely to stumble upon a widespread orgy as they were to come across a pair—or group—of clandestine lovers.

The one place that remained largely untouched was the nursery at the back of the residence. It wasn't that anyone cared about separating the young from what happened at the residence. It was just that it was so far away from the action no one bothered to come here just to have sex.

There hadn't been a child born to Lust in almost nineteen years, so the nursery was covered in a thick layer of dust. Balthasar could still remember what it had looked like before it'd been abandoned. The floor had been carpeted, making it one of the warmer places in the residence. Toys had been scattered across the floor; magical baubles and strength tests, plus the occasional booby trap Caspar had smuggled in.

Balthasar smiled. It had been amusing to speculate how much his little brother could get away with before Melaney found out and flayed him. He'd never learnt, his obsession with Melchior's human blood blinding him. A fact Balthasar had no qualms about making use of.

Pieces were scattered across a forgotten game board, another testament to Caspar's temper. Balthasar picked up the Hell Spider, his favourite, and allowed himself to reminisce about the hours he'd spent defeating his brother in countless ways. He'd always allowed Caspar a few victories to make him feel like he'd finally gained the upper hand, not realising how the spider's web grew tighter and tighter until defeat was inevitable.

He glanced sideways at an overturned cradle, its frame broken in another of Caspar's infamous rages. Melchior had been the last occupant: a squalling, red-faced baby, sometimes blond, sometimes black-haired, with tiny wings. He'd cried for hours while Melaney had enjoyed her many suitors.

Caspar had been annoyed, but Balthasar hadn't paid him any notice. Not until Chay had appeared and finally taken pity on the boy. Balthasar had pretended to be absorbed in his game, but he'd watched as Chay had picked up the baby, using a cloth so as not to touch his skin. But Melchior had freed his arm when he'd finally stopped crying and reached for the only person who'd shown him some care. Balthasar remembered the shock in Chay's eyes when he'd seen what Melchior's future held.

For the next twenty years, Balthasar hadn't paid much attention to his youngest brother. He'd been a child, after all, but the boy had grown much faster than the demons around him. At ten, he'd already killed a demon who'd thought they could get rid of Melaney's half-human bastard. By the time he was twelve, he'd become well acquainted with his mother's sin. Six years later, however, he'd made the inexplicable decision to turn his back on Hescaryn and explore his human side. Chay's influence, no doubt.

And now Balthasar knew why. Melchior was the bearer of the Sword of Amain, the legendary sword of the gods, the sword that broke the world. That in itself wouldn't have been of interest—the Sword of Amain had turned up countless times throughout history—but Chay's interest was. And the other five were.

Balthasar had known about the Prophecy of the Six since Chay had told him nearly a hundred-and-fifty years ago. He'd done his own research since then and felt he had a fairly good understanding of what it involved. The souls of the Twelve Heroes had been reborn countless times since the shattering of the Old World. Three times in Balthasar's lifetime alone, only once in Chay's.

According to the half-demon's research, the last reincarnation had seen six of the souls in one place. St. Alban, a small village in Ashuan. The remarkable thing wasn't just the cluster of souls, but that they'd all died within hours of each other. The other six must've died around the same time. And now they were all reborn, in another small Ashuan town. If Chay was to be believed—and Balthasar had long since learnt to heed his words—the end of all worlds was at hand.

It was a disturbing thought for a demon who'd already lived through a whole millennium. Chay was convinced that no demon would survive the battle with Draken if the dark sorcerer won, although he hadn't told Balthasar why their race was doomed since humans didn't seem to be affected the same way. Still, he believed him, and that would mean entrusting his future to Melchior of all people. His puny, half-human, emotion-ridden youngest brother.

Balthasar shook his head and shuddered. As he saw it, there were two possible paths. He could stand back and trust Chay knew what he was doing, throw his support behind him— and Melchior—and hope the little one didn't screw up when he faced the most powerful mage who had ever existed. Or Balthasar could end him now, give the wheel of prophecy another spin, and hope that the next bearer would be more qualified to carry the fate of their race on their shoulders.

Hollow footsteps sounded behind Balthasar. He let go of the spider, wondering if he was already caught in Chay's web or if it was still him who controlled the threads.

Caspar entered the room, looking disgruntled as usual. His face was scratched and his fair hair was a mess. Amused, Balthasar called him on it. "What happened to you?"

"A stormy encounter," Caspar growled.

"Ah, Shenny." Shenny, or rather Shenecra, was a Stormbride demon, a third-class demon who was as much wind as she was flesh. "She seems to be attacking you a lot these days." Both Caspar and Shenecra served in the Black Guard, with the latter eager to take the reins.

Caspar snorted. "You know how tempestuous she is." He looked around, as if he'd only just now realised where he was. His eyes fell on the cradle he'd destroyed in his rage. "Why are we meeting here?"

Balthasar turned away from the table and took a step towards Caspar. "I thought this place would be suitable. It's secluded and safe. We won't be disturbed."

"And if we are, they'll wish they hadn't."

Balthasar forced a weary smile. "The fearless leader of the Black Guard has spoken. Are you sure Shenny won't be replacing you soon?" Sometimes he wondered how Caspar had managed to hold onto his position for almost four hundred years. He must be doing something right if Volac was keeping him around.

"If she's after my position, she can tear herself to pieces."

"She seems convinced she can tear *you* to pieces."

"All girls can dream, right?" Caspar snorted dismissively. "Volac would never choose a third-level demon over me."

"The Archdemon of Wrath wouldn't care one bit if Shenny managed to kill you."

"But she won't." Caspar looked around once more, not finding anything that pleased him. "Why are we talking about Shenny at all? I thought you had a plan on how to get my hands on that cowardly half-human hiding in Ashuan."

Balthasar still thought that banishing Caspar from the human world had been a stroke of genius. Of course it wasn't Melchior who'd thought of it, but the witch he was obsessed with, Samantha, who carried the souls of Dianthos and Gwydion. The flower-loving, gentle Dianthos was negligible in Balthasar's eyes, but Gwydion had become the God of Magic after his death, and had been the one to put the whole Circle of Magic together in the first place. Obviously, both his affinity for magic and his sharp mind had been passed on to the human girl. In a few years, when she'd outgrown her human sensibilities, she might be a force to be reckoned with. But not now.

He sighed as he looked at the one who was definitely *not* a force to be reckoned with. "Your slowness sucks the fun out of any plan. Why did you have to be the son of a mindless brute?" While Balthasar had been born to Greed and Lust, Caspar had far too much Wrath in his blood.

"Get to the point!" Caspar's patience was already wearing thin. He showed a remarkable amount of restraint by his own standards as he smoothed his hair and looked around the room, instead of going for Balthasar's throat. "How can I kill him if I can't enter Ashuan?"

Balthasar could think of at least a dozen different ways, but none of them were as fun as the plan he'd concocted. "In general, it would be a bad idea to go straight after Melchior. Melaney is..." He thought of the right word to describe his mother's relationship with her youngest son. Obsessed came to mind. Passionate, as so often. Finally he settled on, "...aggressive when it comes to her little darling. Whoever touches a hair on his head won't take another breath. Remember the day you tried to drown him in a sylver stream?"

A dreamy expression spread over Caspar's face. "Oh, yes. He was only four or so, no strength in his arms, but the kicking... Melaney had to pull me away from him." The expression turned sour. "And then she nearly beat me to death."

"What a lovely story," Balthasar said sarcastically. He'd never developed a taste for *unnecessary* violence. Especially not against something as pathetically weak as a child.

Caspar shot at him, "You're the one babbling on here. Get on with it. I still have a bone to pick with Shenny."

"You don't get it, do you? Shenny *and* Melchior. You could catch two cave dwellers with one shot."

"How?" Caspar looked constipated as he tried really hard to understand what Balthasar was hinting at.

It took too long. Balthasar rolled his eyes. "By setting Shenny onto Melchior's trail. With any luck, they'll destroy each other. At the very least, you'll get rid of one of them. If it's Melchior, Melaney won't suspect you and will tear Shenny to pieces instead. Either way, you win."

Caspar's eyes lit up as he finally grasped the idea. "That's brilliant!"

"I know."

It took Caspar almost half a minute to find a flaw in the plan. "Wait! You're helping me... How did Shenny get on your bad side?"

Balthasar grinned. "She still hasn't managed to get rid of you for me."

He jumped straight into his own chambers as Caspar roared and threw energy at him, chuckling at his brother's indignation. So predictable. That was why he didn't bother to get rid of Caspar himself. It would be too easy.

Now, Melchior... he was fun at least.

Fabian

It was a blustery November day when Fabian, Rachel, Samantha, Lucille, and Matt made their way to the town library. Lucille tried desperately to hold her skirt in place, while Samantha clutched a pile of papers to her chest. Just then, another gust of wind blew through them, ripping the papers from Samantha's grasp. Fabian watched in horror as the sheets tumbled in the wind.

No one else was braving the weather, so Matt took the liberty of using his space-jumping abilities to catch each piece before handing them back to Samantha. She looked a little flustered as she mumbled her thanks, almost losing them again in the next gust.

"Please tell me this storm is cursed," Fabian muttered as he braced himself against the wind.

Lucille looked at him and chuckled. "Are you begging for more magic in your life?"

"Come on!" Fabian groaned. "Storms like this aren't normal. Not in Greenvalley."

"Climate change?" Rachel suggested.

"We're here," Samantha announced with relief.

Matt added, "And Jan made it too."

Somehow, they'd reached the library. Jan was waiting just behind the glass door and opened it for them as they approached. "Terrible weather, isn't it?"

As soon as they stepped inside, Fabian sighed with relief. The pressure of the wind fell away instantly and his ears popped. He hadn't realised how loud it had been outside. Once they'd found a table, however, Fabian noticed it wasn't much warmer inside.

"Why is it so freaking cold in here?" he asked as he sat down.

Matt pointed at a sign. "Heating doesn't work."

"Awesome. I've always wanted to freeze to death in a room full of books."

"I bet Lucille could make us a nice little fire," Jan said with a grin.

Lucille scowled at them both. "I'm definitely not going to do that." She shook her head at their silliness, but then her usual smile returned. "We're here today because we have to work on the yearbook."

"And study for exams," Samantha added.

Both things were new to Fabian. He protested, "I'm not on the book committee." It was just like Samantha to sign up for something and then force him to commit to it.

"I'm not even at school," Jan claimed.

Lucille huffed. "Didn't you complain last week that we didn't see enough of each other and you felt left out?"

Jan looked guilty as charged. "Sure, but that doesn't mean I want to study for exams I don't have to take."

Meanwhile, Samantha handed out her pile of papers. "The committee has been working on this profile. The usual stuff: who you are, what you like, what you want to be..."

"To make it more exciting, we're asking everyone to research their family history," Lucille added, her eyes gleaming.

"Excuse me?" Fabian had barely glanced at the profile sheet.

Lucille smiled at him. "We thought that instead of reading the same old self-praising drivel, it would be more exciting to learn about our classmates' history. Like a bunch of micro-biographies. They'll be worth a lot when one of us becomes famous," she joked, then looked at Matt. "Like Archdemon, for example."

Not in the least amused, Matt just raised an eyebrow.

"We also wanted the yearbook to be a little more mythical than usual. Ancient traditions, history, magic..." Samantha explained.

"Has Cheryl heard about this?" Rachel asked.

It was a legitimate concern. The Queen Bee wasn't exactly known for her tolerance of magic. Fabian was convinced she didn't need any more ammunition against Samantha.

But his best friend just shrugged her shoulders. "It's her choice. Either she participates or we leave her out of the yearbook."

"She won't miss a chance to put herself in the limelight," Lucille said, then huffed. "You're absolutely right, though. If she's got a problem with that, tough luck."

Fabian lowered his head and began to read the profile sheet. In his opinion, the last thing Samantha needed right now was to bring the wrath of the Elite Clique upon herself, but clearly, the girls had already had that discussion and chosen a more confrontational path.

The profile asked for all the usual data one would expect, making it look almost normal, but here and there it was sprinkled with magic. If you could have one magical ability, what would it be? Which animal would be your familiar? Vampire or werewolf?

He was about to ask if they were asking what he wanted to be or what he'd rather confront, when he noticed the deadline. "By the end of the month? That's barely two weeks."

"We want to have this part done by Christmas, before everyone disappears or gets bogged down with exams," Samantha explained.

"And why do *I* have to do this?" Jan asked.

"To keep you busy," Lucille joked. "You don't have to do it. You could use the time to write your application for the first responder training—"

Jan snatched the paper out of her hands. "I'll take one."

"I'm sure you'll get in," Lucille said, before looking around. She was beginning to notice the lacklustre atmosphere around the table. "Come on, guys. This is fun!"

Fabian had better ideas of what would be fun, but lately Lucille had been doing everything in her power to avoid hanging out with him in private. With a sigh, he took out a pen and started on the easy stuff.

"This family history," Matt said carefully, "does it have to be true? Like, no one will believe me."

Samantha shrugged. "Worst case, they'll think you're taking the piss out of the assignment." But then she smiled. "It would fit in nicely with our theme, though."

Oddly reassured, Matt started working on the family history section immediately.

"Alright," Samantha announced. "While you do that, I'll start studying."

"Didn't we just finish this round of exams?" Fabian asked, looking up again.

"Yes, but there's only half a year left until our finals."

He groaned. "Sometimes I wonder why I'm friends with you."

"So I can kick your butt when time runs out."

They all laughed while Fabian turned red as a tomato. Apologetically, Samantha brushed his shoulder before disappearing between the shelves. It wasn't long before she was replaced by their classmate Robert.

"Hey guys. Fancy seeing you here."

Suddenly everyone was very busy with their profiles. Only Rachel mumbled a quiet "hi".

Unfortunately, filling out the profile wasn't as easy as it should have been. Fabian complained, "What should I write about my family? My father works at the garage and my mother runs a shop. Do you want me to write an essay about my chickens?"

"Only if you tell everyone how they emigrated to Hell," Lucille joked, gifting him a rare smile.

"Hey, the Magic Circle is cool," Jan protested. "It's *my* parents who are total bores."

"I know what I'm going to write," Robert announced happily. "When I was five, I had a really bad nightmare. I dreamt I was the son of a dark sorcerer. My parents told me I threw this week-long tantrum because I truly believed that they'd lied to me and weren't actually my parents, and that my real father would come and take me away. It got so bad they had to get me a therapist".

They all looked at him now. Jan's lips quirked. "I always knew you weren't right in the head."

Lucille promptly kicked him under the table. "Not funny."

Meanwhile, Matt joked to Fabian, "See, even Robert has a more interesting story than you."

When Samantha returned with a pile of books, Robert took a step back and waved, as usual not offended at all. "See you later, then."

Fabian immediately forgot about him and whined to Samantha, "Couldn't you have thought of something else? I don't know what to write."

"Why don't you *ask* your parents?" Lucille said sharply.

Rachel nodded eagerly. "Yes, your parents generally talk to you."

Samantha cocked her head at Rachel's comment. "I thought you were getting on better with your mum?"

"Better, but... oh, well, it's not like we're suddenly best friends."

"I could write about being the youngest of over two hundred siblings and how my brothers are trying to kill me," Matt said with a grin that belied the gravity of the situation.

He'd finally crossed the line with Lucille, who snapped, "We've been working on this for hours. Could you please take this more seriously?"

"Sorry," Matt whispered, hiding behind his piece of paper. "But it's true."

Fabian sighed. After a few weeks of peace and quiet, he'd almost managed to convince himself that Matt's brothers had given up. Of course, it was likely too good to be true.

When they left the library two hours later, the storm had intensified. It was so strong that Fabian had to lean against the door to open it, and immediately wished he hadn't when the wind blew into his face like a leaf blower.

"Tell me again how this is just a normal storm."

Samantha shrugged helplessly. "All I can say is it's not a spell." She took a deep breath and nodded at Rachel, who returned the look with equal determination. "Alright, be safe, everyone."

The two girls hunched their shoulders to shield themselves and ducked out into the storm. Jan huffed before heading off in another direction, leaving Matt, Lucille, and Fabian alone.

The three of them headed towards the western part of town, where both Lucille's house and Matt's apartment complex were located. Small branches littered the path as they walked.

Lucille leant into Fabian. "Magic or no magic, this storm is worrying."

"You're okay with me not going home tonight, right?" Fabian asked, not wanting to spend any more time outside than he had to.

Instead of confirming straight away, Lucille bit her lip.

Fabian groaned and was about to turn around and follow Samantha and Rachel instead when Matt elbowed him. "What's that?"

He looked ahead and noticed an unusual cloud ahead of them. It was dark and twisted like a tornado, but shaped like an egg. "*This* is not normal."

"Shall we take a look?" Lucille asked.

"I don't think we have a choice," Matt said.

The cloud sped towards them, suddenly letting out a bone-chilling screech. Instantly, Matt leapt in front of them, spreading not only his arms but his wings as he assumed his demon form. The shreds of his shirt fluttered in the wind.

Just before the cloud reached them, the whirlwind dissipated, revealing a white-haired woman dressed in grey rags. "Shenny," Matt spat.

Instead of answering, the floating woman screamed. Matt folded his arms in front of his face, but the storm pushed him into Fabian and Lucille. Branches rained down on them from a nearby tree and there was a terrible crack above their heads.

"Scutum Protecto!" Lucille screamed. The shield appeared half a second before a thick branch came crashing down on them.

Fabian ducked instinctively, but his head had escaped the powerful blow thanks to Lucille and he was still alive.

Lucille grabbed Matt. "We have to go!"

"Can't—move!" Matt forced out between clenched teeth. It was only thanks to his demonic strength that they hadn't all been blown over.

What they needed was a respite from the wind. Fabian swallowed. The strange woman wasn't the only one who could control the wind. He reached into his jacket and pulled out the Feather of Shitaten. Ducking under Matt's wing, he flicked it in the direction of the woman.

For a moment, the wind turned and blew against her. Matt didn't waste any time. He turned and grabbed Fabian and Lucille, pulling them with him as he leapt through space.

Panting, they all reappeared in the middle of the Magic Circle's back room. Suddenly without the strength of the storm to contend against, Fabian stumbled and collapsed to the floor. Breathing heavily, he clutched the feather tightly.

"What the hell was *that?*"

Rachel

The storm had died down a little by the time Rachel got home. Frozen to the bone, she was glad to get back behind walls and near a working heater. As she turned into her street, she saw a man sitting on her doorstep who looked suspiciously like a certain Mick Hadden.

"Daddy!" She ran and threw herself into his arms before he'd even got up.

Her father laughed and kissed her on the forehead. "Hello, Bug. You kept me waiting quite a while. I thought you'd be home by now."

Rachel let go of him and took out her keys to open the door. "I didn't know you were coming."

"Surprise." Mick chuckled and followed her inside, hoisting his suitcase over the doorstep. "It's terrible weather, though. When I left LA, the sun was shining."

"The sun shines in Greenvalley, too, you know, but not as much as in California. And not today." Rachel was boiling over from excitement, almost ignoring his sudden appearance. "Why are you here?" she asked, putting down her bag and dropping the keys into the bowl.

"I applied for a sabbatical and worked something out with the University of Greenvalley. They gave the okay last week, so here I am."

"Wait." Rachel turned. "Does that mean you're staying? Like, for longer?"

A smile spread across her father's face. "Six months—"

With a squeal, Rachel was back in her father's arms.

"I've missed you, too, Bug," Mick laughed.

Rachel wanted to reply, but instead tears streamed down her face. "I can't believe you're here," she murmured.

A key turned in the lock, startling them both. Rachel was still in her father's arms when the door opened and her mother came home.

"What a storm. No style can survive—" She froze. "Mick."

"Hello, Annette," Mick said quietly, letting go of Rachel. "I know I should've called, but—"

"Dad got a job at Greenvalley University," Rachel said, on his behalf. "He'll be staying for a few months. That's okay, right?"

Annette was still staring. "With us?"

"He can sleep in Nico's room." She refused to call it the guest room that Annette had degraded it to.

Slowly her mother came to her senses. "You want him to move in?"

"At least *I'm* asking." When Annette had decided Balthasar was going to live with them, she'd only informed Rachel of her decision after she'd made it. "Besides, it's *Dad.*"

"Yes. I can see that." Her mother still looked like she'd been hit by a truck.

Mick took a step closer to his luggage, his hand wandering to the handle. "Only if it suits you. I could rent a place or—"

Annette took a sharp breath. "Don't be ridiculous." She finally got moving and strode into the living room. "It's not the first time you've come to visit. Make yourself comfortable and don't mind me."

Her mother's reaction to her father's presence had sucked the joy out of their reunion for Rachel. Suddenly she was reminded of the things Annette had told her when they'd both been ill with the plague. How Mick had cheated on her and how he'd never even fought to keep them in his life.

In the living room, her mother uncorked a bottle of wine and poured herself a glass before downing the contents. Meanwhile, her father was still standing by the door, as if he'd forgotten why he was here. Which made Rachel wonder why he truly was. The job was great, of course, but why leave Berkeley for some provincial small-town university when he could have gone anywhere in the world?

Rachel shrugged. She wasn't going to complain about her father making an effort to spend more time with her. Even if she wished he'd done it years ago.

"Come on, I'll show you upstairs."

It was strange to have her father at home. Annette was right, he'd stayed before, but never in Nico's room. Now Rachel was lying in bed, once again hearing noises from the room next-door, and catching herself thinking it was Nico. When Mick had visited after Nico's death, he'd slept on the couch. With a six-month stay that wasn't an option, but it still felt weird.

By now the excitement had faded and conflicting thoughts had taken its place. Rachel loved her dad more than anyone in the world, but she knew the truth now—or at least her mother's truth. And that made things much more complicated. Her father was no longer the faraway hero Rachel could turn to.

She suddenly remembered a conversation she'd had with Nico about him. Rachel had loved their weekly catch-ups—and still did—but when Nico had turned fifteen, he'd refused to continue. He'd blamed their father as much as they both blamed their mother. And once again, their father had never fought back, just accepted it.

A distant knock jolted her out of her dark spiral. It wasn't her room, but the one next door. Sure enough, she heard her mother talking. Curious as to what she had to say in the middle of the night, Rachel got out of bed and opened her door a crack.

"You can't just make split decisions like that. Not when it affects us," Annette complained, sending needles into Rachel's stomach.

"I made the decision for me," Mick said quietly. "I was due for a sabbatical and Greenvalley had a vacancy."

Annette huffed. "Oh, please. I know how you are. You never think things through. Especially when you've got an idea in your head. You should've called."

"I know," he admitted.

"And now you're going to live here?" Annette sounded hurt. "You know I don't want you to."

"You don't want to be around me?" Mick asked, then snorted. "Believe me. I figured that out when you took the kids and moved as far away as you could."

"As if you cared," Annette shot back. "Weren't you all trapped in a relationship you never really wanted?"

There was a moment of silence. Rachel waited with bated breath for her father to defend himself. To somehow prove that her side of the story was wrong.

When Mick spoke again, he just said, "Can't we let the past rest, after all these years? I've matured. You've matured."

"You mean I got old?"

"No! You look great. Really." A quiet shuffle. "Annette..."

"Don't touch me!" Annette snapped suddenly.

Rachel jumped back into her room. What had just happened?

"I'm so over being the victim of your irrational actions. I'm done, Mick." Rachel saw her mother step back out into the hallway.

"I'm sorry, Annette," Mick said, but he didn't follow her.

Annette shook her head and stomped into her room. Rachel was halfway down the corridor when she stopped and turned. In the open doorway she saw her father, dressed for bed. He looked apologetic.

"She'll get over it," Rachel whispered. Even to her own ears it sounded callous. Especially when she heard crying from behind Annette's door. Overwhelmed by feelings that made no sense, Rachel turned on her heels with a, "Goodnight," and returned to her room.

As the door closed behind her, she took a shuddering breath. Her father's presence was a good thing, she told herself twice. It was good because she liked him. And it was good because they'd sort everything out. Hopefully.

If they didn't destroy each other.

Lucille

"I ran away!" Matt moaned as he paced the Magic Circle. "I ran from Shenny!"

Lucille was checking her make-up mirror in an attempt to fix her hair, which had been blown out in the storm. "Who's Shenny?" she asked distractedly. "I mean, *what* is she?" It was obviously the woman in the grey rags who had assaulted them.

"Her full name is Shenecra Delandeva. She hates being called Shenny, so we do it on purpose." He caught himself and frowned, but before he could correct his statement, Fabian jumped in.

"Who is *we?*" He managed to make even that question sound fearful.

Matt leant back against the counter and sighed. "My brothers and I. She's a Stormbride and one of Caspar's lieutenants, but she wants to dispose of him and take over the leadership of the Black Guard. He doesn't take her seriously, and I guess... I never did either." He shrugged uncomfortably. "Call it first-class arrogance."

Lucille half remembered the classification of demons Matt had introduced them to. It didn't surprise her that those at the top looked down on the rest, but it was a testament to Matt's growing humanity that he recognised it, too.

"She looks human and is powerful, so I guess she's a third level demon?" Fabian mused. Now *this* surprised Lucille. Not only had *he* remembered the information, but he also showed some interest, without whining.

Matt nodded. "Yes, exactly. Anyway, I've only seen her in parades, never met the woman. So, her being here..."

"Caspar's back, right?" And there was the fear again.

Lucille snapped her make-up mirror shut. "But we banished him. Surely the ban would last a little longer." She'd wanted to admonish Fabian for his irrational fear, but Matt's falling face didn't fill her with confidence. "What?"

He shrugged. "Caspar is a very powerful demon. You wouldn't be able to banish an archdemon. So maybe... maybe a few weeks is all we get."

Predictably, Fabian moaned and rubbed his face. "That can't be true. A few weeks? We'll never get him again. He... he'll kill us."

"It's true," Lucille said firmly. "If Caspar were able to return to our world, he'd kill us. But he didn't."

"He sent that Stormwitch," Fabian pointed out.

"Stormbride," Matt muttered.

"Exactly. He *sent* her. Because he can't come here." Now that she'd laid out the whole idea, Lucille felt confident in it. Maybe she was grasping at straws, but the alternative was just too terrible, and she refused to always see the worst in everything. "Caspar's still banned, but Shenny's here. So what do we do?"

Matt pushed himself away from the counter again. "I've got to make sure he's not hiding in Greenvalley. So, rain check? Let's tell the others what we've found out and come up with a plan. Do you want me to take you both home?"

"Yes, please." With the wind buffeting the windows of the Magic Circle, she didn't want to cross the town on foot.

"Your place or Fabian's?"

"Me to mine, him to his." She tried to ignore Fabian's frown, but it was impossible not to see the hurt in his eyes. "It's just because of the storm. We might be housebound for a while..."

"And you don't want to be stuck with me," Fabian finished.

Lucille blushed. She wouldn't have said it like that, but the words struck too close to the truth. "I've got a lot to do. Like the profile, you know. This might be the perfect time to ask my dad about his past. In fact, I'm pretty sure it is. Linda's in New York."

"I see."

"We'll see each other tomorrow."

"If the school doesn't get blown away."

Lucille noticed Matt looking back and forth between them. His opinion of their squabble was as clear as day. Shame crept up Lucille's neck. "Let's just go."

"Okay."

When Matt took her hand, Fabian refused to look at her.

As soon as Matt had dropped her off at home, Lucille wished she could take back what she'd just said. She felt like a terrible girlfriend. When she thought about being stuck with her boyfriend while a storm raged outside, she imagined cuddling in front of the fireplace, movies and popcorn, maybe a bath together and hours in bed. The problem was that she didn't see Fabian in these visions. And that made her feel even worse.

Annoyed at herself, she took out her cell phone and typed a message to him: *I'm sorry about earlier. I just think I need some time for myself to sort things out.* Her finger hovered over send before she quickly deleted everything and replaced it with: *I'm sorry if I hurt you, but...*

No, no, she didn't want to start drama. She didn't want to start a discussion about their relationship. She just...

Stay safe. A kiss smiley and the message was sent.

There was no reply.

Groaning, Lucille put the phone down. She didn't have time to deal with his sensitivities right now. Let him mope and she'd call him later when things had calmed down.

Right now she had bigger fish to fry. Namely, her father.

Lucille walked over to his office and straightened her back before knocking and holding her breath.

"Yes?"

Taking the short answer as an invitation, Lucille entered the office. As so often, she found her father on the phone.

He recognised her and sighed. "Can I call you back in a few minutes? I have another call on the line."

"Another call on the line?" Lucille asked, not too impressed.

"I like to keep work and home separate as much as possible," Bastien said, ignoring the fact that his office was at home. "What can I do for you?"

"Do you have some time?" Lucille asked against all hope. She could see that he was clearly busy.

As expected, Bastien shook his head. "Not much. Why don't you tell me what this is all about? Then I can give you a better answer."

Lucille lowered her head. "It's about Mum."

"I thought she was in New York?"

"Not Linda." Her voice almost cracked as she was forced to clarify. "I'm talking about my real mother. Alena."

Her father's face tightened. It took him a moment to smooth it out again. "I see."

"We have this homework," Lucille began to explain. "Well, it's for..." It was her who had convinced Samantha they should write micro-biographies for the yearbook to give herself an excuse to finally dig deeper. "We have to write an essay about our parents. And I thought..." *I thought you'd finally tell me about Mum.*

"What would you like to know about her?"

Lucille gasped. Was he really going to tell her? Just like that? "Um, I don't know anything except her name and that she studied literature. And I've seen pictures, of course, but I can't remember anything else."

"You were only three when she died."

"Yes!" A wave of emotion swept over Lucille. She was so close to learning more about the woman who'd given birth to her. The woman who'd loved her. "It was an accident, right?"

Bastien's lips thinned as he frowned. "A car accident. Are you sure you don't remember anything? You were there, too."

"I... I have nightmares about it sometimes. But..." Lucille shrugged uncomfortably. "I don't know what's really true and what's just memories jumbled together and fed with TV crap." She was trying to sound nonchalant, but hadn't really succeeded.

"Of course." Her father sighed again. "Look, I really don't have time for this. There's an important project that needs to be completed today. I'll tell you about your mother, but not now."

Lucille swallowed hard. "Sure. Thank you for giving me a few minutes of your time." She turned and fled the room before he had a chance to stop her—which, of course, he never even tried.

She put a hand over her mouth and bit down on a sob. Tears streamed down her cheeks as she breathed sharply through her nose. She hadn't expected much from her father. Sure, in her daydreams he always came and sat down with her, sharing his old pain with her now that she was an adult. But maybe he wasn't hiding any pain. Maybe he didn't really think about the wife he'd lost. Maybe he'd never cared at all.

"I don't remember my parents, either."

Pascal's voice startled her. He was standing in the hallway, hands clasped behind his back, watching her with pity in his eyes.

"Eavesdropping isn't very gentlemanly," Lucille snapped, but then his words sank in. "You never got to know her?"

"I was abandoned as a baby. No idea if they died or just couldn't be bothered with a child. Or maybe they were afraid."

Because of his telekinetic powers. "I'm so sorry, Pascal." Lucille bent down and held out her arms.

Pascal came to her willingly. "I just want you to know you're not alone."

She hugged him tightly, grateful for his words. "And neither are you."

Matt

As soon as Matt got home, he cleared the table and drew a pentagram in his own blood. "Caspar, I summon you."

His nerves were on edge as he scanned the room, but his half-brother didn't appear. Matt tried again, to no avail. If Caspar was in Greenvalley, he was ignoring the summons.

He jumped when the door opened, but it was only René. "Sheesh, give me a warning."

"What are you doing there?"

"Trying to find out if Caspar has made it back to Greenvalley, but he's ignoring me."

René frowned. "Didn't you banish him from this world?"

"Sam did." Matt shrugged. "But there's reason to believe it didn't last very long. That storm out there is being caused by a Stormbride he's at odds with. I thought they'd either joined forces or chosen Greenvalley for a duel to the death."

His father dropped his bag and rolled up his sleeves. "I see. Let me try."

"He won't come to you either." If Caspar had ignored Matt's summons, he wouldn't heed René's.

"I know some tricks you don't. Grab that map over there."

Matt had never questioned why they kept a fold-out map of Greenvalley in the bookcase by the couch when everyone had a mobile phone. It was just one of the many things he didn't understand. While René went into the kitchen, he took out the map and looked at it. It looked like an ordinary map, the paper soft and thin from years of use.

René returned with a cloth and a bag of salt. He wiped Matt's blood off the table without commenting on its presence, then waited for the surface to dry. "Spread it out and sit down."

Matt did as he was told and watched in fascination as René covered the entire map with a thin layer of salt.

"Your dagger, please."

He handed René the dagger he'd used to cut himself. Like the blood, the wound was already gone. Now René cut a rune into his left palm. Before Matt could ask what it meant, he pressed his hand into the salt.

"Ouch," Matt commented dryly. The salt in the wound must have burnt like hell, but René didn't even flinch.

Something was happening on the map. The blood mixed with the layer of salt and spread over Greenvalley, then dissolved, leaving a glowing red spot right on top of the apartment complex they lived in.

"That's you," René said as he wiped his hand with a clean corner of the cloth he'd used earlier.

"What does the red mean?"

René chuckled softly. "That I'd be freaking out if I didn't know it was you."

So the map showed those of demon origin. Matt grinned. If Caspar was here, his location would be revealed. "Is that him?" He pointed to a dim spot on the other side of town, worryingly close to Samantha's house.

"No, Caspar would be as bright as you, if not brighter."

"He's definitely *not* brighter," Matt joked, but the joke didn't quite land. Concerned, he studied the map. It was just him and the dim spot that had to be Shenny. No other demon was in town.

Confused, he leant back. He had no doubt that Caspar would send Shenny after him if he could, but why was Shenny listening to him? She didn't usually, and this had nothing to do with Hescaryn—at least to anyone's knowledge.

"There are other things we could try."

Matt looked up. "You really know your stuff, don't you? This whole demon hunter business." It was easy to forget that René had once trained to be a demon hunter. The man taught small children and was completely dedicated to his job. Besides, he was his father.

"Like father, like son," René muttered. Then he sighed. "My father was a demon hunter. He taught me before I could walk or talk. So to speak."

"He was?" Matt had never thought to ask about René's parents. Obviously his father hadn't just appeared out of thin air, but his grandparents had never mattered to Matt and it obviously hadn't been a topic of conversation for René either.

Suddenly he remembered the yearbook profile he was supposed to fill in. "Tell me about him."

René looked up wearily. "There's not much to tell. He was a strict man who travelled the country to fight demons and other apparitions. It was his calling, the family business. I was supposed to follow in his footsteps, but then I met your mother."

"He must have been thrilled."

René winced. "After I protected her with my life—not that she'd needed it—he never spoke to me again. He knows you exist, but don't assume he's ever come to visit."

"Wait! He's still alive?"

"Oh, yes. I mean, I suppose so. I'm his last of kin, so if he'd died, I'd think they'd contact me. And as much as it pains me to admit it, I'm not particularly keen on him showing up now. The last thing you need is a grandfather who knows how to kill demons."

"Sounds to me like that's exactly what I need." A demon hunter would be a valuable asset to have on his side if Caspar and Balthasar continued to come after him.

René's expression turned sour. "Believe me. He may have held back when you were a baby, but he'd have no qualms about killing you now. Let's just forget about him."

So even Matt's human relatives couldn't wait to kill him. "Do you ever regret giving up everything for Melaney?"

"No. And I don't mean because I got you out of it. But once I was out from under his thumb, it was like I saw the world afresh. I no longer studied teaching as an alibi, but really enjoyed it. And I found something that fulfilled me more than killing demons ever did. I love being an integral part of children's lives and giving them the tools to succeed. It's so much better than moving from place to place and getting blood on my hands every day."

Matt was so used to fighting almost every day of his life that he couldn't quite imagine what it would be like to settle down and build a life without violence, let alone raise young children. But he admired his father for it. René was still a formidable opponent, but he'd found happiness in teaching and seemed so much more balanced that way.

"So, what now?" René asked, watching the dim red spot. "This Stormbride isn't as powerful as you or your brothers, but I don't like them hanging out here. The storm will only get worse."

René was right. For whatever reason Shenny was in Greenvalley, she had to leave. Stormbrides were notorious for the wind they brought with them. Unchecked, it would grow and grow until nothing could withstand it.

"Now, I'll get rid of her."

Fabian

Fabian barely slept that night with the storm battering the walls and his emotions in equal turmoil. When his alarm clock finally rang, he almost jumped out of bed in relief. Today he'd force Lucille to talk to him. If something was wrong, he wanted to know so he could fix it. Everything had been so amazing back in the summer.

But summer was a distant memory as he stared at the dark clouds hanging over Greenvalley. The trees outside his window were bent, their leaves falling across the garden. Meanwhile, the old chicken coop had been blown over. It was a good thing all their chickens had gone to Hell.

On his way down, he found Merle cowering under the stairs and sighed. The cat hated storms that made the house rattle. Not that he blamed her. The noises *were* unsettling. He bent down and reached out to pet her. "Don't worry. It'll be all right." If he hadn't had to go to school, he would have picked her up.

His father came out of the kitchen with a bowl of cereal in his hand. "You're planning on going to school?"

"Do I have a choice?"

Joachim laughed. "They've closed everything. No school today. We won't open the garage either. So, relax."

"Awesome." Any day without Mr Herbert was a good day. "Have you put the coffee on?" Fabian tried to go into the kitchen, but his father blocked his way.

"Just wait. Ben's here."

"Ben?" Fabian looked into the kitchen and saw Samantha's father sitting with his mother. They were talking quietly. "What's going on?"

Joachim shrugged. "Just doing his special thing."

"His special thing?"

"He always knew how to reach Caro. They go way back."

Fabian raised an eyebrow. "Longer than you two?"

"I wasn't really friends with your mother until we were well into our teens. But she took classes with Ben's mum, so they knew each other." Joachim grinned. "Didn't help him though, since she picked me over him."

Slightly disturbed, Fabian took a step back. "I don't need to know the details."

Lucille and Samantha might have asked for it by making them do their silly task, but he intended to write just a little about the Magic Circle and then draw something. That should be more than enough for the yearbook. He certainly wasn't going to put his parents' love life in there.

Joachim laughed. "We had a life too, you know?"

"Yeah, don't wanna hear it!" To avoid any more embarrassing details, Fabian bent down to coax Merle out of her hiding place. "Come here, Merle. We've got time for a cuddle."

The cat looked at him, not convinced that his arms were safer than the stairs. His phone buzzed.

Fabian hit his head as he backed away, standing up too soon. "Ouch." He put pressure on his head and fumbled for his phone. When he finally pulled it out, Matt's name flashed on the display and the call ended. With a sigh, Fabian called him back. "What's up?"

"I've got a plan to deal with Shenny. Meet me at the library, and bring your feather."

Samantha

The storm was blowing outside, bending the branches in front of Samantha's windows. She was sitting at her desk, adding to her flashcards, when she heard Cian stir behind her. He'd stayed over last night and completely missed the alarm this morning. Since school had been cancelled, she'd let him sleep and enjoyed the silence to work on her exam preparations.

"Already back at work?" he asked sleepily as he fumbled with his shirt and pulled it on.

"Already? It's almost eleven."

"You always keep me up so late."

Samantha gasped exaggeratedly and turned to him, only to be surprised by a kiss. She hadn't even realised he was standing so close.

When Cian pulled away, he frowned. "Wait a minute. Eleven? Shouldn't we be in school?"

"Look outside." Just then there was a terrible crash. She jumped up. "What was that?"

"Looks like the storm took out one of the trees in your neighbour's garden. Just one of the little ones, but... ugh." Cian shuddered. "So, school's out?" He wiggled his eyebrows suggestively.

"As is pretty much all non-essential work. My mum and Meg are home, and my dad should be back soon. He went over to the Bendtfelds to talk to Caro... Fabian's mother."

Cian sighed, then pulled up a chair and sank into it. "Well, let's study then. Are you already done with Chem?"

"I've waited on it." One of the things Samantha liked about Cian was that he wasn't allergic to studying like Fabian. He actually had ambition and wanted to do well in his finals.

Together, they studied hard, sharing flashcards and information as the storm darkened the sky outside. After a while, the front door opened and slammed shut. It took about five minutes for the fighting to begin.

"They're *still* fighting?" Cian asked softly.

"About something new every day." The constant bickering had become part of their family fabric, and no matter how hard Samantha and Meg tried, they didn't seem to be able to fix it. Even the extra money she'd brought home from her new job didn't help. "I'll tell them to tone it down."

"I could use some breakfast."

She smiled gratefully at him. It would be a lot easier with Cian there. "Then come along."

They left the room together and went downstairs. Her parents were in the living room, standing around the abandoned breakfast table.

"I don't know what your problem is," her father complained as he helped himself to a leftover roll.

"My problem is that there's a century storm out there and you're leaving us to fend for ourselves. Normally I can't even get you out of bed in this weather, but when the Bendtfelds call, you're off in a flash."

Samantha and Cian exchanged glances. Samantha nodded towards a path that would lead them to the kitchen. There was still breakfast on the table, but she didn't want to risk getting caught in the middle.

"Caro needs some help right now."

Juliane crossed her arms. "Oh, and her *husband* can't give it to her? She needs *you?*"

"What's your problem, woman? We're all friends."

Juliane huffed as Samantha and Cian snuck past. "Is that so? Well, you never asked me if I wanted to come. Funny how we're all friends, but it's always just the three of you. I'm just the fifth wheel."

Ben groaned. "Oh god, Juli! You're acting like Meg."

Samantha rolled her eyes at Cian and grabbed some bowls from the cupboard to fill with cereal. Meanwhile Cian poured them some milk.

"Because I want my husband by my side in such doomsday weather?"

"Since when?" Ben retorted. "You always find something wrong with me. Didn't you wish I'd go to hell just last week?"

"Let's go," Samantha said to Cian. He nodded anxiously and together they made their way back through the living room.

"We're *married*. Not that it means anything to you." Juliane threw her arms up in the air. "Hell, your daughter has more sex in this house than we do."

Cian choked heavily on the milk he was drinking. Mortified, Samantha looked at her mother. "Seriously?"

"He didn't stay the night, did he?" her father asked, his voice suddenly lower.

Juliane laughed. "How blind are you? Or rather, how deaf? Of course he did, and it's not the first time."

"Could you please leave me out of your arguments?" Samantha asked angrily.

Her mother barely looked at her. "I'm not a huge fan either, but she's an adult."

"Who still goes to school," Ben added.

Cian put the glass of milk down on the TV table and gave Samantha an apologetic look. "I guess I'd better go." He slipped past Ben and hurried upstairs to collect his things.

Samantha glared at her parents. "What was that about? What do you care what I'm doing in my room?" As embarrassing as it was, it was mostly anger she felt. Her mother was right. She *was* an adult.

"Since I have to listen to it," her mother shot back.

"Juli, please!"

Immediately, she turned back to Ben. "It's either that or your snoring, Ben!"

"You know what? I'm done." Samantha slammed the two bowls of cereal down on the table, not caring about the milk she spilt. Then she marched over to the front door and grabbed her shoes and jacket. "I'm sure Granny needs some help in this weather."

Before her parents could stop her—and before Cian had come back downstairs with his things—she opened the door and stepped out into the storm.

When Samantha finally made it to her grandmother's, she felt like she'd run half a marathon. The storm had made it almost impossible to walk in a straight line. The wind had lessened only marginally in the forest where the trees protected her, but they'd suffered for it. Numerous trees had lost their branches or fallen entirely, blocking the path.

Samantha had to climb over several of them before she finally made it to her grandmother's house. Elda was awaiting her, hurrying her inside as soon as she arrived. They spent the first fifteen minutes securing the shutters outside the windows. At some point, the power was cut and Elda had to light candles and make tea with a magical fire.

Once they were finally settled in front of the fire, it was quite cosy. The wind was howling outside, but the house was secure. Samantha checked her phone and found the group messages from last night. Apparently, Matt, Lucille, and Fabian had come across the supernatural cause of this weather.

"Grandma, have you ever encountered a Stormbride?"

The cup of tea fell from her grandmother's hands and shattered on the stone ledge of the fireplace, startling them both. Flustered, Elda bent to pick up the pieces, but Samantha was quicker.

"Are you alright?" It wasn't like her grandmother to drop her mugs.

Elda's skin went a little blotchy. "Did you say a Stormbride?" She looked at the locked windows as if she could see through the boards. "Is that what's happening?"

"Why...?" Samantha figured her question had just been answered. Her grandmother clearly had some experience with this kind of monster. "What happened last time?"

"Oh dear..."

That didn't bode well. Samantha dropped the shards onto the tray and sat up again, watching her grandmother anxiously. "What is it?"

Elda took a deep breath. "A Stormbride killed your grandfather."

Samantha gasped. Neither her grandmother nor her father liked to talk much about her grandfather's death. All she'd ever known was that he'd died in some kind of accident long before she was born. "Wasn't he... *killed by a tree.*" She sighed. "It was a storm, wasn't it?"

"Yes," Elda whispered. Then she looked lovingly at Samantha. "You have his black hair, darling. Did you know that?"

"Of course."

"And obviously you've inherited his magical talent—and mine." Elda sighed again. "Not like your father, which led to... a lot of fighting. Ben hated the magic he didn't have and what it often meant for him."

Samantha frowned. "What's Dad got to do with Grandpa's death?"

Elda took a deep breath that betrayed a number of complicated emotions. "I don't know exactly what happened that day. Your father refuses to talk about it, but he was there when your grandfather finally defeated the Stormbride and was killed in the process." She straightened in her seat, gathering her composure to tell the story. "We tried to kill her for days, to no avail. She was immune to just about everything. She could even blow magic away. That's how powerful a Stormbride's scream can be.

"When Ben was born, Erich and I were always very careful when we went monster hunting. Often, Erich went out while I stayed at home with Ben, brewing potions, and researching methods. Ben hated how much we worried." Elda winced at the memory. "Well, the year we had the Stormbride, there was a school dance. Erich had forbidden Ben to go, but your father was... in love." She smiled. "He'd been talking about your mother for ages and had planned to ask her to dance. He'd even learnt how to in secret. Anyway, he put a lot of effort into the evening and then his father told him he couldn't go. They had a big fight about it."

Samantha tried to picture it. Her father would have been a teenager, stuck at home while the rest of his friends were having fun at the dance. "But surely he understood the dangers, didn't he?"

"On some level, I'm sure. But he was also a teenage boy. Your father resented the fact that his life was *always* in danger. Of course, his friends' lives were just as much in danger from monsters, but their parents didn't know about it, so he felt singled out. Or he complained we were being too dramatic." Elda laughed softly. "I'd say *he* was the one being dramatic. It wasn't like we kept him locked up all day. But Ben thought it was all a ploy to ruin his life. That we were so worried about him dying that we wouldn't let him live."

This sounded like something out of Meg's playbook. And here Samantha had always thought Meg took after their mother. "Sounds exhausting."

"It was, but I also felt for him. It can't have been easy growing up with all that fear. I mean, maybe we exaggerated a bit. It's just so hard to find the right balance when children are involved. Especially when they don't have any magic to defend themselves. There could always be a monster lurking in the shadows, but you avoid the risk you can. Like that cursed storm. But," Elda's eyes began to water, "your father had other plans. While I calmed Erich down, Ben snuck out the window to go to the dance."

Shocked, Samantha gasped. "He did?"

Elda nodded grimly. "In typical teenage fashion, he defied authority and went to the dance. Erich went after him, and the next time I opened the door the police were outside my house. They'd brought Ben back, who was beside himself, and told me that Erich had been thrown into a tree."

Cold shivers ran down Samantha's arms. "And Dad never told you what happened?"

"He was traumatised. I think he blames himself for his father's death, but all he told me about the fight was that the Stormbride had killed Erich and she was dead now. They must have killed each other at the same time. Unless your father did it somehow."

"How?"

"I don't know. Maybe... maybe he'll talk to you. It's been over twenty-five years."

Samantha bit her lip. If he hadn't talked about his father's death for so long, she had little hope of succeeding now. On the other hand, she had little choice. They *needed* to know how the Stormbride could be killed.

"I'll talk to him."

Jan

Jan didn't mind the storm. In fact, he loved how it had turned things around for him. The Magic Circle was closed for the duration, and Meg had spent the morning at the Kerschers', avoiding her explosive family life at home. And with his mother at the hospital and his father out grocery shopping with Anne, they had the living room all to themselves.

Life was great.

Instead of sticking to his cramped room, they were making out in the living room with little regard for their surroundings. Jan grabbed Meg, intending to lift her onto the sofa, but his foot got caught on the rug and he stumbled, knocking over a vase. They fell over the edge over the sofa and giggled, when something shattered on the coffee table.

Meg startled, holding his hands. "What was that?"

"Don't worry about it." Whatever it was couldn't keep Jan from burying his face between her beautiful breasts.

"Something's broken," Meg pointed out, looking to the side, while running her fingers through his short hair.

Jan spared a quick glance. "It's just an ugly vase." Half-wilted flowers were spread over the coffee table amid blue glass shards, as water ran down the table. A regrettable mess he could deal with later.

"We could get hurt," Meg cautioned.

"I have healing powers."

Meg threw her head back and laughed. Then she pulled his face up and kissed him passionately.

Unfortunately, Meg's parents picked her up at some point, leaving Jan to play video games in his room. After a while he heard the front door open and close. His father and Anne had returned with the groceries. Jan heard them rummaging around in the kitchen, but felt no need to help. The less time he spent around his father, the better for both of them.

Apparently, his father wasn't going to show him the same consideration, roaring from the kitchen, "Jan!"

Groaning, Jan saved his game and dragged himself into the kitchen. "What?"

Anne was busy putting the groceries away, intent on avoiding the drama.

"You have something to tell me?" his father asked in his particularly condescending voice.

"Why?" There was nothing Jan ever wanted to talk to him about. "Nothing?"

"Love you," Jan tried ironically. When that didn't help, he rolled his eyes. "Why don't you just give me a lecture and be done with it? With any luck, you'll even tell me what your problem is."

His father's face predictably darkened. "I don't like that tone."

Jan just glared.

"Explain this!" Stefan showed him the rubbish bin. In it was the broken vase.

Jan shrugged. "I accidentally broke a vase and cleaned it up. What's wrong with that?"

"What's *wrong* with that?" Stefan yelled, causing Anne to drop what she was doing and flee from the kitchen. "That was your mother's anniversary present. I bought it for her three weeks ago."

"So?" It was an accident. "Would you like me to buy a replacement?"

"I don't think you can afford it. Aren't you still unemployed?"

"I have a job."

Stefan's eyebrows crept up. "You do?"

"Yes. I've taken over the Magic Circle while the owner is—"

"The *Magic* Circle?" His father's eyes went wild. "Is that a joke?"

"What's wrong with the shop?"

"What..." Stefan caught himself and rubbed the bridge of his nose. "I can't believe you're still hung up on this magic crap. Will you ever grow up?"

Jan grimaced, his blood boiling. "What do you want, man? It's a job."

"Oh yeah, what's your going rate? How much do you get paid to dabble in make-believe bullshit?"

It took another grunted prompt for Jan to say the meagre number out loud.

His father gasped. "That's not a job, it's a *hobby!* My god, boy, when are you going to grow some brain cells? You know what? I hope you really crash and burn one day."

Jan snorted. "Nice. And here I thought parents were supposed to be supportive and all that crap."

"We *were* supportive!" Stefan shouted. "I worked my ass off at the mine to give you and your sister everything you need. It's not my fault that everything you touch turns to shit."

Jan's anger bubbled over. "Oh, piss off!" He turned on his heel and marched out the kitchen.

It really wasn't his fault that he'd had a bad run so far. Fighting Malcolm had cut into his study time. And he'd lost his job at the hostel because of the gorgon. And it certainly wasn't his fault that the Magic Circle couldn't afford a full-time employee while Caroline was recuperating.

He grabbed his jacket and slipped into his shoes, before slamming the door behind him. While waiting for the elevator, he fumbled for his cigarette pack.

The doors opened with a *ping* and he stepped inside. They were about to close behind him when someone came running after him.

"Wait!" Anne called, slipping into the elevator with him.

Jan groaned. "Anne, please." The last thing he needed was for his goody-two-shoes sister to try to smooth things over. "I don't want to talk."

Anne was a little breathless. "Sorry. I just—"

The lights in the ceiling flickered and the elevator came to a sudden stop, knocking Jan and Anne off balance. Then the lights went out completely.

Jan hammered on the button to open the doors, to no avail. "Come on!" he yelled. "Open, damn it!" The last thing he needed was an elevator malfunction.

"Jan?" Anne's voice was agonisingly meek. "Are we going to die?"

Lucille

While waiting for the storm to subside or Matt to call for reinforcements, Lucille made herself comfortable in the library. The wind was maltreating the giant oak in front of the window and whistling through the cracks. She and Pascal were distracting themselves by playing a game of catch, where Pascal would throw small objects at her with the power of his mind, and she'd try to catch them. When the door opened, they both abruptly dropped what they were doing.

It was only their butler, Albert. "Do you two need anything?" he asked.

"I need my father to talk to me about my mother, but I suppose his work is more essential as usual," Lucille sniped back.

Albert smiled conciliatorily. "I'm sorry."

Lucille sank into an armchair with a sigh. "Don't be. I should be used to it." Then she had an idea. "Can *you* tell me about my mother?"

"Of course." Albert put his hands behind his back. "Alena was a beautiful woman, very delicate and lovely. Your father used to call her fairy-like."

As soon as she heard those words from him, Lucille relaxed.

"She was a quiet woman, well-spoken and incredibly kind. Your father benefited greatly from her presence. And he loved her, put her on a pedestal and the world at her feet. When she died, he locked himself in his room for days and buried himself in work. And he still does, to this day."

As romantic as the idea was that her father could still mourn her mother after all these years, Lucille knew better. It had become a habit, one he felt no need to break.

Pascal piped up. "Then why did he marry Linda? If he loved Lucille's mum so much."

It was a question, which had haunted Lucille for a long time.

"Mr de Cerque never told me his reasons, but if you want my opinion, I think he did it for Lucille's benefit. So she wouldn't have to grow up without a mother."

Lucille laughed. "Oh yes, that's why she sent me to boarding school as soon as she could."

"Mrs de Cerque thought it would be best to provide you with an excellent education."

"Most importantly, it provided an excellent opportunity to get rid of me." Lucille became aware of Pascal watching her. Too late, she thought of how this might affect him. He was already worried they'd send him away because of his powers.

Albert came through with the perfect solution. "That may be so. But adults, like children, need time to grow. Mrs de Cerque was very young when she married your father, and her career was just taking off. It probably wasn't fair of him to expect her to drop everything to bring up his daughter. She had to grow into the role." He looked over at Pascal. "And she's a wonderful mother now."

Pascal shifted back and forth in his chair, not seeming entirely mollified.

"She's changed a lot," Lucille confirmed. "And she *wanted* you." It still hurt that she obviously hadn't wanted Lucille, but Linda and she were on better terms these days.

He smiled happily when he heard that.

Albert cleared his throat. "I'm sorry, I can't tell you much more about your mother. But I *can* tell you about your grandmother."

Lucille perked up immediately. "Yes, please."

"Let me grab a chair." It wasn't often the butler took the liberty of making himself comfortable in their presence, which could only mean that this was going to be a long story.

He nodded at them both and began. "You can't talk about Cecille without talking about Elda. The two struck up a friendship in their teenage years, to the horror of Greenvalley's magical community."

"Horror?" Oh, this was going to be juicy.

"Cecille was the daughter of a long line of witches. Every one of them was called to represent Greenvalley at the annual Witches' Sabbath. And they passed that necklace down from generation to generation." Albert nodded at the Emblem of Power Lucille wore around her neck.

"And Elda?"

"Elda was what they used to call a wild witch. She taught herself magic, first alone, then with Cecille's help. Eventually, she became stronger than Cecille and was chosen in her place."

Lucille remembered the pain at this slight in her grandmother's journals. She'd loved Elda, but she'd grown up expecting to follow in her mother's footsteps.

"And how do you fit into all this?"

Albert laughed. "I'm a distant relative of your grandmother's. A cousin on her mother's side. My family often served the witches, and so I served Cecille."

"By being her butler?"

"Oh no. My services to your grandmother were based on my ability to read people's minds."

Lucille's eyes widened. "Excuse me?"

Albert chuckled. "I can read minds. But don't worry. I've got my powers well under control. Gone are the days when I would randomly pick up thoughts or become overwhelmed by emotions that weren't mine. Nowadays, I only use a gentle probing, rarely more. It has served me well in anticipating the demands of my employers. That's how I initially got the position in your great-grandfather's household. Cecille came to visit me at work where she met his son, Emilien, and the rest is history."

Lucille smiled as she imagined her grandparents' meet-cute. The heir of Greenvalley's richest man and the town witch. What a scandal. Oh, how she would've loved her grandmother to tell her all about it. Life would've been so much easier if she'd had a loving set of grandparents. "How did they die?

"Your grandfather fell ill. And Cecille…" Albert sighed. "The Archdemon of Wrath, Volac, pretty much… tore her apart." He glanced over at Pascal. "I'm sorry. I shouldn't have said that."

"But why?" Pascal asked. If he was disturbed, he hid it behind a good dose of curiosity. "Did he attack Greenvalley?" Lucille found it admirable how quickly her brother adapted to Greenvalley's unique dangers.

Albert shook his head. "Cecille had a dream. She believed that one day we'd be able to work with demons."

"Work with demons?" Lucille thought of those she knew and was a little confused. "That sounds… a bit crazy." Even by her own standards.

"Cecille was convinced demons were just misunderstood. She was friends with one, a half-demon, I think—"

"Chay."

Albert looked surprised. "You know him?"

Lucille felt exhilarated. "Tell me more about her dream." It had suddenly become much more feasible.

"After spending a lot of time with Chay, she came to believe that the origin of all those horrible stories about demons was the human need to make us feel better about ourselves. Say that no matter how evil one of us turned out to be, they could never be as depraved as demons. Debatable, I'm sure," Albert conceded. "But I think what really sold it to Cecille was Chay's theory that demons were humans a very long time ago." Albert shuddered. "Rubbish, if you ask me. But ever since, Cecille had been convinced there was still something human in them."

Lucille couldn't believe what she was hearing. Demons used to be human? "And that Volac proved her wrong?"

"He wouldn't even let her speak." Albert sighed heavily. "If you want, I can show you what happened."

"Me too!" Pascal exclaimed. Both Lucille and Albert glanced at him and he quickly slumped back into his seat, pulling a copy of *War & Peace* onto his lap. "But I want to experience mind reading, too."

"I'll show you another memory later," Albert promised.

Pascal beamed at him and began to read the unwieldy tome.

Albert shuffled his chair closer and raised his hands. "May I?"

Breathlessly, Lucille nodded. She held her breath as he gently placed his fingers on her temples and closed his eyes.

Suddenly, images bloomed in her mind. An owl on a tree. The moon shining through the branches. A green river of magic springing from a moss covered clearing. Lucille recognised the place at once: the Spring of Magic. It must have been the middle of the night, midnight, Lucille knew instinctively.

In front of her, her grandmother stood in a ring of candles. She was exactly as Lucille remembered her. Her grey hair was elegantly braided in a bun at the back of her head and she was dressed sharply, as if she ran a company by day. The Nadellyan Tears, Lucille's Emblem of Power, hung around her neck, complimenting a pair of dangling ruby earrings. Behind her, a younger Elda and Caroline were weaving a spell circle, similar to the one Samantha had used to banish Caspar. Again, Lucille just *knew* it was designed to hold Volac, a flimsy protection against one of the Seven.

"Cecille, this is crazy," Albert's voice sounded. It took Lucille a moment to realise that she was experiencing this memory from his point of view.

"The only thing that's crazy is to never try it," Cecille replied in her calm, gentle voice. Lucille almost cried when she heard it after such a long time.

But Albert didn't give up so easily. "The demons are immoral monsters. Haven't they proven that again and again?"

"What about Chay?"

"Chay is half human. He lived among humans for over a century before he discovered he had demon blood running in his veins."

One day, Lucille would ask Chay about all of this. What a life he must've led.

"According to our research, there are about two million first- and second-class demons in Hell. In our world, there are about five hundred actual demon sightings per year. If that. Less than a third of those ends in death. Every day more people are killed by other humans. Furthermore, almost all of these demonic manifestations follow a direct summoning. They rarely come on their own. Demons aren't interested in overthrowing Ashuan".

Even knowing the outcome, her arguments convinced Lucille. She could hear herself arguing the same case to her friends.

"The protection spell is complete," Elda announced quietly.

"You're making a mistake, Cecille," Albert said, but he stepped behind the boundary of the spell and watched with bated breath.

Cecille closed her eyes and began a litany. Since it was Albert's memory, there was no hope of understanding the Latin.

Red smoke rose from the centre of the circle of candles.

"He's coming," Elda whispered, clutching the Thorak, her husband's demon hunter weapon.

Out of the smoke emerged a demon at least two heads taller than Cecille. Two wounded horns protruded from his wild hair. His eyes glowed red.

The Archdemon of Wrath. Lucille held her breath at his sheer power.

"Who dares summon me?" Volac's voice boomed across the clearing.

Cecille showed no fear and took a step forward. "I, Cecille de Cerque, summon you, Volac of the House of Wrath and head of the Council of Seven, supreme demon of Hescaryn."

Volac hissed and flames erupted around Cecille. Lucille started to take a step forward, but Elda stopped her. Or rather, she stopped Albert. "Let her do her thing," she whispered.

"Do you really think buttering me up is the way to go? I'm not Pride!" Volac roared.

Cecille didn't waver. "I want to propose an alliance. Demons and humans united in a cause."

Volac stomped towards Cecille, his steps shaking the earth. "You want me to ally with *you?* You measly cockroaches? What cause could you possibly have that's of any interest to me."

Tension crept into Cecille's voice. "I think—"

"I don't give a damn what you believe!" Suddenly, Volac grabbed Cecille. Third-degree burns appeared under his touch.

"Cecille!" Now Elda sounded agitated too.

"Stay back," Cecille bellowed. "This is my battle."

Volac laughed. "Battle? You call this a battle?"

"Scutum Protecto!" The shield spell.

The shield appeared as quickly as Lucille had ever seen it, but Volac's energy immediately tore it apart. The remains hit Cecille and she gasped. Magic lit up around Volac as he grabbed Cecille.

Elda had raised her arms. "I banish you, Volac of the House of Wrath. Leave this world and never come back!"

Volac didn't seem to be in the mood to listen. Horrified, Lucille watched as he lifted Cecille up and impaled her with his horns. A terrible scream ripped through the clearing. Albert tried to enter the circle, but the magic repelled him. Caroline stood watching with horror in her eyes.

Then suddenly the magic became so bright they had to avert their eyes. All Lucille could hear was Elda's exhausted grunts.

When the light faded, Volac was gone and Cecille lay in the circle of candles, her empty eyes staring up at the night sky. Blood pooled around her. One of her hands was clasped around the Nadellyan Tears. It hadn't helped her against this enemy.

Lucille pulled away from Albert's touch. Tears streamed down her face as she gasped for air. "Is he... Is Volac still alive?"

Albert's face darkened. "Don't get any ideas, Miss Lucille. Yes, Volac still heads the Council of Seven, and he'll probably continue to do so long after we're buried."

Despite his warning, Lucille shivered. If she ever met that demon, she would disembowel him—and probably die trying. She'd thought Malcolm had been terrible, but he was nothing compared to the Archdemon of Wrath.

In the corner, Pascal cleared his voice. "Was it very bad?"

Lucille wanted to snap at him, but she caught herself and wiped her cheeks again, finding her composure. "Thank you for showing me, Albert. I feel I understand my grandmother a lot better now." Had Chay told her that demons and humans would have to work together one day? *Was* that the future? Or had Cecille gotten it into her own head after meeting the half-demon?

It was hard not to blame Chay for his interference. If he hadn't come to Greenvalley, Cecille would have never tried to summon Volac. On the other hand, he wouldn't have left his book about the Circle of Magic behind. The prophecy that affected them all. Lucille had to believe it would all be worth it in the end. She knew her grandmother would've thought so. Some things were bigger than a single life. Wouldn't she have done the same for the sake of the world?

Her phone buzzed with a message, calling her back to this time and day.

Samantha: A Stormbride killed my grandfather. Apparently my father knows how to get rid of one. Wish me luck he won't have a fit.

Lucille glanced at the dark clouds outside the window and the heavily swaying tree before she replied: *I can come over if you need me.*

Just like their grandmothers, they would support each other.

Samantha: If it's not too much trouble.

Lucille: I'm coming.

She got out of her chair. "Can you ask Tobias to bring the car around?"

"Of course."

"Where are you going?" Pascal asked, suddenly alarmed.

"Samantha's father seems to know how to defeat the Stormbride. We'll talk to him and hopefully put an end to this storm."

Before she could leave the room, Pascal ran over and wrapped his arms around her. "Don't go!"

"Pascal. You'll be safe here with Albert." The butler had already gone to deliver her message.

"But *you* won't be!"

Stunned, Lucille stared at him.

Tears gathered in Pascal's eyes. "Your grandmother died when she faced a demon. It's too dangerous. Why does it have to be *you* who has to face this one?"

Lucille crouched to meet his eyes. "Because it's my destiny. You heard Albert. I come from a long line of witches. It's my duty to defend this city." And this world, she added quietly. "I must go."

To her relief, Pascal was mature enough to nod. He swallowed his tears and hugged her tightly. Then he let her go. "Stay safe!"

He took a step back and Lucille blew him a kiss, before turning towards the door.

Suddenly the world exploded behind her. Glass shattered and wood cracked. Lucille whirled around to see the big oak tree ripping through the window, heading straight at Pascal. In a flash, she was at his side, arms wrapped around his body, braced for the impact.

Rachel

With school cancelled due to the storm, Rachel was able to spend some quality time with her father. They passed the morning catching up, then prepared jambalaya for lunch. Something about the smell of the dish and the companionship with her father in the kitchen grounded Rachel and gave her a sense of belonging. She wished they could cook together every day.

Despite her mother avoiding the downstairs like the plague, Rachel was in a good enough mood to set the table for three. "I'll go get her," she said to Mick, and went upstairs.

As soon as she reached her mother's door, she felt a pang of guilt. Her hand hovered in the air, afraid to knock. Annette had confessed to her what had really happened with the divorce. In her joy at seeing her father again so soon after her visit to LA, Rachel had almost forgotten about his philandering ways.

Sure, she and Annette had their difficulties. Her mother had done too much and cared too little to ever change that. But the man she'd looked up to all her life wasn't as blameless as she'd thought. Had he really not fought for her and Nico? And if so, was it really because he hadn't cared enough?

Rachel decided she wouldn't get any questions if she didn't knock. Lunch could wait. "Mum?"

"Come in."

Nervously, Rachel pushed the door open and poked her head inside. Annette was sitting on her bed, painting her nails and listening to music.

"Lunch is ready," she said as she slipped into the room and closed the door behind her.

Annette looked up and frowned. "Since when do we eat lunch?"

Rachel tried to ignore the barb. How many times had she wished they'd eaten together as a family? Instead, she and Nico had learnt to cook from an early age. "Dad and I made jambalaya. It's delicious."

"I'll have some later."

"Really? You aren't coming?"

Annette hesitated to answer.

Rachel stifled a groan. Instead she asked coldly, "Is it because of Dad or because you can't stand spending time with me?"

"Rachel!" Annette's frown deepened. She put down her bottle of nail polish and shook her hand. "I thought we'd moved on from that."

"I thought so, too, and yet you're all holed up in your room while Dad and I spent the morning together."

Annette was still blowing on her nails as she looked at Rachel. "Isn't that nice? I know better than to come between you and your dad."

"Is it really that bad?" Normally, Rachel would've given up and retreated by now, but she'd done that too many times, condemning her mother just because she made it too easy. "Why are you doing this?"

"Doing what?"

"Taking yourself out of the equation?"

Annette waved her off. "Oh, please. You don't want me down there. You've got your dad, all is well. And for so long this time." Her sudden smile was almost painful. "Go, eat with him. I've got more nails to do."

"Who's not fighting for me now?" Rachel said bitterly.

She turned abruptly towards the door as Annette snorted. "Is that what you want? The two of us fighting for your attention?"

Rachel bit her lip, unsure of what she wanted.

"I'm not going to ruin this for you," Annette said more softly. "Not again."

The words made Rachel squeeze her eyes shut and breathe flatly through her nose. When she'd regained her composure, she opened the door. "Well, the jambalaya's getting cold. Your loss."

She couldn't be sure, but as she left, she thought her mother whispered, "I know." Rachel didn't care. All those complaints about her father giving up on his family, and here Annette couldn't even be bothered to eat lunch with them.

For a shameful moment, Rachel had let her guard down and believed Annette. But her mother's words didn't match her actions. In the end, it didn't matter if Mick had been unfaithful in their marriage. He'd gone out of his way to stay in touch with his kids, celebrating every birthday and Christmas, and always making time for them, while her mother had forgotten almost every celebration, ignored all of Rachel's and Nico's needs for a loving family, and had been criminally neglectful.

If Rachel hadn't grown up and had her own reasons for staying in Greenvalley, she would've packed her bags and followed her father home to LA. Annette and her shattered dreams had no place in her life.

Not anymore.

Fabian

As Fabian crossed the town, getting closer and closer to the centre of the storm, he cursed Matt about a thousand times. Without him, he could've stayed home and cuddled with Merle or spent some time drawing. He hadn't done that in ages and Christmas was coming up. Instead, he had to brave strong winds and fear for his life as everything that wasn't bolted to the ground tumbled through the streets, the trees shedding their branches instead of just their leaves.

"There you are!" Matt was already waiting outside the now-closed library. He'd found a relatively sheltered corner between the large building and the one next to it. "Did you bring your feather?"

Fabian huddled into the corner beside him before opening his jacket just wide enough to give Matt a glimpse of the blue feather quills. "I can follow simple instructions." When Matt raised an eyebrow, Fabian rolled his eyes. "You have a plan?"

"So-so."

"So-so?"

Matt winced. "Don't worry, your only job is to create a wind channel so I can get to Shenny. I'll do the rest."

"I don't like this plan." What kind of plan was it, anyway? Hadn't they already tried that yesterday?

"Noted." Matt nodded, determined. "Ready?"

The right answer would've been *not at all*. Instead, Fabian sighed and shrugged. "Let's do this. Where is she?"

"Over there. I bet if you mess with her storm a bit, she'll come right over."

As if the plan could get any worse. Nevertheless, Fabian took out his feather and held it so tightly his fingers hurt. It wouldn't do them any good if the feather was torn from his hands and blown away.

Together, they left their safe little corner and stepped into the middle of the road. Normally a bad idea, but today there was no traffic. Anyone with more than half a brain cell knew to stay inside. Unfortunately, that excluded the two of them.

Bracing himself, Fabian flicked his feather in front of him. The disturbance in the wind worked like a charm. The grey-cloaked Stormbride appeared almost instantly. She blew the storm back into Fabian's face, causing him to stumble backwards.

Matt caught him and stepped in front of him. Like the day before, he used his wings to shield Fabian. "Shen...ecra." At the last moment, he avoided calling her by her hated nickname.

"At last, you've come out of your hole, Melchior."

"Don't get me wrong, I love seeing you, but what are you doing here?" Apparently, the flimsy plan included a charisma attack.

Shenecra flew a little higher, as if she wasn't already looking down on them as it was. "Caspar wants you dead."

Slowly, Fabian backed away. If he really wanted to duel with a Stormbride—and he didn't want *any* of this—he needed a safety net. Or in this case, a safety wall. With his back to the library wall, he took his stance.

"And since when do you follow his orders?" Matt sounded more than confused.

"If I fail, which I won't, he'll replace me with you."

Matt coughed in a way that told Fabian he'd been on the verge of laughing but had held onto his half brain cell. "That'll never happen," he said instead.

Shenecra's eyes narrowed. "I agree."

In the fraction of a second, her expression changed and she let out her terrible scream. The sudden increase in wind picked up Matt and threw him into a parked car.

The niceties were over and it was Fabian's turn. With his feet planted firmly on the ground, he waved his feather in Shenecra's direction. At first, the wind only died down a little, but then it actually reversed within a narrow channel and headed straight for the Stormbride.

Unfortunately, that attracted her attention. Shenecra spun around and screamed at him. Fabian's efforts were destroyed in an instant, and he was pinned against the wall behind him with such force he couldn't even breathe.

Out of the corner of his eye, Fabian saw Matt struggle back to his feet, using Shenecra's distraction to sneak up on her. Then, just as Fabian's field of vision began to shrink, he drew his sword, leapt through space and brought it down on Shenecra.

Fresh air filled Fabian's lungs as Shenecra's attention shifted. Her storm picked up Matt and threw him into a tree across the road. His sword was ripped from his hands and something snapped with a crunching sound.

Against all hope, Fabian hoped to see a broken branch. Instead, his eyes found Matt once more. He was clinging to the tree with one hand, one wing hanging limply, while he pressed his hand to his chest, looking as if he were in terrible pain.

"Caspar was right. Humans are incredibly fragile." Shenecra sneered, then screamed again, causing Matt to lose his grip on the bough.

With a scream, the half-demon fell to the ground. A shower of branches came down on top of him.

Fabian winced in pity. He could only hope Matt's healing powers would save him from serious injury. Meanwhile, he formed a new plan. Instead of creating a wind to challenge Shenecra's storm, he began to draw metal bars around her, connecting them to form an old-fashioned bird cage.

The drawing was about to become reality when Shenecra spun around. The gusts around her tore the cage apart, sending the bars flying everywhere. One of them came straight at Fabian, who could only stare in horror as it went tip-first into his thigh. The same thigh that had been injured by Caspar.

Fabian screamed in pain as his leg gave way underneath him and he crashed to the ground, driving the metal bar further in. For a few moments, all he could see were stars. The flow of blood in his ears became unnaturally loud and his pants felt wet. Shaking, Fabian fumbled for his leg. *Hot. Sticky.* He touched the bar and screamed again.

Slowly, his vision returned. Despite his bad shape, Matt was attacking Shenecra again, blood covering most of his face. Meanwhile, the storm intensified, picking up everything that wasn't bolted to the ground.

A metallic screech tore through the static in his ears. Fabian's eyes widened as he saw an empty car hurtling towards him.

Samantha

It would definitely be the last time Samantha braved the outside world today—unless it was to kill the Stormbride. Somehow, she made it home in one piece and was able to catch her breath. She took off her shoes and jacket and was about to go upstairs when she saw her father sitting at the table in the living room, staring at her.

"You're back." His voice sounded strangely distant.

"Yes." Samantha shivered. "Terrible weather." She took a step into the living room. "Daddy? Can I ask you something?"

He glared at her and held up his hand. "Does it have something to do with this?" In his hand was her Thorak. The same Thorak she kept safely hidden away in her desk drawer.

"Um. In a way, I suppose." Samantha felt a sudden urge to hug herself. "Why do you have it?"

He ignored her question. "How long?"

"How long what?"

"It's a demon hunter's dagger, you don't have to pretend you don't know that. I'm sure my mother told you when she put it in your hand."

Samantha swallowed, her heart suddenly beating faster. "I thought you didn't believe in magic. You always said it was nonsense." She knew he'd lied, of course, but his denial had always been swift and complete.

"*Idiocy.* Dangerous idiocy," Ben said sharply. He put the dagger down and stood. "I want you to stop this, effective immediately."

"That's understandable." After hearing her grandmother's story, Samantha tried to be sympathetic. "Granny told me how Gramps died." She began to walk towards him, keeping her voice calm as if she were approaching a wild animal. "I'm so sorry, but I need your help. No one knows how to defeat a Stormbride. Only you do. You've seen how. Please tell me how."

"I'm not going to tell you anything!" Ben roared. He grabbed her arm and dragged up the stairs.

Samantha stumbled after him, his fingers digging painfully into her arm. "Dad! What are you doing? Let go of me. Please."

They reached the top of the stairs. "This stops now. I'm not getting my daughters involved in this shit show." He hauled her to her room and pushed her inside.

Staggering, Samantha caught herself on the bed frame. Her entire body had gone into shock mode, but her brain was still trying to make sense of it all. To find a way to appeal to him. "I know it's dangerous. Believe me, I do! But, Dad, I was *born* to do this. I can't just stop."

"Oh, yes, you can. Born for it." He snorted derisively. "Magic is a *choice*."

"Well, I chose it then."

His face darkened further. "And now you're going to *un*-choose it." He marched over to her bookshelf and began pulling out her magical tomes and throwing them into the hallway.

Samantha winced at the mistreatment of her precious books. "Dad, please! Let's talk about it."

"There's nothing to talk about. You're going to stop this right now. I won't watch *you* die because of some misguided sense of duty." As he hurled the words at her, Ben continued to walk around the room, grabbing everything of magical value with frightening accuracy. It all ended up in the corridor.

At one point, Meg showed her face, but when a heavy scrying bowl nearly took her head out, she fled.

Tears streamed down Samantha's face, watching helplessly as her father tore her room apart. He even went through her wardrobe and discovered her secret stash of potions. At the sight of them, some sense returned to him.

"By tomorrow, all this junk will be gone." He pointed at the potions, not daring to throw them around. "Do you understand me?"

Unable to speak, Samantha nodded.

Ben held out his hand. "Smartphone."

"What?"

"You're grounded for the rest of the week. That includes no phone, no internet, and no magic. And if you don't hand over your phone right now, you'll be grounded for life."

Samantha was so stunned she fumbled for her phone and handed it over.

Her father glared at her. Then he marched out of the room and slammed the door so hard she shook.

For a minute or more she gasped for breath, unable to process what had just happened. Not once in her life had her father ever acted so unreasonable. Least of all to her. This display of rage and violence shook Samantha to the very core.

And give up magic? How could she when it was all around her? In the air, in the earth, in the water, everywhere she looked. Giving up all that was like asking her to give up her sight. And what about her friends? How could she let them fight alone when she was supposed to be one of the Six?

No, giving up was out of the question.

Samantha patted her cheeks, though the tears wouldn't stop falling. She stood up. Her legs felt weak, as if her father had drained them of all energy. Sobbing, she made her way to the potions and looked at them.

This was her work. She'd spent weeks testing them to find the most powerful blend. She had a *talent*. A talent she would choose again and again.

Determined, she closed the doors to her wardrobe and grabbed a pair of scissors from her desk. For a moment Samantha hesitated, but then she gathered her courage and cut into her finger. On a piece of paper, she drew a pentagram.

"Melchior. Melchior, please come. Mel—"

He appeared in her room in his demon form, blood streaming down his face, one wing hanging awkwardly from his shoulder, gasping in pain. As soon as he recognised her, he turned into Matt.

"Sam."

She swallowed hard. "You've got to get me out of here. You..." Worry took over. "What happened?"

"Shenny. The Stormbride, I mean."

He took a step towards her and reached for her. An inch from her tear-stained cheek, he stopped. "What happened here?"

"My father..." Her breathing quickened, a sob hovering on the edge of her voice. "I need to talk to Caroline." She was the only one who could reason with her father and fight Samantha's case. Surely she could fix everything. "I..."

The tears overwhelmed her. Suddenly she was in Matt's arms, clinging to him for dear life. The blood on his body mixed with her tears as she sobbed uncontrollably.

For a moment, Matt just stood there, but then he gently wrapped his arms around her. A second later, Samantha felt his hand on her head, caressing her almost cautiously.

"You've got to get me out of here," she whispered between sobs.

"Of course. I..." He cleared his throat. "It's just... we have to get back to Fabian. I think Shenny's about to kill him."

That instantly stopped her tears. Shocked, Samantha looked up at him.

Matt made a helpless face. "I know."

Then he took her with him.

Matt

If it weren't for a Stormbride breathing down his neck, Matt would've been delighted about Samantha summoning him. He didn't quite understand what had happened. Something about her father? The only thing that mattered was that she'd called him.

Well, not the only thing.

Just before he'd been summoned, Shenny had taken aim at Fabian and thrown a car. Even if Matt hadn't been seriously injured, there was nothing he could've done to stop it. Now that they were back at the library, he held his breath in anticipation.

Shenny was gone and the wind had died down. It felt like a dangerous lull, and he expected the Stormbride to attack them any moment, but the area remained calm. There was plenty of evidence of the storm, though. A path of destruction had ripped through the trees across the road and there was the red car, crumpled against the wall of the library.

Matt swallowed. Had he led Fabian to his death? Unable to speak, he pointed to the crash site.

Immediately, Samantha took off. As he followed her, he noticed a trail of blood leading away from the car. And there was Fabian, awake and breathing. A metal rod was stuck in his leg, the pants around it slick with blood. Matt didn't think he'd ever seen Fabian so pale. He gasped in pain as Samantha threw her arms around his neck and sobbed uncontrollably.

Confused, Fabian looked up at him.

Matt shrugged uncomfortably. "She's a bit…" He really had no idea what was going on. "Where's Shenny?"

Fabian's voice trembled as he explained. "She thought you'd fled—again. It made her very angry, but apparently I was no longer of interest." He hissed in pain and Samantha let go of him.

"You're hurt," she said, as if only just noticing.

"Yes." Fabian winced again. "I'm afraid the rod will vanish into thin air in a few minutes, though." When Samantha looked at him in confusion, he admitted: "It's mine, I drew it. Plan didn't work."

"Shit!" Immediately, Samantha went into problem-solving mode and scanned the area. A moment later, she was pointing over Matt's shoulder. "Can you get me that scarf?"

Matt turned to find a scarf tangled in a tree. The wind was tugging at its ends. Instead of wasting more time, Matt jumped into the branches and pulled the scarf from its grip. His own body was already healing, but Fabian didn't have that luxury.

He handed the scarf to Samantha and she carefully threaded it through the hollow of Fabian's knee. "Should we pull the rod out now or risk it dissolving later?"

Fabian groaned softly. "I could bleed to death. This is worse than Caspar's wound."

"Then it stays in." She used the scarf to stabilise the rod as best she could.

Meanwhile, Matt felt the familiar pang of guilt. The Stormbride was here because of him. And he'd drawn Fabian into his plan, thinking the feather would be strong enough to get him a better angle of attack. But Shenny had completely dominated him, and now Fabian might die. It sucked to admit, but he was in way over his head. "I don't know how to beat Shenny. Caspar set her on me."

"Of course," Samantha muttered as she worked.

"There's no way to get close to her. Even my energy can't get through her storm."

Samantha sighed heavily. "My father knows how to defeat her."

"Ben knows how to kill Stormbrides?" Fabian asked confused.

Matt hadn't really paid much attention to Samantha's parents. Unlike Fabian's mother, they weren't very involved in the whole monster-hunting business. And Samantha had never mentioned before that they knew about magic.

Tears were shimmering in her eyes again. "He does, but he won't tell me because he witnessed one kill my grandfather." She gasped for air. "He forbade me to ever use magic again."

"Can he do that?" Matt asked. Samantha without magic was like Ashuan without a sky. Inconceivable.

Samantha shrugged defiantly. "He can certainly try..." She deflated again. "He's just worried about me. I didn't know he felt that strongly about magic. Fabi, I need to talk to your mum. And you need a doctor. Or Jan."

"I'll take you to the Bendtfelds. And then I'll see if I can find Jan." Matt bent down to help Samantha pull Fabian to his feet.

Fabian hissed and groaned as he struggled onto his feet. When he finally stood, he looked like he was about to faint. Matt took his and Samantha's arms and disappeared with them.

Jan

Jan pressed the emergency call button stubbornly as he had for the last fifteen minutes or so. No one responded.

"Hello?" he sang into the intercom, hoping it would somehow connect. "We could use some help, you know…"

"We're gonna fall. We're gonna die," Anne whispered behind him. She seemed on the verge of hyperventilating.

Jan hit the button with his forehead and groaned. "Calm down, Anne. It only stopped because of the storm. Nobody's going to die."

"There's no fresh air," Anne informed him. "We're in a small room, so eventually we'll run out of air."

"Then maybe you should stop breathing so much." Her eyes widened and he regretted his thoughtless words. "Sorry. I'm just—"

"In a fighting mood." Anne nodded rapidly. "You and Dad are always at each other's throats. But now we're going to die and he'll be sorry."

Jan snorted. "As if." He gave up the intercom and sat down. "If we die, you're the only one he'll mourn."

"Don't say that!"

"We're *not* going to die, Anne. The storm just knocked out a power cable. They'll fix it in no time and we'll be out of here. The elevator hasn't moved a bit since it stopped, so the safety traps are working."

"That's not what I meant," she whispered. Reluctantly, she sat down next to him and laid her head on his shoulder. "Do you really think Dad doesn't care about you?"

"He never has."

"That's not true," Anne insisted.

Jan leant his head against the wall and looked up at the dim emergency lights. "Fine, he cares. But everything I do turns to shit, so we fight." As angry as his father's words made him, they'd also hit a nerve. Lately, nothing he touched seemed to go right.

"That's not true."

"Yes, Anne, it is. I just can't help it. That's why I break things or get fired from my job. Or just generally suck."

"What really happened at the hostel?"

Jan shrugged. "I told you. I pressed the emergency button and destroyed the bathroom upstairs."

"Why?"

He cocked his head. "What do you mean *why?*"

"Well, it's a strange story, no offence. But do you really expect me to believe that you'd evacuate the whole building so that you could have a cultivated bathroom destruction in peace?"

Jan snorted. "Cultivated destruction. I love you."

"I love you, too. But I still think you're full of crap."

"You and our parents."

Anne slapped his arm hard enough to hurt. "Stop twisting my words. I don't believe you."

"Fine, tell me what happened then." Jan waited with bated breath.

It didn't take Anne long to come up with an answer. With overwhelming confidence she said, "It was a monster."

"There are no monsters," Jan repeated his father's tired lie.

Anne huffed. "Oh, really? Then why haven't they found the school shooter? The one who didn't even have a gun? And that mysterious disease we all caught and then got cured from overnight?"

"That was due to toxic garbage on the ley line." Or the Rivers of Magic, as Samantha and Lu called them. "Not monsters."

"Ha! So the others were monsters."

Jan stared at her. It had always annoyed him, but his sister *was* smart. Too smart for her own good. "It was a Gorgon. She destroyed the bathroom when she tried to petrify me. I used the emergency button to get everyone to safety. She almost got me, but I was lucky. I tried to explain it to the police, but they suggested I check myself into a mental institution." He pressed his lips together. It had always been like this. No one ever believed him when he told them about the monsters.

"Why didn't you explain that to Mum and Dad?"

He groaned. "Because I've learnt from past mistakes. Normally I wouldn't give a shit, but magic is like a red cloth in our household. They think I'm making it all up."

In her naivety, Anne pleaded, "Try it."

"Okay, here's a story." He pushed away from the wall and crossed his legs to face her. "You know you're a prem baby, right?"

"Of course."

"Well, while Mum was in hospital with you, I met my first monster. I was with Dad. He was supposed to look after me—I was only four—but he was always on the phone asking about you. So I went off on my own and came across this monster under a bush. I don't remember exactly what it looked like, just that it had eyes. Like, a lot of eyes."

Anne listened, her lips slightly parted, hanging onto every word he said.

"When I told Dad, he got angry." Jan still remembered the first time his father had shouted at him for no reason. At least no reason he'd understood. "And then he dragged me home, just to call Mum again."

"I'm sorry," Anne whispered.

"For what? You were a baby fighting for your life. You know what they always say; it looked really bad for a while."

Anne shrugged slightly. She didn't show any signs of having been born prematurely now. "Still. I had everyone worried."

Jan made a face. "You're disgusting. Stop blaming yourself." Not for the first time Jan wondered how his parents could have had two such completely different children. "Anyway, we were back home and he didn't care about the monster. But I knew what I saw, so I put on my knight's armour—I loved that stuff—and snuck out on my own".

Anne's eyes widened. "You didn't."

"Of course I did. Don't you know I was born stupid?"

"Brave." As he stared at her in confusion, Anne smiled. "You were born brave, not stupid."

Flustered, Jan cleared his throat. "If you say so. The fact is, I went down to the playground and faced that monster. It lashed out and cut right through my plastic armour. I probably would've died if that old woman hadn't shown up. She stepped between me and the monster and told me to run back home. I never looked back." Now that he thought about it, there was a good chance the woman had been Elda Kollmer, or maybe even Lucille's grandmother.

"Were you badly hurt?" Anne asked worriedly.

He pulled up his shirt and showed her the three scars on his back. "I was bleeding. Of course, I tried to tell Dad, but he shut the door in my face." All these years, this particular memory had stayed with Jan. He'd really needed his dad, but Stefan had been so worried about the baby he hadn't even noticed the blood under Jan's plastic's armour. Jan couldn't remember exactly how he'd stopped the bleeding, only that he'd thrown away the bloody shirt by hiding it in the garbage. He'd thrown away the useless armour, too.

"He didn't believe me then and he won't believe me now. We're just... He just likes you a lot more than me. They both do." It was a truth Jan had accepted a long time ago.

Anne started to shake her head, then threw herself at him. "I'm sorry my birth was so annoying."

Jan laughed softly. "I forgive you. Just this once."

After squeezing him once more, Anne leant back again. "Why don't you try it again?"

"Anne, please."

"I mean it. He was under a lot of stress back then. I'm not saying it was right because his job was to look after *you*, not me, but I understand. Look, I promise not to be in any mortal danger this time."

Jan laughed. "It won't work. Believe me. Sure, I'll cut him some slack for that time, but that was just the beginning. Dad and I are like water and oil. We don't mix.

"More like two stubborn goats that always go head-to-head."

"Maybe. But it is what it is. He's made up his mind about me, and frankly... I've made up mine about him, too. As soon as I get my feet under me, I'm out of here."

Anne's face fell. "I don't want that."

He shrugged. "Honestly, I do. I just need a bit of luck."

"You will," Anne said with the utmost confidence. "I believe in you. You will get that paramedic job."

"They're not even taking applications now."

"They are in the new year."

"Are they? How do you know?"

She clicked her tongue. "Because I asked them, stupid. You think I'm letting you do this all by yourself?"

"Um, yeah?" It was *him* who needed a well-paid job, not Anne.

"Well, I'm not. I'll look at your application. I'll practice interviews with you until you hate me with a passion. Heck, I'll drag your ass over there if you find an excuse not to go. Unless it's a monster attack. Then I'll let you save the day while I distract the interviewer until you can get there."

Jan burst out laughing. "Man, Anne. You're hilarious." Despite the ridiculousness of it all, he appreciated the passion. It was nice to know he mattered to someone.

"Everything you touch doesn't turn to shit. This is your goldmine."

He didn't know that, but for the first time in a long while he actually allowed himself to hope.

Lucille

Lucille stared at the tree and the shards of glass hanging precariously above her. It was as if time itself had stopped, leaving her suspended in grave danger. She couldn't move, couldn't even think. The only thing going through her mind was that she was going to get hurt really bad. Or worse.

"I can't hold it much longer." Pascal's voice was strained. He had raised his short arms, slowly slipping out from under her and backing away. "Come with me."

Telekinesis. The tree was suspended in the air by his powers.

Before Lucille could properly process her situation and what Pascal had said, the door behind her slammed open. The tree began to shake. Someone grabbed her arms. The tree fell just as Lucille and Pascal were being dragged away.

A few branches brushed against her arms, but they barely scratched her. Instead, she fell into the person behind her, and they both went down with a thud. "Dad?"

Bastien wrapped his arms around her and pressed her against his chest. His heart was beating so fast she could feel it through her back. After a few moments, he loosened one arm to hold it out to Pascal. The boy immediately flew to them. "You're okay. You're okay," Bastien breathed.

Lucille stared at the tree at her feet. If her father hadn't walked in when he did, she would've been crushed. No, if Pascal hadn't held onto the tree at all, it would've been the end of her. Everything had happened so quickly. Her own heart was beating as fast as her father's.

He shifted behind her. "Quick, let's go down to the cellar."

"We have a cellar?"

Bastien laughed softly. "Where do you think we store our good furniture when it's not in use?"

She'd never thought about it.

"Come on."

Together they got up and left the destruction behind. When the last disaster had struck Greenvalley, Lucille had snuck out of her family's house to join her friends. But this time, her family needed her. Or rather, she needed them. After all, her father had come to help her. "How did you get there at the right time?"

"I heard the crash from my office. I came as fast as I could, but..." His eyes fell on Pascal.

There was no way her father could've heard the crash, run over, and made it to the library in time to do anything. The fact that he *had* been able to save her at all was a dead giveaway.

Lucille could see Pascal gulping. It wasn't unwarranted. She remembered when she'd told her father about her magic. He'd flipped out and threatened to send her back to boarding school. She wanted to believe he wouldn't have a fit this time, but she couldn't be sure. Still, she took a deep breath and prepared herself. Better her than Pascal.

As they took a flight of stairs in the servants' quarters Lucille had never noticed before, she said, "Daddy, you have to promise not to freak out."

"Lucille, no," Pascal whispered.

"Have you ever seen me freak out?" Bastien asked.

Lucille winced. She *had*, but then she'd made her father forget about the incident. "Actually... Listen, I know this is a sensitive subject for you. Albert told me how my grandmother died."

He drew in a sharp breath. "Albert did what?"

She raised her finger warningly. "Promise!"

In the cold light of the cellar lamp, she saw the storm in his eyes. The man who'd threatened to send her back was still there, but Lucille was no longer seventeen. She could move out if she wanted to. She hoped it wouldn't come to that for Pascal's sake, but if it did, she was prepared.

Finally, Bastien nodded. "You have my word."

"Good. Well, my grandmother was a witch and so am I." Despite him taking another sharp breath, Lucille continued, "I've known for over a year now. It's dangerous at times, but the truth is the danger will be there whether I get involved or not. I choose to get involved because I have the power to prevent unnecessary deaths."

"Even at the risk of your own life?" Bastien asked in a flat voice. His argument sounded tired, overused.

"It comes with the job."

He hung his head and took a few deep breaths. When he looked up again, his face was pained. "You understand the dangers?"

"A friend of mine died a year ago. Two friends, actually."

He frowned immediately. "I didn't know that."

"I..." Reluctantly, Lucille told him about the spell that had gone wrong and how much it had frightened her. "I couldn't risk it."

"So you went through all that heartbreak and loss on your own?"

Lucille shrugged uncomfortably. "Not on my own. I had my friends, and they'd known Nico longer." He didn't need to know that her spell had also sent Linda away and set fire to the house when she'd started to spiral. In the end, her friends had come through and there had been more pressing matters.

Bastien looked at her, then reached out and hugged her for the second time in an hour. A record, for sure. "I'm sorry."

"You are?"

He winced. "I should've prepared you better. My mother would be horrified if she knew I'd left you alone with this. But after she died... it was so terrible. I'd already lost Alena, then her... I couldn't afford to lose you too. I thought sending you away would keep you safe, but I should've known better. The moment you stepped into Greenvalley, your ancestral magic found you."

Things were a bit more complicated than that. It hadn't been until Lucille had started wearing her grandmother's emblem that she'd come into her powers. But that paled in front of his revelation.

"*You* were the one who sent me away?"

"I told you, it was a joint decision. Of course I never told Linda my reasons. Not in so many words."

Lucille could only stare at him. It was true that whenever she'd asked, she'd been told "Your father and I decided..." but she'd put all the blame on Linda and none on him. It wasn't until she'd moved and tried to get his attention in vain that she'd realised her father wasn't the hero of her story. It still hurt, but it was an old pain. She had so much more to live for now.

"So..." Pascal began. She'd almost forgotten he was there. "Does that mean magic isn't so bad after all?"

"It's not the magic that's bad," Bastien mused. "It's the dangers that come with being one of the Greenvalley witches."

"So if you're not from Lucille's witchline and you're not planning on fighting any monsters," Pascal phrased carefully, "it would be okay to have some? Hypothetically speaking."

Lucille watched her father's face tighten for a moment, but then he turned and faced Pascal. He didn't get down on one knee, but treated him like an adult, as he'd so often done with her. "I know about your magic, Pascal."

"You do?"

"Of course. Do you think I'd let anyone into our family without running a background check?"

Lucille walked over to Pascal and put a protective arm around him. "He's a child."

"It's alright," Pascal said. "Lots of adoptive parents do it."

The flicker of a smile crossed Bastien's face. "But I bet not many adoptive parents have access to a mind reader. I promise it won't happen again. It's a rule of mine not to use Albert's talents on my loved ones. I promised Lucille's mother that. But for security reasons it was necessary." Then he smiled broadly. "I've known from the moment you came into our house, Pascal, and I'm grateful for it, because it looks to me like you just saved my daughter's life."

"Oh, well, she does that all the time. A few weeks ago she even went to Hell to find a cure for the plague..."

Her father looked at her, his eyes wide. "You went to Hell?"

Lucille felt her cheeks burning. Curse children and their unchecked mouths. "Oh, well, you know, that's actually a long story..."

Balthasar

Balthasar was poring over documents his spies had intercepted that were to be presented to the Small Council when a gust of wind blew through the room. He slammed his hand down before the papers made an escape.

"This had better be important, Shenecra," he growled. "We had an agreement. No private meetings." Once he was done with her, he'd have to kill the idiot guard who'd let a Stormbride into the Residence of Lust. If only his mother paid as much attention to their skills at work as she did to their skills in bed.

The Stormbride entered the room, hissing. The wind increased. To be on the safe side, Balthasar put the documents in his drawer before turning to face her. "What do you want?"

"Cut the posturing! You won't be so arrogant when I lead the Black Guard."

He raised an eyebrow. "Your ability to dream is impressive."

Her eyes flashed and a sharp gust blew across the room. It was so vicious it cut Balthasar's cheek. "Don't take me for the fool your brother is. I'm not one of your mindless puppets, Balthasar. Don't forget that."

Unimpressed, Balthasar dabbed at the blood from his cheek with a handkerchief. He took his sweet time to close the distance between them. "How could I forget, my dear Shenecra?"

She looked at him anxiously, swallowing as he raised his hand. A small moan escaped her as he ran his fingers over her shoulder.

Balthasar allowed himself a wicked smile. He stepped around her, close enough for her to feel his presence, and whispered in her ear,

"Let me remind you that we must be careful. Our alliance rests on your ability to keep it secret." His hands moved down her body, slowly and carefully. "It would be a shame if Melaney found out." The Archdemon's name, and the fact his hands had slipped beneath her grey rags, caused Shenecra to moan loudly. It felt as if he'd dipped his fingers into a storm cloud. Delicious electricity ran up his arms. "And now report."

Shenecra closed her eyes, fighting her desire with every breath. She had no chance. "He got away. Twice," she hissed. "Melchior is a coward not worth fighting. I'm bored." She screamed when his hands twisted her insides.

"What are you saying? Are you going to disappoint me?"

"How am I supposed to fight him if he keeps running away?" she asked frantically. "He's not like Caspar."

Balthasar loosened his grip and returned to caressing her. "True. But he's not a coward. You just haven't hit him where it hurts yet. You see, my brother is foolish. He doesn't care about himself. But destroy his city, his friends, and he'll fight you to the death. *His* death."

He had her almost where he wanted her. With one hand, he lifted her chin. Her lips trembled, her eyes glistening with lust. She was irrevocably his.

"Go now," he said, retreating to the other side of the room to wash his hands in the water bowl. "You're not going to let a half-demon play games with you, are you?"

Shenecra breathed hard, but the wind was choppy and undirected. "I don't let anyone play games with me." She hurried away as if he'd shot energy at her.

Balthasar's lips curled in amusement. Shenecra liked to think she was in control, but he'd been playing her for half a century, and she'd always come back for more.

Sadly, she wasn't his only visitor. He turned to see Caspar slip into the room. There was no telling how long he'd been there.

As so often, his handsome face was distorted by a snarl. "That was quite the show."

Balthasar groaned. "Is there no peace here? I'll have to ask the mages to make me a flawless isolation spell."

"You can't afford that," Caspar hissed. "And you forget that I can break spells. It would be easier for you to overthrow Melaney."

"Which brings us to the matter at hand. Nicely done, Caspar." You had to encourage the young ones, even if they didn't appreciate it. "I take it you followed Shenny's report?"

"In detail." Caspar looked disgusted. "I didn't know you had a thing for Stormbrides?"

"I call it politics." Stormbrides had their charms, though it was a risky business and rarely without pain. "I had to take the wind out of her sails, so to speak, while making her believe she was in control." He took a glass of wine.

Caspar growled. "Manipulative bastard."

Balthasar toasted Caspar. "And proud of it."

"You probably think I'm just as easy to manipulate."

"You have proven your capacity for deception more than once."

Caspar frowned, as usual a bit slow with words.

It was time to burst his bubble. "Caspar, you seem to be under the misconception that we're working together."

"I thought that was the plan?"

"We're rivals, have you forgotten?" Balthasar took another sip and put the drink down. "Your death just doesn't have the urgency to bother me much right now. So, go back to playing with your soldiers while I do my job."

Caspar's eyes flashed. "I'd rather play with your entrails."

By the time he shot his energy, Balthasar had already stepped through space and reappeared behind Caspar. He grabbed his brother's arms, twisted them behind his back, and held a stiletto to his throat.

"How predictable. What now?"

Caspar breathed hard, his wrath bubbling beneath the surface. With every breath, he cut himself on Balthasar's knife. Then he exploded.

His wings ripped through his shirt and smacked Balthasar in the face, forcing him to let go. But before Caspar could use his advantage, Balthasar had grabbed one of his wings, stabbed it with his stiletto, and pulled the weapon down, almost severing the appendage.

Screaming, Caspar whirled around and went for his throat. Balthasar leant back and shot energy into Caspar's stomach. Blood splattered across his expensive carpet. As Caspar went down, Balthasar punched him left and right for good measure, then buried his fingers in his hair and yanked his head back.

"Just because I don't attack everyone who looks twice at me, doesn't mean I can't fight." Almost lovingly, he sliced into Caspar's cheek. "Take a breather and heal that."

Caspar tried to get up, but it was too late. Balthasar had already plunged the stiletto into his throat. Blood dripping from his mouth, Caspar bent over.

"Go now!"

This time there was no resistance. Caspar disappeared on the spot, leaving a disgusting puddle of blood in his wake.

Balthasar's face fell at the sight of the puddle and the blood on his suit. The earlier energy shot had gone through his chair and a scroll case on the wall. He could only hope it hadn't destroyed anything important.

Oh, how he hated wrath demons.

Fabian

"I can't find Jan and the phone lines are down."

Fabian sat on his bed, his bleeding leg stretched out in front of him, moaning. The rod had disappeared, and his mother was in the process of re-bandaging him and casting a few small spells to stop the bleeding while Samantha held his hand. So much of his blood had already seeped into the towels underneath, and now Matt was telling him that Jan wasn't available.

"Should I take him to the hospital?" Matt asked.

Meanwhile, Caroline had finished her work. "I think we've got him stabilised for now. The hospital is out at the moment. The storm collapsed the roof over the emergency ward. They're diverting all emergencies to Wernigerode. I'll take him there."

"About this storm," Samantha said softly, her face sticky with shed tears. Fabian wished he knew why—apart from the fact she was worried about him. "It's a Stormbride."

His mother's eyes widened. "A Stormbride?"

"She's after me," Matt said grimly.

"Caro." Samantha's voice almost broke. "Dad found out I'm a witch and that we hunt monsters from time to time."

"What did he say?" Fabian noticed his mother's voice was no less tense.

Fresh tears were rolling down Samantha's cheeks. "He banned me from ever doing so again."

"Oh, Ben." Caroline sighed. "He has his reasons, you know. Especially with this storm."

Confused, Fabian looked back and forth between them. "What reasons? Banning Samantha from using magic is like asking her to stop breathing. It's wrong."

"Thanks, Fabi." Samantha rested her head on his shoulder and took a few shaky breaths. "I know his father died in a storm like this," she told Caroline. "But if he doesn't tell us how my grandfather killed the Stormbride, this storm will kill somebody else."

Caroline sighed again. "I'll talk to him."

"And he'll listen to you?" Matt asked, confused. "Forgive me if I'm wrong, but he sounds... testy."

"Oh yes." Caroline pulled a face. "He can lash out a lot when he's hurt. Believe me, I've been on the receiving end of it more than once."

"You have?" Fabian asked.

His mother shrugged. "We used to be... a thing."

"Wait, what?" Samantha lifted her head again. "What do you mean 'a thing'?"

Caroline waved her off. "It was a long time ago. I went to their house to learn from Elda when I was ten and had the biggest crush on him. But excuse me if I say he can be... a bit of a dick, I suppose. We were together for a while, but he was always fighting with Erich—and to be fair, Erich was not an easy man. He had very little empathy. I don't know what Elda saw in him. But Ben started to hate magic and he wanted me to stop, too. Just like you." She smiled sadly. "I know how you feel, darling. Still, I shouldn't have run to Jo and kissed him instead."

Fabian didn't quite know whether to be horrified or fascinated. "You never told us."

"Of course not. You were kids. But we had a life, too. And in true teenage fashion, Jo and Ben had a public fight about it—at the dance, no less—and got over it. It was ridiculous because he'd already moved on anyway and had his sights set on Juli. But they fought it out. One moment fists were flying, the next they were in each other's arms, crying."

"That sounds weird," Matt commented drily.

"It was. But back to the Stormbride," Caroline said. Her cheeks were a little flushed, as if she regretted telling them about it now. "All I know about that night is Erich marched into the school hall and dragged Ben out. As you can imagine, it was humiliating. And in front of Juliane. The next day we all heard that Erich had died in the storm. That's all I know. Your father refuses to talk about it."

Samantha sighed heavily. "He's such a child." Slowly she pulled away from Fabian. "Very well. My grandfather obviously knew how, so there must be something written down. You take Fabian to the hospital while Matt and I hit the books."

"I'll talk to him," Caroline said quietly. "We'll sort this out."

"We'll start with the books at the Magic Circle." Samantha stood up. "Just be safe, okay?"

"You too." Fabian didn't like the idea of Samantha and Matt challenging the Stormbride again. Hopefully they wouldn't actually face her until they had all the information they needed. Then again, Erich had it, and he'd still died.

Samantha smiled sadly before holding out her hand to Matt. "Let's do this."

Matt nodded grimly and took her head. A moment later, they were both gone.

"Alright," Caroline said. "Can you make it to the car?"

"With some help." Fabian dreaded moving his leg, but if he didn't he'd slowly bleed out on his bed. "I'm sorry I'm causing you extra stress."

His mother's eyes widened. "Oh, please. I'm not *that* sick. You need medical attention, so let's get you some." She put her arm under his shoulders and helped him to his feet.

For a moment Fabian saw nothing but stars. "Dizzy."

"I'll make it quick."

Fabian couldn't remember how he got down the stairs and into the car. His world was still spinning when his mother strapped him into the back seat. It was the only place he could stretch his leg.

"Are you sure you don't want me to come with you?" When had his father arrived?

"I'm fine. I'll call you as soon as the doctor has seen him." Caroline got into the car and blew Joachim a kiss. "Love you."

"Drive carefully. There might be trees on the road and..."

Caroline laughed. "I know, darling. We'll be fine. You take care of Merle."

Joachim gave Fabian a worried look. "Hang in there, buddy." Then he shook his head. "Hiding in his room with a stab wound." He closed the car door and stepped back.

As they pulled out of the driveway, Fabian's head cleared. "You told Dad I was hiding in my room?"

"Well, what else was I supposed to say? Your half-demon friend teleported you to your room after you were hurt in battle?"

Fabian shrugged helplessly. "Wait. So, Dad doesn't know anything?"

In the rear-view mirror, he saw his mother's eyes watching him anxiously. "No, not really. I love your father, but his view of magic was poisoned by Ben. Joachim never took it seriously. He calls me his little witch..."

"TMI!"

She chuckled. "I mean, he teases me about it, but that's about it."

"Haven't you ever wanted to tell him the truth?"

"He has no magic, darling. You know how dangerous that is. Now imagine your father getting involved with no way to defend himself. It's bad enough to see you get hurt." Caroline bit her lip. "It's better this way, believe me." She met his eyes through the mirror and sighed. "If you want, we can tell him together."

Fabian shook his head. "No, you're right. The fewer people involved, the better." It was bad enough that *he* was involved. It was his destiny, but it didn't have to be his father's.

"Alright, let's see if we can call Ben." His mother took a deep breath before asking the phone assistant to call Ben.

To Fabian's surprise, the call went through. It had barely rung when Ben's voice came over the intercom. "Is Sam with you?" He sounded agitated.

"She was," Caroline said irritably.

"What do you mean *was?* Caro, you didn't let her go out in this weather, did you?"

Caroline sighed. "Ben, you have to listen to me. Sammy told me what happened between the two of you. I know you have your issues with magic, but Sammy is a very talented witch. Better than me. She—"

"I don't want to talk about that. I want to know where my daughter is!"

Fabian didn't like the aggressive tone on the phone. He wished he could move enough to put his hand on his mother's shoulder and give her strength.

"She's at the Magic Circle. Looking for the answer you refuse to give her."

"Don't start with that!" Ben shouted. "You know how dangerous it is."

Caroline took another deep breath. "Yes, Ben, I do." She met Fabian's eyes again. "However, I also know how good Samantha is and—"

"My father bloody well died in this weather!"

Fabian saw his mother flinch at the harsh tone. How could this be the same man who'd come over this morning to gently coax her out of her shell?

"Don't you think he had talent, too?" Ben continued. "Did it help him? No!"

"I'm sorry."

"As if!"

"Hey, stop it!" Fabian couldn't hold back any longer. "Don't talk to my mum like that."

Caroline gave him a quick smile. "It's okay, Fabian."

"No, it isn't. I don't care if you two had a thing or if you've known each other for decades. No one gets to talk to you like that."

"Did you *tell* Fabian?" It wasn't quite clear which part Ben meant, but his voice had lost its aggressiveness.

A red light allowed Caroline to give him a dazzling smile. After weeks of seeing her in bed, Fabian's heart felt ten pounds lighter. "Thank you," she whispered. "Yes, Ben, unlike you, I believe in open communication."

"Except with Dad," Fabian muttered.

"When Fabian told me he could do magic, I didn't turn on him, I supported him."

There was heavy breathing on the line. "How long, Caro?"

"How long have our children been honing their powers and fighting monsters?"

A grunt.

"More than a year. And if it weren't for them, we'd all be dead three times over. No joke."

Silence.

"Ben?"

Nothing.

"Ben, are you still with me?"

"I don't like this, Caro," he finally said in a very low voice. "It's not right. It's just not right." He seemed to blow his nose. "I can't lose her, too."

Caroline took a deep breath before saying incredibly gently, "Then you need to stop pushing her away and tell her what she needs to know to keep herself safe."

Fabian could tell by the big sigh on the other end of the line that the words had finally sunk in.

"She's a big girl now," Caroline said.

"I don't think I'm ready for that yet," Ben admitted. "But I guess you're right. Thanks, Caro. And Fabian? Take care of your mum for me, okay?"

Caroline ended the call and sighed softly. "That was rough."

"You know you're amazing, don't you? The way you stood up for Sam?"

She chuckled. "You're pretty awesome, too, kid."

Even though he was on his way to the hospital with a pretty serious puncture wound, held together only by spells and gauze, Fabian thought things were finally looking up.

Samantha

Furiously, Samantha pulled out book after book, glanced at them briefly, and threw them in a pile behind her. Neither of them said anything about storms or wind spirits, let alone storm demons. She needed a better catalogue, ideally an app like those for identifying plants or insects.

Behind her, Matt was doing absolutely nothing. Still, he had the audacity to ask, "Don't you think your grandma would know if it was in one of the books? I'm sure they looked at them all back then."

"That was *thirty years* ago," Samantha snapped. "Surely new books have been written. Besides, my grandfather obviously knew what he was doing."

"Or he got lucky." Matt shrugged. "Or he never killed her. The Stormbride killed him and left."

Samantha gave him a long look. "Everyone says he killed her in the same breath."

"Not everyone. Your father—"

"Has no idea!"

Matt put his hands up in defence. "Hey, I don't know what exactly happened between the two of you, but he obviously upset you a lot."

"Oh, is that obvious?" Samantha hissed in annoyance. Only then did she realise she was barking up the wrong tree. Matt didn't deserve her anger. Not this time. "I'm sorry. You're right. I'm upset. I... He's never been like this. I never thought he could hate me like that..." Now that she'd let go of her anger the despair came rushing back.

"Your father doesn't *hate* you," Matt said firmly. "He's afraid of magic, just like Fabian was back then. And he fears for you." He snorted. "You want to know what hatred is? When your brother tries to drown you in the river."

Samantha grimaced. Matt's demon family was on a whole other level.

"At least he only locked you in your room to keep you safe. He could shun you completely and refuse to even talk to you or meet your children."

The strange tangent made Samantha pause. "Has something happened between you and René?"

"No. But *his* father cut all ties with him. Apparently, he was a pretty serious demon hunter, just like your grandfather. Let's just say he wasn't the biggest fan of my mother. Oh well, you can't win them all, can you?"

Samantha poked him in the chest. "How can you joke about that?"

"Why not?" Matt shrugged, a slight smile on his lips. "I can't help it, can I? I don't even know the guy. He made the decision to cut me and René out of his life before I was even born. That's his fault, not ours. What I'm saying is," he took another step towards her, "if your father decides to shun you because you keep risking your life for this town then, believe me, you're better off without him."

"Thank you." She didn't want to be without her father but Matt was surprisingly right. "That was pretty insightful for a half-demon."

He gave her a wry grin. "I'm trying." Then he took another small step and raised his hand. Unlike back in her room, he didn't shy away and ran his fingers lightly across her cheekbone. "You're amazing," he whispered. "Don't let anyone tell you otherwise."

Samantha caught her breath. Her mouth was suddenly dry and she didn't dare move, as if something big was about to happen.

Instead, something heavy landed on the roof, startling her. Whatever it was, it sounded absolutely horrible, like metal scraping against metal. Samantha looked around wildly, searching for the culprit.

Matt swallowed. "Shenny."

A few seconds later, a storm arose *in* the Magic Circle. It picked up the books that Samantha had thrown around so carelessly and flung them through the room. Even the table moved. A book hit her arm. "Ouch!"

Matt tried to protect her by wrapping his arms around her, but they were completely peppered with books. "We have to go."

A moment later they were outside, looking at the Magic Circle. Her hair whipped against her face as the wind took her breath away. On the horizon, a dark, funnel-shaped cloud had appeared.

"Is that a tornado?" she asked, in horror.

"I'll distract her," Matt said.

He was about to disappear, but Samantha grabbed his arm and was pulled along.

They reappeared a few streets away. Matt looked at her in horror. "What are you doing?"

"You can't beat her!" Samantha reminded him. "We don't know how!"

"Yes, but she's after me. If I distract her, you can get away."

"And what about you?" The Stormbride would tear him apart.

Instead of answering, Matt jumped with her to the other side of the street. A second later, the nearby scaffolding obliterated the pavement they'd been standing on.

Samantha's heart almost burst from her chest. Such was the power of a Stormbride. A wind strong enough to pick up boards, metal poles, and even people—just like her grandfather.

"I'll be fine!" Matt insisted. "Running around with me isn't going to help either. Go and find a solution!" He gave her a firm shove and jumped several metres ahead.

Samantha stared at him. This was madness. He couldn't possibly hold out in this storm. Unfortunately, he was right. They didn't know how to beat her, so if she wanted to help him, she'd have to—

The gust of wind blowing in his direction suddenly turned and hit Samantha with full force. One moment she was on her feet, the next she was flying through the air.

Just as she started to fall, Matt's arms wrapped around her. Together they hit the concrete. Samantha gasped, but Matt had it worse as they slid five metres. "Are you okay?"

He gave her a thumbs up. "Just a little road rash." Quickly, he stood up, dragging her with him. The backs of his elbows were bleeding and his shirt was torn. "Why is she coming after you now?"

"Because I'm with you," Samantha whispered.

Ahead of them, the storm cloud dissipated to reveal a terrifying woman. She was grey from head-to-toe and it was impossible to tell if she was dressed in rags or if her body was nothing more than lightweight shreds in the wind.

Samantha and Matt were so transfixed by the sight they didn't see the car pull up beside them until the wheels screeched. A door opened.

"Get in, quick!"

"Dad?" He was the last person Samantha expected to see out on the streets.

"Come on. Before the wind turns."

Matt gave her a nudge and together they climbed into the back. The door was barely closed when Ben reversed at full speed, turned and sped away.

Nervously, he watched the rear-view mirror. Then his eyes met Samantha's. "Why?"

"Why what?" Samantha felt anger and fear rise in her stomach.

"Why would you risk your life for magic?"

A sudden calm quenched the ugly feelings. Her father didn't hate her, he was scared. "I'm not doing it for magic, Dad. I'm doing it to protect my friends. My family."

His face tightened slightly. "It's another Stormbride, isn't it?"

"Yes, and the only one who knows how to defeat one is you." She didn't believe that the Stormbride who'd killed her grandfather had simply fled. "What happened back then?"

The car took them away from the storm, but the grey clouds followed them. Matt kept his eyes on the rear window, looking tense. Samantha noticed his hand just inches from hers. Acting on instinct, she took it and braced herself. Surprised, Matt looked at her, but she stared ahead, swallowing hard. His fingers returned the pressure.

"I..." Ben sighed. "Very well, but..." He shook his head and took another deep breath. "We ran into the Stormbride on our way home from a dance. I'd snuck out earlier that day and my father had bulldozed into the dance, completely humiliated me, and dragged me out with him. I was mortified. I fought him, but he was stronger than me and didn't show any mercy."

"Caro said he was very strict."

Ben scoffed. "Strict? Other kids got time out, I got cursed."

"What?"

He waved it off and took another nervous look in the rear-view mirror. "I had it up to here, and when I finally managed to free myself, I ran the other way. Right into the Stormbride." He paused for a moment, clearly overwhelmed by the memories of that terrible day. "I couldn't move. There was a tornado coming at me and I didn't know what to do. But my father did. He caught up, grabbed my arm, and told me to hide inside one of those big concrete pipes. You know, like the one down on Kepler Road?"

Samantha remembered it from her childhood. She and Fabian had loved to crawl through it and listen to the echoes. "You hid in there?"

"I did. Meanwhile, my father fought the Stormbride. He used salt. Didn't even bother to open the bag, just threw it in the wind and let nature do its worst."

"Did it help?"

"It lessened the storm, but it wasn't enough. What worked was the Thorak. I suppose because Stormbrides are of demon nature, it was able to cut the wind. He got close to her, but then she screamed at him. My father threw the Thorak and it flew true, even though the storm picked him up and threw him into the tree. He died on impact." He sniffed quietly. "If I hadn't been such a pig-headed brat, he might not have died."

"Oh, Daddy." Pity tightened her chest and she reached for him. "I'm so sorry."

Ben shook his head. "Don't be. It was the life he chose. To risk his life to defend this city. To defend me." His eyes met Samantha's through the mirror. "I'm supposed to defend you, not the other way around."

"But you don't have magic."

"No, but I have this." He held up the Thorak from the seat next to him. Then he parked the car.

Samantha noticed that they'd reached the fields south of the town. There wasn't a tree in sight, just a few power lines. But there was no shelter either and already the storm was gathering. "Dad."

"What? It's a dagger. I can use a dagger. I also brought salt."

Panic overcame Samantha. Her father couldn't possibly think he could face a Stormbride. She wanted to say something clever, something to convince him, but her mind was blank. "You... you can't..."

"I'll do it." Matt let go of her hand and held it out to her father instead.

Ben looked at Matt for the first time. "Boy, this isn't a game."

"I'm not a boy. I've been fighting monsters my whole life. And the Stormbride is after me. She wants this fight. I'm ready to give it to her."

"Matt," Samantha whispered. The Thorak was poisonous to all demon species. Even him.

"Give me the dagger. I've got this."

Reluctantly, Ben handed it over. The aversion to the Thorak was so strong that Matt had to force himself, but in the end he grabbed it and only flinched slightly. Before Samantha could warn him to be careful, he'd opened the door and jumped into the storm.

"Did he just...?" Ben turned to her. "Who *is* that?"

"You said you brought salt?" Samantha snapped, her mind racing.

This time Ben handed her a large bag of salt without hesitation.

Samantha wasted no time getting out of the car. Her father cursed and scrambled to follow. By the time he'd made his way around the car, Samantha had broken the seal. The wind was pushing them both against the car, so instead of throwing it straight ahead, she stretched her arm out to the side and tipped the bag.

The salt blew out of her hands, the grains instantly disappearing into the grey. A few heartbeats later, the pressure of the wind eased. It wasn't much, but every bit could be important.

Unfortunately, that still left the Stormbride herself. She'd appeared above the field, shouting at Matt. He tried to get closer, but the wind picked him up and slammed him into the field. It wasn't a tree, but the ground couldn't have been soft either.

Nevertheless, Matt got up, jumped again, and reappeared behind the Stormbride. He was about to strike her when the wind caught him again.

"That boy is something else."

Samantha couldn't answer. She needed to think of something else. Something that would allow Matt to get close enough. Taking a deep breath, she dove into the magical rivers.

No wonder Matt was having trouble getting close. They were all in turmoil, like great magical maelstroms moving away from the Stormbride. Samantha didn't even know where to begin.

Just then, the storm threw Matt into one of the power masts. He hadn't even got up when a crack went through the pole, burying him under it.

"Matt!" Samantha screamed.

She tried to sprint towards him, but her father threw an arm around her and held her back. She thrashed and kicked, but to no avail.

Somehow, he managed to open the car door again and shoved her into the front seat. He threw the keys at her. "Drive!"

"I can't drive away. Matt's hurt. He... he..." He might even be dead.

"Yes, you can!" Ben shouted. "I'm going. You'll leave!" Then he slammed the door, knocking her knee aside in the process, and hurried towards Matt.

For a moment, Samantha was too stunned. She touched her face and found tears streaming down her cheeks. Matt couldn't be dead. He just couldn't be.

And now her father was going to run into the storm. Without experience. Without magic.

"Dad!"

Samantha threw the door open again and scrambled out of the car.

Matt

Regaining consciousness was no picnic. Matt groaned and tried to roll over, but something was pinning him to the ground. It was so heavy he struggled to breathe. He only noticed the widespread pain later, when the pressure suddenly eased a little.

"Can you get out?"

Matt gripped the Thorak tighter. Even though he wasn't touching the metal, his hand burnt. It was a different kind of pain than the one in his stomach, but it helped him focus. Slowly, he recognised Samantha's father.

Ben's face was distorted as he struggled to lift a pole that had fallen on Matt. Behind him, Shenecra's face appeared.

"You will die now, Melchior!" she hissed.

Matt's eyes widened. He gathered all his strength and jumped through space, hurtling past Shenecra with the Thorak. Judging by the scream, he'd got her.

Unfortunately, his body wasn't in the best shape either. He fell unceremoniously to the ground, unable to move, even though nothing held him down this time.

Shenecra had been wounded, but he'd only grazed her. If it weren't for the micro lightning crackling on her shoulder, he wouldn't even know she was hurt.

Her eyes flashed. She sent a gust of wind at Samantha's father, knocking him backwards over the pole. Hopefully she wouldn't go after him once she'd killed Matt.

His eyes fluttered as he tried to find the strength for another attack. Then he noticed the burning in his hand had gone. He'd dropped the Thorak. He gulped. Without it, death was inevitable.

"Matt!"

Samantha's voice called Matt back with a start. He wanted to tell her to go away, but his tongue wouldn't move.

"What are you doing with my winds, *witch?*" Shenecra hissed. The winds around her had become erratic, sometimes strong, sometimes no more than a breeze. She screamed, but even that didn't straighten them out.

Then Samantha was beside him, her face set. "You don't mind, do you?" She plucked something from the grass beside him. The Thorak.

"Sam... no," he whispered.

But she didn't listen, holding the dagger behind her back. "Come on! Show us what you've got."

Was she mad? They couldn't possibly survive a frontal attack.

Shenecra howled, then shot forward.

Samantha's body bent as she tried to withstand the storm. Matt cursed the slowness of his healing powers that forced him to do nothing but watch. He couldn't even jump away.

Suddenly, Samantha threw herself forward and struck with the Thorak. It sliced through the winds and straight into Shenecra's chest.

The Stormbride gasped, but before she could gather enough air to scream at her, Samantha plunged the dagger in again. And again. And again.

The wind tore Shenecra apart until there was nothing left but tumbling grey shreds.

Samantha's shoulders heaved. She dropped her arms and collapsed onto her back, her head landing softly on Matt's thigh.

He slowly managed to pull himself up on his elbows, wincing at the pain in his stomach and chest. He couldn't have cared less about his injuries. Instead, a silly little smile spread across his face as he watched Samantha's face, exhausted but relieved. Their eyes locked.

"Told you you're amazing."

She just huffed. With a groan, she pulled herself up. "How are you?"

"I'll live." With each heartbeat, Matt felt more and more like himself.

"Good." She stood up and looked past him. "Dad?"

Ben had scrambled to his feet and stared at her as if in a trance. He took a shuddering breath and hurried to close the distance. Before Samantha could say anything, he'd wrapped her in the kind of hug Matt wished he could give her.

Well, maybe not with half his ribs still broken.

"You're alive. You..." Ben held Samantha at arm's length. "That was... terrifying." His gaze dropped to Matt. "Shit, we need to get your friend to hospital."

"I'm fine," Matt said. To prove his point, he slowly pulled himself up to a sitting position. It hurt like hell, but that was to be expected.

Ben stared at him in horror. "You've just been crushed under a pylon. You're probably bleeding internally."

Matt felt around his stomach, poking at his organs. "No, not anymore." His healing powers usually started with the life-threatening conditions.

"Not anymore?"

Samantha gave him a warning look. She probably thought her father had enough to deal with after finding out she was a witch and had succeeded at what either of them had failed to do.

But Matt was done playing pretend to suit human sensibilities. "I'm half-demon. I heal on my own."

As expected, Ben's eyes bugged out. "You... what?" He looked at Samantha in horror.

She groaned. "Really, Matt?"

He dragged himself to his feet, wincing and gasping in pain. "I'm tired of hiding who I am. And you shouldn't be hiding who you are either. Remember, if he can't accept you for who you are, he's not worth it."

Flustered, Samantha turned to her father.

Ben's facial muscles worked overtime, but in the end he sighed. "That's some solid advice there." Slowly, he relaxed and smiled at Samantha. "Of course I accept you for who you are. Even if who you are is a powerful witch—perhaps stronger than both my parents combined—someone who challenges storms head on, and close friends with a demon."

"Half-demon," Samantha corrected softly.

"Well, that explains how you managed to break out of your room with the windows and doors closed."

Samantha started to giggle, then threw her arms around him a second time. Apparently, their fight was over.

They hugged long enough to make Matt uncomfortable. On the other hand, he was healing nicely. He took a step back and cleared his throat. "You probably have a lot of catching up to do." Matt didn't exactly want to be around when Samantha told her father about Daniel or any of the other terrible things he'd done. "Thanks for helping me out there, Mr Kollmer."

"It was the least I could do."

Matt smiled. "I'll leave you to it then." And before Samantha could protest, he jumped away...

...and straight into his bed. Groaning, he ran his hands over his face.

Why had he given in to the urge to tell Samantha's father the truth about him? Now he'd ask a million questions, or forbid her to see him ever again, or—

He'd claimed he had nothing to hide, but there was *plenty*. Matt couldn't help but feel that he'd just ruined his chances with his stupid demon honesty. He'd only wanted to make things easier for Samantha. She shouldn't have to keep his secrets just because they were big and ugly. Just the thought of her having to deal with Daniel's death and everything else without being able to turn to her family for support made him feel sick inside.

But then he thought of that moment in the car when she'd looked to *him* for support. It had been the first time in a year that she'd initiated physical contact. And such a momentous one, even more so than clinging to him in her room. Matt had barely been able to focus on her father's story, his mind swirling around their intertwined fingers and what it had meant.

Were they friends again? Could they ever be more?

He shook his head, of course they couldn't be more. She was with Cian now, and Matt didn't deserve her. Friendship was all he could hope for. And he would learn to appreciate that and stop lusting after her.

Or so he told himself, until his phone buzzed with a series of messages. Achingly, Matt reached for it then almost dropped it when he saw who was messaging him.

Samantha: Next time you drop a giant truth bomb on my Dad, don't run away.

Samantha: Thanks.

Samantha: It meant a lot.

A huge smile spread across Matt's face and stayed there long after his body had healed.

Jan

Just as Jan was about to fall asleep, the elevator came to life with a start. The proper lighting brightened the room and the intercom crackled. "Hello? Is anyone in there?"

"Yes!" Jan shouted, jumping up.

Next to him, Anne stood up more slowly. "We're trapped in the elevator. It's... it's moving again!"

The elevator continued its journey while the voice on the intercom apologised profusely. Jan didn't listen too closely. As soon as the doors opened on the next floor, he and Anne were out.

"Man, from now on I'm taking the stairs!"

Anne nodded emphatically. "Me, too." She looked at him shyly. "Shall we go upstairs? I'm sure Dad's calmed down by now."

Jan groaned, not particularly eager, but he nodded, and together they made their way up to the flat. Anne unlocked the door, but before she opened it, she glanced at him. "I really think you should talk to him. Like, quietly."

It was the last thing he wanted to do, but he agreed for Anne's sake. "Let's see if he missed us at all."

"I'll stay with you," Anne promised.

As soon as they entered the flat, Stefan came into the hallway. "You're back. Good."

"We got stuck in the elevator," Anne explained.

Stefan's eyes widened. "Are you okay?"

"Yeah, I was scared at first, but Jan was amazing. He told me stories while we waited for the power to come back on." She smiled at him.

Jan, however, winced. The public praise didn't sit well with him.

"It's great to hear you stepping up for once."

The words rubbed Jan the wrong way, but he swallowed the provocative retort. Of course his father couldn't compliment him without a reminder of how he'd otherwise failed to impress.

"If you have a minute," Stefan said, "I'd like to talk to you."

Immediately, Anne's face lit up. She gave Jan a nudge. "Funny, so did Jan."

"I'm not going to apologise," Jan declared, but he let Anne escort him into the living room.

Stefan invited him to sit down, which was so out of character Jan braced himself. He hadn't even reacted to his refusal to apologise. "So, boy." He noticed Anne hovering. "Can we talk alone?"

"Can't I stay? I just don't want you two shouting at each other again. Jan asked me to, too."

"I didn't... whatever." He looked at his father. "What do you want to talk about?"

"Well..." Stefan waved his hand at Anne. "That. Your sister is right. We can barely be in the same room without being at each other's throats."

"That's not my fault."

Stefan cocked his head. "Really?" The annoyance in it was unmistakable.

"You never listen to me," Jan explained in a strained voice. "As soon as I open my mouth, you've already made up your mind. I'm the failure, the good-for-nothing son who runs his mouth about magic."

"Well..."

"I know you don't believe me. Like, I could tell you that this storm out there was caused by a supernatural being and *you*," Jan said forcefully, because his father was already opening his mouth, "you'd tell me it's just a side effect of climate change that we suddenly have hurricanes and tornadoes on the streets of Greenvalley, when part of the charm of this town is how protected it is by all the mountains around it."

Instead of yelling at him, Stefan rubbed his face, looking so much older than the fifty-two years he was. "Jan, please, I don't have the nerve to deal with this kind of thing today."

"That's why I didn't tell you the real reason I was fired. Because you wouldn't believe me if I told you I pressed the alarm to evacuate everyone while I was busy fighting a gorgon in the bathroom. You'd rather believe that I somehow put on fifty pounds of muscle mass to throw doors across the room and smash sinks with my bare hands."

Stefan raised his eyebrows. "That's the *real* reason?" He sounded as sceptical as Jan knew he'd be. But for Anne's sake he just grimaced. "Frankly, if you're not on drugs, I'm beginning to think you need psychological help."

"Dad!" Anne protested. "Jan is actually telling you the truth."

"You believe *that?*"Stefan shook his head. "There are no gormens and no supernatural storms."

"Gorgons," Jan corrected dryly. "And you're right. It's all in my head. Also in the heads of my friends—and no, they're not junkies or cult members—and several respectable adults I know, and now even in Anne's head. It's a disease."

Stefan closed his eyes for a moment and inhaled deeply through his nose. "Alright... Listen, the reason I wanted to talk to you is this. You and I—we don't get along. And it's only getting worse. I love you, but I've spent twenty years trying to get you on the right track."

"You've done shit," Jan interrupted.

"Whatever you say," Stefan dismissed him. "The thing is, sometimes you have to take a step back and let your children work things out for themselves. I can't help you, Jan, not while you're so intent on biting the hand that feeds you."

Jan narrowed his eyes. "Is this some weird 'as long as you live under my roof, my rules apply' kind of crap?"

"In a way, I suppose. But here's the thing. I think it would be better for both of us, actually for all of us, if you didn't live under my roof anymore."

As Jan's mouth fell open, Anne gasped. "Dad, no! You can't throw him out. Where would he go? This..."

"It's okay, Anne," Jan said, feeling strangely numb. He searched for the anger inside him, but there was none. Although unexpected, it was only logical. His father would rather cut him out of his life than listen to him for a minute. He stood up. "I'd better go pack, then."

He had no idea where he was going, but he knew he wouldn't stay where he wasn't wanted.

"Jan," his father called after him. "I didn't say you had to leave right away."

Jan turned and glared at him. "I was planning to move out anyway."

Anne looked at him with wide eyes. "Jan."

"I'll see you around, Anne. As for you and Mum." Jan took a deep breath and there was his anger. Neatly wrapped in a thick layer of ice. "It's better if we don't see each other for a while."

Rachel

The storm outside had passed, but the storm inside Rachel was still gathering strength. After she'd spent a lovely day with her dad while her mother had sulked in her room, she'd lain awake that night questioning everything she thought she knew. It had come as a surprise since she'd been so firmly convinced of her father's goodness, but as soon as she'd laid down, she couldn't get her mother's words out of her head.

When she entered the dreamworld, Nico was waiting for her. "What are you thinking?"

"What do you remember about our parents' divorce?" They'd been eight when it had happened.

Nico tilted his head, a subtle reminder that this version of Nico wasn't really him. He didn't remember anything.

"Is it possible to look at memories? I doubt my parents dream about what happened but theoretically it should all be there, right?" It was something she'd been pondering for a while.

Unlike the real Nico, this one knew the answer. "Of course it is. You're the Dreamer, Rachel, just as you can change dreams to take a different direction, you can force new dreams upon them."

"But would they be real? I mean the memories. How factual would they be?"

"That's the question. Even when we dream of things long past, our brains tend to make new connections that weren't there before. Our mannerisms might be the same, but we could do things we'd never... well, we could only dream of." Nico grinned. "It's up to you to recognise the tangents and redirect them. Like a gardener with a fast-growing bush. You have to keep pruning it."

Rachel couldn't help but be intrigued. "I want to try it."

"Where do we start?"

"At the beginning."

And since Rachel had already spent years dreaming herself into Annette's dreams, she started with her father.

When she entered the dream, he was busy chasing a group of rats through the streets of LA. At one point, the rats turned into robbers and started planning a heist, in which her father was suddenly involved.

Rachel joined the group and looked her father straight in the eye. "Show me how you met Annette."

Annette's name was whispered among the robbers, and then her father turned and went to a bar with his now-student friends. While his friends joined others at the pool table, Mick went to the bar to order drinks.

Rachel knew from her parents' stories that Annette had worked in a bar while trying to pay for the glamorous LA life. A few years older than Mick, her hair still its natural colour but styled wildly, she grinned at him. "Are you even old enough to drink?"

Without hesitation, Mick pulled out his card. "Barely."

Annette took her time studying it. "Michael Samuel Hadden?"

"Mick! Michael is my father. And you?"

"Annette."

At the end of the bar, a group of rats gathered for a *Coyote Ugly* performance, but Rachel put them in a cage and sent them into the ether of the dreamworld. What was her father's obsession with rats?

"That sounds..." Mick tried to work out the origin of her mother's name. "Dutch?"

"German," she corrected with a laugh.

"Cool, what brings you to the States?"

Rachel treated the memory like a movie and fast-forwarded to Mick walking Annette home from the bar many hours later. They arrived at a run-down building that Rachel wouldn't have ventured into if it wasn't part of a dream.

Mick seemed to be thinking the same thing. "This is where you live?"

Annette laughed. "Well, what do you think I can afford in this city? Not everyone tips as generously as you do. Do you dare come up?" she asked in a voice that made Rachel wish she could scrub her ears.

"As if I could resist the temptation." Her father's expression was no better.

Then they were upstairs, the dream changing so suddenly that Rachel suffered from motion sickness. The flat looked as bad as she'd expected. In the early sunlight, every hole in the wall was visible. The wallpaper was hanging off the walls and the sink was leaking. There was only an air mattress on the floor, freshly used by her parents for their one-night stand.

Rachel was glad the dream had skipped that part. Then she realised it had skipped a lot more than a few hours. This was no longer a one-night stand but a longer affair.

Mick stood up, wearing nothing but his birthday suit. Horrified, Rachel turned away, cursing her decision to investigate her parents' relationship. The dream shifted around her. Before it could change direction, she spun around again.

Fortunately, Mick had found a pair of boxers. "I'm going to get us some coffee."

"Do you like me?" Annette asked, still under the sheets. Rachel couldn't help but notice how beautiful her mother had been before the alcohol aged her.

Mick laughed. "Do you think I'd keep coming back to you if I didn't like you?" He pulled on his pants. "I can tell you, it's not the room."

Annette grinned. "Spoilt brat." But then the grin disappeared from her face. "I have to tell you something."

Rachel held her breath. Had it really happened so soon? The two of them looked barely a day older than when they'd met in the bar.

"What is it?" Mick asked, pulling a preppy shirt over his head.

"I'm pregnant."

Suddenly Annette appeared with a huge belly, then she was in hospital, then there were twins and feeding problems and—

Rachel stretched out her arms and rewound the onslaught of memories to bring her back to the moment Annette had told him.

"By me?" Mick asked, his mouth slack.

"I know we've only been seeing each other for two months, but you're the only one I've slept with. There must have been some kind of accident."

"Wow."

"Yeah." Annette sighed. "It's not what I planned either."

Mick sat down on the floor with a thud. "What's your plan?"

Annette shrugged. "I can't afford a kid. You know that. So…"

"So we'll get married. I can afford it. I mean, my parents can, but I'll be earning money soon after I graduate. I've even got a trust fund we could use."

Even Rachel was overwhelmed. Annette had just told him she was pregnant and he was planning a whole life for them. After two months.

"You want to get *married?*" Annette asked, stunned.

"It's our child, right? We're both responsible for it. Of course, if you want to get an abortion, I'll pay for that, too, but if you want to keep it, I'll provide for you." Mick grinned boyishly. "Annette, these past two months have been magical. You're the best thing that's ever happened to me. I won't let you down." He took her hands. "Let's get married. Let's do this together. We can start by getting you out of this shithole."

Rachel didn't know whether it was the prospect of better accommodation or a romantic fantasy, but something made her mother smile deliriously, then laugh. "Okay, sure, let's get married."

"No wonder they didn't last," Rachel muttered in disbelief. How could they ever have thought it would work? Mick could've supported her without committing himself like that. Their mother should've been more realistic and told him off. Hell, an abortion would have made more sense, although Rachel was very grateful that hadn't happened.

"They're in love," Nico said, with that wistful smile he'd worn so often. "Can't you tell?"

"Are they really?" Rachel asked doubtfully as she watched her parents get married by a rat minister while the rest of the rats sang an old Millennial hit. "It feels like convenience to me."

"Who hurt you like that?" Nico whispered.

Rachel pointed angrily at the couple. "*They* did!"

Suddenly the scene changed. They were in the wonderful big house Rachel remembered. It was morning and Mick was traipsing around quietly, looking as if he'd slept on the couch in his business suit. As he entered the living room with its magnificent open-plan kitchen, he found Annette pouring herself a glass of wine, while Rachel saw herself and Nico blissfully playing in the corner.

"Look who's finally home," Annette greeted him.

So, not the sofa, rather a very long night. "You're already awake."

"Daddy!" Little Rachel toddled up to him and threw herself against his legs so he'd pick her up.

Rachel's heart ached. She'd always been a daddy's girl, even though it was her mother who'd stayed home all day.

Annette turned away from them in disgust and sipped at her glass.

"Mummy's mad at me, eh?" Mick asked little Rachel.

"Mummy calls you a mannore."

Through the connection in the dream, Rachel immediately understood it to mean a manwhore. And so did Mick. He pulled a face. "Do you have to teach her those words?"

"It's the truth, isn't it? Or did you have to *work late* again?"

"Mannore, mannore," sang little Rachel. "Daddy, what's a mannore?"

"It's a bad word. You shouldn't be using it," Mick told her before looking back at Annette. "Seriously, you need to watch your language around the kids." He put Rachel down again. "Go and play with your brother, darling. Mummy and I need to talk."

Rachel felt conflicted as she watched them. He was right, of course. She wasn't supposed to know such words at the tender age of three. But she didn't like the way he was telling Annette off. It didn't seem right.

And now he went over to take the bottle of wine from her. "It's not even eight and you're already drinking."

"Why do you think that is?" asked Annette mockingly. "It's after seven and the man is still at *work.*"

"Sorry, it got late. I slept at the office."

"With who? That pretty teacher's aide I always find in your office for some reason?"

Disgusted, Rachel pushed the dream away, but Mick's mind had now caught on to the memories and they kept coming at her. It was a mixture of him playing with Rachel and Nico while ignoring Annette's needs and fighting with her. Her barbs became sharper and more bitter, but she always forgave him.

Until the day she didn't. It was night and they were both in the master bedroom. Mick was just standing there while Annette packed.

"I get it, Mick. We only got married for the kids. You were twenty-two, way too young. You weren't ready for this. Still aren't."

"What was I supposed to do instead? Leave you?"

"Be honest. Do you love me?"

"I love my children."

Annette smiled softly. "I know you do."

"And you want to take them away from me."

"It'll be a relief for you. You've got all these big plans and dreams. Mick, your work schedule is only possible because I'm here, looking after the family you never wanted. I know you've got more money than me and that your parents know a bunch of lawyers who'll take everything from me if you ask them to. Please don't do that. Let me have my children. I want nothing more from you."

Mick stood there, saying nothing. Just as her mother had told her, he never really fought her. He just watched her go. At first, they'd lived nearby in a tiny flat. Then he drove them to the airport and held them tight while Rachel cried and Nico wouldn't look at his father. And then they were gone, and Mick was alone in the big, beautiful, empty house, where only abandoned toys reminded him of what he'd lost.

Rachel started the next morning much more subdued. The dreams had changed her. Nico had warned her that not everything she'd seen was necessarily the truth, but at its core the memories matched what she'd seen in Annette's dreams. Her mother's story was true. Her father was at least as much to blame for the break-up of their marriage.

Part of her wished she'd never seen that side of him. The beginning of their love was like a fairytale, but fairytales didn't happen in the real world. And what had started as a romance had quickly turned into a nightmare that had trapped them both for the better part of a decade.

At the breakfast table, Rachel made a decision. Once again, Mick had gone all out. There was French toast and bacon, pancakes and fresh fruit. He must've gone shopping as soon as the supermarket had opened. Rachel hated the exaggerated gesture of it all.

"I don't think you should stay here," she said, well aware that her mother was lurking in the kitchen, getting ready for work.

Mick frowned. "What do you mean?"

"What I just said. Mum's right, you can't just spring these kinds of decisions on us, and we shouldn't pretend to be a happy family when we're anything but."

Annette came out of the kitchen with a curious look on her face. "Rachel, are you sure? You love your dad."

"I do." Although she wasn't sure anymore if he deserved her love. "I just don't think it's healthy for us. You and I have come to an understanding that, frankly, is important to me. More important than Dad living in the house with us. I want to honour that and give each other a chance."

Mick sighed heavily. "You're right, of course. I shouldn't have pushed this on you. I'm going to stay in one of those cosy little inns in town until I find some temporary accommodation. Are we still going to see each other, though?"

Rachel nodded, relieved. She didn't want to lose one parent for the other. "Of course."

"How about weekly Friday dinners?" Annette suggested. "That wouldn't hurt anyone, would it?"

"Are you sure?" Mick asked her.

"We can be civil, right?" Annette gave him a warm smile.

Mick swallowed and then nodded. "Of course. Friday dinner then, if that's all right with you, Rachel?"

"I'd love that."

Lucille

Later that day, Linda came home early. As soon as she was through the door, she called for Pascal and Lucille. Curious, Lucille went to see what the fuss was about, only to be pulled into an unprecedented embrace.

"You're okay!" Linda exclaimed, hugging Pascal to her chest. "I came as soon as I heard the news. And then I saw the tree outside." She brushed her fingers over Pascal's face, then noticed the scratches on Lucille's. "You must have been so scared."

"Pascal took care of me," Lucille quipped.

"I did what I had to do."

Linda just laughed and pulled them into another hug. "I'm just glad you're safe. The news was terrible. They said the hospital had collapsed or something, and cars had been pushed across the road. Climate change, right? Who's ever heard of a hurricane in the Harz Mountains?"

"Definitely climate change," Lucille assured her, sharing a secret little smile with Pascal.

Having flown home early from Fashion Week, Linda decided to spend the whole afternoon with them while a repair crew arrived to deal with the tree in the garden and the window. Her father had gone back to work, picking up where he'd left off. Lucille didn't mind. She knew now that he cared. He'd never be Father of the Year, but it wasn't out of indifference.

To her surprise, though, he came to her as she was getting ready for bed. "You're not trying to talk me out of it, are you?"

Bastien chuckled and shook his head. "You'd just put a spell on me." He winked at her, then looked at the couch. "Can we sit down?"

"Sure." Lucille surprised herself by how quickly she sat down.

Her father followed much more slowly. "You asked me earlier if I could tell you more about your mother. I'd like to do that now."

Lucille's heart almost skipped a beat. "Really? It won't hurt too much?"

"It will always hurt." Bastien shrugged slightly. "But that's fine. It doesn't mean that I don't love your stepmother or that I can't be proud of the woman you've become. Only that your mother was special. Beautiful and tender... a true angel."

"How true are we talking?"

Bastien laughed. "To be honest, I've never met an angel. But if they exist, I'd like to think your mother came pretty close."

Lucille exhaled in relief. She didn't know if she could have handled another supernatural family history. Instead, she settled in as her father told her how he'd met Alena and how wonderful and kind she'd been. How close she'd been to her mother-in-law, who had adored her as much as he had.

"Did you ever have any doubts?" Lucille asked. As much as she loved the way he talked about her mother, it felt more like a fairytale than reality. In her own experience, relationships never felt like that. "You must have been annoyed with her sometimes."

"Annoyed?" Bastien laughed, but then thought about it a bit more. "I'm not saying we never argued, but I never doubted our love." He cocked his head. "Do you have doubts?"

Lucille waved him off with an awkward laugh. "No. I'm... Fabian's great. Annoying sometimes, but like you said, that's not a deal breaker."

"Darling," Bastien said sternly. "Never settle for less than you deserve. If he doesn't make you happy, find someone who will."

"I didn't say he didn't make me happy."

"You just asked me for relationship advice, the person who had doubts about this boy's suitability from the very beginning," her father pointed out. "Well, I'm not saying he's a bad guy. I'm sure he's lovely, but is he who you want?"

Lucille sank into her couch. "I don't know what I want." She shook her head. "No, I do. I want what you and Mum had. The fairytale."

Her father smiled and stroked her hair. "It didn't have a happy ending."

Sadly, she snuggled against him. "I wish it had."

It didn't bode particularly well for her own love life.

Part 2

Rituals & Sacrifices

Caspar

The news of Shenny's demise did little to improve Caspar's mood. He'd spent the better part of a day clawing his way back to life after Balthasar had betrayed him. A betrayal he should have seen coming a mile away.

A common goal. Ha! Only one brother could take Melaney's throne. There were no common goals, no alliances, nothing. Caspar knew better than to trust Balthasar or anyone else for that matter.

Anyone but his sister.

When Menuha heard he'd been badly injured, she'd flown to his side in an instant. She hadn't said much, but she'd watched over him while he was out of action, doing some human crafting project he'd never have had the patience for. Even after he'd recovered, she'd stayed close, though Caspar couldn't quite figure out why.

Menuha was sweet. Many demons thought she was weak and malleable, with a strange obsession with humans. But Caspar knew better. He saw the rage simmering under her skin with every stab of the needle. He heard it in her silence and felt it in his gut when she decided to look at him.

"Why are you so angry with me?" he asked sullenly.

"Find out for yourself."

Caspar groaned. There was only one reason he could think of, and it grated on his nerves. Menuha was *his* sister, not Melchior's. She'd always belonged to him. "Balthasar sent Shenny to Ashuan, not me."

"Oh, really? I must have imagined the moment when you two made a deal. Or the fact that you *were* Shenny's superior."

He seemed to have hit a nerve. "So what? Your precious little half-brother is alive. It was only a Stormbride."

"He's not my *precious* little half-brother," Menuha hissed.

"Oh, please. You were all over him from the moment he was born." Caspar mimicked her. "'Look, Casp, he's half human. Look how fast he is growing. He called me Menu. And he's not even two!'" He barely dodged the blast of energy she shot at his face in response. "What? It's true."

"It's not true!" Menuha stabbed her cloth furiously, then tossed it aside and stood up. "If anyone is obsessed with him, it's you!" Now she mocked him. "'He's *human*. Better kill him now rather than later.'"

Her impression was much better than his, Caspar had to admit. "And look how much trouble that would've saved us."

"What trouble? You're the only one who's ever caused trouble!" Menuha flung her hands at him and pushed him hard enough to send him tumbling into the drawers behind him. Furiously, she glared down at him. "You didn't have to pick on him. Just like you didn't need to get involved in this stupid scheme of Melaney's."

"She nominated me."

"She's *playing* you. All three of you."

Caspar got to his feet and frowned. "What do you mean?"

"I've spoken to the other residences. They're all surprised to hear about this alleged council decree. It's a *lie!*" she hissed again. "Why would the Seven decide to get rid of one of their own for some arbitrary reason, while at the same time allowing her to choose her own killer?"

"So..." Caspar tried to understand what Menuha was hinting at, but his mind was blank.

Menuha clicked her tongue in annoyance. "It's a ruse, Casp. *Melaney's* ruse."

"But why? Why does she want to be killed?"

"She *doesn't!*" Menuha threw up her hands. "I know you have a brain. Put aside your wrath for a moment and use it."

Caspar would have pulverised anyone else who dared talk to him like that. From Menuha, he was used to worse. And she was usually right. "Just tell me," he begged.

She sighed heavily. "Fine. I don't know what her endgame is, but the whole thing is designed to test Melchior and bring him back to Hell. She's only interested in him. You're just a tool to get what she wants. And *that's* what makes me so angry. Because, once again, you're letting her use you." Menuha pushed him again, but much less forcefully than before.

"I'm nobody's tool!" Caspar roared. The words stung more than Menuha could ever know. Even after five hundred years, the anger was still there. He shook his head and let it consume him. "I don't care what Melaney wants. *I* want *him* dead. You say this is a test for her precious little boy? Well, I hope she's okay with him failing."

"She'll kill you," Menuha warned, crossing her arms.

"Let her try. I'll show her how deadly her little games can be."

Menuha sighed. "Is that what you want? Killing her will make you the Archdemon of Lust. Let's face it, you'd make a terrible archdemon. It's not your sin."

Caspar's eyes darkened and he snarled as he took a step towards Menuha. "You think I don't know about sins?"

A lazy smile spread across her face. She threw her arms around his neck. "I never said you were free of it."

Jan

"It's almost ten," Meg said to Jan after a glance at her phone.

Instead of getting up, he wrapped his arms around her and nuzzled his nose into her neck. "I don't want to go."

Meg threw her head back and laughed. "You have to. Dad will kick you out if you don't."

"Let him try," he growled, then kissed her neck.

There was a simple reason why Jan didn't want to leave. He had nowhere else to go.

"Where are you going to sleep tonight?" Meg asked. She was the only one he'd told so far. Or rather, Anne had told her before he could think of a lie.

Jan shrugged. "Here," he joked.

She clicked her tongue and turned to him. "I'm serious."

"So am I." Now that she was facing him, it was time to distract her with a good old-fashioned kiss.

Meg melted like butter in his arms, but before they could get much further, her father knocked on the door. "It's past ten."

With a sigh, Jan dragged himself out of bed, showing that he was fully dressed, just as the rules demanded. He and Meg had long since found a way to conceal their activities. The number one rule was not to do it close to curfew—or dinner time; that was a bad one, too.

"Can't he sleep here?" Meg asked, apparently deciding to take matters into her own hands. "I promise he'll sleep on the couch. Or in the guest room. Jan could sleep there."

Ben shook his head. "You can see each other tomorrow. After school." He jerked his head towards the corridor. "Off with you."

Jan could have told Meg it wouldn't work, but he was grateful she hadn't outed him to her father. The last thing he needed was for her parents to think she was now dating a homeless bum.

Unfortunately, that was exactly what he'd become. True to his word, he'd packed as soon as his father had mentioned it, not even waiting for his mother. She'd called later that day, but he'd ignored her. There wasn't anything he wanted to talk to either of his parents about. Not for a very long time.

Jan kissed Meg one last time and dragged out his time at the Kollmer house until Ben Kollmer looked like he was about to physically kick him out. Then he left the warm house behind and set off for the Magic Circle.

He knew it wasn't right and that he should probably talk to Fabian about it. But Fabian and his mother had their own problems, so he let himself in through the back door and locked up behind him.

Once inside, he put the kettle on in the little café and grabbed a leftover roll. It was a lousy dinner, but at least it was dinner. With the money he made running the shop Jan could have bought some food, but there were no proper cooking utensils, just a hot plate for the cauldron, and he knew better than to mess with Samantha's cauldron. He'd rather not curse himself for a pot of spaghetti. Besides, he wanted to save money for a permanent place to live.

The clothes he'd packed were in the back of the storeroom, hidden in a couple of delivery boxes. Jan put his food on the table and got his sleeping bag out. By the time he'd arranged the chairs, his tea was ready.

He ate as he scrolled through job listings. Nothing really caught his eye. Either he was woefully underqualified, or the jobs paid little more than the Magic Circle, without the benefit of doubling as his emergency accommodation.

For the millionth time, Jan checked the first responder course. A new one was starting in February, applications were due on the fifth of January. But how? How could he afford the training without a permanent roof over his head? He couldn't give up his job at the shop without losing his sleeping place, and he wouldn't have time for the course if he had to work at the shop.

Frustrated, he checked the group chat for monster sightings. It annoyed him that he'd missed the last one because he'd been stuck in a lift. He hadn't even been able to help Fabian with his leg. What a fine first responder he made.

With a groan, Jan turned the phone off and put it on the charger. Then he brushed his teeth in the small sink and climbed into his sleeping bag. It was anything but comfortable. The chairs were hard and their seats slightly concave, leaving him with no less than three uncomfortable ridges. And when he tried to shift, the row disintegrated, leaving him with twice as many ridges and crevices. Yesterday he'd found himself on the floor at three in the morning. Suffice to say, it hadn't left him well-rested.

Maybe he should just sleep on the floor, Jan thought as the middle chairs split, leaving his bottom hanging out. Then again, the very thought of sleeping on the cold stone floor made him shiver. Maybe what he really needed to think about was what to do about the whole situation.

Samantha

Once again, Samantha fled home to spend the night with Cian. After the embarrassing confrontation with her parents, they'd both decided his house was the safer option. Cian's mother didn't seem to mind her frequent visits and always welcomed her with open arms.

They were upstairs in his room watching a movie Cian had chosen: some kind of horror movie with a giant snake. Samantha had tried to pay attention, but the plot was threadbare and the giant snake was so obviously fake it was distracting. Instead, she leant into Cian and scrolled through her phone.

After a while, Cian glanced at her. "Anything interesting?"

Samantha frowned. Interesting wasn't quite how she'd describe the news ticker. Disturbing was more like it. "They found the body of a girl in the woods." She studied the accompanying picture of a plain girl, perhaps sixteen or seventeen, as she smiled awkwardly at the camera. She looked vaguely familiar, like someone they went to school with.

Cian tilted the phone in his direction and his eyes widened. "That's Leonie."

"Leonie?" It didn't ring a bell with Samantha.

"Oh, we're in the same athletics club. She's nice—unbeatable over long distances—but a bit quiet... kind of like Rachel." He sighed. "What happened?"

"Don't freak out," Samantha warned, "but according to the Greenvalley View, she was bitten by a snake."

Cian's eyes automatically went to the TV screen where the giant snake was viciously attacking one of the main characters. Without making a face, he turned it off. "Scary."

"Yeah. Especially when you consider that there are no snakes in the Harz Mountains, at least no poisonous ones. And even if there were, they would've gone into hibernation long ago. It's much too cold for snakes."

"Wait a minute." Cian reached across the couch for his phone and showed her a WhatsApp message. "Do you think it has anything to do with this?"

"What's this?"

"The Serpents of Ishtar. There's a party in the old mines this weekend. Super secret and exclusive. We were thinking of going."

"Who's we?"

He winced. "You know, Alan, the girls."

"Right." Samantha shivered. In the privacy of his room, it was easy to forget he was part of the Elite Clique. "I take it you were all invited, then."

"You weren't?"

She snorted. "Please. Like I ever get invited to exclusive parties."

"Sorry." He put his arm around her and pulled her close. "You know I'd take you, but you have to be on the list."

"It's fine, really." The last thing she wanted was to humiliate herself at another party in front of Cheryl. Besides... "The Serpents of Ishtar... That is indeed worrying. A girl's killed with snake venom just as some snake organisation throws a party. We should probably check it out."

"Right now?"

Surprised, Samantha looked up. "What? No, I meant me and my friends."

"I want to come."

"Absolutely not." She immediately thought of Daniel who'd paid so quickly with his life for accompanying her on a monster hunt.

Cian took his arm away. "Why not? Because I'm not some reincarnated hero of old? I was the one who gave you the idea."

"It could be dangerous."

"Come on. Okay, maybe I can't do magic, but neither can Jan."

"Jan can heal. And he's got a black belt in karate."

Cian shrugged, irritated. "I can hold my own in a fight. What about Rachel? I know she can wander through dreams, but that can't possibly be in handy in a fight."

"Rachel's very skilled with a crossbow."

He raised an eyebrow. "You want to bring a crossbow to a party?"

Samantha sighed. "No, of course not."

"Then I don't see the problem."

"The problem is that I don't want to lose you," she said, raising her voice.

Stunned, Cian could only stare.

Samantha felt the heat rise in her cheeks. She hadn't meant it to be so dramatic. Like he was the love of her life. With a sigh, she knelt and cupped his face. "You know what happened with Daniel. Please, I can't go through that again. Promise me you'll stay away from this party."

"I..."

"Cian, please. It's not worth it."

With a heavy roll of his eyes, Cian conceded. "If it makes you feel better."

She smiled and kissed him. "It would."

For a while she lost herself in the kiss, but the ominous Snakes of Ishtar and Leonie's unsolved murder never quite left her mind. Eventually she broke it off and grabbed her things.

"I'd better get home before my parents freak out again."

"What? We haven't even finished the movie."

"I've already forgotten what happened in the beginning. And I want to do some research on those Serpents of Ishtar. I'll see you at school, okay?" She kissed him again, feeling a pang of guilt for cancelling their date for a potential monster, but her heart wasn't in it tonight, and she knew she wouldn't get any rest. "Tell your friends to skip the party."

"Sure. That'll go down well with Cheryl."

"Oh, she can go," Samantha joked, drawing a laugh from Cian.

With a final wave, she left the room, eager to get back to her research.

The next morning, she met the others at the Magic Circle. Fabian yawned and Jan looked like he'd fallen out of bed. On the other side of the table, Rachel, Lucille, and Matt looked well rested and ready for the day.

Samantha quickly explained about Leonie's suspicious death and the party planned by the Serpents of Ishtar. "I did some research, and it turns out Ishtar was a Syrian war goddess. She represented destruction, sex, and healing."

"Sounds like my kind of girl," Jan joked.

Samantha rolled her eyes. "Sure, Jan. Anyway, the snakes were her sacred animals. According to the myths, she rode in a chariot pulled by two basilisks, so that's already worrying enough, but I also found something on these Serpents of Ishtar." She pulled out a printout of a news article. "Apparently, they're a cult from Spain: Serpientes de Ishtar. They've gotten into a bit of trouble, but nothing that suggests murder."

"Spain?" Fabian repeated dully. "What are they doing here?"

"Throwing a party," Jan said. "Didn't you get the invitation?"

"I did," Matt announced.

Lucille shrugged. "I got one too."

"So did I."

Both Samantha and Fabian stared at Rachel, causing her to raise her hands. "I didn't plan to go."

Samantha winced. "That's okay. Guess I should be glad my number wasn't in the data leak that led to this." She knew perfectly well her exclusion hadn't been an accident.

Fabian crossed his arms and sat back sullenly. "Looks like Sam and I are sitting this one out."

"I'm not going either," Matt declared. "I've got something else planned for the weekend."

"Do you?" Samantha couldn't help herself. It sounded like Matt was dating. She'd known it would only be a matter of time.

Matt couldn't even meet her eyes. "Yeah, but I'll try to get back early in case things go south."

Lucille sighed. "I was hoping for a good party. Oh well." She looked at Jan and Rachel. "Shall we discuss a plan?"

Samantha sank back in her chair, feeling inappropriately dejected. She should've been happy she had an excuse to stay away from murderous cults. And she really shouldn't have cared that Matt was going back to his old ways. She was still seeing Cian, so why should she mind if he dated someone else?

Matt

As soon as school was out, Matt headed for Hescaryn to meet up with Menuha. She was waiting for him in one of the alcoves, looking apprehensive. Below them, the city of Lucin glowed in the darkness of the caves. There was no sky above Lucin, but a combination of cleverly placed light sources and mirrors made it the brightest spot in all of Hescaryn.

Today, the city was full of demons. Like Matt and Menuha, they crouched in alcoves or on rooftops, or lined the streets of the city, leaving only the main road empty. At the top of the stairs leading to the Residence Square, six of the seven archdemons lorded over the city. Not surprisingly, Sloth was skipping the ceremonies.

"All this fuss for what?" Matt complained.

Menuha shrugged. "It's a great victory against the vampire covens in the south."

Matt snorted. He'd faced vampires before and no one had thrown him a parade.

"It's Wrath demonstrating his power," Menuha said quietly. "A reminder not to mess with the house. If you want my guess, it's Volac and Hel at it again."

Matt shot her a look. "Volac and Hel are fighting?"

"When aren't they?" Menuha laughed. "Oh, Matt, it's time you learnt a little more about the dynamics of the Seven. It's important if you want to stay alive."

"As if they'd care about a half-demon."

"They'll care if they think they can use you." She sighed. "Volac leads the Seven. Not because he has the most skill or experience. By the gods, no. He's been an archdemon for less than three hundred years. Compare that to Hel's millennia. And she's the epitome of pride, so you can imagine how she'd take it if some young hotshot thought he could tell her what to do. So, yes, those two are always fighting. Some fights are subtle and some are flashy, like this one."

Matt had never had the displeasure of crossing paths with either Volac or Hel. The Archdemon of Wrath was notoriously short-tempered, and the Archdemon of Pride oozed contempt even as she sat on the stage, her long black hair falling over her shoulders as straight as her back.

That would change today.

He felt a tingle of nerves as he watched the great cave entrance that would soon be swarming with the most dangerous demons Hescaryn had ever seen.

"Don't do it," Menuha warned. "It's too risky."

"They won't care about me." His eyes were fixed on the entrance where demons were beginning to take shape. "He messed with my friends. It's high time I returned the favour."

When the Black Guard finally emerged from the Dûr Lôrac, it was led by none other than Caspar. Even Matt couldn't quite escape the impact of his entrance as he rode in on a Blood Steed. The horse-like creature stood about three metres tall, with leathery skin and fiery eyes.

The demon atop it was no less terrifying. Caspar was dressed in blood-spattered full armour. Spikes protruded from his shoulder plates, close enough to his neck that a lesser demon would've impaled themselves. His face was covered by a gruesome black helmet that seemed as much a weapon as the demon who wore it.

"The Guard definitely needs a fashion update," Matt commented dryly, trying to shake his unwanted awe. "Can he even move in that?"

"Ask the vampires."

Matt snorted. Anyone could handle vampires.

Behind Caspar, his Blood Riders followed, decorated officers in their own right, each of them on another terrifying Blood Steed. Demons who'd gotten too close to the path retreated quickly, whispering and pointing at the creatures. Matt had heard it said more times than he could count that his brother had been the one to tame them, just one of his many martial achievements.

After the officers came the rest of the guard. What distinguished the Black Guard from the Army of Death, the Small Council's force, was the heterogeneity of its members. While the Army was uniformed and made up of exclusively first- and second-class demons, the Guard celebrated chaos. Its ranks included as many bipedal first-class demons as multi-legged creatures of the lower classes. None of them were any less dangerous.

There were bog witches and djinn, humpback wolves and giant arachnids, and many more creatures that haunted Matt's nightmares. All under Caspar's control.

"Did he have to bring the spiders?"

"They're his favourite."

Matt rolled his eyes. "Well, it's all very impressive, but—"

"Matt." Menuha looked at him warningly. "You can't do this."

As if on cue, Caspar looked up and found them. Matt couldn't see his face from the distance and through the helmet, but he knew without a doubt his brother had taken notice. "Payback time."

Before Menuha could stop him, Matt jumped into Caspar's path. With a challenging grin, he spread his arms. "Come and get me, oh terrible General of Terrors."

It was a gamble Matt couldn't lose. Caspar immediately broke rank. He shot energy at Matt, narrowly missing him.

Matt was already jumping away, leading his brother on a wild goose chase across the rooftops of Lucin, disturbing and terrifying the demons who'd come to watch the parade. With every missed shot and outraged cry, Matt felt his excitement build. It wasn't something he'd ever pull off in Ashuan, but on his homeworld, nothing was more exhilarating.

"Come on, old man!" he teased Caspar, not bothering to shoot through his armour. "You're slow!"

With a roar, Caspar ripped off his helmet and threw it at Matt.

Matt dodged it by unfolding his wings and taking to the air. Some unfortunate bystander was impaled and knocked down instead. "Oh, that's not looking good for the Guard's aim."

More chunks of armour followed. "I'll tear you to pieces!"

Time to step it up. Instead of continuing his flight through the inconspicuous onlookers, Matt dove straight into the Black Guard.

They were all wedged in so tightly the large monstrous demons could barely move, while simultaneously blocking the smaller ones' reach. The ranks wobbled as they tried to accommodate their own raging general. Some were brave enough to throw magic at Matt, but he dodged them as easily as he had Caspar, his adrenaline surging.

Officers snapped at those who'd reacted, desperately trying to keep order. An order Caspar couldn't care less about as he stomped through them, shooting energy left and right.

"You're going to kill your own troops," Matt laughed.

Out of the corner of his eye he saw a hand shoot towards him. Within a split second, Matt had drawn his sword and sliced off the arm of what turned out to be a Blood Rider.

With more officers and Caspar approaching, it was high time he got out of there. He plunged his sword into the chest of a wraith, then jumped away from Lucin, landing in one of the larger caves in the Dûr Lôrac.

A wide stream of sylver thundered past him. Its water cooled Matt's flushed skin. His head felt a little dizzy as he tried to process what he'd just achieved. The whole point had been to embarrass Caspar in front of his superior, to hurt him where it really mattered. Never in his wildest dreams had he imagined he'd take on half the Black Guard and not only come out unscathed but also maim a Blood Rider—they were Caspar's most dangerous fighters.

Surely, that was enough to show his brother he wasn't—

"Got you!"

Matt was yanked back by his neck and slammed to the ground. Quickly, he rolled around and kicked Caspar into the stream of sylver. Then he turned and ran.

Fabian

Despite his injury, Fabian accompanied Jan and Rachel into the forest. Neither of them had bothered to get ready for the party. Rachel because she just wanted to do the snake thing, and Jan because he never put effort into anything. By the looks of it, he was wearing the same shirt he'd worn this morning.

Fabian held his tongue, but he would've given an arm and a leg to get an invitation. The only party he'd ever been to had been the football team's last year, and that had ended with a terrible hangover and very few memories.

It wasn't so much the party he was dying to go to, but the fact he felt so excluded. Like he wasn't cool or good enough. A feeling that was only exacerbated by Lucille's recent flakiness. Even tonight she'd claimed a delay in getting ready to avoid meeting him.

He was losing her. Just as he'd lost Rachel and Samantha before that. And like all the times before, there was nothing he could do about it. He was just not cool or interesting enough to keep a relationship going. He didn't even have a say in it.

"What do you think their plan is?" Rachel asked.

"It's a party," Jan said irritably. "There's no plan. Maybe it's a kinky one. I've never been to a cult party."

"Yeah, cults aren't exactly known for throwing epic parties." Fabian struggled to keep up on the uneven forest floor. "Personally, I wouldn't go. It's probably a trap."

"Lucky you can't, then!" Jan joked, jabbing his elbow into Fabian's side.

Fabian winced. "Yes, so lucky."

Just then they caught up with another straggler. One who looked strangely familiar. "Robert?"

Their school friend turned around, his eyes wide with delight. "Fabian. Jan. And Rachel. Fancy seeing you here."

"You got an invitation?" Fabian asked incredulously. How far down the social ladder was he that even Robert was invited?

"Invitation?"

"To the party at the old mine?"

"There's a party?" Robert sounded genuinely surprised.

Jan groaned. "Hey, dude, you're literally on the Old Mine Path."

"I'm just going for a walk. So, a party, huh? Can I come?"

"It's invitation only," Rachel muttered.

"Well, that makes sense. Nobody ever invites me to their parties. But have fun! Drink one for me, okay?" He took the next path down and disappeared between the trees.

Fabian snorted. "Hey, at least Robert thinks I'm cool."

"Sad," Rachel commented dryly.

Jan threw his arms around his shoulders and grinned at him. "Man, Fabian, if you want to go to this party so bad, sneak in."

"How do I sneak into a mine?"

"There's another entrance, isn't there? Down by the gravel lake. The bars are pretty banged up, so you should be able to squeeze through."

"I don't want to sneak in."

"And here I thought you were cool enough." Jan thumped his chest and laughed before letting him go. He wrapped Rachel's arm around his like a gentleman as they came in sight of a small group waiting patiently outside the old mine entrance. Glancing over his shoulder, he said, "Live a little. It's fun."

Fabian stayed back and watched as Rachel decidedly freed herself from Jan's arm and joined those already waiting. Everyone seemed to be in an exceptionally good mood, chatting excitedly about the party ahead.

For a moment, Fabian glared at them all. He was so tired of standing on the sidelines while everybody passed him by. Maybe he *was* going to sneak in.

Abruptly, he turned and started to make his way downhill towards the lake, wincing every time his barely healed leg carried a little too much weight. Tucked away in the woods, it was a popular swimming spot in the summer and could get almost as crowded as the open-air pool next to the river. Just the sight of its dark waters peeking through the trees made Fabian feel at ease. During the day the lake was crystal blue, almost turquoise, but the sun had already set on the early winter's day, turning into a black hole instead.

A loud splashing sound startled him. It sounded like a big fish or...

A girl.

Fabian froze halfway down the path. In front of him, a girl rose from the water, black hair pooling around her shoulders. There wasn't even a hint of a swimsuit strap—in early December.

The girl's eyes widened in shock when she saw him standing there. "You're not allowed to see me!"

Her words broke Fabian's shock and he promptly turned around. "Um... I was just... Aren't you terribly cold?" He reflexively glanced over his shoulder, only to find her glaring at him.

"The Serpents of Ishtar don't feel the cold." She began to step out of the water, exposing more skin with each step.

Fabian quickly turned around. "You're one of them? This murder cult?" He bit his tongue. What had happened to normal small talk? *Hi, nice weather, isn't it? Killed anyone lately?*

The shadows in front of him drew closer. If it hadn't been for the full moon, Fabian would have been completely blind.

Still, he was surprised when the girl suddenly pressed her wet body against his back and held a snake-like dagger to his throat. "Who are you calling a murder cult?"

Whatever blood had rushed to his cheeks before was now draining away. "What are you doing?"

"No mortal is to see me tonight."

The dagger nicked his neck. Fabian racked his brain for the right response. Should he fight her? Let her slit his throat with this vicious weapon? Instead of doing something, he kept talking. "Mortal? Aren't you...?"

"Ishtar's chosen one."

"Awesome." He had no idea what that meant, but he remembered what Samantha had said about the ancient goddess. "Absolutely charming." The dagger pressed a little deeper into his skin. "What are you doing?"

"Sacrificing you, of course," the girl bit back, but her voice trembled slightly. "Hopefully she'll forgive me for letting you see me."

Sacrifices were never a good thing, Fabian thought, especially when he was the one being sacrificed. "Or you could let me go and continue your winter swim. I'm sure Ishtar won't mind. It's not like I was watching you on purpose or anything."

He tilted his head back to escape the dagger and glanced at her.

The girl's pretty eyes were still glowering at him. "You're looking again."

"Right, I—"

Something bit his calf. Fabian screamed as he felt its teeth sink into his flesh. Immediately, icy cold spread through his body. He wanted to say something, but before long, the shadows took him.

Rachel

Rachel regretted her decision to go to the party about five times in the half hour they stood outside the old mine. For one thing, it was terribly cold—nothing that would change much once they were inside. And secondly, the people who'd gathered here were exactly the sort she usually avoided. To make matters worse, three of the girls from the Elite Clique had arrived just after them.

Cheryl, Ani, and Jennifer giggled and chatted, but kept giving her disparaging looks, making it easy to guess their conversation's subject—or rather target. Cheryl grimaced at her before turning to her friends. "Who invited her? She's still wearing the same clothes," she said, without any care over whether Rachel would hear.

It was true. Instead of fashion, Rachel had opted for warmth and comfort. She was wearing heavy boots, jeans, and three layers under her winter jacket. The Elite Clique girls, on the other hand, were all dressed to the nines, with bare legs and thin jackets that were more decorative than practical. All three wore heavy make-up.

"If this is any indication of what this party's gonna be like, let's go somewhere else," Ani said.

"Where?" Jennifer asked, a little confused. "The *Maverick* is so lame lately. And they let anyone in."

Cheryl rolled her eyes. "We're not going anywhere. But *she's* going home. They'll turn her away as soon as the doors open."

"Ignore them," Jan whispered.

Rachel just shrugged. "Been doing that for years." Cheryl's barbs didn't hurt her. In fact, her opinion didn't matter to Rachel at all. And unlike Samantha, there was no personal undertone to her attacks. She was just collateral damage, nothing more.

"Are you guys dating?" Jennifer asked them suddenly. "You make a cute couple."

"The loser dropout and the wallflower. Could almost be a teen film," Cheryl continued. "If one of you were interesting."

"I'll show you interesting," Jan said, clenching his fist.

Rachel tugged on his sleeve. "They're opening the doors."

"That's as much as you're going to see of the inside," Ani said, pushing past her with a giggle.

"You might as well turn back now," Jennifer added.

Cheryl was the last to walk past. "Save yourself the embarrassment and go home."

"I don't get it," Jan said. "How come they never get murdered?"

Rachel didn't bother to point out the fallacy in his comment and followed the others into the old tunnels.

They walked for about fifty metres in near darkness. Just as the teenagers pulled out their phones, the flickering lights of torches appeared ahead of them. As they got closer, they found two people in black robes in front of a passageway. Two others, a man and a woman, stood off to the side, watching the proceedings as if they were guiding pigs to the slaughter.

Rachel pushed the uncomfortable thought out of her head and regarded the cultists closer. Her eyes were immediately drawn to the tallest of them: a young man of around twenty, with long black hair he'd tied back. The tattoo of a vicious snake crawled up his neck and bit his cheek. As if he'd noticed her gaze, his eyes met hers. A lazy smile curled his lips and he leant over to whisper in the woman's ear.

Annoyed, Rachel rolled her eyes. Was it really so offensive for her to be here?

The girls from the Elite Clique flashed their invitations and were waved through without a problem. Jan held up his phone and reminded Rachel that she'd better get hers out too. She was about to grab it when a hand wrapped around her wrist.

"You're not going in there."

Her heart skipped a beat as she recognised the man. Ahead of her, Cheryl's laughter echoed through the mine. "See? I told you they'd throw her out."

"I have an invitation," Rachel muttered.

"Sure you do." He tugged at her hand. "Come with me."

"Rachel?" Jan, who'd already been let through, looked ready to fight the man.

Thinking they wouldn't get anyone in if Jan didn't go, she shook her head. "I'm fine. Just go. Have... fun!" She'd figure something else out with Samantha or meet up with Fabian to try sneaking in at the back.

It wasn't until they were alone in the corridor that Rachel realised the man wasn't leading her back outside. Instead, they'd ducked into a side passageway.

"Where are you taking me?" She tried to free her wrist, but his grip was too tight.

The stranger looked over his shoulder, his eyes almost black in the darkness. "Rachel, was it?" When she refused to answer, he grinned. "Don't worry, Rachel. You're destined to be the star of the party."

Confused, Rachel stumbled along. Her? The star of a party? And how did he know her name in the first place?

The man opened a hidden door and pulled her inside. Again, torches lit up the room, which seemed to be some sort of preparation chamber. Immediately, Rachel's eyes were drawn to a bald woman with several snakes tattooed on her head. She was sitting in a chair while more snakes were painted on her face. For a moment, Rachel thought even her yellow eyes were slitted.

"What's the meaning of this?" Rachel whispered, her voice failing.

"Eresta." The man gave her a brief nod, something that seemed to displease the woman. "This is Rachel Hadden, one of the chosen ones. Do tell. Is she worthy?"

The woman gave her a long look that made Rachel feel as if she stood there naked. "We'll have to see." She waved to another cultist who picked up a small box and carried it to her. "Bring her closer, Enrico."

Enrico changed his grip so that his hand was now wrapped around her upper arm, and pulled her forward until her knees almost touched Eresta's.

Slowly, as if she had all the time in the world, Eresta opened the box and pulled out a fancy bracelet in the shape of a snake. It didn't quite bite its own tail. Instead, two sharp needles protruded from its mouth.

"What are you doing?" Rachel tried to free herself, but Enrico had her firmly in his grip. "Let me go."

"This, child," Eresta said, taking her hand, "is a test. Only those who can withstand the snake's venom are worthy of Ishtar."

"Venom?" Rachel squealed. Her heart leapt into her throat as she squirmed in Enrico's grip.

He was relentless, bending her arm down so Eresta could place the bracelet around her wrist. With a gleam in her yellowish eyes, she pressed the snake's head down. Rachel screamed as the two small needles bit into her wrist. Burning pain spread up her arm almost instantly.

Rachel's vision swam and her body felt heavy. Before she could form words, her knees buckled under her. The snakes on Eresta's face coming to life were the last thing she saw.

Lucille

Lucille was running late. She'd been getting herself ready when her father had come in for a chat. Naturally, she couldn't say no to such a rare occasion. It had been nice, but now she'd missed the meeting with her friends.

When she finally reached the forest, they'd already left. Faced with a dark, wet path through the woods, Lucille almost asked the chauffeur to turn back, but that would have been a waste of a good dress and make-up, so she sucked it up, took her phone out of her bag, and got out of the car. She barely made it ten steps in her high heels before the ground slipped out from under her.

Her fall was broken when a young man caught and steadied her. Lucille immediately noticed how handsome he was. He wasn't a stunner, but he had warm brown eyes, a five o'clock shadow, and a fashionable haircut. A camera hung around his neck, softening his smart appearance slightly. "You okay?"

"Thank you." Lucille gathered herself, then held out her hand. "Lucille de Cerque."

"Oh, I know." He nodded towards the car pulling away from the kerb. "That BMW is a dead giveaway."

Lucille didn't quite know what to say. She'd never had a stranger recognise her.

He took her hand with a charming smile. "Philipp Vendenberg. I work for the *Greenvalley View*."

"You're the weirdo who specialises in local paranormal news." Her cheeks immediately flushed with heat. "Oh, I'm sorry. That was so inappropriate. I apologise."

Philipp just chuckled. "I've heard worse. But to honour the facts, my editor made that call. I'm just really good at it."

He had a confidence that inspired her. It could have come across cocky, but the easy smile told her he was just joking with her. "Well, if that's the case..." Lucille checked out his camera. It seemed to be an expensive one. "Are you working tonight?"

He patted his camera lightly and nodded. "That gave *me* away now, didn't it? Yes, I'm working tonight. There's this party, but obviously you already know about it. I suppose you don't usually go walking at night in high heels."

"More than you'd think." Suddenly emboldened, she slipped her arm into his. "Thanks for volunteering to get me there safely."

Philipp barely missed a beat. "My pleasure."

They started down the path. It didn't take Lucille long to appreciate Philipp's presence as she stumbled over uneven ground and protruding roots. "That's one star less for accessibility," she joked.

"I'll be sure to mention it in my review. By the way, I don't mean to be a party pooper, but you might like to know that these Serpents of Ishtar are a Spanish cult."

"I knew that."

"You did?"

Lucille grinned. "You're not the only one who does their homework."

Philipp looked impressed and confused at the same time. "And you're still going?"

"Of course I am! In my opinion, that makes it all the more exciting." That wasn't the reason, of course, but it worked as a perfect excuse for Philipp, who looked at her with new appreciation.

"You're much more interesting than I thought."

"Ouch."

He laughed. "Sorry. That was meant as a compliment."

Lucille pretended to be offended and gave him a side-eye. "Okay, weirdo."

"Snob," Philipp teased back.

This caused Lucille to break character and burst out laughing. "Oh, we're going to have so much fun together."

"Are we?"

Delighted, she patted his arm. "Oh, yes."

A little later they had made it to the mine and inside. The party was held in an old storeroom large enough to hold a hundred people. Terrariums of snakes lined the room, distracting from the food and drink. The centrepiece was a bronze statue of a woman with at least three different snakes wrapped around her body. Ishtar.

Even though they'd arrived, Lucille still clung to Philipp. They tried some of the food, finding it rather bland, before checking out the snakes in their terrariums. Subtly, Philipp snapped a few photos, and Lucille amused herself by shielding him from detection by the handful of black-clad cult members in the room.

As they made their round, they reached the back of the room only to discover it was a black curtain. Philipp pushed the curtain slightly to the side to take a peek.

"I'm afraid we have to part here," said Philipp.

"Why?"

Philipp shrugged, looking a little embarrassed. "I'm going to have to use some journalistic tricks and I wouldn't want to get you into trouble."

Lucille grinned. "You want to know what's behind the curtain."

"Potentially."

"Like I said, I'm terribly curious." She nodded at him. "Go ahead. I'll follow your lead." She liked the journalist enough not to let him go into potential danger alone.

"Aren't you afraid of the consequences if we're caught?"

"Oh, I *am*. Very much so. That's why I'm coming with you." Lucille gave him a winning smile. "I want to make sure no one steals you from me."

Philipp raised an eyebrow. "Are you hiding your concern behind a little flirting?"

"Potentially."

He grinned, then cast a quick glance around the room. "Alright, let's do this." He lifted the curtain for her, and they both slipped behind.

The curtain separated the party room from a hollowed-out pit. Thanks to the loud music, Lucille didn't hear the hissing until they reached the edge. Below them, more than a hundred snakes coiled on the old mine floor. Some of them were small, others large enough to crush a limb. None were held in place by anything other than the depth of the hole.

"This is insane," Philipp muttered as he took a few pictures.

Lucille noticed his hands trembling. It must have been the first time one of his articles had brought him face to face with actual paranormal activity. *If* this cult was involved in something paranormal. "I wonder what they're doing with them."

"Whatever it is, it can't be good." Philipp sighed. "I'll probably have to notify animal control and the police."

"I don't think so."

Lucille and Philipp spun around to come face to a face with a group of black-clad figures. A man with long black hair and the tattoo of a snake on his cheek glared at them. Four more cultists stood behind him.

"Ishtar has offered you a glimpse into your future. A rare honour. Especially for the uninitiated." Then he turned to his companions. "Seize them."

Jan

So far, the party had been pretty lame. Sure, there was free beer and soda and the Serpents had hired a DJ, but the vibes were off. The many colourful snakes in their terrariums along the walls didn't help matters either. Jan felt more like he was in a zoo than at a party. Still, he wasn't going to say no to a free beer.

It tasted okay and gave him an excuse to wander the room looking for sinister activities. Even the cultists seemed bored, although the sheer number of them standing between the terrariums creeped Jan out.

He was still watching them over his shoulder when he ran into a couple of familiar faces: Alan and Cian.

"Of course you two idiots are here. Can't miss a party, no matter how lame, can you?"

Alan sneered at him. "Speak for yourself. You're probably just here for the free beer."

Jan rolled his eyes. "It's the only thing that makes meeting you bearable."

"You..." Alan lunged forward, but Cian put a hand on his arm before searching Jan's face. "We're not here for the party."

"We aren't?" Alan sounded confused.

Jan crossed his arms. "Then why?" What else could have brought the two Elite Idiots to this place?

"We're here because of Leonie."

"Who's Leonie?" Alan asked.

"She's a Year Twelve. From my athletics club."

Alan rolled his eyes. "Oh, her. Why are we here for her? I thought you were sleeping with—"

Cian punched Alan's arm. "Because she was murdered. Poisoned. With snake venom."

Jan raised an eyebrow. Could it be that these two idiots were here for the same reason? If so, they'd be way out of their comfort zone and would only get themselves, and by extension him, in trouble. He had to find a way to make them leave.

He gave Cian a mocking sneer. "And you think one of those snakes did it? Have you interrogated them yet?" He hissed for good measure.

Immediately, Cian's face darkened. "I don't think it's coincidence. First the snake bite, now this snake-themed party. There's something going on here."

"So you two are wannabe cops now?"

"Careful what you say, Kerscher." Alan was all up in his face again.

Jan had no interest in a fight, so he changed tactics. "Relax. I agree with you. Something's off about this place. So, why don't we beat it and find a proper party?" He'd get rid of them as soon as they were outside.

"I don't know." Cian glanced over his shoulder, as if expecting his dead friend to appear behind him.

Alan, however, was more responsive. "Kerscher's right. This party stinks. All these snakes give me the creeps. Let's go."

Cian sighed. Together, they turned towards the entrance, only to find it had been locked by a set of bars. With a sinking feeling, Jan tested the bars, feeling the glare of at least two cultists in his neck. The bars wouldn't budge. The door was locked, leaving them trapped with at least a dozen cultists, a handful of snakes, and the creepy statue of a goddess.

Matt

Matt and Caspar's cat-and-mouse game led them into the Dûr Lôrac. Energy was shot back and forth, causing several collapses. From time to time, Caspar would get hold of Matt and they'd roll over the ground, sparing no punches. Matt had just managed to extract himself from one such scuffle, when the ground split beneath them and they were free falling. Matt spread his wings, but a rock hit his left side, sending him crashing into the pile of rocks below.

Groaning, he struggled to his feet. His face and entire left side were burning. When he touched it gingerly, pain shot through his core and his hand came away bloody. But there was no time to dwell on the injury. Not with his brother running amok around him.

He searched for Caspar and found a wingtip sticking out of the pile of rocks. A slow smile spread across Matt's face. He might be hurt, but Caspar had it worse. The rocks were shifting, so he was definitely alive, but with any luck he wouldn't recover fast enough to follow his trail through the abstract space. Especially if he was never actually jumping.

Across the room was the entrance to a cave. Carved runes emitted a soft blue light, the only source of light down here. Matt dragged himself up and hobbled down the pile of rocks, making sure he stepped on Caspar for good measure. Then he ducked into the adjacent cavern.

Nothing could've prepared him for the sight that awaited him. Countless silver threads spun from the ceiling, just high enough for people to pass under, but not so high that they couldn't be touched. Some threads were so thin they ended in the middle of the room, while others were tangled. In the back, a thick golden thread cut through the silver ones.

Matt entered the room with a quiet awe. He knew many wondrous and beautiful places in Hescaryn, but none like this.

Suddenly, the image of a young demon working in Hell's Gardens flickered alive, followed by a grunt. He whipped around and saw that Caspar had followed him, wiping a low hanging thread out of his face.

Irritated, Caspar paused, resting his weight on the leg that hadn't been crushed. "What is this place?"

The gardener had vanished.

"You tell me," Matt replied. "You've been around longer." Curious, he reached for a thread above him.

Two demons flickered alive. "You killed her?" the one on the left said.

The other looked absolutely miserable. "It was an accident."

"If anyone finds—"

Matt let go of the thread and the demons disappeared. Slowly, an idea formed in his mind. He looked around for a thread to test his theory on and found one starting a few metres in front of him.

Running his hand along the thread, he witnessed a baby grow before his eyes. These threads represented lives. But whose?

"Hey, come back."

Even Caspar didn't sound like his usual self. He looked around anxiously, clearly reluctant to attack Matt in here. A small comfort.

"If I did, my life would literally be hanging by a thread." What if one of those was his? Would it show him the future as Chay had seen it?

"I'm warning you!" Caspar said, but his heart wasn't in it. Instead, he followed Matt and wiped some of the blood from his face. He grabbed a thread and brought up another image. "I think they're memories."

"Memories?" Matt couldn't believe what he saw.

Caspar's face was transforming. Instead of hatred and anger, fascination took over his features. "This must be the Web of Memories."

"There are monsters who weave webs of memories?"

Caspar shook his head. "Not monsters. Mishkarian priests."

"The Goddess of Time?" Matt asked. A multitude of gods were worshipped in Hescaryn. Matt had never cared much for any of them.

"I thought Balthasar was only joking when he told me about it, but the web exists."

"For what?" As beautiful as it was, Matt couldn't quite understand why someone would want to preserve these particular memories. The ones he'd seen so far hadn't exactly been captivating.

Caspar shrugged. "I suppose it's some kind of archive. This is all of them. The memories of every demon who has ever existed. Hescaryn's collective memory."

"All of them?" Matt asked, the awe returning three times over. "Does that mean our memories are here too?"

"Obviously. Why?"

"I just had an idea." Matt knew it was a long shot. There were thousands and thousands of threads in this cave system. Millions, if Caspar was right. The demon population wasn't even remotely comparable to Ashuan's, but there were still far more threads than he could ever explore in his lifetime.

Still, he touched one here and there, pulling himself deeper and deeper into the web.

"What are you doing?" Caspar barked behind him as he struggled to keep up.

"It's somewhere..." It was as if the threads were calling out to Matt. He ignored most of them, trying to find the one he wanted. The one that would set his brother on edge.

Suddenly, a familiar face appeared. Balthasar, carrying a heavily bleeding, fair-haired boy over his shoulder. "Bad weeds grow tall," Balthasar said nonchalantly.

"Got you."

"Don't you dare!" Caspar growled.

Matt grinned at him, his hand hovering over the inconspicuous silver thread that held all his brother's memories. "Sorry, I can't resist the temptation."

He didn't feel a shred of remorse as he grasped the thread and brought Caspar's memories to life.

It was as if a cinema screen opened between him and Caspar, but the figures on it were in 3D and Matt could feel the draft from the corridor where Caspar and a little girl, Menuha, were hiding. If his siblings had been human, they'd be about eight or nine.

Behind the walls, he heard the familiar moaning that told Matt they were in the Residence of Lust. Five hundred years before he was even a thought.

Menuha pushed aside a curtain. "The way is clear."

To Matt's surprise, Caspar hid in the shadows. "Melaney forbade us to leave the residence."

"It's safe this time," Menuha declared, clearly the braver of the two.

"That's what you said last time."

Menuha groaned. Then she walked back and grabbed Caspar's arm. "Come on." When he still didn't move, she looked at him as sweetly as she could. "Please!"

Caspar was like butter in his twin sister's hands. He only hesitated for a moment before following her into the corridor. The two of them hurried through the residence, and slowly, Matt got a lay of the land.

They had almost reached the exit when a man appeared in the corridor. He immediately reminded Matt of Caspar with his white-blond hair and large muscles. It was obviously the twins' father; Dorian from the House of Wrath. If Matt remembered correctly, Melaney had disembowelled him many centuries ago.

Startled, Menuha let out a scream, but the man grabbed her and covered her mouth.

Caspar looked absolutely terrified. Still, he took a stance and fired a weak blast of energy into Dorian's face. It didn't hurt the older demon, but he let Menuha go and grabbed Caspar instead, slamming him into the wall.

Matt winced as blood splattered. Moaning, Caspar cried, "Run, Menuha!"

Menuha left immediately, but her father raised his hand, ready to blast her out of existence. "Oh, no, you don't."

Caspar rammed his head into Dorian's side, causing the energy to hit the ceiling instead. Two heartbeats later, Menuha was gone.

With a furious scream, Dorian drove his knee into Caspar's stomach.

Caspar folded instantly. His father pushed him to the ground, pinned his chest with his knee and wrapped a large hand around the boy's throat.

"Please," Caspar whimpered. Now that Menuha was safe, his bravado quickly faded. "I'll do anything you—"

Dorian grinned as his son fought for life beneath him. "You want to bargain with me? Very well. I wanted your sister, but you'll serve well enough." He lifted the boy by the throat, threw him over his shoulder, and disappeared.

The memory changed instantly, taking the shape of a circular room lined by brick walls, a tower of sorts. Matt discovered medieval-looking laboratory equipment, scrolls of parchment, herbs, cauldrons, and dead animal parts. The closer he looked, the creepier it was.

Dorian dropped Caspar in front of a man in his forties—if he was human. And since demons rarely looked older than thirty, he probably was. The man had a wiry frame, looking half the size of Dorian with his bulging muscles. His salt-and-pepper locks were unkempt and fell to his shoulders. Pale blue eyes glared at the demons, as if he was thinking about blasting them out of existence.

"An endless supply of demon blood, just like you wanted," Dorian declared, not even looking at the boy coughing and sputtering on the floor.

"That's a child."

"My child."

Little Caspar, who hadn't Matt's future knowledge of his heritage, looked up in shock. He'd never even seen his father before.

Dorian ignored him. "He's from the Houses of Wrath and Lust. That should do for your purposes, Alecto."

Matt's stomach began to turn.

"We'll see," Alecto said, poking Caspar with the toe of his shoe. The boy whimpered.

"Are we done now?"

Alecto nodded. "It is fulfilled. The boy stays with me."

Dorian grunted. Without another look at Caspar, he disappeared. The fear and confusion in Caspar's face as he was abandoned with this frightening stranger was enough for Matt to let go of the thread and stagger back.

Shocked, he stared at Caspar. "Your father sold you to a... sorcerer?" Judging by his laboratory, the man obviously knew something about magic.

Caspar spat. "Don't worry, he paid with his life."

"Melaney." Matt nodded, though Caspar just grunted. Like father like son. "Where did he take you?" If it had happened five hundred years ago, it might have been Ashuan. But there were many other worlds just like it.

"Nowhere," Caspar snapped. When Matt raised his eyebrows, he grunted again. "To a *human* sorcerer. Alecto summoned him or something. He taught me everything I know about magic, and once I got bored, I ripped his throat out."

Matt replied flatly, "How innovative."

"You know me," Caspar said.

In Matt's opinion, his brother was trying a little too hard to appear unaffected by the memory they'd dug up. If he didn't know better, there was a hint of fear in Caspar's eyes.

Matt moved his hand a little, careful not to skip too many years. "Not good enough."

And there it was. Caspar's eyes widened in genuine fear. "Don't."

There was no way Matt could stop now. He grabbed the thread again.

Samantha

While the others were at the party she wasn't allowed to attend, Samantha made the fatal decision to have dinner with her family. The days of happy chatter were long gone. Every now and then one of her parents would ask how school was going, and she or Meg would answer "good". Then there'd be silence again.

The family TV was on to fill it. Since none of them was interested in watching anything, it was whatever was on free TV these days. As usual, her father was in control of the remote, zapping through every commercial break. It was a habit that annoyed her mother immensely, but she kept her mouth shut until—

"Stop!"

Irritated, Ben stopped and looked at her. "Stop what?"

But Juliane's eyes were glued to the screen. For the first time in a long time, she looked delighted. "That's Max."

On the screen was a smart-looking, dark-haired doctor who told his patient the devastating diagnosis. The acting was mediocre, like most early evening shows, but he was handsome enough to keep people invested.

"Who's Max?" Ben asked, a little annoyed.

"Max is Max," Juliane said with gleaming eyes. "He's my... ex."

Meg gave Samantha a pregnant look and Samantha felt her heart sink.

"And when was that, if I may ask?" The tension in her father's voice didn't bode well.

Juliane waved him off. "Before you. We were just children. Fourteen or fifteen. He was my neighbour and we both did theatre. One day at camp, we made each other promise we'd make it big one day." She looked dreamily at the television again. "And he did. He looks so good."

The TV went black.

"Hey!"

"I'm not going to watch you make goo-goo eyes at some mediocre actor slash future reality TV star."

"And off we go," Samantha muttered. Her meal was only half eaten, but her appetite was gone.

Juliane huffed. "Are you seriously jealous of someone I dated over twenty years ago? Give me the remote!"

"Looks to me like you're still into him."

"How?"

"'He looks so good,'" Ben imitated.

Meanwhile, Meg took out her phone and started typing.

Annoyed, Juliane clicked her tongue. "He's a handsome man. Am I not allowed to look at anyone anymore? Is that how it's going to be?"

Abruptly, Ben stood up and threw the TV remote at her, almost taking off Samantha's nose. "Go on, watch your goddamn heart out. But without me." Then he stalked off, his steps pounding the stairs like elephant feet.

Instead of apologising for the interruption, Juliane bent down to pick up the remote control and turned it back on. The scene had moved on, and Max was having a tense confrontation with his colleague.

"Max Schönborn," Meg said, as if their parents hadn't just had the most ridiculous fight. She looked at her phone. "He's got a few acting credits. This is his first leading role, though."

"How nice," Juliane said, looking at what seemed to be Max's Wikipedia entry. "I wonder if he's on Instagram."

While Meg immediately started the app, Samantha got up from the table and cleared her and her father's plates. She was about to go upstairs when the doorbell rang. "I'll get it," she called, then opened the door to a familiar yet unexpected face.

"Hi," Shayna said with a fake smile that set Samantha on high alert. "I hope you're not busy." The smile faltered. "Because I need your help."

"My help?" While Shayna was the most easy-going girl in the Elite Clique and Cian swore up and down that she was cool, Samantha couldn't bring herself to trust her.

"We have a pair of idiots to save."

Samantha frowned. "Who are you talking about?"

"Alan and Cian went to check out that cult party. You know who I mean, the Serpents of Ishtar." She rolled her eyes.

Panic washed over Samantha. "What? He promised me he wouldn't!"

"Well, looks like he lied. So, are you busy or not?"

It could still be a trap, but Samantha wasn't willing to risk Cian's life on it. She could already see him dead on the floor, eyes blindly staring into the night sky. "I'm coming. Let me just get my shoes and my bag."

"Okay, but hurry."

#

The walk to the mine was the weirdest experience. Shayna kept nagging about the boys' stupidity as if she and Samantha were best friends, while Samantha mostly kept quiet, unsure of how much she could say without inviting ridicule. When they finally arrived at the mine, they found the entrance guarded by two cultists.

"You're too late."

"So?" Shayna asked, not used to being denied entry.

"The doors are locked."

Shayna started rummaging through her bag for her phone. "I have an invitation."

"Late means late. So go home and pray to Ishtar to spare your life." It was said with such venom that Samantha doubted Ishtar was likely to grant the favour.

"Let's go," she said to Shayna, pulling her away.

Shayna didn't come willingly. She kept looking over her shoulder, her body as tense as if she was about to punch someone. "Look, hoping bad things go away might be your M-O, but that's not how you get things done."

"Well, bullying your way in might be yours, but there's another way."

Surprised, Shayna stared at her. "Did you just...?" Then she smiled, and this time there was nothing fake about it. "Not bad, Kollmer. So, what's this other way?"

"There's another entrance to the mine down by the gravel lake. It used to be blocked off, but it can't hurt to have a look."

"Not bad at all. Let's go."

Together they made their way down towards the lake. It was almost pitch black under the trees, and the wind whistled through the leafless branches. It didn't help that their friends might be trapped with a bunch of snakes.

Desperate for a distraction, Samantha asked, "What do you mean 'hoping bad things go away is my M-O'?"

"Well, listen, I don't blame you, but part of the reason Cheryl keeps picking on you is because you make it so damn easy. You just stand there, retreating into yourself, hoping she'll go away soon."

"So now it's my fault you guys have been bullying me all these years?"

"Oh no, that's not what I'm saying. I just wish you'd spoken up sometimes. For me, it got boring real quick."

"Sorry my torment wasn't more entertaining for you."

Shayna's eyes lit up. "See, more of that! Honestly, I love seeing that confidence, and I know there's more where that came from."

"You're weird."

"And proud of it," Shayna declared. Then she linked arms with Samantha's. "As *you* should be. Look, Cheryl may think being a witch is boring, but in this town, it's just part of the vibe. And I love a good vibe. So does Cian." She wriggled her eyebrows suggestively.

Samantha was still fighting the whiplash of Shayna's moods. "If you say so."

"He's crazy about you, Kollmer. I hope you know that."

Unsure what to say to that, Samantha cleared her throat. "Um..." As much as she liked hanging out with Cian, she wasn't crazy about him.

"I really hope it's worth breaking his heart, because he's pretty great," Shayna added in a voice that wasn't quite as nonchalant as it should have been.

It occurred to Samantha that Cian was to Shayna what Fabian was to her. Just as it hurt her to see the way Lucille was treating him lately,

Shayna was worried about Cian. Unlike her, though, Samantha had vowed not to interfere in her friends' relationship. They were both adults, after all.

"He knows how I feel." Or rather, what she didn't feel.

"I'm well aware," Shayna said with just a hint of reproach. "I know he's going into this with eyes wide open, but that doesn't mean I'm comfortable watching."

Samantha wasn't quite sure if that was because she was the low-hanging fruit Cheryl had always made her out to be, or because of the potential heartbreak Shayna believed was inevitable. She wasn't intending to break Cian's heart. That had never been part of the plan.

Fortunately, they reached the lake before she had to answer. In the pale light of their smartphones, they saw several footprints in the snow. It looked like something heavy had been dragged to the entrance. Someone had definitely been using this part of the mine.

They found the bars covering the entrance broken and bent, and the rocks blocking much of the tunnel pushed aside.

"They've kept themselves busy," Samantha observed. A tightness wrapped around her chest as she looked down the dark corridor. Everything inside her was screaming not to go into this maze of unknown dangers. But between the abrasive guards uphill and the cult's background, Samantha would never forgive herself for turning her back on her friends.

She exchanged glances with Shayna, who nodded and went in first. In the darkness, their footsteps left a hollow echo that seemed to match their heartbeats. They walked in silence for a while, but then Shayna stopped suddenly.

"Did you hear that?"

"Hear what?" Samantha whispered. Then she heard it too. A dragging sound near her feet.

She turned her light towards the ground and immediately wished she hadn't. Gasping, she pointed to her feet. "Snakes."

Shayna's light joined hers and a small cry escaped her. Several snakes of all shapes and sizes were writhing around their shoes. "Are they poisonous?"

"How would I know?" Samantha swallowed. "The only snake I've ever seen in these parts was a grass snake. Could be."

"What do we do?"

Samantha's mind raced. Then she remembered the potions she'd packed in her bag before leaving. One of them was supposed to ward off small creatures like mice or rats. As she took out the purple vial, she sincerely hoped the potion would work for snakes too.

"What is that?" Shayna asked.

Ignoring her question, Samantha uncorked the vial and let a drop fall to the ground between her feet. Foul-smelling steam rose in response. The snakes hissed and retreated.

"Um... caproic acid." It wasn't, but it was close enough to use as an excuse. "It smells bad, as you clearly noticed." Shayna held her nose and gagged a little. "Animals are more sensitive to it, so they stay away. It's alright now."

Shayna winced at her explanation. "Then why aren't you continuing?"

"You want to go first?"

"Take your time."

Samantha swallowed again. By the looks of it, there were a lot more snakes ahead of them, and she only had the one vial. Fortunately, one drop seemed to go a long way, so she decided to trust the potion, took a few steps, dropped another, and continued.

"May I ask why you have caproic acid in your bag?" Shayna asked after a while.

"Sure... Well, I took some from class yesterday."

Shayna raised her eyebrows. "And you're allowed to do that?"

"Exam prep." Of course they weren't allowed to take any of the chemicals. Not that it had stopped her when she'd taken Robert's explosive mixture last year.

"I see. Are you saying that Cian made some, too, and took it home?"

Hopefully she wouldn't question Cian about it, because they'd left acids and lyes in Year Twelve.

"He could have... if he'd paid more attention in class."

"Didn't he get twelve points in the last exam?"

"Well, twelve isn't fifteen." The highest attainable mark.

Shayna snorted. "Nerd."

"Ssh."

They'd left the snakes behind and had reached a larger room full of sleeping bags and backpacks. No one was home, which did nothing to ease Samantha's worries.

"There must be a lot more than I thought."

Shayna nodded anxiously. "We're still going, right?"

"Of course." Now more than ever.

Fabian

When Fabian regained consciousness, he found himself lying in a small alcove with his hands and feet bound. Groaning, he tried to lift his head and get his bearings. Somewhere behind a wall or two he could hear bass thumping, but his surroundings looked more like a temple than a party.

The only one present was the girl who'd knocked him out. She knelt over a bronze bowl and was dressed now, though the snakeskin leggings and tight black corset didn't leave much to the imagination, and the memory of her bare breasts immediately came back to Fabian. Then he remembered the snakebite and that he was lying here, trussed up like a pig.

Panic rose in his throat, threatening to overwhelm him. Fabian forced himself to swallow. Just as he was about to speak to the girl, a man strode into the area. He had the same black hair as the girl, but while hers fell over her shoulders, his was tied at the back.

"Ophelia! How far along are you?"

The girl looked up worriedly. "I've bathed and cleansed my blood."

The man picked up the bowl and tilted it. To Fabian's horror, he suddenly realised its gruesome contents. Meanwhile, Ophelia held her arm where she'd cut it, bled drops welling through her fingers.

"You know what happens to those Ishtar doesn't approve of," the man said, putting the bowl down.

"She chose me," Ophelia said in a feeble show of defiance.

He merely snorted. "That hack Eresta chose you!"

"Enrico!" Ophelia clapped her hands over her mouth. "She's the Goddess' mouthpiece."

"That's what she claims." He grabbed her upper arm and pulled her to her feet. "Eresta is afraid because I'm rising through the ranks. Already more brothers and sisters listen to me than to her. She chose you to humble me. And when Ishtar destroys you, she'll say it was my blood that failed."

Due to his words and their similar looks, Fabian assumed they must be brother and sister.

Ophelia stared at Enrico, her pretty face full of doubt. "You think she'll kill me to teach you a lesson?"

"Isn't it obvious?" Enrico took a strand of her hair and twirled it between his fingers, pulling on it as he did so. "Why would Ishtar choose someone like you? You're too meek and gentle."

Fabian almost snorted. There had been nothing gentle about her at the lake.

"Gentle?" Ophelia huffed. "I'll show you how gentle I can be."

Instead, it was her brother who showed her, tugging hard enough on her hair to make her yelp. "Call it imbalanced, then. One day this, the next day something else."

He let go of her hair and his eyes fell on Fabian. "Who's that?"

Ophelia looked around in surprise, as if she'd already forgotten his presence. "He was sneaking around."

"Did he see you bathing?"

"Of course not," Ophelia hastened to say.

Seeing her bathing in the moonlight seemed to be an even bigger deal than Fabian had thought.

"Look, I—" Fabian began as he saw Enrico's eyes harden.

"I'll take him to the other sacrifices."

Sacrifices? Fabian's eyes widened.

Ophelia grabbed her brother's arm. "No!"

"No?"

"*I* will sacrifice him to Ishtar. To ask for her blessing."

Enrico raised an eyebrow. "You? You've never sacrificed anyone before. It takes more to draw a blade through skin, muscle, and sinew than a belly full of rage."

The description alone terrified Fabian. He and his friends had known these so-called serpents weren't above a little poison murder, but full-on sacrifice? What kind of freak show had he gotten himself into?

Defiantly, Ophelia lifted her chin. "I can do it. I'm not *gentle*."

Enrico turned to her with a smile. "Very well. Sacrifice him to Ishtar. I doubt it'll change her mind about you."

He was about to leave when Ophelia called after him. "Enrico?" Suddenly, her voice was as meek as he'd accused her of being.

"What?"

"Do you really think she's going to destroy me?"

Enrico didn't answer immediately. His facial muscles were working overtime, and for a fleeting moment, it almost looked as if he was going to take her in his arms. But then he stared past her and said, "No one would blame you if you chickened out and disappeared into the night. It's probably for the best, anyway. Not everyone agrees with Eresta's choice."

"Ishtar's choice," Ophelia whispered.

His eyes hardened instantly. "If you say so." Then he left the room before she could say anything else.

Fabian watched her stand there for half a minute, just breathing. Then Ophelia turned and came towards him. She pulled a knife from a small scabbard at her waist and cut the bonds around his feet.

"You know," Fabian cleared his throat, "you should take his advice. Ishtar seems a bit aggressive if you ask—"

She slapped him surprisingly hard. "Don't dirty the name of the goddess with your foolish prattle." She pulled him to his feet by the hands. "Come on. Let's get this over with."

Once again, Fabian had to fight down the wave of panic inside him. "You're not really going to kill me, are you?"

"Shut up and walk."

As soon as they stepped out of the alcove, Fabian discovered a small altar and a deep pit full of snakes. He stumbled after Ophelia, his heart bopping up to his throat, until she pushed him to his knees in front of the altar.

Fabian swallowed several times as he watched her light the candles. He knew he had to do something, but his mind was black, and it didn't help that the shadows in the cave were freaking him out.

When he opened his mouth, a strange, jumpy laugh came out. "You're not really going to kill me, are you? Look, I don't doubt that Ish… she's an amazing goddess, but human sacrifices? This isn't ancient times, you know?"

After ignoring him most of the time, Ophelia grunted in annoyance. "Ishtar demands blood and obedience from her followers."

"I always say, never trust a god who thirsts for your blood."

"What do you know of gods?"

"Not much," Fabian admitted. "But come on! You don't really believe this goddess exists, do you?"

Ophelia went back to her work. "Of course she exists, and tonight she'll choose me as her vessel."

"And you're looking forward to that?" Fabian asked doubtfully. He couldn't imagine anything more terrifying.

She looked at him again. "Why shouldn't I?"

"I don't know. The goddess of destruction, war, sex…" Now that he thought about it, the last thing he wanted was for Ishtar to choose a vessel to walk the Earth tonight.

Impressed, Ophelia asked, "You know Ishtar?"

"Only what's on her Wikipedia page."

Ophelia rolled her eyes and picked up her dagger, cleaning the blade in the fire.

Things were going to go South soon if he didn't do something about it. "Think about it. When your beloved goddess chooses your body as her new vessel, what will happen to you?"

"Me?" she asked, as if concern for her own health and safety had always been an afterthought.

Fabian almost felt sorry for her. It was obvious to him that she'd grown up in this cult, probably dragged into it by her older brother way too young. "Yes, you. How old are you? Fifteen?"

"Sixteen," Ophelia hissed.

"Sixteen, and you want to give your life for this goddess? Even your brother thought it was a bad idea."

"My *brother* never believed in me."

"I'm sorry," Fabian said and meant it. "Really. But if you ask me, I think he was at least a little worried about you. He says you're going to be destroyed. Whatever that means."

Annoyed, Ophelia explained, "Others have tried before and failed. I *won't* fail."

"Of course not." It was always better to agree with people on such matters. Especially people with knives in their hands. "But what will become of you?"

"I'll be her vessel, so she can walk the earth."

It still sounded pretty bad. "And that's a good thing?"

"For all true believers."

"But not you," he pointed out.

Ophelia glared at him. "Do you always talk so much?"

"When my life depends on it, yes."

"Why should Ishtar's awakening be bad for me?"

"Because you'll cease to exist. Or do you think you'll share your body with her and she'll let you out from time to time?"

It seemed to only now dawn on Ophelia what she was trying to do. "It is a great honour to be chosen as Ishtar's vessel."

"Sure, I'd say that too if I were the leader of a cult. It neatly excuses killing a bunch of innocents." Fabian noticed her hand trembling. He was getting somewhere. "Ophelia? That's your name, right?" She nodded slightly. "You don't have to do this."

She sighed. "Yes, I do." Then she stepped behind him, grabbed his hair to pull his head back, and held the knife to his throat.

"Wait!"

"For what?"

"My name is Fabian." He looked up to see her frowning at him. "I've just turned nineteen and I'm going to finish school next year. Then I'll probably study Biology, because I like nature a lot."

Ophelia rolled her eyes. "Why are you telling me this?"

Fabian went on. "I don't have any siblings, but I have a best friend who's practically my sister. My mum runs a magic shop. Pretty weird, I know, but it's actually quite cool. I like to draw, and I've got a cat. Her name's Merle."

"Great?" Her voice sounded strained.

"I just thought you should know." Her bewildered expression told him he'd completely confused her. It was a start. "I'm not just some nameless sacrifice. I'm a person. With a family and plans for the future, dreams and hopes. I have a life." Slowly, his voice softened. "At least as long as you don't take it away from me."

The knife at his throat trembled, but it never cut. Finally, Ophelia lowered her hand and his head, cutting the ties around his hands instead. "Well, I don't."

"Don't what?" Fabian asked, not quite daring to breathe yet.

"I don't have a life. At least not outside of Ishtar's Serpents. Enrico is all I have." Her voice cracked. "If I run tonight... if I fail Ishtar..." Her eyes glistened in the candlelight. "What should I do?"

Slowly, Fabian turned and placed a hand on her cheek. The poor girl had been brainwashed by this cult since she'd been a little girl. It wasn't her fault she was surrounded by a bunch of psychos.

He rubbed a tear from her cheek. "We'll figure it out. I promise."

"We?"

Fabian gave her a wry smile. "I owe you one, don't I?" He took her hand and pulled her a little away from the altar. "Let's pack your things and go, shall we?"

Ophelia looked at him as if in a trance. Then she nodded and followed him.

She was just about to grab a few things and stuff them into a backpack when they heard footsteps coming down the corridor. Panicked, Ophelia pushed Fabian into the alcove and put a finger to his lips.

"Are you packing?" The new arrival was a woman, her question full of glee. "I knew it! You're nothing but a child, not worthy of Ishtar."

"She *chose* me," Ophelia hissed back.

"Oh, did she?" The woman approached quickly. Judging by Ophelia's yelp, she'd grabbed her. "Where's your snakebite, huh?"

The next thing Fabian heard was Ophelia protesting as the other woman dragged her away. He dared to look and saw a dark-haired woman hauling her to the snake pit.

"Why don't we see if Ishtar really likes you that much?"

Fabian saw the blank look of incomprehension on Ophelia's face as the woman threw her into the pit..

Caspar

The moment the memories flashed before him, Caspar was back there; in that cramped little tower with its million contraptions and experiments and that horrible human who treated him like shit. His throat tightened as he noticed the heavy iron ring around the neck of his much younger self. It was inscribed with runes that made it both impossible for him to slip it off and for him to use most of his demon magic.

But the worst part was how weak he was. How he toddled after the mage, always alert and present, eager to please.

He'd spent thirty years there, though this particular memory was still early in his apprenticeship. There had been nothing he'd called his own. Even the dirty tunic he wore belonged to Alecto. As did he, something the mage had never let him forget.

In his current memory, little Caspar was running after the mage with a heavy notebook, writing down everything Alecto said as he went through his experiments. The workbench was full of complicated apparatus and bubbling liquids. Above them, high in the roof, a raven looked down and croaked.

"Tube six is turning purple."

"That's good, isn't it?" his younger self said eagerly. "It means it's working." He'd learnt a lot about magic over the years.

Alecto's withering stare hit him. "Did I ask you to comment on my work?"

"No, Master."

"Ugh. Why do I bother with a demon child like you?" A stare to freeze the blood in one's veins. "Tell me."

Tired of repeating himself, little Caspar said, "You need my blood. It carries the power of Wrath and Lust and several magical properties that will strengthen your potions."

"Let's see about that."

Without hesitation, his younger self closed the book and held out his right arm. Alecto hauled him to the table where he picked up a bowl and a knife. The little one held his arm over the bowl without being told to, but Caspar saw the nervous twitch in his throat and the tension in his face. The boy knew what was coming.

Alecto cut so deep little Caspar screamed. Blood poured down his arm, quickly filling the bowl before the cut had a chance to heal itself. As Alecto took the bowl, little Caspar stepped back, trying his best to ignore the blood-smeared, aching arm as the mage mixed his blood into tube six. The potion turned so dark it looked almost black.

"Why aren't you taking notes?" Alecto barked.

Little Caspar snapped back to attention. He wiped his arm on his tunic and opened the notebook again.

"We'll start with live probes now." Alecto opened a nearby box, from which they'd heard a loud squeak.

From its depths, he pulled a fat little mouse by its tail. He placed the animal on the table, on top of a rune, which glowed blue. Immediately, the mouse sat still, immobilised by the magic in the symbol.

Alecto took tube six and poured it over the wretched creature. The mouse began to grow, and little Caspar took notes.

Soon it changed, and instead of simply growing, the mouse began to blow up like a balloon. It was one of the most grotesque things Caspar had ever seen, and although he knew what would happen, he flinched as the creature exploded, taking half the lab with it.

Shrapnel and debris rained down on them. Little Caspar protected his eyes with his arm and the cuts he received healed quickly. His master wasn't so lucky.

Alecto rolled on the floor, shrieking in pain as he covered his left eye. "Boy!" he cried. "Where are you? Heal me."

Little Caspar rushed to his side, only to be hit by Alecto's flailing arm. Still, he pressed on and put his hands over Alecto's eye. The memory showed the damage. Irreparable if it hadn't been for his magic. And though it hurt like hell, the younger him gritted his teeth until his master could see out of it again.

As soon as the damage was repaired, Alecto pushed him away. "You useless dolt! What am I training you for?" He spat at the boy at his feet. "What are you doing down there? Get up!" Alecto hauled him to his feet. "Clean up this mess and make a note. The experiment failed. We'll start again tomorrow."

Then he stormed out of the room, leaving an exhausted boy behind.

Before Caspar could stop him, Matt had moved on to the next memory. This one took them almost ten years forward. His younger self was now what humans would call a teenager, although he was far beyond his teens.

In the years since the last memory, his situation had improved slightly. His clothes were still simple but clean, and Alecto trusted him enough to let him run the experiments on his own while he researched more complex spells. As before, Caspar's younger self took meticulous notes. When he heard footsteps coming up the stairs, he immediately stopped and stood to attention.

The years hadn't been kind to his master. He'd aged twenty years. Most of his hair had fallen out and one of his hands had turned permanently black, the result of a curse gone wrong. Caspar remembered how he'd been starved, beaten, and worse for a month because he'd been unable to cure the affliction.

"Any progress?" Alecto's bark was as harsh as ever.

And despite all that time in the tower, little Caspar was still eager to please—or perhaps too frightened not to. "The decaying elixir should be ready tomorrow. The first results have been impressive." He'd never seen anything die so quickly.

"Then I want you to prepare it for trial for tomorrow. My enemies are growing bolder."

"Yes, Master."

"Have you done your exercises?" Over the last years, Alecto had begun to teach him his runes.

Caspar nodded and pulled a roll of parchment from the pouch at his waist to show him.

Alecto tore the paper from his hands and studied it. After a while he threw it back in Caspar's face. "It's getting there."

He went on to check the experiments, looking for something to complain about. But after all these years, Caspar had mastered the expected lab conduct. He kept better order than his master. Everything was clean, tidy, and well documented. Not a single ingredient was wasted. Even the most malicious person couldn't find fault with his work. Neither could Alecto.

Instead of praise, he grunted.

Encouraged, Caspar asked the question he'd been thinking about all morning. "Master, may I spend my lunch hour in the gardens?"

The tower was surrounded by extensive gardens where Alecto grew his own food, poisonous plants, and even flowers. Caspar, who was never allowed outside the tower grounds, loved the gardens. They made him feel better, and he enjoyed working in them more than experimenting on defenceless animals. He was well aware he could never let Alecto know how much it meant to him or he'd never see the gardens again.

Even now, Alecto seemed to be about to say no. Instead, he grunted again. "You can finally dig up the herb beds and pull out the weeds. And harvest the poison thistles."

"Thank you, Master."

The memory stopped when Matt finally let go of the thread. After all, Caspar had been through, Matt seemed *amused.*

Caspar glared at him. "What?"

"Are you sure these are your memories?"

"You have a problem with that?"

"Nope." The amusement vanished. "I just wonder what happened to turn this obedient, submissive boy into... well, you."

Caspar growled. "Nothing happened. I grew up."

"Why don't I believe that?"

"Are you done now?"

Matt raised an eyebrow. "Done? After seeing this?" He snorted. "Far from it." His hand moved back to the thread.

Caspar knew he should stop it, but something deep inside immobilised him as much as the rune had frozen the mouse. Could it be that he *longed* to see more?

As Matt's finger brushed the thread, the face of a brown-haired girl appeared.

"Jeyne," Caspar whispered, causing Matt to raise his eyebrows and close his fingers around the thread.

Matt

The girl was no more than fourteen, which probably put her in the same maturity range as Caspar. She was pretty in the same way Samantha was to Matt. Not a stunner who turned heads left and right, but someone who could blow you away with a single smile meant just for you. Her auburn hair was braided around her head with a green ribbon, while tiny curls framed her face. A smattering of freckles covered her nose, drawing attention to her hazel eyes.

Eyes, which looked absolutely terrified at the moment.

Matt had missed the start of this particular memory, but they were in the aforementioned gardens. Behind them a dark and twisted tower rose up, casting its shadow over the hedges that surrounded beds of poisonous plants.

It was neither the tower nor the poisonous plants that frightened the girl. It was Caspar who had cornered her, looking almost as ferocious as Matt knew him to be. "Who are you?" he growled, one hand raised. The effect was only slightly marred by the fact that his tunic and arms were dirty to the elbows.

Tears formed in the girl's eyes as she stuttered, "Jeyne. I'm Jeyne. Jeyne Wynter."

"What are you doing in this garden?"

A tear rolled down her cheek. "I... I was just curious. A stupid test of valour."

Already, Caspar's face softened. "A test of valour?"

Jeyne took a deep breath and blinked away the tears. "I was supposed to sneak into the enchanted garden and bring back a flower as proof.

I'm sorry." Her voice broke and the tears returned. "It was foolish of me. Please don't hurt me."

Caspar let go of her and took a step back. "You shouldn't be here," he told her. "The master doesn't like visitors."

After drying her eyes and blowing her nose, Jeyne looked at him curiously. "What about you?"

"Me? I'm his apprentice."

"Really? Are you..." Her eyes widened suddenly. "You're the demon boy, aren't you?"

Every bit of courage Jeyne gained seemed to drain right out of Caspar. Anxiously, he kneaded the hem of his tunic. "You've heard of me?"

"My father is the mayor down in the village. We get a lot of visitors. They talk about you."

"About what?" The way Caspar asked the question made Matt wonder if he'd seen *anyone* other than his abusive master in the decades he'd already spent in this world.

Jeyne's tears were completely forgotten as she explained, "That it's only a matter of time before he sends you to kill us all."

Now Caspar's eyes widened. "Why would he do that? Why would *I* do that?"

Jeyne shrugged before asking naïvely, "Aren't you evil and bloodthirsty and... I don't know?"

Caspar stared and then he began to laugh in a way Matt had never heard him before. "Me. No, not that I know of."

Now, Matt *really* needed to know what had happened between then and now, because the Caspar he knew was just that; evil and bloodthirsty.

"You don't look it," Jeyne confessed. From the way she regarded him, Matt knew her curiosity was about to turn to interest.

"What do I look like?" Caspar asked.

"Normal. Like one of the boys from the village." A soft blush covered her cheeks. "Only better."

Immediately, she giggled then covered her mouth and looked at him with her big hazel eyes.

Caspar wasn't unaffected. If anything, he looked almost as red as she did. And when he opened his mouth, all that came out was, "I've got wings."

"Really?"

Apparently that was an invitation for Caspar to shrug off his tunic, which sent Jeyne into another breathy giggle. Then his wings unfolded, black and magnificent. The way he had turned for her, she saw more wings than torso, but what she saw fascinated her immensely.

"Can I touch them?"

Caspar had no idea what he was in for. "Sure."

Carefully, Jeyne held out her hand and ran her fingers over the leathery skin. Her touch was so soft Caspar couldn't help but tremble.

The innocence at play was almost painful for Matt. He couldn't remember exactly when he'd learnt how sensitive the wings were, but it had been at a much younger age. Then it suddenly hit him. He'd grown up in Hescaryn, while Caspar had spent most of his formative years in a human world. And he'd come home from it hating humans.

Matt figured the way Caspar had been treated by his master was part of it, but Jeyne seemed sweet. A welcome distraction from Caspar's daily torment. Suddenly he was very worried about her.

"Are you alright?" she asked.

Flustered, Caspar tucked the wings back in and put his tunic back on. "Yes, yes. Very."

Jeyne crossed her arms as if to protect herself, but her eyes still roamed over Caspar's body. "You're quite something."

"If you say so." Caspar's voice was a bit thin.

"What about this?" She pointed to the iron band around his neck.

"Those are holding runes. They prevent me from... jumping away or summoning someone to me. Demons can jump through space, you know?"

Jeyne frowned. "Doesn't that make you more of a prisoner than an apprentice?"

She had a very valuable point, Matt thought. One that Caspar hadn't quite grasped yet.

"I belong to him," he said, repeating what had been hammered into his brain since his father had sold him to the mage.

"Like an animal?" Embarrassed, Jeyne covered her mouth. "I'm so sorry. I didn't mean to offend you."

Caspar just shrugged. He'd been called much worse. "That's alright. I'm not human, after all."

"Are demons so different?"

"My master says so. I'm evil, stupid, rotten, lazy, and irredeemable. Worse than an animal, in fact." He looked around until his eyes fell on a bush with large pink flowers.

Jeyne jumped when he plucked one and handed it to her. "Here. To prove your valour."

They never broke eye contact as Jeyne carefully took the flowers from his outstretched hand and tucked them into her hair. Caspar's gaze followed her movements and settled on the flower. He swallowed.

"Thank you," Jeyne whispered.

Matt let go of the memory to ask Caspar what had happened to the girl. But when he turned, his brother was staring at the empty place with a kind of longing that was almost painful. Not daring to disturb him, Matt moved his hand along the thread.

Lucille

"I'm not saying I don't like the company, but this is a bit too intimate for a first date, don't you think?"

Lucille had to agree with Philipp. The cultists had seized them, tied them back-to-back, and shoved them in a room filled with even more terrariums. They'd also tied their feet so they couldn't escape. Worse, two of the cultists had been left with them, and were now sharpening their knives near the small altar of a female goddess. It didn't take much imagination to figure out what they'd planned for them next.

"It's going to be alright," Lucille said, her voice a little too high. "I'm going to get us out of here." So far none of the cultists had shown any real magical power, which gave her the edge. If it had been just her and the cultists, she would've already freed herself, but she was wary of casting spells in front of the charming reporter.

"When?" There was a hint of panic in Philipp's voice. "They're going to disembowel us at any moment!"

"I know."

He trembled against her back, clearly fighting down a panic attack. "I'm sorry. I didn't want to snap at you," he said in a tight voice. "It's not your fault, it's mine. This just wasn't what I meant by taking a risk. I didn't expect something like this."

Lucille held her tongue. This was still pretty tame compared to what she was used to.

"Wait, did you...?" He tried to turn his head. "Did you expect this?"

She sighed. "Something like it."

"Why didn't you tell me?"

"And reveal all my tricks?" Maybe flirting wasn't the right thing to do in this situation, but Lucille couldn't help herself. "I promise you won't die."

Philipp swallowed and seemed to relax a little. Just then, the cultists finished their preparations. "I'll get Enrico," one of them said, and walked out the door. The other came towards them, the knife still in his hand.

"Now would be a great time to make good on that promise," Philipp said, panicking again.

"Agreed."

"You'll go behind bars for this," Philipp managed to squeak at the cultist.

The cultist sneered. "And your blood will nourish Ishtar."

"I have no interest in that kind of blood," said a deep, raspy, sultry voice, which sounded a lot like Matt's mother.

The cultist whirled around in shock. The statue in the corner was glowing, the snake wrapped around it moving slowly.

"What kind of sacrifice would that be? Weak and bound? Is that all you have to offer me?"

Philipp gasped. "Lucille? Am I hallucinating? Is this statue talking?"

Lucille ignored him. He was indeed hallucinating, as was the cultist. Or rather, they were both victims of her illusion. "Why don't you kneel before your goddess?" she made Ishtar say.

The cultist nearly fell over his feet as he followed the suggestion. His knife clattered to the floor. "Oh, Ishtar, bless me."

"Follow the snakes and you will find me," the goddess said. "*Don't* follow them and I will find you." The threat was followed by two massive snakes that wound around the man's knees before slithering down the corridor.

He hesitated. The statue began to glow redder and redder, sending him scrambling to his feet and running after the snakes. As soon as he was gone, the statue returned to its normal form.

"I hope Ishtar doesn't mind that I spoke for her."

"You did that?" Philip asked. "How?"

"Drama class." Lucille laughed nervously. She liked Philipp and didn't want him to think she was crazy. Or worse, expose her in the newspaper.

"Drama?" He didn't sound convinced, but instead of pressing the case, he tugged on the rope. "Do you have any idea how to get out of here before he or the other one comes back?"

Lucille sighed. "Yes, but you're not going to like it." There was little she could do to hide the next step in her plan.

"I'm open to anything right now, you know?"

"Is that so?" Lucille teased him before taking a deep breath. It had to come out sooner or later anyway. "Viscus Viperion Vivarens."

Despite knowing what to expect, Lucille shuddered as the ropes around her limbs and torso turned into thin snakes—ironically fitting for the Serpents of Ishtar. Philipp jerked into her back, before wiping off the snakes and leaping to his feet. Panting, he retreated to the far corner of the room, his back pressed against the wall. There he stared at her, eyes wide.

"I don't think they're poisonous." Lucille couldn't be sure with a spell like that, but she hoped whoever had conceived it had been sensible enough not to turn one predicament into another more dangerous one.

Philipp was still staring. He wet his lips about three times before he said, "You're a witch."

Lucille sighed. She'd enjoyed his company, but this would change everything. After all, he worked for the *Greenvalley View.* "We have to go," she said, ignoring his claim.

Slowly he calmed down. "That wasn't an accusation."

"The cultists could come back at any time." And if they did, Lucille would have to do a lot more magic, further damning her in Philipp's eyes. She got to her feet, making sure no snakes were hitchhiking on her, and turned towards the only exit.

As she walked out of the room, Philipp hurried after her. "So you're just going to ignore me? You're not going to confirm you're a witch? Even though you sent that cultist fleeing with that *drama* trick and turned our bonds into snakes?"

"It's a snake cult, Mr Vendenberg." The corridor led into another, which seemed to be the main shaft, connecting all the rooms occupied by the Serpents of Ishtar. Overwhelmed, Lucille was tempted to use another spell to find her way out.

Philipp huffed. "Oh, is it Mr Vendenberg now?"

Lucille half turned to him. "I'm not going to confirm such an outrageous claim just so you can put it in your gossip column: 'De Cerque's daughter involved in occult coven'."

Philipp raised an eyebrow, slightly amused. "Oh, that would sell. Too bad I don't do the gossip section." He grinned. "So, it's a whole coven?"

"Forget it!" Lucille chose to turn left and walked on, not knowing where it would lead.

"I can't. Curiosity is an occupational hazard."

Lucille couldn't help but chuckle. "Looks like we have that in common." His charm was beginning to work on her, but the threat remained. "I'm serious, though. You can't write about this."

"Of course not. You think I want to torpedo my career?" He shook his head when Lucille looked at him in surprise. "Look, a little mysticism is all well and good and part of the *Greenvalley View*'s branding. But claiming the de Cerque heiress is a witch who speaks for goddesses and turns ropes into snakes will get me fired faster than writing out Serpents of Ishtar."

"Then what *will* you write about?" Lucille was well aware they needed to escape the tunnels first, but Philipp was providing a wonderful distraction from the problem.

"That a mad cult from Spain was delusional enough to attempt an occult ritual to awaken an ancient goddess." He suddenly bit his lip. "I can't leave yet."

"You can't leave?" Surprised, Lucille stopped. "Philipp, this is dangerous. Really dangerous."

Philipp nodded. "And that's why you should go and call the police. But I need to know what's going on. Besides, there could be other victims."

"And you think I'm going to leave them to fend for themselves?"

Just then, she heard footsteps coming down the corridor and pulled Philipp into a corner. Suddenly she became very aware of the firmness of his body and the heat of his breath as it brushed across her forehead.

Lucille felt her stomach tingle and her heart beat faster. If only she could turn her face up a little...

"Do you even know where you're going?" a familiar voice made Lucille forget her excited feelings.

"I've led us this far, haven't I?"

Lucille pushed past Philipp as two people approached. "Samantha?" For some reason her friend was with Shayna, of all people. "What are you doing here?"

Samantha lifted her torch. "Lucille. And...?"

"Philipp. This is Philipp *Vendenberg*. You know, the journalist."

"Oh." Fortunately, Samantha caught on quickly. "Hello."

Philipp cleared his throat and joined them. "I take it you two are not human-sacrificing crazy cultists?"

"Human-sacrificing?" Shayna yelped. She tugged at Samantha's arm. "We have to hurry."

"You know where to go?" Lucille asked, assuming Samantha was using magic to find her way.

"Yes, I do, actually."

"She has a *hunch*," Shayna said, sounding slightly annoyed.

"Well," Philipp said, "I've learnt to trust *hunches* lately."

Lucille grinned at him. "Good man. Shall we, then?"

"After you." He offered Samantha the lead.

As Samantha passed them, she gave Lucille a look that was equal parts reproach and curiosity. In the presence of both Philipp and Shayna, she didn't say anything, though. "Let's hope they haven't started the sacrifices yet."

Jan

Jan was still baffled by the locked gate Alan was now trying to force open.

"They can't lock us in. It's not safe," Alan said. "I need to talk to the manager."

"Sure, Karen."

Alan glared at him, but before Jan could accidentally start a fight, Cian called their attention. "People are coming over."

Four cultists were approaching them, clearly not happy to see them mistreating the gate. "Get back to the party," their leader barked.

"Or what?" Alan snarled.

Without further ado, Cian grabbed his arm and pulled him along. "Let's just do what the nice people say."

"Why?"

Cian waited with his answer until they were clear of the cultists. Then he hissed, "Because they had knives!"

Jan looked over his shoulder, only now noticing the subtle sheaths. The four cultists followed them with intense glares that suggested little good. They were joined by others, who subtly herded the crowd of partygoers towards the altar.

The music faded. There was a tension in the air that made Jan nervous. He really wished he wasn't the only one of his friends here, with only a bunch of Elite Idiots around. But no matter how often he scanned the room, he couldn't find Rachel or Lucille.

His attention was drawn to the front, where a bald-headed woman was leading a creepy procession. Jan's stomach turned at the sight of the giant snake around her shoulders and the many more tattoos of the creature on her skin. Behind her came a row of cultists, including a young woman with long black hair wearing nothing but a white nightdress.

"What kind of freakshow is this?" Alan asked.

He was immediately silenced by the nearby cultists.

"Welcome children of Ishtar!" the bald-headed woman, who Jan assumed was their priestess, said with a powerful voice that filled every corner of the mine. "You have been rewarded the honour of aiding in the return of our mistress."

"Why do I doubt I'd want this honour?" Jan mused.

Cian passed him a worried look.

The priestess turned her back on them and addressed the statue instead. "Oh mighty Ishtar! Hear our plea. The hour of your return is at hand. Tonight, the blood of the Blessed One will awaken you, so you may once again take this world by force." She began to sing a strange song full of hisses and low notes that crawled through the cave.

Jan swallowed hard. "Yeah, that doesn't sound good at all." He looked back at the gate, wondering if he could break them out. Or perhaps there was another exit. Where had the priestess come from? His gaze fell on the shifting back wall. "Wait a minute." That wasn't a wall but a curtain!

The singing reached a crescendo, sending goosebumps across Jan's arms. The priestess raised her arms. "Bring me the Blessed One!"

Sure enough, the curtain moved as two cultists walked through, dragging a third person between them. When Jan saw who it was, he gasped. The Blessed One the priestess had been talking about was Rachel.

She must have been drugged or something because her eyes were barely open and she needed the two cultists to keep her upright. It also explained why she didn't fight them when they carried her to the statue and tied her to a wooden table with deep grooves in front of it.

Slowly, the people began to understand what was happening and shuffled nervously. One by one they realised they were surrounded, and the door was barred. Jan noticed more and more panicked faces.

"Is that Rachel?" Cian asked.

"Who cares?" Alan asked, eyeing the nearest cultist as if he was considering taking him on, knife or no knife.

"I do." Jan had no idea what he was going to do, but as everyone backed away, he stepped forward. Unfortunately, the Elite Idiots were right behind him. How was he supposed to take on all those cultists, save Rachel, and protect all these people by himself?

Just then, there was a series of sliding noises. Hisses arose. To Jan's horror, the cultists had opened the terrariums.

People started screaming, which gave Jan an idea. "Alright, let's have a civilised little panic." He stopped and shouted at the top of his lungs. "They're going to kill us all!"

Cian stared at him, confused, but the rest of the party guests picked up his shout. Suddenly, they were all screaming and crying, but most importantly, they were rushing towards the door, overwhelming the cultists. Some of the snakes were trampled, others hissed and bared their fangs. The cultists drew their daggers, but they were outnumbered and hesitated making use of them. Meanwhile, the priestess began to sing, her own ceremonial dagger raised high above Rachel's body.

Jan ran forward, away from the mass, as a flicker caught his eye. A few seconds later, the curtain burst into flames.

Fabian

Fabian had to wait until a bunch of cultists had crossed the room and left for the party. When he was finally certain he was alone, he crept towards the snake pit, hoping against hope there was something he could do for Ophelia. Few people survived a fall into a pit of dangerous snakes.

"Ophelia?"

To his surprise, he found her sitting in the pit surrounded by snakes. A viper was winding its way around her torso, up to her neck.

"Shit."

Ophelia blinked, then smiled blissfully. "I'm fine. The snakes won't hurt me. Ishtar *has* chosen me." Her smile faltered. "I think I broke my ankle, though."

Fabian breathed a sigh of relief. "Do you think..." He swallowed. "Do you think Ishtar has a problem with me coming down there to help you?" What was he doing? Climbing into a pit of snakes to save a girl who'd tried to slit his throat just an hour earlier?

"I will ask the snakes not to harm you," she promised.

Against better judgement, Fabian decided to trust her. He swung his legs over the pit, causing some of the snakes to hiss menacingly. This was it. Running was not an option. Taking a deep breath, he dropped into the pit.

The hissing intensified and several snakes crawled towards him. Then Ophelia whispered to them in what he thought was Spanish, and slowly the snakes slithered to the side, leaving a path for him.

Fabian raised his hands in amazement. "You've convinced me. You are the chosen one."

Ophelia shook her head. "It's not that. You convinced them by walking among them. That was brave. Ishtar rewards the brave."

He wasn't so sure of that with all these fangs and slithering bodies around him. "You guys didn't just move in yesterday, did you? This kind of pit doesn't dig itself."

Ophelia chuckled, stroking the viper around her shoulders gently. "We've been preparing for Ishtar's return for half a year."

"Half a year?" Fabian was almost at her side. "Well, you certainly know a thing or two about subtlety."

"Outside of ritual time." She suddenly looked worried. "Has the ceremony started?"

"I suppose so. A bunch of your people headed over there a few minutes ago." He bent his knee beside her and lowered himself between the snakes. The viper around her shoulders seemed to be staring at him.

Ophelia took a shuddering breath. "Then it's too late to run. Help me up... please."

"That's why I'm here." Fabian turned his back on her. "Climb up."

The viper slid to the ground as Ophelia scrambled up. Wincing, she climbed onto his back. Fabian grabbed her under her thighs and lifted her up. She wrapped her arms around his shoulders and nuzzled her face into his neck.

"Thank you," she whispered, blowing hot breath over his ear.

Fabian's throat suddenly tightened. He told himself it was from fear. The snakes or even Ishtar could strike him down at any moment. But he didn't let the fear consume him. Instead, he kept going, putting one foot in front of the other. Somehow, he'd get them out of here. First the pit, then the cult.

Matt

Matt's mind was blown as he watched his usually so irate brother act like any human in love. Caspar had been in a long-term loving relationship. He was completely smitten with Jeyne. Their relationship began slowly, innocently, but over the years, as Jeyne grew and Caspar remained much the same, it became more physical.

Matt was so fascinated by this other side of Caspar—both the one in the memories and the one who stood transfixed beside him—that he couldn't tear himself away.

The two lovebirds spent every minute Caspar managed to sneak out of the tower together in the garden. Through Jeyne, he learnt about the world around him and how much it feared his master, and by extension, him. Not that Jeyne was ever afraid of him.

They were lying naked in the grass. She stroked his biceps, a lazy post-coital smile on her lips. "I wish time would stand still."

"Why?"

Jeyne grinned. "Because if it did, I wouldn't get old and wrinkly while you stay fifteen forever."

"I'll get old, too, just a bit slower."

But Jeyne was right. She'd already overtaken Caspar, even though he was probably older than her parents. And she'd die of old age before Caspar would be considered an adult by demon society. It was a doomed relationship. They both had to know that, but instead of running away from it, they spent as much time together as possible, savouring every moment.

Jeyne sighed, her hand now resting flat on his arm. "I know. But if I could stop time, I wouldn't have to marry some stupid guy I don't even like that much."

Pain flashed across Caspar's face. It wasn't the first time he'd heard this, but so far, he'd chosen to ignore it. Until now. "Why can't you marry me?"

Matt nearly doubled over. Caspar had *proposed* to a human? With a demon's lifespan being so inconceivably long, very few ever saw the need to marry. Matt knew some demons tolerated each other enough to have long-term partners—like his mother and her lover Frennys—but he'd never heard of anyone making such a commitment. Eternity was too long to be promised lightly.

Jeyne went through a dozen emotions at Caspar's question. If she'd had any say in the matter, she would've married him on the spot. "My father would rather die than see me marry a demon. You know how he is."

Since these were Caspar's memories and not Jeyne's, Matt only knew her father from what she'd told Caspar: how he met with warriors and mages to discuss the growing threat of Alecto, how he thought Caspar was a dangerous beast that needed to be put down, and how he'd promised his daughter's hand in marriage with no regard to her own wishes to broker a weapons' deal.

"Still better than mine," Caspar joked.

In a surprising turn of events, he'd confessed to Jeyne how homesick he was. How much he missed his twin sister and how worried he was she'd forgotten all about him, because that's what demons were like. These were all feelings Matt would never have associated with Caspar. Who would have known that so many tender emotions had once filled his brother's heart?

Jeyne rolled her eyes at his tasteless joke, then leant forward to kiss him on the lips before pulling her dress up. "You need to be careful," she said, in a worried voice. "They're getting restless down in the village. They're planning an attack."

"They'll get killed," Caspar said, not boasting, but matter-of-factly. "The tower is protected by an almost infinite number of runes, and the things my master's cooking up... you don't want to meet them."

Jeyne swallowed hard. "They'll still try." She turned her back to him so he could lace her up.

Instead, he kissed her neck.

"Casp!" Jeyne turned her head, and he kissed her lips instead.

It didn't take much from there to turn her onto her back and continue the kisses. Caspar's voice was dark when he said, "I don't want you to marry another man. I love you."

Matt gasped. He quickly checked with his brother, but the grown Caspar just stood there, only a tiny tremor betraying his emotions. A terrible realisation dawned on Matt. Caspar *still* loved her. Still loved this human girl who must have died at least four centuries ago.

"I love you, too," Jeyne whispered, her hand on his cheek.

"Then come with me," Caspar pleaded. The tower is big and empty..."

Jeyne's eyes widened. "Are you mad? They'll think you kidnapped me."

For the first time, Caspar's eyes showed the hard look Matt knew. "Maybe I'll do that," he growled. But the hardness wasn't his thing yet and the expression quickly left his features. Desperately in love, he rested his forehead on her exposed collarbone. "I don't want to lose you."

Jeyne wrapped her arms around him. "No matter what happens, I will always be yours."

For three years, they'd been lucky, and neither Jeyne's family nor Alecto had suspected a thing. False loyalty changed all that. Worried by what he'd heard from Jeyne about the villager's preparations, Caspar took it upon himself to warn his master.

"And you know that how?" Alecto asked in a soft voice that sent shivers down Matt's spine. Suddenly, he wanted Caspar to shut up, to stop giving away his only happiness.

But the young demon hadn't had that kind of experience. After all he'd been through, he was still too trusting. In a way, Alecto had raised him, and his cruelty was all Caspar had known for three formative decades. Stuttering, he told him about Jeyne. "I didn't tell her any of your secrets. Jeyne…"

"For how long?" Alecto rose from his desk and slowly approached Caspar.

"How long what?" Caspar swallowed.

Alecto's eyes narrowed. "How long have you and this Jeyne Wynter been meeting?"

"I met her three years ago."

"Three years," Alecto repeated in a dangerously low voice. "For three years you've been deceiving me? Betraying me?"

Caspar's eyes widened. "No! I would never betray you. We just… I love her."

Suddenly, Alecto burst out laughing. "You love her?"

Nervously, Caspar kneaded his hands. "I'd like to marry her if—" He stopped talking when Alecto started laughing again.

Still amused, he left the room, motioning for Caspar to follow. As always, the young demon hurried after him without a hint of rebellion.

The sight of it made the hairs on the back of Matt's neck stand up. He wanted to scream at Caspar to run, but there was nowhere he could run to, not with the rune-carved iron band still around his neck.

Alecto led him up to the laboratory. There he touched a rune, which in turn activated a pulley, lowering chains and a hook. Caspar looked up, worried. As soon as it was in range, Alecto grabbed the chain. "Come here, boy!"

Despite knowing what awaited him, Caspar followed the call. His face showed pain and fear, but he'd been abused for too long to run now. The moment he was within reach, Alecto grabbed his upper arm and hauled him into the centre of the room. Then he used the runes to chain Caspar's wrists, wrapping the chain around the hook. With another rune, he lifted the device high enough to force Caspar onto his tiptoes.

Panting, Caspar began to plead. "Master…"

"You're a demon, Caspar!" Alecto barked. "A wild animal that knows nothing but death and ruin. An animal that I have spent *thirty years* civilising. And you think you understand love?"

"I'd die for her," Caspar said, defiant for the first time.

Surprised, Alecto gasped. "As you wish."

He grabbed a tube-like object with a pointy end from the laboratory table and connected it to a hose. Then he picked up a pail, activated a cleaning rune, and brought everything over to Caspar, who watched nervously. Without even looking at his face, Alecto plunged the tube into Caspar's thigh, right into the main artery. Caspar screamed in pain as his blood rushed into the bucket at an alarming rate.

"Master, please." With the device stuck in his leg there was no chance for his innate healing powers to do their work.

"A disciple who doesn't obey his master is useless. *You* are useless." Alecto smiled as he looked into the pail. "But your blood will be of great use. These villagers won't know what hit them."

Desperate, Caspar begged again. "I've served you for thirty years."

"You want me to praise you for that?" Alecto laughed at him. "Your father brought you here for me to use. You're a tool, nothing more. But like any tool, you're worn down."

"I'm more than a tool!"

Alecto shook his head. "When are you finally going to get it, boy? You're a demon, scum, a hell-spawn. If you had an ounce of decency, you'd have thrown yourself off this tower or drowned yourself in the bath."

Caspar shuddered. The words slowly sank in. Whatever lie he'd been telling himself all these years was being brutally torn away, leaving nothing to hold on to.

"Bastard," he whispered.

Alecto raised an eyebrow. "What was that?"

"You're a bastard!" Caspar shouted at him.

"Don't talk to me like that, vermin." Alecto walked over to him and used Caspar's own blood to paint a rune on his chest. "Jirkris!"

The rune lit up and Caspar screamed in wild pain. If he hadn't been strung so taut, he'd have convulsed more. Even so, his muscles spasmed until the rune faded again, leaving him exhausted and panting.

"So, let's talk about this girl. Jenny."

"Jeyne."

"You know I have to kill her now, don't you?" Alecto buried a hand in Caspar's hair and yanked his head back. "And it's your fault. Think of that when I send you to the Realm of the Dead."

A fire lit in Caspar's eyes. Suddenly he grabbed the chain above him and pulled himself up with his superior strength. With a twist of his torso, he swung around and wrapped his legs around Alecto's neck. The tube fell out and blood splashed into his master's face. Without the device, the wound was now healing quickly. Meanwhile, Alecto was gasping for air, his face rapidly reddening. He clawed desperately at Caspar's legs.

"Break the runes and let me go, and I will spare your miserable life!" Caspar hissed.

Alecto was defiant at first, but the lack of oxygen quickly made him reconsider. Caspar loosened his thighs a little, just enough to let him breathe. Shuddering, Alecto pulled a rune stone from the folds of his robe. When he hesitated over his next move, Caspar tightened his grip.

Hastily, Alecto used his finger to draw the rune backwards. The stone crumbled in his hand. At the same time, the iron band around Caspar's neck fell apart, flooding him with even more power than before.

With a flick of his wrist, he yanked down the pulley and half the structure with it. As he landed lithely on the ground, his master collapsed, gasping and sputtering. Caspar watched with growing disgust. Then his instincts took over and he wrapped the chains around Alecto's neck, pulling them so tight they crushed his windpipe and nearly tore his head off.

Without a flicker of emotion, Caspar watched as his master's body fell to the ground. "Shouldn't have trusted a demon's word."

He removed his chains and eyed the pail of his precious blood. Snarling, he kicked it over, wasting every last potent drop. Then he left the tower.

Now that he was free, he would surely have his bittersweet happy ending with Jeyne, Matt thought. After all, there was nothing holding him back any longer. But he had a feeling the sight of his wild, unleashed, bloody self would frighten Jeyne away, causing her to call him a monster, just as his master had done all these years.

When Caspar arrived in the quaint village he'd never set foot in before, the streets were empty. Confused, he stumbled about. "Jeyne?"

A window was slammed shut behind him. Caspar looked over his shoulder but saw nobody.

Eventually he found his way to the marketplace. Most of the village seemed to be gathered there, their attention on something in the front. Still looking for Jeyne, Caspar pushed his way through the crowd. People hissed and complained about him, but no one really paid much attention. They were all too focused on what was happening in the centre of the square. And then he heard the dreadful words.

"Jeyne Wynter, daughter of Hert. You stand accused of fornicating with a demon. We have sentenced you to death. You may say your last words."

Shocked, Caspar turned. His eyes finally found her. Her head had been shorn and she was wearing a dirty linen dress. Bruises and juices of unknown origin covered her face, hair and skin, as if she'd been run through the streets. She knelt in front of a wooden block with the executioner behind her, her eyes glazed over. Beside the judge stood a stout man with a gold chain, his face stiff and turned away from Jeyne. Her father, the mayor.

"I love him," she whispered.

"Recalcitrant to the end," the judge condemned her. "May the gods have mercy on you."

Tears streamed down her Jeyne's face as she laid her head on the block. The executioner raised his axe.

Caspar finally moved. He pushed through the crowd when he should have jumped. But the shock was too deep, and he'd lived a limited life for so long that the instinct was lost on him. "Don't. Don't. Don't..."

The axe fell.

Caspar stopped cold. For a moment he lost control of his body. Then the crowd began to cheer.

His wings unfolded so quickly they slammed the people around him into the ground. The cheers turned to cries of horror.

Madness filled Caspar's eyes as he shot energy left and right, drenching the square in human blood.

As if stung by an adder, Matt let go of the thread. He'd recognised the feeling of madness. It had been the beginning of Caspar's Blood Night. His awakening.

Panting, he looked at his brother, but Caspar still seemed lost in memory, his eyes staring blindly ahead. It took Matt a few tries to clear his throat. "That was... that was horrible." They'd *murdered* his love. Her own father had stood by as his daughter was killed for falling in love with a demon. A demon who'd never lifted a finger against them. Who'd even gotten rid of the evil sorcerer who'd tormented them for so long. Not that they'd ever found out.

"That's humans for you," Caspar said in a strange, toneless voice.

Matt swallowed. "Is that why you hate them? Because humans killed her?"

"They killed her because she loved me." Slowly Caspar's eyes shifted to Matt. "That was the only reason. They didn't know me, never wanted to know me."

Overwhelmed with pity, Matt blurted out, "I'm so sorry."

"Save your pity!"

"What you've been through—"

"Oh, please. Shut up." Caspar's voice slowly gained strength.

Matt sighed. "I'm just trying to say that I understand now. I—"

Caspar strode towards him, his face promising a world of pain. "Stop feeling sorry for me and I owe you one, okay?"

It wasn't what Matt had expected.

"Just to be clear, I won't spare your life."

As little sense as it made, Matt understood. In a way, Caspar was sparing his life this very moment. There wasn't enough fight in him to continue their wild chase.

"Let's leave this place," Matt offered.

Caspar grunted and immediately turned around. Strangely side by side, the two made their way out of the Web of Memories.

Near the end of the cave, Caspar turned to him. "If you talk, you're dead!"

Matt only gave him a weary look. The threat was nothing more than a defence mechanism.

"I didn't tell Menuha or Melaney. All they know is that I was gone for thirty years and came home after killing an entire village of humans."

Matt snorted. "Of course. Death and ruin."

Caspar's face darkened at the hateful words his master had thrown at him. "That's all we demons are good for."

"Caspar." Matt paused, not willing to let him internalise that lie again. It all made sense to Matt now, the obsessive hatred, the unfiltered brutality, even the lack of sexual activity.

His brother turned with a glare. "Just shut up!" He stormed on, leaving Matt to follow more slowly.

Just as they left the Web of Memories, they ran into Menuha. "Caspar... Matt." Curiously, she watched them both. "There you are. And in one piece."

"For now," Caspar growled. It sounded forced to Matt's ears.

Menuha's face was full of concern as she turned to Caspar. "You're in big trouble. The Seven want to talk to you. Melaney seemed tense."

"Whatever." Caspar shrugged and disappeared.

"You got what you wanted," Menuha said to Matt.

It took Matt a moment to realise what she meant. It seemed like years since he'd interrupted the Black Guard's parade. "Well... he shouldn't have reacted like that."

"Caspar and not react?" Menuha snorted, then shook her head. "I ran into Chay. He saw snakes and blood in Greenvalley?"

Matt's eyes widened. Samantha's face immediately came to mind. "I have to go."

"Of course you do." Menuha smiled sadly at him. "Say hello to everyone."

Matt left without answering.

"Of course you do." Menuha smiled sadly at him. "Say hello to everyone."

Matt left without answering.

Samantha

Samantha had no idea where the fire had suddenly come from, but the curtain was suddenly in flames, providing the perfect distraction—and a way for people to escape.

It was absolute carnage. People were screaming, some were being trampled, and amid the chaos of it all, snakes were hissing. Samantha felt for the animals as much as the people, but her attention was quickly drawn to the statue of a naked woman and the friend tied up in front of it.

Rachel was completely out of it, her head lolling from side to side. A bald priestess with snake tattoos was chanting, despite the chaos around her, a ceremonial dagger raised high. A couple of cultists shielded her and a woman in a white dress. Knives were coming out.

"Kill them!" A long-haired cultist shouted. "Kill them all for Ishtar!"

"We must find Cian and Alan!" Shayna tugged at Samantha's arm again. "They must be here somewhere."

As far as Samantha could see, they weren't in any immediate danger. Unlike Rachel. "You look over there," she told Shayna, freeing herself. Then she locked eyes with Lucille. Her friend was close to Philipp Vendenberg, who'd taken out his camera and was taking pictures for the Greenvalley View. "Get everyone out of here and keep him safe."

Lucille nodded and Samantha ran towards the statue, gathering magic in her hand. Just beyond, a familiar figure emerged from the crowd. Jan.

"Come and get me!" he shouted at the cultists guarding the priestess and her victims. "I can take you." Despite being heavily outnumbered, he was ready to fight.

The cultists weren't lacking in courage. One of them lunged forward, knife flashing, when suddenly a voice rose. "In the name of Ishtar, stop!"

The last burning scraps of the curtain fell to reveal a young girl with glistening black hair and glaring green eyes. Standing next to her was none other than Fabian, licking his lips anxiously.

To Samantha's surprise, the priestess stopped her chant, eyes widening. The long-haired cultist who'd been shouting for everyone to be killed stepped forward. "Ophelia? Then who's..." He looked at the woman in the white dress beside him as if he hadn't noticed her before. "Mara!"

"Mara?" the priestess repeated, almost hissing the name.

The woman lifted her chin defiantly. "She does not deserve this honour. I—"

The snake around the priestess's shoulder lunged and bit Mara. Gasping, the woman went down, convulsing heavily.

"Does anyone else wish to test the will of the goddess?" Eresta asked.

Most of the cultists looked elsewhere. The man with the long hair glowered, but he kept his mouth shut. It was the girl next to Fabian, Ophelia, who spoke up, "I do. But it's your will I'm contesting, not Ishtar's."

"What are you talking about? She chose you!" The priestess was seething.

"Ishtar values free will. It's not my time to lay down my life. I want to live first. You'll have to find another vessel for your plans."

Samantha had no idea what was going on, but she welcomed the distraction as she wove a shield around Rachel. From the looks of it, she had Fabian to thank for the unplanned intervention.

"You're weak," the male cultist said, sounding both disappointed and relieved.

Ophelia gave him a withering look. "No, Enrico. I'm strong. I follow my own heart and go my own way."

The priestess snorted. "Ishtar will awaken whether the little brat wants her to or not." She turned to Rachel and brought her knife down.

It was only stopped by the thick layers of magic Samantha had woven around her.

Her eyes widened. "Ishtar…"

"Looks like blood sacrifices are out for today," Jan said, suddenly standing at Eresta's side and striking at her.

The snake hissed, and Jan barely escaped the fatal bite. Before he could gather himself, Eresta growled at him and suddenly an invisible force lifted him up and hurled him across the room. He collapsed on impact.

"Jan!" Samantha ran after him.

The room was once again thrown into a frenzy as the cultists began stabbing people left and right. Meanwhile, the fire had consumed the curtain and spread to other objects. Smoke filled the room.

Samantha made it to Jan's side and quickly pulled out her flowers when she noticed how groggy he looked. Changing the colour of her pollen was a quick process. When the flower had turned yellow, she blew the pollen on him to stabilise him.

His eyes widened. "Watch out!"

She half turned to see the cultist with the long hair coming after her when someone tackled him from the side.

"Cian!" Shayna yelled.

To Samantha's horror, Cian and the cultist rolled across the floor, fighting for the upper hand. Cian had managed to wrap a hand around the wrist holding the dagger, but the other man struck him with his left. They rolled twice more before suddenly disappearing from sight.

Samantha stood up, fearing the worst. "Cian!"

She ran towards a pit, pushing aside a few panicked partygoers and cultists, before coming to a sliding halt at the edge. Below her, hundreds of snakes filled a hole in the ground. The cultist had managed to get on top of Cian, but he'd lost his dagger somewhere among the snakes. While the animals had given them some space at first, they now slithered closer, fangs bared.

"Cian!" Samantha began to weave another protective web just as someone jumped in after them, grabbed the cultist by the neck and tore him from Cian to throw him into the snakes. "Matt?"

For some reason, Matt was suddenly there—*saving* Cian. He offered the other boy a hand. Samantha watched the snakes around them nervously, but they were all after the cultist. Some of the larger ones started strangling him, while others bit him. His eyes bulged and his body froze. The air was squeezed out of his lungs, turning his face into a mask of horror.

Meanwhile, Matt pulled Cian to the edge and crossed his hands to help him up. "Come on, before they move on to the next victim."

Cian nodded and climbed up. Samantha reached down to help him, and within seconds both boys were out of the pit and safe. Annoyed, Samantha boxed Cian in the chest. "You idiot! What were you thinking?"

"He was going to hurt you." Despite his earlier bravery, he looked incredibly pale.

Samantha sobbed. "You're still an idiot." She threw her arms around his neck and held him close to her chest. "Don't ever do that again."

"You should go," Matt said, his eyes fixed on the snake pit. "I'll follow later when the snakes have been dealt with."

Cian took a step back. "Matt, I don't know how to thank—"

"Just go! I don't want to save your life again, you know?"

Samantha couldn't help but chuckle. He'd saved Cian for her, despite himself. "Thank you."

By the looks of it, Lucille had the evacuation under control, while Fabian and the cultist girl had joined Jan at the statue. Most of the cultists had fled, but the priestess was still standing tall—and Rachel was still tied up.

"We're not done yet."

Cian swallowed before nodding. "I'll watch your back."

Matt snorted, but he kept his back turned on them, facing the snakes. Samantha took a deep breath, then she ran back into the fray.

Fabian

Despite the chaos—which would've proved a perfect distraction to escape—Ophelia seemed determined to make her stand. Fabian followed her through the crowd, despite her insistence that she could take care of herself. Together, they reached the big altar. There, he was surprised to find Rachel tied to a block of wood. Her eyes were fluttering, as if she'd just regained consciousness.

"You can't make me Ishtar's vessel," Ophelia told the priestess.

"You have been chosen, child. Do you really think Ishtar cares about your wants and needs when hers are so much greater?"

Uncertain, Ophelia looked at Fabian. He nodded at her. "She's brainwashing you. Surely Ishtar would tell you herself if that's what she wants."

"Who are you?" the priestess glared at him. "What do *you* know of our goddess' wishes? Seize him."

Too late, Fabian noticed the two cultists nearby. They grabbed his arms, bent them backwards, and dragged him a few steps back. Ophelia's eyes widened, distracting her from Eresta, whose eyes gleamed devilishly.

"Watch out!"

The priestess grabbed Ophelia and dragged her over to the statue. There, another cultist dutifully helped her bind Ophelia's arms to the snakes wrapped around Ishtar's body. In the meantime, Rachel had woken, and started thrashing in her ropes.

"What are you doing to me?"

The priestess turned with a smile. "Your blood will show Ishtar the way." She closed her eyes and began to chant again. Then she raised her dagger. Fabian threw himself against his captors' grip to no avail. The knife came down, Rachel screamed, but it didn't cut. Something stopped it an inch in front of Rachel's chest.

"Someone is interfering," the priestess whispered.

Then she listened to an invisible speaker, and Fabian was convinced he heard something hissing. And indeed, the priestess was leaning into the snake around her shoulders. Suddenly her eyes met Fabian's.

"Ishtar says your blood will serve as well."

Fabian jerked in the grip of his captors. If anything, their hands tightened around his arms. "You're all mad!"

The priestess didn't care for his accusations. Without further ado, she slashed at his chest. Pain burnt through his body. Then she dipped her hand into his blood and used it to draw arcane symbols on Ophelia's skin.

"The blood of the Blessed One will show Ishtar the way to her new vessel."

Above Ophelia, the eyes of the statue began to glow.

The priestess resumed her chant as she used more and more of Fabian's blood to draw her occult symbols. Ophelia tried to free herself, but the ropes held tight, while the serpents she was bound to lost their grey hue, revealing shimmering scales. They were coming to life.

Just then, someone grabbed the cultist to Fabian's left and punched him. Matt. He turned around and went for the second one.

Fabian staggered to his knees as his injured leg gave out under him. The pain in his chest and the thickening smoke were starting to overwhelm him. His eyes were watering and his chest felt like it was on fire. Then Jan was suddenly at his side and put his hands on the cut. Seconds later, it began to heal.

"Better?" Jan asked.

"Go get Rachel." Fabian pulled himself up again, careful to put his weight on his other leg. The smoke made him cough, but he forced himself to stay upright.

Ahead of him, Ophelia's body began to glow through the bloody symbols. The statue's eyes burnt like twin stars. Ophelia strained and struggled, but she had no chance against the bonds and the goddess trying to possess her.

It was then that Fabian remembered the words of the priestess. *His blood* was showing Ishtar the way. Shaking, he raised his arms and pointed his hands at Ophelia and the goddess. Water burst from them, washing away the blood on her skin.

"No!" the priestess screamed.

It worked. As soon as the symbols were gone, the statue turned to stone again. Ophelia stared at him, eyes wide.

The priestess turned around, furious. Before she could go after him, Matt brought his sword down, severing both the head of the massive snake and that of the priestess from their respective bodies. He turned to the remaining cultist, who took one look at the sword and ran.

Jan rushed to Rachel's side, where Samantha and Cian were already sawing on the ropes with a dropped dagger. "Let's get everyone out of here before the whole place burns down."

Fabian sighed as he heard his cue. With a quick glance, he identified the fires in the room and extinguished them, replacing smoke with steam.

Meanwhile, Matt went over to Ophelia. The sword cut through the ropes easily. As soon as she was free, she came running and threw her arms around Fabian.

"You *are* blessed. You can do magic!"

"Um... yes, I guess."

Matt patted him on the shoulder. "Come on, Blessed One. We've got to leave."

"I need my stuff," Ophelia said.

Fabian nodded at Matt. "You go. I'll follow later."

"Don't be too long," Matt warned, before helping the others free Rachel.

Ophelia let go of him and took his hand instead. When she noticed him favouring his leg, she slipped under his shoulder as if she were always meant to be there. Together, they made their way back to the living quarters to pick up Ophelia's abandoned stuff.

"I'm really glad you decided *not* to become a snake goddess."

"As am I." Ophelia sighed in relief. "I was so afraid she'd take me anyway." She looked up. "Why didn't you tell me you could do magic?"

"You knocked me out and tied me up like a pig?"

Ophelia's cheeks flushed. "You could've struck me first."

"I don't usually walk through the woods and strike down pretty girls."

"You think I'm pretty?"

Fabian bit his tongue. He shouldn't say things like that. Even if they were true. "You know you are."

To his surprise she shook her head. "No one's ever told me I'm pretty. Or useful."

"They at least thought you'd make a good vessel." He winced at his ill-aimed joke. "I'm sorry."

Ophelia's eyes dropped and she stepped away from him. She looked so lost all of a sudden.

Feeling bad about his words and the way the cult had treated her, Fabian took a step forwards and gently placed his fingers under her chin. "They lied to you... no, they cheated you out of everything. Your talents, your childhood, and they almost cheated you out of a future too." She hung on to his every word. "You *are* beautiful and brave. Strong-willed and skilled." He lowered his hand to take hers. "Come with me and I'll show you how wonderful you really are."

"With you?" she whispered, her big green eyes looking up at him.

Flustered, Fabian rubbed the back of his neck. "You need a place to stay, don't you?" At least for now.

Ophelia's face lit up in a smile. "I'd like that."

She picked up her backpack and the two of them turned to leave. They moved past the snake pit, which had turned to absolute carnage. Not a single animal had survived. Ophelia gasped as she recognised her brother among the dead snakes, pulling Fabian to a halt.

"I'm sorry."

She shook her head. "Don't be." Her voice trembled slightly. "He was terrible to me. If I didn't listen to him, he'd lock me in the dark for hours, sometimes days." She sighed. "I suppose there was a silver lining, though."

Fabian asked, horrified, "What good could have possibly come from that?"

"Because of him, I learnt to appreciate the shadows. I'm also blessed by Ishtar. That's why she chose me. I command them like you control water."

Fabian remembered the snake bite that had knocked him out. There had been no real snake lurking in the shadows. "Are they good shadows?" he asked, worried.

Ophelia laughed. "Shadows are shadows. Everything has one. There's no need to be afraid of them." She cast a last glance at Enrico. "He hated that Ishtar chose me. It had always been his goal. Just like that stupid Mara's."

Fabian snorted. "Well, the snakes made their opinion clear."

"Poor things." Ophelia turned away. "Let's go."

Hand in hand, they left the lair of the Serpents of Ishtar behind.

Lucille

Getting Philipp out was almost impossible. It wasn't until the smoke and steam were so thick his images were practically useless and he was coughing heavily that he finally gave up. Lucille had kept an eye on the fleeing masses and crazed cultists the whole time, throwing shields left and right.

"Ready?" she asked Philipp as he ducked down the corridor everyone else had fled down long ago.

He gave her a pained smile. "You should've left."

"I kept myself busy."

"I noticed."

Lucille tensed. There was still the danger he'd spill everything he'd seen today in the local paper. Sure, most people wouldn't believe it any more than they'd believed his other articles, but Lucille preferred not to be the butt of a public joke.

"Philipp, you can't—"

"I told you. I won't write about you."

"Promise?"

He smiled softly. "Promise."

Lucille relaxed slightly. They followed the procession of partygoers until they came out at a lakeside. She breathed in the fresh air, only now truly realising how stuffy the mine had become. All around them, people were collapsing. Some were crying, others continued to run. Someone said the police were on their way.

Philipp pulled them aside, keeping an eye on the exit. Lowering his voice, he said, "But you have to help me."

"Help you with what?"

"What to write. Or rather, what not to write." He pointed at Matt, who was leaving the mine with Jan and Rachel in tow. "He had a sword and I'm pretty sure he killed someone with it."

Panic rose in her throat. "To defend us all." Philipp raised an eyebrow at her. "He's a friend."

"Then let's skip that part."

Now Lucille was staring at him. "Just like that?"

"Look, I don't want to cause any trouble. He was obviously on our side. If he hadn't killed that crazy priestess, who knows what would have happened? I'm a journalist, not a policeman."

"Aren't you committed to the truth or something?"

"That's a pretty way of putting it, but the way I see it, there's the truth and then there's the part of the truth the world is ready for. Besides, if I break this story now, I'll lose my most valuable source." He grinned boyishly. "You."

Lucille raised her eyebrows mockingly. "I'm your source now?"

"I think we can be mutually beneficial to each other. You give me the inside scoop, and I make sure you and your friends and this magical community or whatever it is stays protected. And to make it official, I'd like to invite you for an exclusive interview with coffee and maybe a piece of cake, far away from any crazy cultists."

Lucille had the distinct feeling that this was not the kind of interview that would lead to a feature in the *Greenvalley View*. "Are you paying?"

"Of course. I'm a gentleman through and through." He glanced at the exit as two more figures emerged from the mines.

To Lucille's surprise, it was Fabian and the girl who'd confronted the priestess—and they were holding hands. "Huh."

"What about that part? I'm not quite sure what happened, but it looked like he was shooting water from his bare hands."

Startled, Lucille looked up at Philipp. "Oh, yeah, no, don't mention that. He's... he's a friend too. And she's... I don't really know her."

"Oh well." Philipp sounded only slightly disappointed to have missed out on that particular twist. "So, what about that date... interview?"

Butterflies danced in Lucille's stomach. The way Philipp looked at her made her all flirty and giddy, but there was still the small matter of her "friend". A matter that might have taken care of itself. "Let's pencil that in."

\#

Once the police had arrived and the smoke had cleared, Lucille walked over to the rest of her group and nudged Fabian's elbow. Surprised, he turned around.

"Lucille... you came."

It took Lucille a moment to realise why he'd say that. "Oh, yes, I was just a bit late. Can I talk to you for a minute?" She leant over to catch a quick glimpse of the girl he'd escorted out. She was gorgeous. "Hi. It won't take long."

Fabian frowned, but he stepped aside with her. "What's going on?"

"Who's she?"

His instant blush told her all she needed to know. "Um, her name is Ophelia. She—"

"—looks really hot. No wonder you're all over her."

"What?"

She laughed. "Oh, please. I can sniff a crush out from a mile away. You like her."

His expression became pained. "Lucille..."

"Oh, don't worry! Look, you and I, we had a wonderful little summer romance. No regrets. But summer's over. It's time to move on, don't you think?"

Fabian looked quite confused. "Are you breaking up with me?"

"Don't you want that, too?" She glanced over and found Ophelia watching them anxiously. "She's definitely dying to get to know you better."

"She was brainwashed by a cult and just lost everyone she knew, including her brother. I don't think she's looking for romance."

"Oh." A pang of guilt washed over her. Here she was, trying to set her boyfriend up with someone else to free herself from any commitment, while he was his usual sweet, caring self. "I'm sorry, I didn't know—"

Just then Philipp came up the path. "Hey, Lucille, the police said we could go. If you want, I can take you home."

Fabian followed her gaze and raised an eyebrow. "Time to move on, huh?"

Lucille felt even worse. "Fabian…" she whispered.

"Hi," Philipp said with a big friendly smile, offering his hand. "Philipp Vendenberg. You're one of Lucille's magical friends, aren't you?"

"I'm actually—" Fabian started, sounding slightly annoyed.

Lucille gave him a sharp look, silently begging him not to screw this up for her. She felt terrible, but the truth was that their relationship had run its course, and she *was* ready to move on.

Fabian sighed. "A water mage, yes. You knew about that?" He stared at Philipp's outstretched hand and gave in. "Fabian."

Philipp smiled as he shook his hand. "Fabian, nice to meet you. Lucille has only told me a little so far, but I hope to see and hear more of you soon. Now…"

"Actually, please could you give us a minute?" Lucille's guilty conscience had finally reached its boiling point.

Philipp took a step back. "Of course. Would you like me to wait?"

"Yes, please. If it's not too much trouble."

"Okay, I'll be over there when you're ready." He nodded to Fabian and withdrew.

Lucille sighed. "Fabian, I'm sorry. I only met him today."

"So you weren't secretly going to the party together?" His flat voice betrayed his hurt.

"Not until I met him on the way. I didn't plan this."

"But you planned to break up with me," Fabian said with a heavy sigh.

Lucille bit her lips. "You've been a great boyfriend. I just—"

Fabian snorted. "Don't. Please. I don't want to hear about how I'm so great, but not great enough."

"You're just not the right person for me."

Somehow that seemed to make it easier for him. Fabian nodded thoughtfully. "Look, I'm not going to force you to stay in this relationship. Do you like this Philipp guy now?"

"I mean, I barely know him," Lucille admitted, "but there's a connection I'd like to explore. And I really think this Ophelia girl has a big crush on you. She'll scratch my eyes out if I talk to you any longer."

Curiously, he glanced over, but then his gaze returned to Lucille. "Like I said—"

"—she needs time and understanding. Sorry, I'm being a real ass today." She was obviously trying to push him towards the girl, because that would make her feel better about moving on with someone new. "I'm sorry."

"Vendenberg. He's the journalist, right? Your father will be impressed."

Lucille's face fell. "It's not like that."

Fabian shrugged. "What? It's true. He never liked me."

Now she wondered if that had had any influence on her falling out of love with Fabian. But if she was honest, it just seemed like another excuse. "It's not my father. It's me." She couldn't let her father take the blame when he hadn't been bothering her about Fabian.

"Oh well. I guess... good luck?"

"If you need any help with—"

"I've got it. Thanks," Fabian said curtly. With a sharp nod, he returned to Ophelia, who was eagerly awaiting him.

As Lucille watched his tender way of reassuring the girl, she felt even worse. He was a catch, but it couldn't be helped. He wasn't the one for her. Philipp on the other hand... The way he smiled at her made her feel excited. Maybe he wasn't the right one either, but Lucille would be damned if she didn't at least give him a chance.

She walked towards him, feeling the guilt melt away as freedom took over. "I'm ready now."

"Are you?" he asked, his voice hinting that he had an inkling of what had been going on.

Lucille laughed softly. "Perhaps, instead of coffee tomorrow, we could have a drink today?"

"We could write my article together. In a bar."

"Sounds good." She linked her arm with his and decided this would be a good thing. And maybe one day, Fabian would see it, too.

Caspar

Caspar knelt on the cold stone floor, his head bowed before the Seven. Directly in front of him was Volac, the Archdemon of Wrath and his immediate superior. He'd only risen to his position less than three hundred years ago. Before that, they'd served side by side in the Black Guard, slavering under Balboa.

None of which mattered when the archdemon was caught in a tantrum. "He must have lost his mind! Not only walking out of his own damn parade but leaving it a complete mess!"

"Maybe he thinks he is better than us." The Archdemon of Pride, Hel, was a tall, gaunt woman who always had her nose turned up. She rarely agreed with Volac, but she missed the opportunity to put others down even less.

"I wouldn't dream of it," Caspar said, because it was expected of him, not because he meant it.

To his left, Yash, the Archdemon of Sloth, yawned. She was stretched out on her throne. "Let him go, Volac. This parade was far too long and tiring anyway. I would have left much sooner than him."

"You weren't even there!" Volac shot back.

Yash held up her hands, as if that proved her point.

"Maybe he wanted more attention," the Archdemon of Envy, Pyke, hastened to suggest. "He's jealous of your fame."

"I just wanted to kill my half-brother," Caspar explained. He couldn't even muster enough anger at Melchior, which was unlike him. It usually didn't take much more than the mention of his brother and all his privileges to set him off.

"With my Guard?" Volac shouted at him.

Hel chuckled instead. "That must be one dangerous half-demon. I take it he's dead at least?"

"He's not."

She smiled secretly, as if she'd already known that and he'd just played into her hands. Balthasar would probably know what that meant, but Caspar didn't have the head to deal with the Seven.

Volac leant back in his chair. "Perhaps I should look for another general. Someone who won't let disruptive troublemakers escape and who'll show more responsibility with the Guard."

"Someone who doesn't forget whose leash he's on," Hel added.

"Someone who won't ask for more than he deserves," Pyke said.

"Or maybe someone who produces less work for us," Yash added cheerfully.

"It won't happen again," Caspar forced himself to say, although he couldn't truly bring himself to care. None of it really mattered at the moment.

"It won't!" Moloch, the massive Archdemon of Gluttony, said with gleaming eyes. "He should be drawn and quartered, burnt, drowned, and—"

"That's enough!" Melaney finally added her voice to the council. "Caspar will not be killed." From the look she was giving him, a worse fate awaited him if he dared show his face in her residence any time soon.

Hel snorted. "It would be a fitting consequence for his lack of respect. I'm with Moloch. Let's vote to kill him."

"You're not voting on anything, old hag!" Volac shouted. "He's mine."

"Take everything from him," Pyke suggested. "Leave him with nothing but his life."

Yash groaned. "That sounds way too exhausting."

"We might have trouble finding someone as capable as he is if we got rid of him."

Caspar paused and glanced at the new Archdemon of Greed. Her name was Iyaga and very little was known about her. She'd ascended after those kids in Ashuan had gotten rid of Malcolm. The magic had chosen her, something that hadn't happened in Hescaryn for as long as demons could remember. Caspar didn't give her more than a few years before a more worthy challenger would emerge.

For now, Volac welcomed her contribution. "Exactly. The Guard needs him," he said, though only a minute ago he'd considered replacing him. "If Shenecra hadn't been so foolish as to seek her death in Ashuan, she might have been an option, but without her—"

"What is it with the Black Guard and these humans? Your second-in-command has to go to Ashuan personally, and your general has to drop everything for some half-blood? And let's not forget Malcolm's embarrassing demise. Are we at war with Ashuan?"

"Oh please, not again," Yash groaned. "Wars are so tiresome."

"It's not Caspar's fault that Stormbride couldn't handle a few human children," Melaney said, her support wavering in and out.

Hel snorted again. "He can't handle that half-demon either. How many times has he tried to kill his half-brother and failed?"

"Maybe this half-demon would be a good replacement, then," Iyaga mused.

Normally, Caspar would have balked, but right now he felt more like a sloth demon than a wrath demon. He couldn't even bring himself to care.

"No, no, no," Pyke argued. "It can't be a half-demon."

"I will not accept a half-demon!" Volac roared.

And for once, Hel agreed. "That would be outrageous."

"In that case," Melaney began, "we have no choice but to pardon him."

"He must be punished," Moloch insisted. "A million punishments."

To everyone's surprise, Yash stood up. "He shall be thrown into the Dark Cells. The meeting is over." She disappeared before anyone could protest.

"I lead this council," Volac shouted into the void as the other archdemons disappeared one by one.

Melaney gave Caspar one last withering look before she left.

The last to remain beside Volac was Hel, who stood and looked down on him. "You lead this council only so long as the Black Throne remains empty." Then she disappeared.

The veins on Volac's forehead bulged, as if his head was about to explode. Then he roared at the guards, "Throw this traitor into the Dark Cells!"

Two guards from his own regiment appeared and took Caspar by the arms to hoist him up. Caspar stared blindly ahead, ignoring Volac's tantrum as he was led from the Council. It would've been easy to fight these two or exert his authority, but the thought left him as quickly as it came.

The Dark Cells were true to their name. As soon as the guards dropped him in and activated the runes that would prevent him from jumping away, complete darkness engulfed him. There was no window, no door. Nothing, just a hole in a rock with nowhere to go and no one to talk to. No one to see him.

The mask Caspar had worn during the council meeting crumbled. As he allowed himself to feel again, a deep searing pain shot through his body. *Her* image flashed before his eyes.

"Jeyne," he whispered.

For five hundred years he'd pushed her memory to the back of his mind. Her beauty and kindness, her intelligence and curiosity, and the pain. All the pain he'd caused her. The pain she'd caused him.

It all came back to him then, drowning him in a flood.

Caspar wrapped his arms around his knees and buried his face in them as the tears fell.

And fell.

And fell...

Part 3

Friends & Ghosts

Rachel

After almost being sacrificed at the altar, the last thing Rachel needed was to visit a club. At first, she'd been cautiously excited to spend some time with her friends, but less than an hour in, she was the only one sitting at the large table they'd secured.

Lucille was busy with her new beau, the reporter *Rachel* had always admired. Not that she'd been very impressed with the real deal. His articles were great, but the rest of him? Surprisingly boring. Mostly because he was more concerned with flirting with Lucille than finding out his stories happened to be closer to the truth than he'd ever imagined.

As she watched them on the dance floor, smiling at each other and taking every opportunity for their bodies to touch, Rachel wondered if this was why Fabian had refused to come. She had no idea why they'd broken up, just as she had no idea why they'd been together in the first place, but then she remembered he wasn't here because he was coddling one of the cultists who'd kidnapped and tried to murder her.

Jan, of course, took advantage of the fact that his underage girlfriend was allowed in the club until midnight. The two of them were also on the dance floor, although apart from a bit of swaying there wasn't so much dancing as there was snogging.

And as for the only two not in a relationship... Rachel glanced over at the bar. She didn't know who they were kidding. Samantha might be sleeping with Cian, but she only had eyes for Matt. And he was, of course, as smitten as no half-demon had any business to be. They were supposed to order another round of drinks but seemed to have completely forgotten their task.

Rachel looked around the club again, annoyed that she'd left her e-reader at home. There was a book in her bag, but there wasn't enough light to read it. And books didn't change the fact she felt lonely.

"Sixteen years and he's never fallen in love again."

To Rachel's surprise, the two *non*-lovebirds had managed to pry themselves from the bar and were making their way over with a tray of shots.

Samantha's eyes were glued to Matt, though. "Not a single relationship?"

Matt put down the tray and pulled out a chair for her. "He said he had a short fling here and there, but that he never really felt ready to settle down with anyone." He laughed as he sat down next to her. "And he's trying to teach *me* about commitment."

They both sat as far away from Rachel as they could. An oversight, probably, but one that Rachel felt keenly. She still didn't know who they were talking about, not that she cared since it was all about sex again.

"It could be trauma. Your mother probably hurt him pretty badly."

So they were discussing the sex life of Matt's *father* now. The same man who'd taught Samantha at primary school.

Matt raised an eyebrow. "It happened sixteen years ago."

"He might still be in love with her," Samantha suggested.

"I know my mum is supposed to be a real firecracker in bed, but..."

It was too much for Rachel. This fixation on sex, all those sparks in the air, those longing looks. If they wanted it so much, they should just do it. Instead of saying what was on her mind, though, she just grabbed her bag and got up. "I'm going home."

"Already?" Samantha asked.

"I still have homework."

"Oh, okay, well, goodnight."

Matt simply held up his hand in greeting. Rachel nodded at him and made her way around the table. Before she was even gone, he continued his story: "I'm just saying, like mother, like son."

Samantha *laughed.* She actually found the immature boast charming.

Rachel shook her head and hurried away as quickly as she could. Sometimes she thought there was something wrong with her. It was the only way to explain why everyone else acted like idiots and yet she was the one who was always alone. Always on the outside.

Tears suddenly stung her eyes. Annoyed, Rachel blinked them away, cursing the fog machine under her breath. She was fine, absolutely fine.

Of course, nothing was fine. Her friends were always in relationships, her brother was dead, and her mother was never home.

Rachel stood in the dark living room and watched the shadows shrink and grow as a car drove past the house, mimicking snakes. Tears formed in her eyes, and this time there was no fog machine to blame. She'd been through something horrific but there was no one to talk to. Sure, her friends had saved her, but now their duty was done, she'd been dropped like a hot potato. A cult member was getting more attention than she did.

Furiously, Rachel wiped the tears away and stomped up to her room to throw herself onto the beanbag by the window. For a moment, she just sat with her feelings. Thoughts of inadequacy welled up. She wasn't interesting enough for her friends. For anyone, really. All she had were her dreams, but Nico had told her to live in the real world. The real world where madwomen tried to sacrifice her to bring back old gods.

Nico.

The pain should have been an old friend by now, but it still hurt just as much as it had back then. It didn't even make sense. If Nico were alive, he'd be out there in the club. He'd probably have another girlfriend or be hanging out with those good-for-nothing guys. He wouldn't have stayed at home to keep his introverted sister company.

Rachel rubbed her face, trying to push the toxic thoughts away. Beating herself up wouldn't change anything. She didn't deserve it, either. Annoyed, she bent over her bag and took out the book she'd been reading. *Making Friends with Ghosts.*

She'd found the book in the Magic Circle and had bought it because of the ghosts in the title, but now she thought how much better ghost friends would be. Without a body, at least their conversations wouldn't revolve around sex this and sex that.

It was a pseudo-magic book, of course, like the dozens of others the Magic Circle carried. She doubted the author had ever actually seen a ghost, let alone befriended one. Most of the book was about how to respect the ghosts living in a place you moved into, or how to turn their negative energy into positive. It was a lot of woo-woo but written in such an entertaining way, Rachel devoured it.

She finished the chapter on creating a ghost-friendly environment and turned the page. *Chapter 13: Inviting Ghosts. Now that you've made your home more welcoming, I'm going to show you how to invite kind spirits to visit.*

At first, there was a lot of hogwash about opening your mind and visualising your ideal guest, but then she found a ritual. Intrigued, Rachel read on. She had everything she needed at her fingertips, and no magic was required. Sure, there was a spell, but the words weren't in a foreign language, easy to pronounce.

Excited, she ran down to the kitchen and grabbed a bowl, a candle, a bunch of dried herbs and a knife. It was supposed to be a proper athame, but since the spell only required a drop of blood, Rachel figured any knife would do.

Back in her room, she lit the candle and carefully measured the herbs into the bowl. Cutting her thumb was surprisingly easy, and Rachel watched in fascination as her blood fell onto the dried leaf crumbs. The smell was uncomfortably delicious.

When the candle had melted enough, she carefully dribbled hot wax over her herbs. Although it now looked like a disgusting little lump, Rachel decided to continue and read the words from the book. "Spirits of the day, spirits of the night, hear my call, come forth to my side. Come as quickly as you can, follow my voice and my plan. Taste my blood and my fears, follow the trail of my tears. I need you here, I need you now. You're welcome here, this much I vow."

The flame flickered. Rachel listened and looked around the room. But all she saw was a sad girl in the mirror, calling out to ghosts because her friends weren't around.

Frustrated, Rachel blew out the candle and went to bed.

Jan

"The police won't drag you home when the clock strikes twelve," Jan whispered in Meg's ear.

She giggled. "I know that. But my sister will."

Annoyed, Jan threw his head back and glanced at Samantha. While she was still talking to Matt, she looked like she was about to get up. And indeed, they both stood and hugged before Samantha grabbed Meg's bag and came over.

"Told you." Meg laughed. "I can't wait to turn eighteen and be done with all this. It's a stupid law anyway. What changes at midnight that makes it any less safe than before?"

"Meg," Samantha called. "It's time to go."

"I know." Meg took another look at Jan. "Will you take me home? Please?"

Jan didn't really want to. Not because he was the worst boyfriend in the world, but because once he'd taken Meg home, he'd be on his own. And then he'd have to go back to the Magic Circle to sleep on a bunch of chairs while the temperature dropped below zero.

"Sure. Let's go."

The three of them put their jackets on and left the club. The shock between the heated club and the snow-covered world outside was unexpected.

"I hate winter," Jan complained. He put his arm around Meg's shoulders in search of warmth. "We should call this place Whitevalley."

Samantha laughed. "You know, you can always go to the clearing in the woods. It's always green."

"Is it warm there?" Maybe if he camped in the Spring of Magic, he'd be more comfortable at night.

"Not really."

There went that plan.

Meg touched his hand over her shoulder and looked at her sister. "What's up with you and Matt? Are you two a thing? I thought you were into Cian."

"What?"

"Wait, what?" Jan asked. "You're into Cian? *The* Cian?"

Samantha clicked her tongue. "It's nothing."

"Obviously, because you were all into Matt today," Meg said before Jan had a chance to ask for clarification.

"I wasn't!"

Meg shrugged. "Well, you should have been. That boy only had eyes for you. And we're talking about Matt Traidous. *The* hottest guy in school, notorious for sleeping around—"

"He doesn't do that anymore."

"Because he wants you?" Meg asked, laughing, as if the very thought was ridiculous. Then she looked at Jan. "Do you get it? What's up with all the hot guys circling around my sister?"

"You know, I thought you found me hot," Jan joked, in a bad attempt to draw some heat from Samantha.

Meg slapped his chest. "You are, but not like Matt."

"Ouch?"

"Or Cian for that matter." Meg's attention was on Samantha again. "Who are you going to choose? Or are you going to have them both? I bet Matt would be into that."

Samantha looked absolutely horrified. "Meg! Stop talking. Please!"

Meg threw her arms up in the air. "Seriously, I don't get it. You're so boring!" She walked to the door and turned to Jan, "Wait here. I've got your laundry ready."

As she disappeared inside, Jan cast a cautious glance at Samantha. "You and Cian?"

"It's complicated," Samantha said, staring straight ahead.

"Does Matt know?"

"Yep."

That surprised Jan. "Really? And he's okay with it?" Maybe Meg wasn't too far off with her suggestion of a threesome. Props to Matt for finding a much healthier way to deal with his rivals.

Exasperated, Samantha turned to him. "Why is my sister fetching your *laundry?*"

Busted. "Um, they just got dirty the last time I was here."

"And then you left the house naked?"

Jan blushed. "No, I..." Oh, well. He supposed he couldn't keep it a secret forever. "My parents kicked me out. I'm living in the back of the Magic Circle at the moment. Don't tell Fabian or he'll—"

Something slammed into his back, filling him with a searing heat. Jan gasped. He felt as if he'd been pushed aside, squeezed thin to accommodate whatever else had taken his place. Then he looked into Samantha's eyes and saw a kind of fire there that made his knees weak and his trousers uncomfortable.

"My darling," he said in a raspy voice that didn't belong to him.

Samantha smiled wickedly. Then she grabbed the back of his head and pulled him into a kiss that turned his whole body to jelly.

"What the hell?" Meg stood in the doorway. His clean clothes were strewn across the step at her feet.

"Go away, little girl," Samantha purred, her hands digging into Jan's collar. "He's mine now."

Before he could protest, Jan was pushed away even further. The last thought he had wasn't even his own.

Together at last.

Rachel

Rachel was lying in bed buried under pillows and blankets, when a loud thump woke her from her sleep. Tired, she sat up and looked at her phone. It was only a few minutes before her alarm. She sank back into her pillows just as there was another knock.

"What?"

When the door remained closed, she threw open her covers and got up. Annoyed, she shuffled to the door. Her mother knew better than to bother her in the morning, so she hoped there'd be a good explanation for it at least.

But when she opened the door, no one was there. "Mum?"

There was another knock. This time the sound came from her left. From *inside* her wardrobe. Someone, or something, was knocking on the inside of her wardrobe.

Suddenly wide awake, Rachel grabbed the kitchen knife from the night before and made her way over. Could it have worked? Was Nico in the cupboard?

Her hand hovered around the handle for half a second before she gathered the courage to open it. "Nico?"

The door fell open. Sure enough, there was a man in her cupboard. But it wasn't Nico. Instead, it was a white man in his early thirties with an old-fashioned beard and a waistcoat.

Rachel screamed and jumped back. "What are you doing in my wardrobe?"

"At last," the stranger said with a relieved smile. "I thought I'd never escape this cruel dungeon." He noticed the knife in Rachel's hand. "Easy, milady. I come in peace."

"Do you?"

The stranger stopped, one foot in the cupboard, the other outside. "Pardon me, but you're the one holding me at knife point."

"I'm..." Rachel looked at her ridiculous kitchen knife and threw it on the table. "You're in my wardrobe, in my stuff."

The man turned and pulled a pair of jeans off his left leg. "These garments are yours? What a strange fabric."

She snatched the pants from his grasp. "It's not strange! Who even are you?"

"Forgive my lack of manners." He bowed to her. "Hugo von Hohenstetten. At your service."

Rachel couldn't help but chuckle at his exaggerated mannerisms. "Well, I'm Rachel. Now, Hugo, could you please come out of my closet and explain how you got in there in the first place?"

"I'd love nothing more. If you could help me. I think I'm tangled in another garment of yours." He held out his hand. It was slightly transparent in the light.

"You're a ghost." It all began to make sense now.

"Apparently, I am," Hugo said, a little embarrassed. He got rid of another pair of pants and stepped out. "Your closet is not the most comfortable place, but it far surpasses the dungeon I spent my last days in."

"You lived in a dungeon?"

Hugo straightened his back and assumed a noble posture. It made him almost as tall as Fabian. "Indeed, until your call tore me from my draughty chambers. I was just about to haunt the halls and frighten the new night watchman they'd hired, as you would expect from a proper castle ghost."

"You're a castle ghost? With rattling chains and all."

"I have to beg your pardon. We no longer live in the Middle Ages. The modern ghost of today uses the blaring horns of your rolling metal boxes."

"Cars?" Rachel giggled. She sat down on her bed. "Oh, Hugo, you must tell me everything."

Her ritual had worked. Sure, she hadn't managed to call her brother, but then again, she already knew he hadn't become a ghost. Instead, this most interesting ghost from another time had come to her aid.

They were going to have so much fun!

Matt

Tired, Matt stumbled into the bathroom. He relieved himself, then washed his hands and face, trying to wake himself up. He ran his hands through his hair and looked in the mirror.

Instead of his own reflection, Daniel was looking back at him. "Good morning, hellspawn."

Panting, Matt grabbed the sides of the sink. After a few seconds he desperately moistened his lips. "You're just an illusion." It was like that one time with Dion.

Daniel sneered. "You know I'm real."

"No, you're not."

"I'm inside you."

"You're dead."

Daniel paused. "Right. There's that."

Matt shivered. If this was an illusion, it was as good as the last one. But he was no longer in denial. There was no inner turmoil to exploit. At least not much.

"What do you want?" he asked his false reflection.

"What belongs to me."

"Samantha," Matt whispered. No, it couldn't be. Not now, when they were finally getting along again.

Daniel smiled darkly. "Revenge."

Matt snorted. A dead man couldn't take revenge. Even if Daniel had been alive, he wouldn't have had it in him to take the kind of revenge Matt deserved.

He turned away from the mirror, intending to ignore it, when he suddenly felt his head exploding. Daniel's thoughts filled his head. Matt clawed at his temples as he realised what was happening.

"Oh no, you don't," he tried to say, but his mouth didn't open, and the thought just stayed in his head.

It was answered by another and unbearable pressure. *"Oh yes, you're mine now. Get used to it."*

With a grunt, Matt doubled over and lost control. Suddenly he was inside his body, yet outside of it. Another presence filled his limbs and mind. Daniel's. *"Get out!"*

There was a knock at the door. "Hey, Matt. Everything okay in there?"

"No, it's not. I'm possessed. I'm—" Not a single word left his lips.

Instead, Daniel straightened up, smoothed his shirt, and opened the door. With a smile he told René. "Everything's perfect."

\#

Matt fought and struggled inside his own body, but none of it made it to the outside. Daniel had him completely under control. It seemed that death had made him stronger and more bitter. As they walked into school, Matt had to endure an onslaught of vitriol that only got worse with every piece of information Daniel managed to drag out of his memory.

He suddenly knew how Caspar had felt when Matt had seen those terrible scenes. Nothing was safe from Daniel. Not his experiences, not his thoughts, and least of all his feelings.

"You really love her?" Daniel thought amusedly. *"You? A monster?"*

"I'm more than that," Matt insisted. He remembered how the villagers and the sorcerer had condemned Caspar just because he was born a demon.

"Yes, but you're not like him. He became a monster. You are one."

They were interrupted when they saw Lucille emerging from a classroom. Lucille was equally surprised to see them. "Good morning! Did you sleep in? We missed you in French."

"No," Daniel said coldly. "Where's Samantha?"

"She has Physics with Fabian and Rachel. You know that." Her face suddenly lit up. "Wait, are you two an item now? You looked awfully close last night."

Immediately, Daniel found the relevant memories. It had been a great night. They'd talked for hours, joked, and laughed. It had been as if... as if the thing with Daniel had never happened.

"How is that possible?" Daniel asked, disgusted.

Lucille laughed. "Quite simply. You apologised, just as I'd told you to a million times, and she forgave you. The rest is just the natural attraction between you two. You're practically made for each other."

"I'm gonna throw up."

"What?" Lucille frowned. "Look, you don't have to—Oh, there's Fabian and Rachel!" She waved down the corridor. "Good morning. Is Sam not with you?"

Fabian shook his head. "No, she skipped Physics. Rachel was twenty minutes late, too. Herbert threw a massive tantrum."

Next to him, Rachel shrugged good-naturedly. "It happens. Sam's probably just sick."

"Or she's hanging out with *my* boyfriend." Meg joined them, Anne in tow. Her eyes were red, as if she'd been crying all night.

"What do you mean she's hanging out with Jan?" Fabian asked.

Meg lifted her chin. "Well, I caught them kissing last night." Everyone stared at her. "It's true!"

"Sam and Jan?" Fabian repeated doubtfully.

Matt's jealousy reared its ugly head at the very thought.

"Easy there," Daniel mocked him. *"I thought you were so much better now."*

"I know!" Meg began to sob. "It doesn't make any sense. Why does everyone suddenly want to bang my boring sister?"

Anne took her in her arms. "I'm sure there's an explanation."

"Agreed," Lucille added. "Meg, Jan loves you. You've been together for over a year and Sam... Sam would never do this to you."

"Especially not with Jan. Sorry, kid," Fabian said.

Meg crossed her arms. "Then explain it."

"We have to find them first," Lucille reminded her.

"I'll do that," Daniel offered.

"What about school?"

Daniel had already turned. "Who cares about school?" He remarked to Matt, *"Unlike you, I've already graduated."*

"Good for you? Who's possessing her?" It was the only possible explanation for her kissing Jan and skipping school.

"How should I know?" Daniel laughed softly. *"But let's go pay her a visit."*

Matt was suddenly filled with fear. What would Daniel do once he found her? Would he have to watch another man kiss her? With his own body, no less? While he took a back seat, screaming into the void?

"Tempting, but no. You'll just have to wait and see, I guess."

Unlike his own thoughts and memories, Daniel's were a closed book to him. Slowly it dawned on Matt that Daniel had all the power. And he had none.

Balthasar

"Selima is back."

It was the last thing Balthasar had expected after the Council of Seven had summoned him to their hall. He'd come immediately, abandoning a Small Council sitting mid-discussion. One did not ignore a summons of the Seven. But this... This couldn't be true.

"She's dead," Balthasar pointed out as politely as possible while throwing a glance at Melaney, the very reason Selima couldn't possibly be back.

Long ago, when he'd been but a little boy, Selima had been the Archdemon of Lust. Melaney had killed her to succeed the position.

"Apparently, an aspect of her found a way to possess somebody," Melaney explained patiently. "Her lover Sokaris, too." She batted her eyelids. "And he's in close proximity of the Staff of Seth, which will allow them a true resurrection."

"That's not allowed to happen," Hel said, sneering. "That insolent Selima thought too highly of herself and lusted for the Black Throne. Every trace of her needs to be destroyed."

Next to Hel, Volac grunted. "You've gotten rid of her once. You will do it again." No question, just an order.

Balthasar knew better than to argue. He lowered his head. "It will be my pleasure."

"But not too much pleasure," Melaney warned, reminding Balthasar of how they'd tricked Selima last time. If that was what was necessary, he wasn't above it. Though he doubted Selima would fall for the same trick twice.

"May I inquire as to where Selima and Sokaris have taken up residence?" The Council of Seven was notoriously stingy with details. He wondered how they'd even learnt of it.

"Oh, you know the place," Melaney said with a sneer that rivalled Hel's. "In Ashuan. Greenvalley, to be exact."

What had his brother and his short-lived friends done this time? Balthasar nodded again. "I'll leave immediately."

"Everyone's always rushing," Yash complained, lounging in her chair as usual. "It took Selima decades to prepare her coup last time. She won't take over Hescaryn tomorrow."

"She won't take over anything!" Volac bellowed, loud enough to make everyone jump.

As the Council of Seven descended into chaos as usual, Balthasar checked with his mother. Melaney waved him off. "You're dismissed." Then she mouthed, "Don't let that bitch come back."

Balthasar didn't intend to. As he left the Council of Seven, he thought about the first time he'd crossed Selima's path. It had been the first time he'd met his father too. Back in Sephira.

Sephira had been Hescaryn's old capital and home to the Black Tower, which was the source of all demon magic. It hadn't been as well-lit and engineered as Lucin, but rather dark and twisted. Plants had grown between the buildings and silver waterfalls cascaded down the streets.

Balthasar had heard the archdemons were visiting and found them gallivanting arm-in-arm along one of the tower roads.

"My offer is only valid for a short time," Selima had said in a sultry voice. Unlike Melaney, she was a blond bombshell with lips as red as blood and striking blue eyes.

Malcolm had stroked his beard. "It's an ambitious plan."

"But not impossible. Don't you want more power?"

"I'm an archdemon. I *have* power."

Selima had given him a cunning look. "But do you have enough?"

A fire had lit in Malcolm's eyes as his greed came to the fore. He could never have enough.

Balthasar had only been a boy, but he'd decided he had one chance or none. Dressed in simple clothes with scrolls tucked into his belt, he'd stepped into their path. He'd bowed to Selima first. "Your Lust." Then he'd done the same to Malcolm. "Your Greed. I'm Bal—"

"I know who you are," Malcolm had barked. "You're Melaney's offspring."

"Who's Melaney?" Selima had asked, sounding both amused and offended.

Malcolm had snorted. "My little sister."

"I'm *your* son, too," Balthasar had said, hoping it would give him just the little edge he needed.

Selima had been delighted to hear of Balthasar's lineage and slapped Malcolm's arm. "Naughty."

"What do you want?" Malcolm had been far less enamoured with the whole thing.

"A position in the Small Council," Balthasar had said with all the confidence in the world. "As an ambassador for Greed." The other younglings made fun of his bookish ways, but Balthasar had outgrown every single one of them. Their rough-and-kill play bored him. He had wanted more and his father was the key to getting there.

Malcolm had sneered at him. "You want me to take you into my household and trust you to represent my interests in the Small Council? How old are you even?"

"Thirty-three. I'm not a child."

"You're not?"

Called out on his youth, Balthasar had admitted, "I mean, I'm not like the others. They're stupid. I'm not."

"I like him," Selima had said, amused.

Malcolm had given her the smile he didn't have for his son. "Then perhaps we should put him in your household."

Balthasar had frowned, annoyed. "I want to go into politics, not into bed." He'd seen where sex led. After him, his mother had had four more children. They'd all held her back, forcing them to live on the streets like scum.

"One doesn't preclude the other," Selima had lectured, with a hint of something depraved. Then she'd leant over to Malcolm and whispered in his ear.

While he'd thought little of the Archdemon of Lust, Balthasar had hoped she'd put a good word in with Malcolm. Sure enough, his father had nodded. "I'm impressed by your ambition. But you lack experience."

Balthasar's face had lit up. "I'm willing to learn. I work hard and—"

"Good. Let's go then."

Before Balthasar had a chance to react, Malcolm had grabbed him by the shoulder and the three of them had leapt through space into a blindingly bright hall. It had been noisy there, filled with the cries of children and infants. Demons dressed in blue took care of them, and Balthasar had a sinking feeling he knew the place.

Malcolm had pushed Balthasar towards one of the caretakers. The demon had looked up in annoyance, but quickly changed his tune when he recognised the two archdemons. "Your Greed, your Lust, what can I do for you?"

"My son." Malcolm had nudged Balthasar.

"How old is he?" the caretaker had said with little interest. "Can he talk? Can he read?"

"Of course I can read. I'm thirty-three." Panic rose in his throat, but Balthasar had forced it down. He couldn't lose it, not now.

Malcolm's hand had landed on his shoulder and squeezed so hard it hurt. The caretaker didn't appear to take notion. Then he'd nodded.

"We'll start him in the third ring. If that's not too hard for him, he can move up to the fourth."

Balthasar had whirled around in a panic when his worst fears were confirmed. Malcolm had brought him to the City of Youth, the centre of education in Hescaryn. If one could call stuffing adolescent demons into a hostile environment and watching who'd make it out alive an education. "Malcolm, I—"

"Shut up, boy!" The pressure on Balthasar's shoulder had been enough to bring him to his knees. "You're ambitious, but you're still a child. The City of Youth will teach you. I expect you to bring me honour."

He'd let go of Balthasar, who'd trembled with rage but managed to control himself. He'd taken a deep breath and nodded briefly. "I won't bring you shame." It was going to be worse than the streets of Sephira, but he'd outsmart them. He'd always outsmarted everyone.

Selima had laughed. "You're adorable." She'd stroked Balthasar's face with the back of her fingers, letting them linger under his chin. "Come find me when you're all grown up." Then she'd leant into Malcolm and the two of them had jumped away.

Sixteen years. They'd derailed Balthasar's plans for sixteen years! He'd paid her back for that, and Malcolm had found his own demeaning end. Balthasar had risen through the ranks faster than anyone before, which was precisely why he couldn't let Selima ruin this for him. He'd brought upon her downfall once; he'd do it again.

"Balthasar," a voice called him from the shadows outside the Council of Seven.

Balthasar turned around and cocked his head. "Chay. What are you doing here?" While Chay was a frequent guest at the Council of Seven thanks to his skills in premonition, he usually didn't hang out outside the council rooms.

"The Seven have commanded me to stay put." Chay winced. "They're sending you, I suppose."

"*You* told them about Selima and Sokaris," Balthasar surmised. The half-demon must've had a vision. "I assume you know *who* exactly they've possessed."

Chay took a step forward. "Jan and Samantha, but Balthasar—"

Balthasar knew what was coming. Chay would ask him to save them or something ridiculous like that. "I serve the Seven, not you."

"You serve yourself." Chay snorted. "And we had a deal."

"One on which you haven't delivered yet." As much as Balthasar enjoyed working with Chay, he was a little wary to trust him completely. Chay only had one interest and it wasn't Balthasar's success and glory. Still... "I'll see what I can do."

Before Chay could try and convince him otherwise, Balthasar jumped to Ashuan. It was time to find Selima. Or Samantha. He'd decide what to do with her once he got hold of her. After all, he was nothing if not flexible.

Fabian

School was weird today. Not only had Samantha skipped class without explanation, but the projector in Politics did the same and walked straight out the door. In Art, the chalk wanted to join in and drew caricatures of the teacher on the blackboard. The act only spurred everything else on, too, and soon they had to flee from wild paintbrushes and flapping sheets of sketch paper.

Looking out the window, they saw the caretaker fending off a hose behaving like a cobra, spitting water whenever he got too close. Two PE students were running after their shoes.

"What's going on?" he asked Lucille, the only friend he had in Art class. He hadn't really talked to her much since the break-up, but this warranted an exemption.

"I thought it was just our home."

"What's going on at your house?"

"We had breakfast with Lady Macbeth."

Fabian stopped short. "Come again?"

"We were having breakfast with Lady Macbeth. She was plotting murder. Then she left through the wall." She shook herself. "You don't have ghosts at home?"

"Not that I know of..."

Just then the door opened, and a Year 11 class was ushered in. At least half of them were in tears and immediately huddled in groups to comfort each other. Only one of them seemed completely unaffected and also completely alone.

"Ophelia?"

Her eyes lit up as she saw him, which changed her entire appearance. And an appearance it was. She was dressed all in black, with a laced corset and skin-tight leather pants. The outfit was complemented by a long cloak she wore over her arm, as if it were too hot outside.

She came over to him straight away. "Fabian, hi."

"How's your first day been so far?"

"We just found a dead girl in the school pond. Apparently, she drowned herself," she explained cheerfully.

Fabian swallowed. "You found a body?"

"No, they wouldn't let us look for it. It was quite creepy, actually." Ophelia giggled. "We went into the garden and there was this girl sitting on the bank, facing away from us, crying. The teacher asked her what was wrong, and she turned around and showed us her waterlogged face."

Fabian almost threw up in his mouth. "What a disturbing start for you."

"Disturbing? It was glorious. Everyone was screaming, even the teacher. Two people even fell into the pond in their panic. It was hilarious."

The comments were overheard by some of her new classmates, who glared and distanced themselves.

"Hilarious... yeah," Fabian said wearily. "We only had self-drawing chalk and paintbrushes."

"So, what do we do about it? *Are* we going to do something about it? I mean, it's all pretty harmless. Not like anyone's trying to murder anyone."

"Lady Macbeth is," Lucille cut in. She glanced at Fabian. "I have to check if it's safe for Pascal to go home, but we could meet at the Magic Circle later. Maybe Matt will have found Sam by then."

Ophelia looked back and forth expectantly. "The Magic Circle? That's your mum's shop, isn't it?"

"How do you know that?"

"I listen," she said proudly.

Embarrassed, Fabian remembered the word diarrhoea he'd used to keep her from sacrificing him. "Well, yes. It's my mother's shop. We often meet in the back of it to deal with"—his eyes fell on an approaching parade of musical instruments, all playing themselves—"this."

Slowly, Ophelia's class was herded into a classroom. "Alright, I've got till seventh period today."

"Same."

Ophelia beamed at him. "Wonderful. Pick me up at the gym and we can go together." She followed her class, hips swaying.

Lucille leant in. "Do you believe me now?"

"Believe you what?" Fabian asked, his eyes still on Ophelia's ass.

"That she's into you." Lucille slapped him on the arm and giggled. "And so are you."

Fabian shook himself from his stupor. "We don't have time for this. There's, like, an army of poltergeists out there."

"And normal ghosts, too," Lucille added cheerfully.

"Nothing about this is normal."

#

It was sheer stubbornness that kept the school open throughout the drama, including a visit from the police. Somehow Fabian made it through his classes. He was one of the few in his age group who did. Lucille left early to take Pascal home when his classes ended early, and Rachel faked period pains and wrote herself an apology.

Fabian was over it, too, but he'd sucked it up and went to the gym as promised. When he arrived, Anne and Meg were just leaving, both too engrossed in gossip to notice him standing there. One by one, the rest of the class left, leading Fabian to believe that Ophelia had skipped out early as well.

He was about to leave when the door opened and Ophelia came out. This time she was wearing her cloak, which looked more like a pretty dress than a jacket. She didn't look too happy, but as soon as she saw him, her face lit up. "You came."

"Of course I came."

As if it were the most natural thing in the world, she locked arms with him. "No more dead people on the schedule, but we had a dodgeball ultra fight. Just the balls against us. Lots of shrieking and crying, as you can imagine." She rolled her eyes.

As they started to leave, Fabian asked, "Are you okay?"

"Sure. Why do you ask?"

Fabian shrugged a little. "No reas—Just that you came out last."

"It took me a while to lace up the corset by myself."

"By yourself. You were standing by yourself before, too," he said gently.

Ophelia made a face and laughed. "Of course I did. I'm the new girl, remember? People don't know me yet."

"It didn't look like they wanted to get to know you."

Fabian regretted his words when the good mood faded from Ophelia's face. She chewed on her lip. "If it were up to me, I wouldn't go to school. But the people from the Youth Service said I didn't have any qualifications, so it would be easier to send me to school while I'm still under eighteen. That's why they're making me sit the Year 10 exams at the end of the year. I'm bored already."

"Have you been home-schooled before?"

"I home-schooled myself. Enrico never let me go to school. He was too afraid I would talk about the cult or something. So officially, he homeschooled me, but he never cared about school, so I did it myself."

"You did it yourself?" Fabian asked. He couldn't imagine her reading more than a book or two between snake feeding and rituals.

She nodded. "You know he didn't think much of me. I was often excluded from the affairs of the cult. And since I wasn't allowed to go out alone, I did schoolwork." She paused and gave Fabian a long look. "They gave me some tests to see which class I should be in. I'm actually quite clever, you know?"

"I didn't," Fabian admitted.

Ophelia bit her lip. "Neither did I. Enrico always said I was dumb. But, apparently, I got top marks or something." She shrugged. "It's nothing."

"It's everything!" Fabian exclaimed, turning to her. "Okay, maybe not everything, but it's fantastic." Seeing Ophelia light up again was worth every word. "I mean it. You've had, like, the hardest upbringing and your brother was wrong. About everything."

She giggled as he used the word again. "Thank you. Well, they put me with people my own age, so I guess that's a good thing."

"It is." When Ophelia lowered her face, Fabian asked, "What's going on?"

Ophelia groaned. "Word got out that I belonged to the cult. Now they're calling me a murderer and a witch. Or crazy. That's popular too."

"A murderer?"

She sighed. "Apparently one of Eresta's victims went to this school. People knew her and blame me."

"People are stupid," Fabian snarled. "You had nothing to do with this."

"Well, I almost killed you, didn't I?" Her voice cracked. "I'm really not much better than Enrico."

Fabian put his hand under her chin and lifted it. Tears glistened in the corners of her eyes. "Ophelia..."

"Lia," she whispered. "Ophelia is what he called me when he was mad."

Fabian smiled gently. "Lia. You grew up in a murderous cult. I won't pretend to know what that was like, but from everything I saw that night and from everything you told me, I know the fact you *didn't* murder me is what matters."

"I only did it because you were cute."

He chuckled, feeling more than a little flattered. "I'll take it. But what I'm saying is that when you had to sacrifice me, you chose to take a stand instead. That must have taken an enormous amount of courage. And for me, that makes all the difference. You're a good person, Lia, and you shouldn't have to suffer for your brother's sins. You've suffered enough already."

Her tongue flicked over her lips as she looked up at him, hanging onto every word. Fabian gazed into her green eyes and got a little lost in them. She had such a beautiful face.

Suddenly, she frowned, looking past him. "What's that?"

He turned around and stared straight into a cloud of tiny elf-like creatures.

"Elemental!" they screamed, and swarmed him.

Lucille

"Lucille! Come quick!"

Lucille had just managed to avoid catastrophic water damage in the bathroom when Pascal came running to her. He was as white as a sheet of paper. "What's wrong?"

"There's a girl in my room."

"And?"

"She's tearing up paper, but she... she can't see. I mean, she doesn't have any eyes." Pascal began to pant and whimper.

Lucille pulled him into a hug. "Shh, did she hurt you?" She felt him shake his head. "Did she say anything?" Pascal mumbled something. "What was that?"

He pulled his head back. "She didn't have a mouth, either."

Lucille pressed him against her stomach again and hugged him tightly. "I'm so sorry. Don't worry, we'll get to the bottom of this." She offered his hand. "Let's go to my room, shall we?"

She made sure the taps were off before she took Pascal's hand and walked down the corridor to her room. A ghost floated out of the wall in front of them and disappeared into the next one without looking at them. Lucille let out a shuddering breath. "Please tell me you just saw that."

"Mhm," Pascal said quietly as he pressed himself against her.

Lucille took a deep breath and opened the door to her room... and closed it again. "Nope. I'm out of here."

"What was it?"

"Nothing." There was no way she was going to tell Pascal about the corpse hanging from her ceiling. Noticing his sharp look, she fibbed, "I've also got a faceless girl."

Pascal pulled a face. "What are we going to do?"

"We'll call in reinforcements. Don't worry, all these creepy squatters will be gone by tonight." As they marched down to the lounge, Lucille took out her phone.

The group chat was surprisingly quiet. She'd thought they'd all be on it by now, but not a single message awaited her. Instead, several from Philipp flooded the screen.

Despite the eerie atmosphere in the house, she found herself smiling. Before she knew it, she'd pressed his number to call him.

He picked up almost immediately. "Hey, you."

His voice almost made her melt. "Hey."

"How's your day been so far?"

"Good. I..." She noticed Pascal staring at her, eyebrows raised in doubt. The reality of her situation returned to her. "Actually, it's been a bit of a nightmare. I don't know if you noticed, but—"

"There are a lot of extremely mysterious accidents and strange sights?" Philipp asked.

"Yes."

He sighed. "My boss sent everyone out to cover the apparitions. Did he send his local mystic news guy? Nope. I have to cover the Mosby exhibition and write about ancient curses or something."

"Ancient curses?" Maybe the key was in the exhibition. Lucille hadn't heard of it before but now she was intrigued. "What's the Mosby exhibition?"

"It's a critically acclaimed moving exhibition about an Egyptian pharaoh that was unearthed a few years ago," Pascal said as Philipp rattled off something similar.

"The pharaoh was called Mosby?" Despite her love for dead languages, Egyptian wasn't a language Lucille was familiar with. Mosby wasn't it, though.

Philipp laughed at the other end, while Pascal rolled his eyes. "The archaeologist who found it and published her findings is called Mosby. Katherine Mosby," her brother explained.

"I see. How do you know all this stuff?" Then she said into the phone. "Sorry, my brother's here, too."

"We went with the class last week."

If the exhibition had been in Greenvalley since last week, it couldn't be the reason for the sudden chaos. Unless something had happened to it last night. "Can you come here?"

"To your house?" Philipp asked. It was a bit early for house calls in their relationship.

"We can compare notes. The thing is, I can't leave the house alone right now. We've got at least three different poltergeists and... just come here."

There was silence on the other line. Philipp had only just discovered how magical Greenvalley really was. Perhaps she was asking too much. But then he snapped right back. "Sure. I'll be there in fifteen minutes."

\#

While waiting for Philipp, Lucille posted a message on the group channel asking everyone to come to her place and bring any books on exorcism or ghosts. Fabian replied with, "I'll try". Rachel had seen the message, typed something, but never sent it. The other three remained silent.

"This is so weird." She and Pascal made themselves comfortable in the lounge, which at least seemed to have no permanent ghost inhabitants.

Meanwhile, she'd told the staff to go home, keeping no one but Albert.

"What are we going to do?" Pascal hugged himself, glancing over his shoulder frequently. "Do you think it's getting colder?"

Lucille was still wearing her comfy jumper from school, but Pascal was right. The temperature did seem to have dropped. "Probably just a ghost playing with the thermostat. We'll wait for Philipp and—"

Just then, Albert announced Philipp and led him into the room. The young journalist looked around in amusement, but waited until Albert was gone to deliver his verdict. "This is even better than I thought."

"Philipp!" Lucille jumped up and fell into his arms, feeling a sudden relief to have someone else there. "You're here."

"You asked and I came running. Isn't that how it works in the de Cerque world?"

"Very funny." Lucille let go of him and sat down again.

He was about to sit down next to her when a couple of ghosts in medieval garb floated through the room.

"He hath almost supped. Why have you left the chamber?" the woman hissed.

"Hath he asked for me?" The man sounded nervous.

"Know you not he hath?"

"We will proceed no further in this business. He hath honoured me of late, and I have bought golden opinions from all sorts of people, which would be worn now in their newest gloss, not cast aside so soon."

The woman groaned. "Was the hope drunk wherein you dressed yourself? Hath it slept since? And wakes it now to look so green and pale..." They disappeared into the other wall.

"What are they talking about?" Philipp asked.

"They want to kill their king," Pascal said, sounding surprisingly cheerful.

Philipp frowned. "Sounds like Macbeth."

"It *is* Macbeth," Lucille said, slumping back in her chair with a sigh. "Or at least its historical model." She sat up again, remembering that she wanted to impress Philipp. Slouching was definitely not the way to do it. "There are so many ghosts in this house. People have died here, or it's just a magnet for the most disturbing ghosts in existence."

"There's a faceless girl ripping paper in my room," Pascal piped up. "In Lucille's room, too."

Lucille smiled weakly. "Yes, a girl." Not a hanging man, just a faceless girl. She sighed. "Someone's turning on all the taps, and there's a jealous housewife in the kitchen throwing pots around." As if on cue, the sound of breaking china rang through the house.

Philipp jumped. "Charming."

"The others will be here soon." At least she hoped so.

"Okay, so how does this work?" Philipp leant forward, approaching the situation with professional interest.

"Well, usually we compare notes and then Samantha..." Samantha, who hadn't answered yet and who might be MIA with Jan of all people. And where the hell was Matt? "Okay, um, so—"

Just then, the house rumbled like an earthquake and the temperature dropped drastically. Pascal leapt into Lucille's arms while she dug her fingers into the armrests. White clouds rose in front of her face.

"Philipp?"

He looked at her, eyes wide. His throat bopped once.

"I'm scared."

Rachel

As soon as the ghostly incidents at school started increasing, Rachel rushed home with a bad feeling. This morning she'd had the most amazing conversation with Hugo von Hohenstetten. His opinions were a little dusty, but he was polite to a fault. She was hoping he'd stuck around, because she could use a friend right about now.

To her relief, she found him sitting in her room, just as she'd left him. "You're still here."

"I'm a man of honour who keeps his promises."

"How charming," Rachel said with delight.

"Were you able to accomplish your important things?"

Rachel frowned until she realised what he meant. "School? Yes, I went to school." She clapped her hands. "And now I'm back... because we have a problem."

Hugo rose from his chair. "If there is a problem, we must tackle it immediately."

So much enthusiasm. If only she knew what to do. "It's not that simple. The thing is... you don't seem to be the only ghost who answered my call." It was the only explanation Rachel could come up with. She'd called the ghosts and then Hugo had appeared, and with him a whole bunch of others. Only the one she'd actually wanted had stayed away.

"Your call was very strong."

She winced. "Wonderful. Just wonderful." She suddenly felt heady and on the verge of a breakdown. All she'd wanted was a friend. "They have to go. The ghosts have to go. It's pure chaos out there."

"You want me to leave?" Hugo asked.

Rachel had only known him for a morning, but they'd had so much fun together that the thought of losing him so soon was too much to bear. "Yes. No. I'm sorry. I didn't mean to force anyone to come."

"No," Hugo said surprisingly forcefully. "I've told you this before. Don't apologise for dragging me away from my post. I haven't seen the sun for four hundred years, all because I wanted to take revenge on my sister. She cheated me out of my inheritance, you know?" His face softened. "Now I can feel things again. This blanket." He ran his fingers over her bed. "So soft. The warmth of the winter sun. It's like I'm *alive* again. I'm very grateful to you, Rachel."

Rachel stared at her blanket, processing his words. "Maybe you don't have to go." Surely there was another way to get rid of everyone else. The others hadn't even bothered coming to her. Only he had.

Just then, her phone buzzed. She took it out and read the group message from Lucille. Apparently, her old villa was haunted. And now she wanted everyone to come running.

As Rachel stared at the phone, Fabian replied that he'd be there. Rachel's fingers hovered over the keyboard. She would need the others' help. But that meant telling them what she'd done.

She sighed. "Let's go." The phone slipped into her pocket without a message.

"Go? Go where?" Hugo asked as she went downstairs to put her shoes on.

"To meet my friends." Her stomach churned at the thought of their indignation. "They'll be so angry."

"Angry?"

They left the house.

"Yes. Because I made a mess." Bitterness spread through her mouth. "This is all my fault. And they'll tell me how stupid and reckless I was to try an untested spell." That was what she'd tell herself if she weren't the one behind it.

Hugo frowned. "Are you sure we're visiting friends?"

"They're right. I mean, they will be right. I shouldn't have done it."

"Then why did you?"

Rachel bit her lip. *Because she'd been lonely.* But how could she say that when she had a whole group of friends around her. All of whom were in relationships or should be. "Do you really want to know?"

"I wouldn't have asked otherwise."

Warmth filled her from head to toe. Hugo was really something else. So attentive and polite. It wouldn't hurt to trust him with her inner darkness. "Okay, so..."

Just then she noticed Fabian and the snake girl he'd "rescued" from the mine on the road ahead. They were on their way to meet her but were too busy fending off what looked like a swarm of hornets to notice her.

Only the hornets spoke. "Good spirits! Bad spirits! You're our friend. You play with us."

A small shower poured down on the two of them. Alarmed, Rachel walked towards them, Hugo in tow.

What looked like hornets from a distance were tiny human-like creatures with wings. Like fairies out of a storybook. When they noticed Rachel, a ball of fire formed in front of her. It came with a face and was grimacing. "Woah. What's that?"

Ophelia noticed her. "These elemental spirits think Fabian is their new gang leader or something." She looked at Hugo. "And who's your transparent friend?"

Hugo didn't take offence and bowed instead. "Hugo von Hohenstetten. It's my honour to make your acquaintance."

Ophelia giggled. "I'm Ophelia and the guy preventing a fire over there is Fabian." She pointed at Fabian, who was using his water to put out the fire, which had gotten out of control.

Rachel didn't like Ophelia very much. What was Fabian doing with her anyway? She'd belonged to the cult of Ishtar, who'd tried to kill her. They'd also tried to kill Fabian. In fact, he'd said that *Ophelia* had tried to kill him. So what was going on in his head, running around with her like that?

"I can't play with you!" Fabian said to the spirits. "I've got something important to do, and besides, I've got more than enough friends."

The cloud of elemental spirits made an unhappy face. "DUMB!"

An icy wind blew through the street, freezing the wet ground. Fabian, Ophelia and Rachel all slipped in surprise. Only Hugo remained standing, hovering a centimetre above the ground.

The ground rumbled and a mound of earth tried to push itself between Fabian and Ophelia. Even the spirits didn't like the snake.

Rachel was about to make a terribly snide remark when Balthasar appeared between them. He also slipped but caught himself with another space jump.

"What's *he* doing here?" Fabian asked.

Balthasar fixed him with a look. "I'm here to kill someone." Fabian swallowed as Balthasar slapped away a bunch of elemental spirits. "What are those?"

"Elemental spirits," Ophelia said again as she stood up. "They like Fabian. Who are you? And how did you just do that?"

Before Balthasar could answer, Rachel interrupted, "Who are you trying to kill?"

Balthasar was about to answer when his gaze slipped past her. Rachel looked over her shoulder and saw Jan and Samantha walking arm in arm down the street.

"Was Meg right?" Fabian asked, confused. The elemental spirits settled on his shoulders and head, equally fascinated.

Balthasar leapt forward, dodging the ice. "So, Chay spoke the truth. You found a way to wriggle yourself out of your grave."

The way Samantha looked at Balthasar was so uncanny Rachel knew immediately what had happened. A spirit had possessed her friend. And not just her. Jan, too.

"I'd hoped Melaney would have scratched your eyes out by now. But I guess she's not even capable of that." Samantha gave him a wicked smile that was equal parts threat and seduction. It was not a smile Rachel had ever seen on her friend's face. "It leaves the pleasure to me. Bring him to me."

Instantly, Jan leapt forward and charged at Balthasar. The demon grabbed him and pushed him away, but Jan just took the fall and pulled out a silver shimmering stone. He closed his eyes and mumbled something, then held out his hand.

The sudden flash of blue lightning made them all jump. It struck Balthasar, knocking him to the ground. Stunned, the demon lay motionless.

Jan pulled out a knife and walked over, looking terribly relaxed. Rachel looked at Samantha and saw her smile in anticipation.

"Jan?" Fabian asked, making Jan pause. "Since when do we take on dangerous demons alone? In broad daylight?"

Energy shot towards the group. The elemental spirits built a wall just fast enough to protect them all. Hugo was the only one who got hit, though he just sighed.

Balthasar was back on his feet and threw himself at Jan. Fabian raised his hands to shoot water at the demon. As soon as Fabian took a stance, the elemental spirits joined the fight. The earth split beneath Balthasar and Jan, wind blew left and right, and lightning struck.

A blast of energy struck Balthasar and separated him from Jan, who ran to hide behind Samantha. It took Rachel a moment to realise that it was her friend who'd been shooting energy like a demon.

Now Samantha was facing them. "I don't know who you are or what you want, but I'm warning you. Don't ever cross my path again." She took Jan's hand and disappeared with him. Like a demon.

"Oh god, she's been possessed by a demon." Rachel whimpered. What had she done?

"Not just any demon," said Balthasar, spitting blood on the ground. His clothes were torn and he was putting pressure on a bleeding wound in his side. He looked angry enough to tear them all apart. "Can't you children just stay out of this for once?"

"Stay out of it when you're attacking *our* friends?" Rachel asked, aghast.

"I doubt those two were your friends," Hugo mused. "They were evil. Truly evil."

Ophelia snorted. "You're Rachel's ghost. Shouldn't you have her back?"

"Don't tell him what to do, snake," Rachel hissed.

Ophelia looked taken aback. Rachel didn't know why she thought they were all friends now, but she was wrong.

Actually, she *did* know why when she saw Fabian put a hand on her shoulder and squeeze it comfortingly.

"The ghost is right," Balthasar said with a grim expression. "You might as well forget about your friends. They no longer exist."

Lucille

When Lucille had thought of inviting her friends, she hadn't expected them to bring so many extras. Ophelia was fine with her. There was clearly a connection between her and Fabian, and Lucille would do anything to support it. But they came with a cloud of elemental spirits, some of whom had built a fire in the fireplace while others explored the lounge. Rachel had brought along an old-fashioned ghost who was polite but rather possessive. And to top it all off, there was Balthasar. Matt's demon brother, who was currently trying to kill Matt—and them by proxy.

Not that he was actually killing anyone right now. Instead, he was pacing the room, looking like he wanted to be anywhere but here.

"Fabian, can you please tell your pixies that my house is not a playground?" Ten of the little sprites floated an expensive vase around the room.

"I've got my eye on it," said Pascal. He watched the vase intently, which made Lucille feel a little better.

Meanwhile, Fabian groaned. "They're not mine. They just follow me."

Just then, a cold shower fell on Lucille. Screaming, she jumped out of the way. "Stupid girl," the spirits said in unison. "We are elements, not pixies. Good spirits, bad spirits, we want to play!"

"Hey, listen," Fabian said.

The vase continued to float around the room, and some of the spirits pulled on Fabian's hair, clearly not wanting to listen to anything he was about to say.

Fabian's face darkened. And then the impossible happened: he started to shout in a rather authoritative voice, "LISTEN TO ME!"

Suddenly all the spirits stood still. They looked at Fabian, who raised an eyebrow, then continued much more calmly, "Thank you. You air spirits will put down the vase. The rest of you, show some manners. We're guests here. If you can't do that, I'm no longer your friend."

"DUMB!" shouted the elemental spirits, but they did as he said and sat down on the furniture and his shoulders.

Lucille was impressed. She hadn't known Fabian had it in him.

Balthasar, however, growled at them. "Can't you be a bit quieter? I'm trying to think here."

"No one said you had to do it *here*," Ophelia said. She obviously didn't know who she was talking to.

Before Balthasar could put her in her place, the house groaned. The elemental spirits all hid behind Fabian and Pascal pressed himself against Lucille's side. "I'm scared."

"It's all good. We'll get to the bottom of this." She looked at Balthasar. "It was you, wasn't it?"

"Me?" Balthasar pointed his hand to his chest. "You think this giant mess is my fault?"

"Who else would do such a thing? This is one of your ploys to get rid of Matt, isn't it?"

He stared at her a little longer. "How is this getting rid of Matt?" he finally asked.

Matt wasn't here, whatever that meant.

Rachel cleared her throat. "Um, actually... it's my fault." Everyone looked at her in surprise. "Last night, I summoned a ghost and... well, this morning Hugo turned up in my wardrobe and Greenvalley had gone mad."

"You what?" Lucille couldn't believe what she was hearing. *Rachel* was responsible for this?

"I summoned the ghosts."

"But why?" Fabian asked. "I mean, who does that?"

Rachel gave him a withering look. "*I* do."

Meanwhile, Balthasar rubbed his temples. "Was there a mirror nearby?"

"A mirror?" Rachel asked. "Well, my wardrobe has a mirror."

"And may I be so bold as to presume you didn't cover it up?"

Rachel nodded shyly.

Balthasar groaned. "Why do you guys have to make every rookie mistake in the book?"

Lucille still didn't know what had possessed Rachel to do such a thing, but she wasn't going to let a demon get away with giving her shit. "So professionals like you have a job to do. If you're so omniscient, you're welcome to share your knowledge. If not, you can leave my house and think somewhere else."

Balthasar held onto the back of an empty chair and leant forward. "Mirrors act as gateways between the world of the living and the world of the dead. Your little ghost whisperer offered Selima and Sokaris their return on a silver platter."

"And who are they?" Philipp asked, as if the others already knew. Lucille didn't blame him. It was a lot.

"They're the most dangerous couple Hescaryn has ever seen. Selima was the Archdemon of Lust before Melaney, a power-hungry viper who wanted to conquer the Black Throne. Sokaris was a human sorcerer she'd taken as her lover, binding his life to hers for all of eternity."

"That's the one in Jan, right?" Fabian asked. "He seemed stronger than you."

Balthasar's eyes narrowed. "He used elemental energies concentrated in gems. What I don't understand is how he managed to get his hands on a hematite so quickly."

"Probably from the Magic Circle or his own collection. Jan loves crystals and gems," Lucille explained helpfully, before asking, "Demons can bind people to themselves?"

"The Archdemon of Lust can. They take a lover, usually a demon, whose life is bound to theirs. The archdemon can survive them, but the lover can't. It's the ultimate devotion. Other sins have their own structures," Balthasar explained.

Lucille raised her eyebrows, her mind already racing. She wondered if Matt was aware of this perk. "Does your mum have one?"

"Sure. His name is Frennys."

She hadn't expected that. "But she still sleeps with others?"

"He's her lover, not the other way around," Balthasar said irritated, then groaned. "You mean whether she's in love with him? No, no, they're partners. Business partners, if you like. Just like Selima and Sokaris. Sure, there's a lot of sex involved, but Selima didn't choose Sokaris because she developed feelings for him. She chose him because of his magic, because of her master plan."

Lucille struggled to follow. "The Black Throne?" She wasn't sure if she'd heard of it before. Maybe Matt had mentioned it when he'd talked about the Council of Seven. "Isn't it empty?"

Balthasar looked at her as if she was particularly slow today. "That's the point. It's empty, there for the taking. After Lucifer fell from the heavens, Marialle killed him. Not a great achievement, the angels had pretty much finished him off already, but it made her the Queen of Hell. Then the vampires attacked, and she was killed. Her energy went nowhere, just like Malcolm's. Since then, the Council of Seven has jealously guarded the Black Throne. They don't want to lose their power, but Selima was one of them, and she tried to take it for herself."

Lucille's head was swimming from the amount of information Balthasar had thrown at her. Lucifer was real? Vampires were attacking Hell? There were angels? "What was in it for Sokaris?"

"You mean besides eternal life and all that power? Ashuan. Selima promised him Ashuan as a reward. If they'd succeeded, this world would've looked very different."

The thought made Lucille shudder. Her world would have been bound to Hell and ruled by a megalomaniacal sorcerer.

"But they didn't succeed," Fabian said, looking terribly pale.

"Obviously. But they came close. Very, very close. The Black Guard was hers, she had our priests and mages under her spell, and she had an army of undead ready to be unleashed if the other six archdemons didn't cooperate."

Lucille swallowed. "What stopped her?"

"Not what. Who!" Balthasar smiled wickedly. "I did. Or rather, I helped Melaney kill her."

"That explains why she was so happy to see you," Fabian quipped joylessly.

Balthasar's explanation was interrupted when the two Macbeth ghosts floated through the room, still discussing their murder. When they were gone, he straightened up and clapped his hands. "I've wasted enough time here. According to Chay, I must get to them before they get their hands on the Staff of Seth."

Shocked, Lucille jumped to her feet. "Wait, what? What do you mean you have to get to them?"

"The Council of Seven sent me to make sure there is no proper resurrection. I will find them and destroy them, ensuring there'll be not a trace of ghostly energy left."

Lucille licked her lips nervously. "Surely you can do that without hurting Samantha or Jan, right?"

"I doubt it," Balthasar said sarcastically, making it clear he wasn't even interested in trying.

Rachel gasped and the house howled as if in pain. Lucille grabbed Philipp's hand in panic.

"Probably just the wind."

"Are you sure Samantha and Jan are lost?" Ophelia ignored their eerie surroundings. "What if they're still in there? Jan paused when Fabian spoke to him."

Balthasar shrugged. "Maybe. But I have neither the time nor patience to find out."

"You can't kill them," Fabian protested. "We won't let you."

Immediately, the elemental spirits sprang into action and surrounded Balthasar. "We won't let you."

A muscle twitched in Balthasar's face as he tried to remain calm. "Both our worlds are at risk. What else do you suggest?"

Lucille looked at the others in panic. According to Balthasar, their time was running out. Which meant... No, they couldn't let Balthasar get away with his ultimate solution. Ophelia was right. Samantha and Jan were still in there. They just had to get through to them. But how?

Then it hit Lucille. "Matt! Matt can get through to Samantha. I know he can."

Balthasar grimaced. "I don't know if you've noticed, but Matt's not here."

Lucille clicked her tongue. "Luckily, he's half-demon. We can summon him."

Matt

Matt was more terrified than he'd ever been in his life. To feel Daniel moving in his body, controlling where he went, what he saw or what he said, was more frightening than the pit of hellworms Caspar had thrown him into as a small child. That had hurt; this was worse.

"What are you going to do with Sam?" he asked Daniel as they walked through the streets. Samantha hadn't answered her phone, and she hadn't been home either.

It should've irritated Matt that he was more worried about her than about himself, but there was no time for doubt. Somehow, he had to stop Daniel.

"I'm taking what's mine," Daniel said in his mind.

"You were together for a week!" For once it wasn't jealousy that reared its ugly head, but genuine concern. This wasn't the Daniel Samantha had fallen head over heels for. The Daniel Matt had hated so much had been kind and sweet.

"Too bad you killed him, huh?" Daniel commented dryly.

There was that. *"She's still not yours."*

"But she'll never be yours."

Matt lunged at him. For a moment he felt as if he was gaining control, then he was thrown back into the depths of his mind.

"You can't fight me," Daniel said, with a contemptuous sneer that ripped through Matt's mind. *"Your body is mine now and I'll do with it as I please."*

"And how are you going to convince Sam that it's you when all she sees is me?"

Daniel laughed, a sound that only frightened Matt more. *"Oh Matt, do you think I'll do you a favour and have a relationship with her in your body? Give you what you so desperately want?"*

"Then what's your plan?"

"I won't stay a minute longer in your blood-stained body. And I'll be taking her with me."

"What?" Once more, Matt threw himself against Daniel's presence in his mind. He might as well have thrown himself against a brick wall. Whatever had given Daniel the power to possess him was too strong for him. *"Please, don't. Daniel, this is crazy. You can't..."*

If it hadn't been clear before that Daniel had lost his mind, it was clear to Matt now. This wasn't love anymore. This was obsession. Worse than he'd ever been.

"You're not exactly an expert in this area," Daniel pointed out. But then a shift went through him and the hatred faded. "Samantha."

It could have been Matt's chance, but instead he was just as distracted when he saw her walking down the street towards them.

In an entirely un-Samantha-like fashion, she rolled her eyes at the mention of her name. "What now?" her voice was harsh and unforgiving with a hint of dark promise behind it.

Daniel didn't care about her obvious annoyance and hurried towards her. Warmth swept through Matt as Daniel's old feelings came to the fore. He smiled at Samantha. "There you are."

Her posture changed as she finally took notice of Daniel. A devious smile crossed her lips, reminding Matt of his mother, of all people. "Well, aren't you a handsome boy?"

"I'm not Matt," Daniel said, a little annoyed.

Samantha put her hand on his neck. "I don't care who you are." Her other hand went straight between his legs, making Daniel gasp. "Just entertain me."

"It's not her," Matt told him, mortified. *"Samantha's not like that."*

The other ignored him. "Daniel. I'm Daniel."

"Okay," Samantha breathed, but then she stopped and seemed to listen to the wind. Amused, she suddenly gasped. "Oh, oh. You're Daniel... and Matt. How delicious."

"I've missed you," Daniel said, still blind to what was going on. He put his hands on her face and kissed her, despite his big speech earlier.

"It's not her, you idiot! Can't you see she's just as possessed as I am?" Matt had no idea who'd possessed Samantha. If it didn't have to be a ghost, he would've guessed his own mother. Was that possible? Would she go that far?

Whoever it was certainly didn't have a human sense of decency. She kissed Daniel like there was no tomorrow and worked his nether regions almost more. Matt refused to think of this as a kiss between him and Samantha. They had nothing to do with it.

Meanwhile, Daniel was taken aback by Samantha's intensity and slowly came to his senses. Unfortunately, this meant he returned to his original plan. His hands slipped from Samantha's face and wrapped around her neck.

She immediately retaliated by squeezing his balls, anger flashing in her eyes.

For the first time, Matt was glad to be out of control of his body. Daniel screamed but held onto her neck as if his life depended on it.

There was a dangerous glint in Samantha's eyes. Her other hand moved from his neck to his chest and suddenly energy burst from her. Daniel was thrown halfway across the street.

"How dare you?" Samantha's eyes blazed. "You unworthy wretch."

Daniel tried to get up, but she kept shooting energy at him. *"Demon. She's a demon. Why is she a demon?"* His thoughts spiralled.

"Let me get us out of here. We need to recoup and—"

Another energy bolt nearly knocked them unconscious. Daniel rolled over and came to a halt, breathing heavily. Blood streamed down his body, and he flashed back to that night in January when Matt had done something similar to him. Samantha was going to kill him. Or rather, both of them.

"I can jump away. Get us to safety," Matt begged him. *"Just let me take over."*

"Never!" Daniel gritted his teeth. *"Show me how."*

Matt wanted to stand his ground and refuse, but then he saw the ice in Samantha's eyes as she raised her hands.

A moment later, Daniel had jumped them out of harm's way. On weak knees, they reappeared a few streets away, holding on to a streetlamp. *"Heal, you damn body,"* Daniel demanded, almost collapsing from the pain.

"I thought you wanted me dead," Matt replied coldly.

Daniel laughed sharply. He was clearly losing his mind. *"Dead? I don't want you dead, Matt. Oh no. Oh no. You will live. And suffer! For all of eternity."*

Matt almost feinted. *"Ass—"*

"—hole."

Suddenly Matt was standing in the familiar lounge of Lucille's villa. His feet were planted on a tiny pentagram drawn in blood. Next to him, Fabian was suckling on his index finger. Next to him sat Ophelia and Lucille. Everyone was assembled. Everyone except Jan and Samantha. Instead, there was his brother.

"Give it back!" A voice inside him shouted. Daniel.

It wasn't until then that Matt realised he had assumed his demon form. His hair was black and a pair of wings sprouted from his back. His friends had summoned Melchior, which in turn had pushed Daniel aside.

"There you are!" Lucille said. "You didn't answer a normal call." Only then did she seem to notice the blood on him. "What happened?"

"Caspar, I suppose," Balthasar said. "Oh, no, he should still be locked up."

Matt shivered. He had control over his body again, but something told him it would only last as long as he remained Melchior. "No. Samantha."

For some reason, his brother wasn't even surprised. "Oh, that wasn't her but Selima. Melaney's predecessor. She doesn't like her children very much. Samantha's gone."

"Samantha's *not* gone!" Fabian hissed.

Suddenly everything made sense. The vibes he'd felt from Samantha... it wasn't Melaney, it was the sin of lust. Samantha was not only possessed by a demon, but by an archdemon.

Balthasar rolled his eyes. "You still haven't given me another plan."

The window opened and closed. It kept doing that without anyone around or a breeze blowing. Lucille's new boyfriend got up and held the window shut but seemed to be having trouble with it.

Matt wet his lips. "Another plan?"

"Selima has to be destroyed," Balthasar said, as matter-of-factly as ever.

"Selima, yes," Fabian said emphatically, "Sam, no."

"Or Jan, for that matter," Rachel added meekly.

Matt gave up. "What's going on here?"

"It's complicated," Lucille said. "Would you please return to your human form? You're a bit creepy." She squinted at a spot over his shoulder.

Matt turned his head. His wings looked perfectly normal. Their shadows did not. Instead, they loomed over them as if they were a creature of their own.

"I can't. If I turn back, he'll take over again." In the back of his mind, Daniel lurked, ready to pounce.

"Who?" Ophelia asked.

"Daniel."

The collective gasps from Lucille, Fabian, and Rachel confirmed they all understood the gravity of the situation immediately.

Rachel paled. "Oh no."

Meanwhile, Ophelia leant over to Fabian. "Who's Daniel?"

"Samantha's ex. He's... he's dead."

Lucille clapped her hand over her mouth. "You've been possessed by Daniel?"

"It's all my fault," Rachel cried. "I summoned the spirits."

There was a strange ghost beside her. A man with a lot of facial hair and a fancy suit. "Don't lose hope, Miss Rachel."

"You summoned them?" Matt asked. "Have you gone mad?" What could've possibly possessed her to do such a thing?

Her face hardened. "No."

Lucille sighed. "Samantha and Jan have been possessed by Selima and Sokaris, the former Archdemon of Lust and her lover. Together, they want to take over Hell. Balthasar is here to stop them."

"And time is running out," Balthasar remarked. "Can I go and kill them now?"

"Daniel's with you there," Matt told him. "He wants to kill her to get her back."

Fabian's eyes widened. "He *what*?"

"Yeah. His death must've made him go insane or something."

Balthasar clicked his tongue in annoyance. "Death doesn't make you go insane. It takes your life. Daniel's soul is in the Realm of the Dead like everyone else's. This is just a spectral image of him. Probably based on his last minutes. Don't you know anything about ghosts?"

That made a lot more sense. Matt knew about the Realm of the Dead, but nothing about how ghosts were created.

"Samantha killed her ex-boyfriend?" Philipp asked Lucille quietly.

She sighed. "No, Matt did. It's complicated."

"There must be a way to send the spirits back to where they came from," Rachel said, her eyes practically glued to Balthasar.

He finally gave in. "You'll need an obsidian. Pull the spirits in there. The stone will do the rest."

"How?" Lucille asked, her eyes narrowing. "How do we pull the spirits in?"

"I don't know the spells. I'm not a ghost summoner like your friend. I'll give you two hours. If you haven't finished by then, I'll continue with my original plan."

"There might be something in my book," Rachel said hopefully. "It's at home, though, and I have no idea how to get obsidian so quickly."

Balthasar shrugged. "That's your problem."

"Jan." Fabian said. "There might be one in his collection."

"Great idea." Lucille pointed at him and Ophelia. "You two go to Jan's. Rachel will get her book." She rolled her eyes at the ceiling. "And I'll look after the house."

"What about me?" Matt asked.

She looked at him with trepidation. "You should just stay here. If Daniel really wants to kill Samantha, you'd better stay as far away from her as you can. But maybe you could wash all the blood off you before you ruin our carpets any more than you've already done."

Beside her, Philipp cleared his throat. "I don't know if this is helpful, but I'm writing an article about the Mosby exhibition. The centrepiece of the exhibition is the Scepter of Ombos, also known as the Staff of Seth. That's what they want, isn't it?"

"Where is this exhibition?" Balthasar asked.

"In our one and only museum."

Balthasar disappeared before Philipp had finished the sentence.

Lucille cursed. "Come on guys, we need to fix this. Preferably before Balthasar decides our time is up." She shot a dark look at Rachel, who returned it sullenly.

"You know," Ophelia piped up, "the way Samantha's been acting, I'd be more worried about Balthasar."

"Go!" Lucille shooed them all out of the room. To Matt she said, "The bathroom is over there."

Matt dragged himself to the bathroom, feeling exhausted. It didn't help that the toilet called out to him in a hollow, indecipherable language. Ignoring it, he began to wash his face.

When he looked up, Daniel was staring back at him from the mirror. Just like this morning.

"You don't think you're safe from me, do you?" Daniel asked, madness dancing in his eyes.

Matt knew he wasn't. The demon form gave him some protection, but he couldn't walk around like that forever. "Look, Daniel. We have bigger problems. Samantha needs our help."

"There is no us, Matt. Just me."

"Damn it, man!" Matt slammed his hand down on the sink, almost breaking it. "Can't you try and work with me here? You loved Samantha."

Daniel just scoffed at him. "You heard your brother. She's gone. That Selima woman owns her body now."

Matt refused to give up that easily. "We'll find a way." Balthasar had told them how. He fully believed Rachel would set things right.

"Right." Daniel grimaced. "And lucky for you, that means I'll be gone too."

He hadn't thought about it yet, but Daniel was right. Once Rachel had cast her spell, he'd be free.

"If I can't take Samantha with me," Daniel continued, "I'll have to kill you. I won't let the two of you be together after what you did to me."

"What about living and suffering?" Matt asked.

"Times change."

Matt swallowed. "You can't get to me while I'm in this form."

Daniel's lips curled upwards. "Is that so?"

Screaming, Matt went down. Daniel struggled for control, digging his fingers into his core, tearing and fighting without any regard for Matt's safety. Matt felt his wings being pulled back and pushed them out with enormous effort. As he lay writhing on the ground, he switched back and forth a few times.

And then it was over.

Daniel stood up and looked at himself, while Matt was the one trapped behind the mirror. "Time to end this unworthy existence once and for all."

Matt screamed and hit the mirror, but Daniel walked away, his grip on Matt's body merciless.

Rachel

While Rachel had rushed home to get the book, her candles, and the bowl, now she dreaded going back. If Samantha's and Jan's lives hadn't been hanging by a thread, she wouldn't even have bothered. She'd have locked herself in her room and let the town sink into chaos. What did she care?

"You don't look well," Hugo noticed. "Are you unwell?"

He was the only one who'd accompanied her. The only one who'd cared enough.

Rachel shook her head. "Just disappointed."

"About what?"

"It doesn't matter. I screwed up and got the receipts for it. Everything's fine." It shouldn't bother her that much. If it had been Lucille's spell that had gone wrong, Rachel wouldn't have had much sympathy either. She shouldn't have tried a spell she didn't know in her bedroom. It didn't matter that she didn't normally do spells, or that the book was a trivial piece of literature. She'd *wanted* it to work. Just not quite that well.

"I don't believe you." Hugo said, to her surprise. "I don't think you're being honest with me or yourself."

Rachel was so shocked that someone hadn't immediately backed off when she'd claimed everything was fine that she could only stare at him. Hugo was a man from a time that had been very unkind to women. His views were antiquated. And yet he paid her more attention than her friends had lately.

"Okay..." He'd be gone in a few hours, so what was the point of keeping her feelings to herself? "I'm angry that they're blaming me for this. Even though they're right. It's just that none of them ever thought to ask *why*. It's all about their own dramas. I'm just Rachel. I'm always fine."

Hugo frowned. "They *did* ask. You didn't answer."

Called out like that, her cheeks blushed. "Because they don't really want to know. And they wouldn't understand."

"What is there to understand?"

"That I feel like the third wheel in our group of friends."

"What's so special about being the third wheel?"

"It's useless." Rachel sighed. "It's just a figure of speech. Everyone's in a relationship. Lucille and Fabian broke up, only to couple up with someone else straight away. Don't ask me what's going on, because it makes no sense. Especially that Fabian would be interested in a cult member. From the cult that tried to *kill* me. But hey, it's just Rachel. Jan has his long-term relationship, which is fine. They're solid. And Matt and Samantha aren't in one, but they only have eyes for each other, even if they don't want to admit it. Especially Sam. That leaves me. Nobody wants me." Not even Fabian had ever wanted her. He'd only tried for her sake.

Hugo's frown deepened. "I think that is absolute hogwash."

"How do you know? You don't know them. Back then it was just Fabian, Samantha, my brother and me. Now... now Nico is dead, and the other two are always off doing their own thing. Samantha hangs out with Lucille all the time because they're both witches and I... I always feel like an afterthought." Her throat tightened and she swallowed heavily to avoid bursting into tears.

"Did you tell them that?"

Rachel shook her head. "It wouldn't do any good. I mean, I get it. They have a common interest and I have my dreams, which nobody understands. I just wish... I just wish I wasn't so alone all the time."

Hugo floated towards her. "You're not alone. I'm here for you."

Overwhelmed, Rachel fell into his embrace. A few tears fell, but she quickly gathered herself. "Thank you, Hugo. I appreciate it." She sighed, well aware that time was running out. "We really must go now.

I can't let Balthasar kill Sam and Jan. I wouldn't be able to live with myself if that happened."

He nodded seriously. "Agreed. Well then. Your quest awaits. Onwards."

She chuckled softly. "Onwards."

Balthasar

Balthasar had no trouble locating the town museum. He didn't quite understand why it displayed all these broken items, but he assumed it was some sort of temple. Thanks to the information boards everywhere, he quickly made his way to the room Sokaris would be headed to.

To his great relief, there was no sign of Jan or Samantha, just another young human with shaggy brown hair. He was marvelling at a long glass box, which held the Staff of Seth.

Balthasar stepped closer, fearing for a moment that the staff had already been stolen. He felt the magic before he saw the artefact. It was a long slender staff. Once coated in red gold, time had taken its toll, letting the dark wood underneath shine through. Egyptian symbols had been carved into the shaft. At the top was the undefinable animal head of the god Seth, his eyes made of red rubies.

"Pretty cool, right?" the human next to him said. Balthasar ignored him, but the boy just kept talking. "The old Egyptians knew their stuff." He laughed, then shuddered for some reason. "Hopefully, Seth isn't coming out of it."

Irritated, Balthasar looked at him. Did the boy know something he didn't?

"I'm just saying." The boy laughed nervously. "It's quite spooky today, right? Have you seen a ghost? I saw three. One of them followed me for five streets." He looked at the staff again. "So creepy. I'm Robert, and you?"

Before Balthasar could answer, he felt the pull of a summoning. One moment, he saw the Staff of Seth, the next, he was drawn to the outside, involuntarily jumping to the riverside.

Ready for anything, Balthasar landed in front of Samantha, who was leaning seductively against a wall. "Selima." He had to remember who truly looked at him from those green eyes.

"Who do we have here?" Selima drawled. "Malcolm's little boy. You look good."

Balthasar growled. "Can't say the same for you." While the human girl didn't even come close to Selima, the change in attitude had a disturbing effect. "Where's your little bed warmer?" Balthasar asked, trying to play it cool. The truth was that the Egyptian sorcerer hadn't been chosen by Selima for his qualities in bed.

"My trusty Sokaris brings me a gift."

The Staff of Seth. Balthasar tried to return to the museum, but an invisible web kept him locked in place. Selima was powerful, but she was no witch, which meant... this spell had been woven using Samantha's potential. Balthasar tested the web subtly and found not a single weakness. A scary thought.

He was caught in here with Selima and the only way out was by killing the witch. Chay would be *so* mad with him.

Selima pushed herself off the wall and walked over. "Not so hasty, my dear. You and I have unfinished business, don't we?"

How long would he be able to hold out against a witch of Samantha's calibre when led by someone with Selima's ruthlessness? Would it be long enough for her little friends to come through? Or would he have to kill one of the six and ruin Chay's plans for the future? It galled him that he was even giving the matter so much thought.

"What's wrong, dear?" Selima cocked her head. "You didn't hesitate last time."

"It's not time yet." Perhaps he could stall her by other means.

"Time?" Selima laughed abruptly. "Don't tell me, you promised those human brats you'd hold back." She clapped. "How charming. I always thought you were ruthless. Well, I hope you don't expect me to waste my time waiting like you."

Her words were followed by a jolt of energy.

Balthasar managed to dodge the fatal shot quite easily. "You've gotten slow. The Council of Seven will have a good laugh when you challenge them."

"You're as arrogant as your mother." Selima's eyes blazed. "No, your father. He thought he could betray me, seize power for himself. How did that work out for him?" she asked.

"I didn't maintain a relationship with Malcolm. He bored me." Malcolm had never given him the time of day and so neither had Balthasar. He'd had all the power he'd wanted through his mother's hand.

Selima laughed again. "Oh dear, you're so adorable. It's a shame you're such a mama's boy." Suddenly, she was right in front of him, running a finger up his chest. "I would respect you more if it had been you, but to pull a coup like this just to put your dear old mummy on the throne." She clicked her tongue.

Balthasar remembered it as if it was yesterday. Once he'd finally escaped the City of Youth, he'd plotted against Selima. It hadn't been revenge—not necessarily—more like there had been an opening. Selima had the Seven quivering in their seats. She'd controlled the Black Guard and the Army of Death. And she had Sokaris. She was invincible, in reach of her goals. And at a point in her plan where someone as insignificant as Balthasar couldn't possibly have posed a threat.

He'd waited for her in front of her residence, knowing exactly how to present himself to catch the archdemon's eye.

She'd stopped and run her gaze up and down his body. "Who are you and what do you want from me?"

Balthasar had returned the favour and regarded Selima as if he was already undressing her. "Everything."

Selima had laughed. "Humility is not your strength, is it?"

"You told me to come back when I'm grown up." Balthasar had spread his arms. "Well, here I am." It had been the key piece of his plan, the one Selima herself had handed him herself.

"You're Malcolm's boy!" she'd said with delight. "Has your father finally come to his senses? Will Greed swear fealty?"

Balthasar had snorted. "I don't care about my father. I'm here for my own sake."

Selima had liked what she heard. "How exciting. Are you staying the night?"

A sly smile had crept across Balthasar's face. "I thought you'd never ask."

She'd led Balthasar into her residence, past the scantily clad guards, to a wondrous bedroom. Artefacts, mostly of Egyptian origin, had decorated the room. The centrepiece had been a huge golden bed with red curtains.

Selima had pushed Balthasar onto it and straddled him before kissing his neck. She'd begun to open his shirt, her tongue following her fingers as Balthasar had unfastened the front of her sheer robe. She'd pushed him down again and kissed him, one hand tangled in his hair. When her dress fell to her hips, she'd sat up again and placed his hands on her breasts.

Balthasar's fingers hadn't stayed there for long, moving deeper instead. They'd barely left her when the tip of a dagger had appeared between her breasts. Selima's eyes had widened just before death claimed them. Behind her, Melaney had pulled out the dagger and pushed the blond woman aside.

"Why did that take so long?" Balthasar had asked. He'd spent far more time with Selima than he'd planned to.

Melaney had shrugged. "I enjoyed the view."

He'd snorted. "Very well." A wicked smile had slipped onto his lips. "We did it. All this is ours now."

"So is the Lust." Melaney had locked eyes with him, her eyes burning with the newly awakened fever...

"You know," Selima's voice called Balthasar back to the present. "What I don't understand is how you got her in there? You can't just walk into a residence or jump in. My guards would've caught her."

"A summoning rune," Balthasar said. Sometimes the simplest plans were the most effective. "I dropped it on the threshold while you were busy seducing me. It took me months and a small fortune to fashion, but it got you right where I wanted you."

"You see, such a clever little boy, and yet you let her take the prize."

Balthasar snorted. "I intend to take what is mine soon." As soon as there'd be an opening, Balthasar would end Melaney's charade.

"Too late. You had your chance." Selima took a sudden step back and dropped another web. One Balthasar hadn't seen coming.

Screaming as if his skin was on fire, Balthasar dropped to his knees and writhed on the floor. Selima stepped on his face, already weaving another terrible spell.

"You know, the little witch may not be much to look at, but boy, does she have a lot of potential."

He'd thought the web blocking his space jumping was already intricate. It was nothing against the next spell. Balthasar's skin burst in over a hundred places. Pain engulfed him, so terrible he couldn't even think.

The only thing he knew was this: it had never been about him holding back for as long as he could. All he could do was survive long enough. And with Samantha's true potential unfolding, Balthasar doubted he had it in him.

Fabian

Fabian and Ophelia had little trouble retrieving an obsidian from Jan's room, although Anne had been very surprised to see them and uncharacteristically brusque as she led them to his room. While the rest of Greenvalley descended into chaos, Jan's room looked immaculate, as if he hadn't set foot in it for days.

His crystal collection had been stowed away, but thanks to Ophelia and her experience with rituals, they quickly identified the obsidian and were back at Lucille's villa with a good hour to spare. Rachel was already back, flipping through a book, while Lucille and Philipp searched through a pile of diaries. Lucille's little brother was gone.

"Where did Pascal go?"

"I sent him to the park with Albert. It's getting creepier and creepier in here." As if on cue, the walls began to moan. Then she looked at Fabian. "You're still running with them?"

The elemental spirits followed him wherever he went. At Lucille's comment, a few flew towards her and tried to set her hair on fire. "Bad girl. Doesn't like us."

"Hey!" Fabian shouted. "Leave Lucille alone! She's my... friend." He'd almost said girlfriend. "Please just go. I don't have time to play with you." If they didn't find a solution quickly, two of his best friends would die.

His words only served to send the spirits into a frenzy. Some flew around his head until he was dizzy, a storm arose to his left, and rain fell from the ceiling. The earth rolled a few times beneath his feet.

"Hugo," Rachel said, clutching her book. "Can't you do something about them?"

"I can certainly try, milady." The ghost floated towards Fabian, then past him. "I'll play with you."

To Fabian's surprise, the elemental spirits followed him curiously. Hugo lured them into a corner where he just stood there, letting them play with him and the objects nearby.

Lucille winced when an old-fashioned globe flew into the air. "I can't watch."

"I've got it!" Rachel suddenly shouted.

Immediately the others crowded around her. Fabian felt his heart beat faster as hope filled him.

"The stone must be placed in the centre of a chalk pentagram," Rachel quickly summarised. "Ideally in the heart of the affected area. There needs to be a white candle in each corner, and here's the spell. Oh... and we need a ghost to lead the procession. Someone who will willingly enter the stone, like a lure".

Fabian handed Rachel the obsidian. "Here you go."

"What about Hugo?" Lucille asked. "He seems quite reasonable."

"I would be honoured to be of assistance," Hugo said, without missing a beat as the elemental spirits blew through his body, freezing his hair into ridiculous shapes.

Rachel closed the book. "No! Hugo stays."

Fabian stared at her in shock.

Lucille widened her eyes. "Rachel, we need a ghost. You just said it." Her voice trembled. "I don't think I can convince Lady Macbeth to put her murder attempt on hold for this."

"There must be another ghost in Greenvalley who'll do it," Rachel insisted.

"We're running out of time," Fabian shouted. "Balthasar will kill Sam and Jan, and if not him, then that Selima woman will. Hugo already agreed to it!"

"He's just being nice. He doesn't want to go."

"But he has to," Ophelia pointed out quietly. "He doesn't belong here."

Suddenly, Rachel's eyes narrowed. "You're the one who doesn't belong here."

Stunned, Ophelia pressed her lips together and gave Fabian a troubled look. It broke his heart.

He angrily told Rachel, "Hey, leave Lia out of this. She's got nothing to do with this mess."

Rachel's eyes glistened, but she looked as feral as he'd ever seen her. "Yeah, I know it's my fault. Thanks for rubbing it in."

Lucille raised her hands in a reassuring gesture. "But we're going to fix it together," she said calmly. "With Hugo's help."

Instead of coming to her senses, Rachel crossed her arms and shook her head. "No. I summoned Hugo. He's staying."

"Are you really going to put a ghost above the lives of your friends?" Fabian asked, horrified.

"Oh, and what great friends you are."

Nothing she said made any sense. "What are you talking about?"

"Nothing," Rachel said stubbornly.

Next to him, Lucille groaned in exasperation. "We don't have time for this."

"You *never* have time for me," Rachel suddenly shouted.

Everyone fell silent, including the elemental spirits and the house.

Rachel rubbed her eyes quickly and swallowed. "Hugo is mine. He... he's a good listener and he cares about me. He's on my side for once."

"Of course I am. Now and forever," Hugo said gently.

"When he leaves, I'll be all alone again."

Fabian didn't know what to say. He still agreed with Lucille that they didn't have time for this. Any other day, yes, but not now.

Lucille, on the other hand, cautiously reached out to place her hand on Rachel's knee. "Rachel, we're on your side, too. I'm sorry if I ever gave you the impression that you weren't important to me. You are. Look, when this is over, we'll do more things together."

"You mean you'll all bring your partners so I can sit in the corner and look stupid?"

Lucille shook her head. "No, just the six of us. Or just us girls."

"Two of whom might soon be too dead to do that," Fabian muttered, earning himself an elbow between the ribs, courtesy of Lucille.

"I'm afraid we don't have a choice," Hugo added quietly.

Rachel closed her eyes, and a few tears ran down her cheeks. Suddenly, all Fabian wanted to do was hold her. The moment he thought about it, he got over himself and just did it. "I'm sorry, Rachel."

Hugo spoke again, "You said it yourself: you can't risk your friends' lives. Believe me when I tell you this life is short enough as it is."

Rachel opened her eyes and gently pulled herself out of Fabian's embrace. "It's not fair," she said, wrinkling her nose. "But you're right. We don't have time to find another solution."

Relieved, Fabian sat down again. "Thank you."

"Now we just need to find a central location." Lucille immediately switched back into problem-solving mode.

"We could do it at the town hall. I mean, the whole town is infested," Rachel suggested.

Fabian glanced at the elemental spirits and lowered his voice. "What about them? Will they follow, too? They're not like the others, are they?"

"I think the surplus of spiritual energy has drawn them here. Once we banish all the ghosts, they'll probably leave."

"Let's do it right away," Ophelia said, jumping to her feet.

But when they turned towards the door, they found it blocked by a wall of elemental spirits. Meanwhile, Hugo hovered frozen in the air. "Good spirits. Bad spirits. We not want in dumb stone! Won't let you out."

"Hugo!" Rachel cried out. She ran towards him but the spirits suddenly grabbed her and lifted her into the air. Terrified, she flailed her arms around.

"Hey!" Fabian shouted. Some of the spirits stopped and formed a grim face. "There's no need to get upset. Nobody's trying to imprison you in a stone." The face turned into an arrow pointing at Rachel. "Put her down! Listen, she can't do this to you. You're far too strong and too clever to be lured into a dumb stone."

The elemental spirits paused. "Promise."

Fabian held up three fingers. "Scout's honour."

They dropped Rachel and cleared the door, but when Lucille opened it, she found only a brick wall. Terrified, she let out a scream.

"What's happening?" Ophelia asked, clinging to Fabian's arm.

Suddenly, the house moaned and groaned. The temperature dropped to freezing and the door slammed shut again. A series of clicks went through the house. Locks.

"I think there's someone else who's not happy about going into a stone," Fabian whispered.

Lucille turned around, eyes wide. Her voice was shaking. "You're not going to promise the house ghosts can stay, too, are you?"

An eerie howl rose.

"By the way," asked Philipp, who'd been quiet the whole time, "where did Matt go?"

"We could call him!" Fabian said, enthused. "He can jump us out—"

The coat hanger suddenly sprang into action and ripped Ophelia from his arm, its iron wrapping around her chest and neck as if threatening to kill her if they didn't do as it said.

Fabian ran to her and tried to pry the iron from her body, but it wouldn't bend, no matter how hard he pulled.

"Let's do it here." Lucille's voice cracked. "Right now."

"We can't," Rachel said. "It has to be central, otherwise only some of the ghosts will be drawn in."

"But the ghosts here would be," Philipp pointed out. "We'd just have to do it twice."

"It wouldn't work!" Rachel insisted. "The obsidian would be sealed. We only have one chance."

Under Fabian's fingers, the iron moved in the wrong direction and Ophelia gasped for air. "We won't have a chance if we can't get out of here alive!"

A few elemental spirits came to help. The others found it funny how the wall kept shaking and used it to get a free massage.

"There might be a way," Hugo said quietly to Rachel. He looked at the fireplace.

Rachel understood immediately. "Lucille, distract the house!"

"Distract the house?" Lucille repeated, probably stunned to hear those words in combination. "Sure." She stared at the wall. "This is just an illusion. It's not real."

Fabian kept trying to free Ophelia from the coat hanger, glancing over his shoulder frequently to see Rachel and Hugo climbing into the fireplace. The ghost wrapped his arms around her and began to float her up.

The house didn't like it at all, and the fireplace came to life, bursting into flames.

Fabian let go of Ophelia and turned his water on the fireplace. The flames went out, but the safety bars slammed down, sealing off the exit for everyone else.

"We're screwed."

Rachel

When Rachel and Hugo arrived at the market square in front of the town hall, she was completely out of breath. The ghost was fine, but Rachel needed a moment.

The outside world wasn't much better than Lucille's house. Three ghostly children were playing catch with oranges from a fruit stall, while a ghostly dog chased visitors, and a woman in grey went on and on about her suffering. Rachel pushed past her and knelt on the ground.

"Hand me the chalk, please." They'd stopped by her house to pick up the candles and chalk before coming here.

Hugo passed her the chalk and Rachel began drawing a pentagram on the ground. People gave her a wide berth, which aided her incidentally. She took the obsidian pyramid from Jan's collection and carefully placed it in the middle. Meanwhile, Hugo placed the candles in the corners for her to light.

"It's time to say goodbye," he said gently. "It has been a pleasure to know you, Rachel. I sincerely hope you find someone who will make you less lonely. Or that your friends will treat you better."

The tears were back, much to Rachel's annoyance. "I don't want you to go." She looked at the grey woman, thinking she was the perfect bait. If only they could convince her.

"It has to be done. Your friends' lives are too precious."

"What about yours?"

Hugo smiled sadly. "Taken from me a long time ago. I know my place, Rachel. It's time to part."

She stood and threw herself into his arms. Hugo held her just as tightly. "I'll miss you."

"I'll miss you more."

Rachel took a deep breath. Hugo was right, this had to be done. She shouldn't have summoned the ghosts in the first place. She had friends. Friends who depended on her.

A little calmer, Rachel sat down cross-legged and opened her book. She cut her thumb and let a drop of blood fall onto the obsidian. Despite its hardened appearance, the stone absorbed the blood like a sponge. "Spirits of the day, spirits of the night, hear my call, come to my side." The second drop fell, and the pyramid began to vibrate. "Come as quickly as you can, follow my voice and my plan. Taste my blood and my fears, follow the trail of my tears." A blue light shot from the top, high into the sky, before widening.

Hugo was hit by it and gasped. Moments later, all Greenvalley seemed to converge. Ghosts, blue in the light, were drawn into Hugo until he glowed.

Rachel watched in fascination. Then she remembered she wasn't done yet. "Get out of this world, get out of here fast. You're no longer welcome, not meant to last."

As the last word fell, Hugo stepped into the centre of the blue ray. "Goodbye, Miss Rachel."

Tears streamed down her face, but she repeated the formula. Hugo disappeared. The beam of light collapsed, leaving only the small black pyramid. Her friend was gone.

Rachel burst into tears.

The town quietened. People paused as the apparitions vanished. Abandoned objects clattered to the ground and the noise level dropped considerably. There were no more ghosts. No more Hugo.

She was all alone again.

Lucille

The house was going wild. Earthquake after earthquake shook the walls, ghostly voices howled, and the temperature dropped lower and lower. Philipp had wrapped his coat around Lucille, but she was still hugging herself it was so cold.

"Come on, Rachel," she whispered.

Behind her, Fabian finally managed to free Ophelia from the hanger with the help of his elemental friends. Shaking, she collapsed into his arms. "Any luck with the wall yet?" he shouted at Lucille over the rising wind.

"There's nothing I can do!" She'd already tried throwing her black magic arrow at it, but the house had just swallowed it.

"Good spirits, bad spirits. Want to play?" sang the elemental spirits. They were the only ones having fun here.

Fabian groaned. Then he began to plead. "Listen, please. If you don't help us, we're all going to die here, and then no one will play with you."

Immediately, the spirits formed a battering ram and smashed through the wall. It seemed like spectral energy was the only thing that worked against their possessed house.

Lucille grabbed Philipp's hand and ran through the wreckage before the house could rebuild its barrier. The others followed.

As they ran down the corridor, the wind picked up, throwing small statues and potted plants at them. A piece of paper hit her face, sticking so hard it almost suffocated her.

Lucille stopped and ripped it from her face. She was about to throw it behind her when she noticed the signature. *Matt.*

Alarmed, she began to read while Philipp dragged her into the foyer. There, the elemental spirits blew open the door, using the wind around them.

"Hurry!" Fabian shouted, already at the door.

"NO!" Lucille came to a halt. "We can't leave."

Ophelia stared at her, eyes wide. Bruises covered her neck. "Why the heck not?"

A new fear had gripped Lucille's heart as she tore her eyes from the letter. "It's Matt. He's trying to take his own life."

Fabian let the door fall shut again. "What?"

Lucille spun on her heels and ran back into the house, trying every door in front of her. They were all locked. Panicking, she turned to the others. "I don't know where he is."

"Melchior!" Fabian yelled. "Melchior, come here."

"Blood. We need blood." For a moment, Lucille had almost forgotten how to get blood from her body. Then she remembered something else. "I know where he is!"

She led the group to her room and threw the door open. There in front of them was Matt, standing on a chair with a rope around his neck. "Matt, don't!" Lucille cried.

He just grinned at her and kicked the chair out from under him. Lucille screamed as Philipp surged forward and got his shoulders under Matt, holding him up. There was a brief struggle, then a blue light left Matt's chest. Almost instantly, he grabbed the rope with one hand and shot energy at it.

Both he and Philipp collapsed to the floor. At the same time, the locks in the house clicked open, the wind died down, and the temperature rose again.

"What the hell, Matt?" Fabian ran over to Matt and helped him remove the rope. Matt rolled onto his back and took deep, frantic breaths. Lucille sank to her knees, sobbing uncontrollably.

Matt croaked, "Daniel. It was Daniel."

Lucille looked up. "Daniel wrote the letter?"

Philipp came over and hugged her. "It was just a ghost. It's gone. It's all over."

"Philipp's right," Ophelia said, hugging herself. "Rachel must have come through. The house doesn't feel hostile anymore."

As all the tension fell from her shoulders, Lucille only cried more. Fabian collapsed into a chair and rubbed his face. Meanwhile, Matt's breathing had calmed, but he'd put his arm over his eyes and remained lying on his back.

An hour later they were all settled in the kitchen with a big pot of tea and biscuits. When Rachel joined them, looking completely devastated, Lucille pulled her into a big hug. "I'm so sorry, Rachel."

"It's okay," she said dejectedly.

"No, no, it's not."

Rachel took a deep breath. "I got what I deserved."

"Nobody deserves that. Here, have a cup of tea."

Not long after that, Jan arrived with his hands raised in defence. "Guys, this is the last time I go to the museum. Even if it's just so I never have to come across security again." He shook his head. "They didn't want to believe me that I had nothing to do with the broken display. I don't even know how I got there."

Without words, Lucille hugged him as well. "I'm so glad you're back."

"Was it one of your spells again, Lu?"

Lucille shook her head, close to tears once more. Between sobs she quickly told him what had happened. As it turned out, unlike Daniel, Jan didn't remember anything. Sokaris had completely overpowered him.

With a sigh, Jan patted her back. "Now, now, Lu, let's not make your boyfriend jealous."

She let go of him and grimaced. "I heard you made your girlfriend jealous."

Jan pulled a face. "Oh yeah, I kissed Sam, didn't I? Great, that'll be fun to explain. Do you think she'll believe me when I tell her I was possessed by an Egyptian magician?"

Fabian started to giggle. "That's worse than 'the dog ate my homework'."

Lucille found herself giggling, too. And slowly she felt the tension ease from her shoulders. It had been an intense day. There would be a lot to discuss, but for now, making terrible jokes was more than enough.

Jan had hardly sat down, digging into the biscuits as if he'd been starving, when Balthasar appeared with Samantha in tow. Matt stood up immediately, on full alert. By the looks of it, Samantha was fine, while Balthasar looked as if he'd been put through the wringer.

"There she is, unharmed and back in control of her body." Balthasar rubbed his neck. "I almost killed her by accident, though."

"Of course you did," Matt said, casually putting himself between his brother and Samantha.

"Well," Samantha said quietly. "Apparently, *I* almost killed him on purpose. Or rather Selima did." She shook her head. "I'm still trying to wrap my head around it?"

"You don't remember anything?" Matt asked, swallowing.

"Very, very little. She... she was just too horrible... and powerful." Samantha shuddered.

Balthasar narrowed his eyes as if to argue but turned to Rachel instead. "The obsidian," he demanded.

Wordlessly, Rachel handed over the pyramid.

"Is that mine?" Jan asked.

Balthasar closed his hands around it. "No. It's mine. I'll make sure Selima never comes back."

"I'm sorry," Rachel whispered, looking as if she was going to fall apart at any moment.

The demon just snorted. He turned to Matt and Samantha, regarding the latter thoughtfully. "Remind me to never cross you." Then he disappeared.

"What was that about?" Lucille asked.

"Apparently, this Selima used my magic to torture him." Samantha shuddered. "I don't even want to know." She looked so tired.

Fabian got up and wrapped her in his arms. "It's over now. Selima's gone."

Rachel hunched her shoulders, her lips pressed together before she spoke. "If you don't mind, I'll go home now. I'm really sorry about what happened, especially to you guys." She looked at Jan, Samantha, and Matt. "I promise it won't happen again. I'll burn the book or something."

"It's alright," Lucille told her sympathetically. "We've all made a mess before. You didn't mean for it to happen."

There wasn't even a smile in response.

"Don't you want to stay, hang out a little?" Fabian asked.

Rachel shook her head. "Not today. I need to be alone for a while. But another time, yes."

She waved to the group and opened the door.

"Miss Rachel."

Rachel took a step back. In the door was Hugo, though he'd changed a lot since Lucille had last seen him. Where he'd looked perfectly normal before—apart from the floating thing—he was now as transparent as frosted glass. When Rachel leapt into his arms, she passed right through him.

Slightly embarrassed and shaking, Rachel stepped back. "How?"

It was a question Lucille wanted to know too. The obsidian was supposed to be sealed. If Hugo had escaped the stone, someone else might as well.

But Hugo smiled gently. "I told you your call was very strong. You needed a friend, so here I am."

Even though there was nothing to hold on to, Rachel hugged him again.

Lucille turned to Philipp, who offered her his hand. She squeezed it and snuggled back into his embrace. If Rachel was happy with her ghost friend, she wouldn't judge her.

Fabian

After they'd finally escaped Lucille's haunted house and all was well again, Fabian walked Ophelia home. The social workers had set her up in a group home with some other teenagers who'd fallen on hard times. It gave her just enough freedom and a social worker to turn to if she needed anything. But it didn't make up for a home or friends

"I'd promise you Greenvalley is not always this dangerous... Unfortunately, it is." Fabian said.

"I had fun," Ophelia said, chipper.

He turned to her in surprise. "Fun?" His eyes fell on her neck. After Jan's healing there was only a faint trace of the bruises she'd received from the coat hanger. The last thing they needed were intrusive questions from her social worker. "You call this fun?"

"Eyes up here." Ophelia pointed with a finger, grinning slightly.

Fabian immediately blushed. "I wasn't..." His eyes hadn't dropped any lower than her collarbone.

Ophelia laughed. "You're so cute."

"Cute?"

"The way you blush, the way you get flustered so easily. It's adorable." Shyly she lowered her eyes.

Fabian didn't know what to say. "Um... thanks."

When she looked up again, she was more serious. "You're not going to abandon me now, are you?"

"Abandon you?" Fabian repeated, appalled. "Why would I do that?"

She shrugged dejectedly. "Oh, you know, you've done your duty. More than that. You brought me to a safe place, helped me settle in.

You're done. I'm nothing to you. We barely know each other, and you've got your friends." She took a deep breath. "I'm fine now. So don't feel obliged to stay."

It was a lot to swallow. While she was telling him she was fine, every look and every drop of her voice was saying the opposite.

"What if I want to hang out with you?"

Ophelia looked surprised. "Do you?"

"Only if you want me to, of course. I'm just... Lia, you're not a burden. I haven't just done my duty. I genuinely want you to be safe and... and happy." Fabian was surprised, too, but he really *did* care about her. "You've been through a lot, and I understand that there will be a lot to learn and unlearn, but you don't have to do it alone. I could be there."

"Do you really want to be there?" she asked cautiously. "Like I said, you don't have to. You—"

He stopped her there, taking her hands in his and looking deep into her eyes. "I want to."

"Why?" she whispered.

It was such a loaded question, as if it was impossible for her to understand why anyone would want to be around her.

"Because I like you." It was the easiest answer.

"But why?" Ophelia lowered her voice. "I tried to kill you."

Fabian couldn't quite understand why it didn't bother him as much as it should. He tried to put his feelings into words. "Maybe I'm naïve, but I don't think you ever *wanted* to kill me. You did it because it was expected of you. You wanted to impress your brother and your goddess." He rubbed his thumbs over the back of her hands. "I'm glad you didn't. Not just because I got to keep my life, but because there's no going back after that. You'd be a completely different person."

She laughed nervously. "You don't know me. I might be exactly that person."

"I don't believe that."

A sigh escaped her lips. Cautiously, as if unsure if she should, Ophelia leant in and put her cheek against his chest. Fabian made sure she didn't have to second-guess herself by putting his arms around her.

"Your heart's beating pretty fast," she said after a while.

"Is it?" Now that she'd said it, he noticed it too. If anything, his heart was beating faster by the second.

Ophelia tilted her head back and smiled up at him. "You know, I like you, too."

"Do you?" Fabian barely resisted the instinct to lick his lips.

"Like I said, you're cute." She chuckled nervously. "But you're so much more. You're brave."

"Brave? Me?" he laughed. "See, you don't know me, either. Ask my friends—they'll tell you I'm scared of everything."

Ophelia shrugged slightly. "Maybe so, but you don't let that stop you. It's easy to be brave when there's nothing to be afraid of. You may be scared, but you still show up. You still risk your life to help other people, like me. And you don't run away. Ever."

He swallowed hard. It had never occurred to him that he might not be as much of a coward as he thought. The monsters still frightened him and he would much prefer a quiet life without the constant drama. He didn't think it was *fun*. But running away wasn't an option. Not when his friends' lives were at stake. Or anyone else's. He'd been given powers to defend what he loved, and he'd be a true coward if he didn't use them.

"You're also kind," Ophelia continued. "And frankly, you're a good person. Admittedly, I don't have much to compare you to."

"So, what you're saying is that the bar is pretty low?" Fabian joked.

"I suppose it is. But still, I think most people would've just handed me over to social services and felt their job was done. Which it was," she added hastily. "I didn't expect any more." Her face softened again. "But you've given me so much more. You made sure I got settled. You checked in on me at school. And you let me hang out with you today."

Fabian snorted. "And as a result, you got trapped in a haunted house."

Ophelia grabbed his jacket and pulled him close. "There's no one I'd rather be trapped in a haunted house with."

"I can also offer running from demons, being sucked into Hell, and being turned into monsters, if you're into that sort of thing."

She laughed again, then shyly put her hand around his neck. "I *am* into that. A lot, actually." She bit her lip nervously.

Fabian swallowed unintentionally as his gaze fell on her red lips. "I don't want to take advantage of you," he whispered, reminding her of what she'd just escaped.

Ophelia frowned. "I'm not some sad, vulnerable thing. I can take care of myself if I need to. Remember, I can speak to snakes and command the shadows. I can hold my own."

He laid his forehead on hers. "I know you can."

"Good. Because that's how I need you to see me. Strong, independent, not someone who needs saving. Can you do that?"

He thought for a moment. Reason told him she'd been through hell, she needed time to heal. But then he remembered her sitting among the snakes like a queen, comfortable, at ease, and he knew she was far stronger than he'd given her credit for. "Yes," he whispered.

Instead of answering, Ophelia pulled him closer and pressed her lips to his. Her arms wrapped around his neck as he tightened his own grip. There was nothing shy about this kiss, no cautious testing. She *wanted* this, and all doubts were swept from his mind as he felt the supple softness of her lips and the warmth of her breath.

Maybe it was wrong, or not the right time, but if so, it was all the right kinds of wrong.

Samantha

Balthasar had informed her of what had happened. It had been quite the shock to suddenly find herself holding a web in her hands as cruel as it was intricate. Disgusted with the evil intention, she'd dropped it, only for Balthasar to wrangle her down. She'd thought she'd drawn her last breath, when he'd stopped himself and took a deep breath instead.

When he'd told her about Selima, Samantha hadn't known how to react. The thought of someone else driving her body, of doing things to it and *with* it without her consent made her feel sick. She only vaguely remembered when Selima had first entered her. Before she'd even realised what had happened, Selima had already kissed Jan.

What a giant mess. Meg would be so mad. Samantha would have to talk to Jan and find out who else she might have accidentally offended—or kissed. But what really made her stomach churn was the haunted look in Matt's eyes. He didn't say a word to her during the dinner, but he never stopped watching her either.

From Lucille, Samantha learnt that Daniel had possessed him. Only Daniel's ghost hadn't been able to drown Matt's soul completely. Instead, he'd tormented him. And while a small part of her thought he deserved it, she couldn't ignore how messed up it was.

"Can I walk you home?" Matt asked softly as they left Lucille's. *Walk* not jump. He obviously wanted to clear the air.

Samantha nodded. "Sure."

"How are you feeling?" he asked quietly as they walked down the driveway.

"Exhausted?" she guessed, still unsure of what to make of all this. "Disgusted with myself?"

His eyes widened. "Disgusted? Sam, nothing Selima did was you."

"It was still my body."

Matt bit his lip. "You don't remember, though? Do you?"

Samantha swallowed. She tried to remember then, but Selima's overpowering depravity made her shirk away. "Not really, no. Was..." Her lip quivered. "Was it really Daniel?"

"Balthasar said ghosts were just an image, one facet, not the whole person. In Daniel's case, it was... I shouldn't speak ill of him, because it's my fault he's that way, but he was consumed by hate."

Samantha swallowed again. "Can you blame him?" Her voice nearly broke.

"That's what I'm saying. I can't, but Sam... he wanted to kill you." His brown puppy eyes were full of despair.

Shocked, Samantha gasped. "What?" That didn't make any sense. Why would Daniel want to kill her? She hadn't done anything to him.

Matt gave her a one-sided shrug. "He wanted me to suffer so you could be together."

"As ghosts?" Samantha asked, horrified. *What* had happened? Clearly, she'd met Matt while Selima had been possessing her. "Matt, what did I miss? Please, you've got to tell me."

When Matt reluctantly told her of their encounter, Samantha groaned. She'd not only almost killed Balthasar, but Matt too. And she'd *kissed* him. Samantha shook her head. No, she refused to accept it.

"I'm sorry," Matt said, as if he was the one to blame for this.

"Don't... It wasn't us. Selima tried to kill you. And Daniel..." She swallowed heavily. "Daniel tried to kill me. And they kissed. Not us, right?"

Matt raised his eyebrows. "Technically."

"Good. Because I don't want our first kiss to be like—" What was she saying about their *first kiss* there? Panicked, she turned to him. "I mean, I don't even remember it and you, you know, just..."

She stopped when she saw Matt grinning. "Agreed. I wouldn't want our first kiss to be like that either."

"I didn't say I *wanted* a first kiss," Samantha said hastily. Her cheeks were burning now. Why couldn't she just shut up?

Innocently, Matt nodded. "I know."

"Stop it."

"Stop what?" He couldn't help laughing.

"Nothing, I... Let's just go home, okay?" She began to walk faster, leaving him to catch up.

By the time he did, his amusement was gone. "I'm really sorry."

"Not your fault," Samantha repeated.

"I know, but even though Rachel was behind it, you keep getting pulled into demon drama. That's my fault."

Samantha turned to him, shaking her head in disbelief. "I doubt this had anything to do with you or your family."

"Balthasar was the one who killed Selima initially. If that hadn't happened..."

"You mean a thing that happened nearly a thousand years ago?"

Matt shrugged helplessly. "Yeah?"

"Oh, Matt. It's not just you." Samantha chuckled softly. "You're not responsible for your brother's actions. Frankly, I think the fact that we're the Six has much more to do with all these monsters and demons than your brother disposing of a madwoman a millennium ago."

Slowly, Matt began to grin. "You're probably right."

"I often am."

A twinkle appeared in Matt's eyes. "You are. And you're one powerful witch. Did you hear Balthasar? He's afraid of you."

Samantha groaned. "I don't believe it."

"He doesn't want to face you ever again."

Suddenly the scene she'd awakened to came rushing back to her. Balthasar's skin had been split all across his body. And his body had been suspended in the air, twisted beyond repair—while she'd held the strings to his torment.

Samantha stopped and looked at her trembling hands. "I have this power within me." Just the thought of what she was capable of made her head spin. She couldn't even blame Selima. The first web she'd ever perfected had been a web of death.

Tears fell on her hand.

And then Matt was there. He took her hands in his and kissed them, searching her eyes until she held his gaze. "You have the power, yes, but you're in control of it. You don't have to use those kinds of weaves. You can make your own. Beautiful, life-giving, protective weaves. We're all capable of darkness. You know I've fallen deep into it, but you're stronger than I am. And I know in my dark little heart that you'll use those powers for good. Because you're one of the good ones." He smiled. "One of the very best."

Samantha blinked. Matt's speech had touched her more deeply than she'd ever thought possible. He'd understood her worries and turned them into hope. But she didn't know how to deal with it. Everything still felt so raw.

Matt blew another kiss on her hands and let them go. "Daniel was wrong to try and kill you. You still have too much to give. You belong in this world, not the next."

A weight lifted from her shoulders, and she was left feeling a little exhilarated. Matt believed in her. Perhaps she should believe in herself, too. "Thanks." After a moment she teased him gently, "I didn't know you had it in you to be emphatic."

He laughed softly, a wonderful sound like the pitter-patter of a summer rain. "I had a good teacher."

They spent the rest of the way home stealing glances at each other, unable or unwilling to say anything else.

Jan

After the others told him what had happened, Jan hurried to the Kollmer house. There, he rubbed his face about five times before he finally found the courage to press the doorbell. While he knew that he and Samantha had absolutely no choice in what Sokaris and Selima had done while possessing their bodies, Jan had enough imagination. He also knew Meg wouldn't understand. She'd always skirted around magic, never quite acknowledging more than his healing powers.

Meg opened the door, but when she saw who it was, she tried to close it again. Jan jerked his hand out, feeling the impact of the door in his wrist. "Ouch."

"You've got some nerve," Meg hissed at him.

"We need to talk."

"I have nothing to say to you."

Jan winced. "But I've got plenty. It wasn't what you thought." What a terrible turn of phrase. In a way, it had been exactly what it looked like. God, just the thought that he'd kissed Samantha disgusted him. She was a friend, nothing more.

"It was my *sister!*" Meg hurled at him.

"See, that's the thing. It wasn't."

She frowned. "So you made out with another black-haired girl on our doorstep?"

"No. Meg!" She shut the door on him again. "I was possessed."

"Goodnight, Jan."

"You know today was crazy, right? There were ghosts everywhere."

She narrowed her eyes. "I wouldn't know. I cried my eyes out all day."

"I'm sorry." Damn it! He'd never meant to hurt her. He'd never even thought about other women. "I really am, but I'm here to explain, because that wasn't me, and it wasn't your sister."

Meg groaned and crossed her arms. "Alright, spill. What was going on in your head?"

"Rachel opened some kind of portal that let all kinds of ghosts into Greenvalley. Samantha and I were possessed. So was Matt, by the way, and probably a lot of other people." Jan sped up to get the whole story out before Meg decided she'd had enough. "Apparently, I was pushed out of my own body by an Egyptian egomaniac. He wanted to take over the world or some shit. Your sister was possessed by a demon, his lover. *They* were making out. Not us."

Meg dropped her arms and rubbed the bridge of her nose. A chuckle escaped her lips, then another. "Sorry, but that's your excuse? Possessed by an evil mage?"

"Meg, it's true. Ask your sister. Ask Rachel or Lucille—or the security at the town museum. Apparently, I tried to steal some old stick!" He'd regained his consciousness standing in a pile of glass shards with the alarm blaring. "Can you imagine?"

Instead of coming to her senses, Meg made a face. "Are you on drugs again?"

"No!" Jan forced a deep breath. He could hardly blame her. His story sounded wild even to his ears. "Meg, it was magic. Magic is real and so are monsters and ghosts. Come on, you know that. Your sister is a witch."

"You mean she pretends to be a witch."

Jan shook his head. "Meg, I love you. I would never deliberately do anything to hurt you. It wasn't me." If she still didn't believe him, he had no idea how to convince her.

"You love me?"

"Is that such a surprise?" Had he really never told her?

Just then, Samantha arrived with Matt. It took her one look to realise what had happened. Dismayed, she rushed over to Meg and hugged her tightly. "I'm so sorry, Meg! I wasn't myself. I was—"

"Possessed by a demon, apparently," Meg said coldly, trying to free herself from the unwanted affection.

"Does that mean you believe me?" Jan asked hopefully.

"Not. A. Word. Ghosts, magic, demons. You all spend t-too mu-much—" she suddenly stammered, staring over Jan's shoulder.

Curiously, Jan looked too and saw Matt had changed into his demon form.

Wings outstretched, he spread his arms and slowly turned around. "Does that help?"

Samantha coughed. "Pretty."

Matt winked over his shoulder.

"Those are real?" Meg asked, despite the fact Matt's wings were clearly growing out of his shoulders.

"Very. Do you want me to leave the demon way to convince you?"

Meg crossed her arms again. "What's the demon way?"

Matt had finished turning. "You'll see." He looked at Samantha. "See you at school." Then he disappeared.

"That's the demon way. Very annoying," Jan explained.

Meg didn't even look at him. Instead, she stared at Samantha. "Matt's a demon?"

"Half-demon. His father's human." She sighed. "If you're open to it, I can explain it all. I can also show you my magic."

"I'm not sure I want that." Meg sighed. She looked from Samantha to Jan and back again. "So, it's true? You were both possessed by evil spirits?"

"I swear to you!" Samantha said. "Do you really think I would kiss Jan? Out of the blue like that?"

Meg shrugged. "You slept with Cian just like that, so..."

"*Slept with?*" Jan thought Samantha just had a crush on the Elite Clique boy, not that she was having a full-blown affair. "You and Cian are having sex? Are you—?"

Samantha winced. "It's complicated. And before you ask, yes, Matt knows that, too. Rachel, too, but no one else."

"I get the goss before Lu? Nice."

"Hello," Meg called out, "focus, please. I've made my decision."

Concerned, Jan turned back to her. "What decision?"

"Whether to keep you." She took a deep breath and gave him an evil look. "I'll believe your outrageous story on one condition. Unless it concerns me directly, I don't want to hear anything about magic. I can't handle all the ridiculousness."

"Um okay…" Jan found it a bit strange, but if that was what it took to make Meg forgive him, he was fine with it. "No magic talk."

"And I need some space. No touching until I've erased those images from my mind."

"Fair enough." Now that she'd said it, he felt a sudden need to take a shower. Who knew what else Sokaris had done with his body. "You don't think I can hop under your shower? I want to scrub my skin."

Meg balked at the idea. "Does it have to be here?"

"I don't have anywhere else." Jan's voice did an odd little hop.

"Jan…" Samantha said faintly.

"Hurry!" Meg told him with a stern look.

Jan didn't need to be told twice. "You're the best."

Annoyed, she said, "I know. Now go. Go, go! Mum's watching TV and Dad's still working."

"At this hour?" Samantha asked, as it was well past closing time.

Meg shrugged. "Don't expect him to be home for dinner."

After Jan had a chance to rest, he'd find a way to make it up to Meg. Her personal life was bad enough. She really didn't need any more complications. But first, he needed to cleanse his body and make sure not a trace of evil Egyptian mages remained on his body.

Lucille

Although it was a little early in their relationship, Lucille invited Philipp to spend the night. After tucking Pascal into bed, she was grateful for his presence. They sat in front of the fireplace, doing nothing but holding each other and talking.

"Do you need more material for your article?" she teased. "I could add a few chaotic spells."

Philipp laughed. "Please don't. I'm a full believer now." He kissed her forehead. "After I looked into the Staff of Seth, I was able to spin a fantastic yarn and blame it for everything that has gone wrong. The exhibition will either have to pack up or open the doors wide, because people will want to see this."

She snuggled into his side, utterly content.

"Don't tell me you do this every day."

"Just every other Monday." Lucille grinned at him. "Don't worry. It's not usually this intense. I mean... no, that's not true. Magic can be very dangerous and there are monsters you don't want to mess with. But we've got each other and that makes it okay."

Philipp put his arm around her shoulder and pulled her closer. "And now you've got me."

She looked up at him and found his lips. It was a soft, sweet kiss that reconciled her to so much that had happened. Like a warm chocolate pudding on a cold winter's night.

But then her phone buzzed. Thinking it was her parents checking in, Lucille leant back and looked at it.

Samantha: I didn't want to out him in front of everyone, but just before Selima possessed me, I found out Jan was kicked out by his parents weeks ago. He's been sleeping at the Magic Circle. Can you take him in for a few days until we figure something out?

Philipp read the text message over her shoulder and nudged her gently. "Come on, friends are more important."

She agreed with him. After hearing about Rachel's silent suffering, she knew she had to do better. Even though they were fighting monsters, they were all just people deep down inside.

Half an hour later, Lucille stood in the Magic Circle and looked at Jan, freezing his ass off in a sleeping bag. She'd woken him up, causing him to fall off the flimsy row of chairs he'd built. Confused, he looked up at her.

Lucille sighed. "Come on. Pack your things. You're moving in with me."

Part 4

Fire & Snow

Jan

Jan stared at the dilapidated building in front of him and Lu. It looked as if the architect had been in his goth phase and drunk when he'd designed it. All the walls and the roof were black. It was three storeys high, but it didn't look like it could support them, as all the angles suggested that the next gust of wind would knock it over.

A lone tower rose on the left. Looking up at the top window, Jan thought he saw movement, but quickly realised it was nothing but a whirl of snow.

"I can't afford a house," Jan pointed out, not for the first time.

"You can afford *this* one," Lu said, as optimistic as ever. "My father pulled a lot of strings to find something in your budget." She winced. "You'll probably still have to take out a loan, though."

Jan snorted. "Have you seen my credit rating? I'm a low-income high school dropout."

"You'll have a proper job and education soon." When they'd discussed his future, he'd told Lu he was thinking of becoming a paramedic. The interviews were early next month, and now that he'd told her, he couldn't back out. "Besides, your loan is from the de Cerque bank."

"You're lending me the money?"

"Of course not. But my father will act as your guarantor." Lu gave him a stern look. "I'm vouching for you here."

Jan was a little overwhelmed. There were too many expectations and responsibilities. None of which were in his wheelhouse. He was no homeowner. And he shouldn't go anywhere near a mortgage. "How did you convince him to invest in me?"

Lu batted her eyelashes. "As if Daddy could say no to me."

"Well played." He looked at the house again and found several broken windows. "Is it safe?"

"They wouldn't sell it otherwise, would they?"

Jan gave her a long look. "*How much* am I paying for this?"

Lu mumbled something under her breath, but before he could ask her to speak up, she said, "Look, it's a bit of a fixer-upper, but I'll help you. We'll all chip in and I'll pay for the necessary renovations. It's all part of the loan." Then she suddenly jumped up on her toes and raised an arm.

A silver car pulled up in the driveway.

"That's Mr Jensen!" Lucille announced, as a tall man with thinning hair and an immaculate suit got out of the car. A big cheesy smile flashed across his face as he walked over to them. A smile that Lucille matched. "Good morning, Mr Jensen. We spoke on the phone yesterday."

The man shook her hand. "Miss de Cerque, it's a pleasure to finally meet you. Your father is one of my favourite business partners." He turned to Jan and repeated the gesture. "And you must be the lucky Mr Kerscher. May I congratulate you on your first home? It's a beauty, isn't it?" He looked at the house a little too long. "Full of history. Built by the author Jonathan Blackstone in 1960. It has all the charm of his Gothic novels."

That explained the dark exterior.

"Let's have a closer look, shall we?" Mr Jensen led them to the garden gate, which looked as if it had been kicked in a few times. The garden itself was desolate, even considering it was winter. "This house was way ahead of its time, thanks to Blackstone's eccentricity. You have to admit, it has a lot of character."

"If it's so charming, why is it so cheap?" Jan asked, earning a dirty look from Lu.

Mr Jensen laughed, slightly flustered. "Oh, well, you see. It's been owned by the bank for a couple of decades. It's become quite high-maintenance. If it wasn't a listed building, the land would have been sold a long time ago."

"A listed building? Does that mean…?"

"You can't tear it down or change the exterior. As you can see, it needs a few repairs, but I can only emphasise that we've got an unpolished gem here. This house has over sixty years of history behind it. Its builder was a well-known writer."

Jan narrowed his eyes. "You said that already." He nudged Lu as they walked around the house. "You can't be serious."

"You need a roof over your head. It's a bargain."

"It sounds like the roof is going to collapse on me as soon as I get the keys."

They reached the front again and faced the entrance. Mr Jensen looked very pleased. "And here we are."

Jan waited for him to continue the tour. "Can we see the rooms now?"

"The rooms?"

"I wasn't planning on camping in the garden." Although that seemed a lot safer at the moment.

Once again, Mr Jensen appeared a little *too* nervous. "Well, if you insist, we'll go inside."

At last, Lu was catching on and shared a confused look with Jan. "We insist."

Mr Jensen fumbled with the keys. When he finally got the right one and turned the knob, the door opened with a loud creak.

Jan pushed past the useless estate agent and stepped into a dark and dusty foyer. A door opened to the right into what looked like a living room, while a dark staircase with crooked steps led to the upper floors. Two other doors beside the staircase were closed.

"This is way too big," Jan said.

"I told you. It's a bargain," Lu said, though her voice was a little shaky.

Jan took another step when an icy gust blew into his face. "Great, it's drafty as hell. How is that better than sleeping in the Magic Circle?"

"For one thing, you don't own the store. And you're not moving in today. We'll fix it up and it'll be spring soon."

The temperature continued to drop. Jan sighed. "Spring can't come soon enough. Very well. Let's seal my fate."

\#

A few days later, when he'd been given the keys, Jan showed his friends around the house. It was still far too cold and drafty, so his plans to move in were still on hold. But he had to admit that it was pretty cool to have such a big house full of nooks and crannies, with an air of mystery about it.

"And this was the author's office." The office itself had been emptied, leaving only a fireplace and a massive, ink-stained oak desk in the room.

Fabian stared up at the uncharacteristically high ceiling. "This place is just creepy. Didn't we just deal with a haunted house?"

"It's not haunted," Lu said. "Just a bit eccentric."

"Those sloping angles are definitely something else," Samantha said doubtfully. "Alright. Where do we start?"

"We?" Jan asked.

Matt clapped his shoulder. "You weren't planning on doing this yourself, were you?"

"I mean... do you have the time? I thought you had exams coming up?" Their most important exams.

"We can test each other while painting," Lu said with a cheesy smile.

Jan stared at her. "Lucille de Cerque will take up a roller and paint my walls?" Slowly he began to grin. "Okay, you've convinced me. I have to see this."

Everyone laughed, while Lu made a face. "Ha-ha. It can't be that hard."

"What was that?" Fabian suddenly turned around.

"What was what?" Jan hadn't noticed anything out of order.

"I feel like someone—or something—is watching us. I told you this house was creepy." Fabian shuddered.

Lu clicked her tongue. "Nonsense. That yellow tapestry is creepy. It just needs redecorating."

"How about a lush rosé?" Rachel deadpanned.

"I'd say black. To match the exterior," said Fabian's new girlfriend. In her tight corset and long skirt, she looked absolutely ready to move into the house.

Meanwhile, Samantha crouched in front of the fireplace and picked up some sort of shard. "Look at this."

Jan had little interest in rubbish and said, "Great, we'll have to clean that, too."

"With this much dust, at least three times," Matt joked, much to Jan's dismay.

Lu clapped her hands together with another cheesy smile. "Well, I think this house is exciting. Who knows what we might find in here."

All Jan wanted was a warm place to sleep. "Probably a bunch of secret passageways, a hidden torture chamber, and the crypt of Jonathan Blackstone."

Samantha suddenly hissed and dropped the shard. "Cold!"

The room grew a little darker, and Jan had the feeling they were being watched. Meanwhile, their breath turned to white clouds in front of them.

"Shall we go into the living room?" Fabian suggested in a panicked voice.

"Good idea," Jan muttered. His feelings about the house were changing rapidly. He didn't want a haunted house. Not when he had to live here on his own.

They reached the living room to find a gruesome ice statue in the middle of the room. It looked like an ugly gnome with a distorted face that made Jan's stomach turn. "That wasn't there when we came in."

"It was just too good to be true," Fabian said with an exasperated sigh. "Of course, we couldn't do something as normal as buying a house without encountering a monster."

Next to him, Lu swallowed. "It was a bargain."

"It's snowing," Rachel exclaimed. They looked up at the ceiling where thick snowflakes were falling.

Jan wanted to believe the roof was in desperate need of repair, but there were two floors above them, their floors as solid as they could be.

"Time to go," Fabian announced, already marching towards the front door.

The others followed. At the door, Jan turned and faced the house grimly. "I'll be back. This is my house now." As it was, he was stuck with it. Whatever spirit was possessing it would have to leave.

Samantha

Something had changed between Samantha and Matt. Maybe it was because he'd finally been punished for what he'd done. Or maybe it was because they'd both been through the same terrible experience. On the other hand, she wasn't any closer to Jan. Mortified was more like it. After explaining to Meg what had happened, they'd both sworn never to speak of it again.

Samantha had no problem keeping her distance from Jan, but she found herself drawn to Matt instead. She found his new honesty refreshing and half expected him to turn up at school with his beautiful wings.

But when she left the music room, he was his usual human self. Although the smile on his lips when he saw her was out of this world.

"Good morning," he said, falling into step beside her. "How was class?"

"Lots of theory," Samantha complained. Usually, her music lessons had at least some singing component, but lately it was all theory review for the few people lucky enough to take the music exam. "How was PE?"

"Lots of theory," Matt replied with a laugh.

"Poor boy." Theory had always been a part of the PE major, much to every male student's dismay. In Samantha's opinion they just got what they deserved for choosing the seemingly easy-grade option.

Matt shrugged, still chuckling. "I'll survive. It's not too bad. You wouldn't know anything about biomechanics, though, would you?"

"Sorry, I don't have any biology. I might be able to tell you about the chemical processes." She doubted that the little organic chemistry she'd learnt would help him much.

Matt wriggled his eyebrows. "You know, we both have chemistry."

She laughed at him. "True." Regardless of the innuendo, chemistry was his third chosen written exam. "If you need help with—"

"Yes!"

Samantha started to giggle. Matt was a good student, so she doubted he really needed the help, but explaining it to him would also help her prepare for her exam. "Okay, okay. I'll prepare something for when we paint Jan's house later."

"Alright." They'd reached the cafeteria. "I'm off to French. Could teach you some of that in return."

Mouth agape, she watched Matt walk down the corridor backwards with a big grin on his face. With an amused snort, Samantha turned around and bumped into someone else. "Cian."

Cian growled. "Really?"

"Really, what?"

"You and Matt?"

Samantha sighed. "There is no me and Matt. We're just friends."

He shook his head and shuddered. "I don't know how you can even stand to be in the same room with him after everything he's done."

It was a good point, but... "He's apologised."

Cian's eyes widened in disbelief. "I don't think you can apologise for that."

"Cian, please."

He pulled her aside so they wouldn't block the entrance and put his hands on her arms. "I'm sorry. I know what we have is only temporary, but Matt? Really?"

Samantha pulled away. "I told you, there is no Matt and me. Now if you'll excuse me." Her feelings might be messed up, but they were her mess, and in her opinion, Cian had no right to judge her. It made the simple thing they'd had so far unnecessarily complicated.

She left him standing there and entered the cafeteria for her free period. At the back of the hall, Rachel was reading a book, providing the perfect cover.

"New book?" she asked as she sat down. "*The Mask of Fire*. Sounds exciting. What's it about?"

Rachel put the book down slightly. "It's about a man who comes into possession of the Mask of Fire and uses it to summon the devil. The book's only been in the shops for three days and has already shot to the top of the bestseller lists. I bought it yesterday."

"Since when do you read such things?" Rachel usually preferred thick historical novels.

"Since Jan bought the author's house. I thought it wouldn't be a bad idea to do a bit of independent research. So far, the book reads a bit autobiographically."

Samantha gasped. "You think the devil's residing in Blackstone's house?"

"Not really, but maybe the Mask of Fire exists. Remember the shard you found by the fireplace?"

Cold dread filled Samantha. "It felt more like a Mask of Ice."

"Artistic licence?" Rachel suggested with a shrug.

Samantha remembered Lucille's insistence on what a bargain the house was. How eager the bank was to get rid of it, despite its size and historic value. "Oh dear. The house *is* haunted."

Matt

Matt and the others stood outside the Blackstone house waiting for Jan and Lucille to arrive. Despite the recent snow, the garden looked desolate and sad.

"I wish it was spring," Samantha said. "Then we could work outside, make this place pretty."

"Work outside," Fabian eagerly picked up the thread. "I'm in. Anything to avoid going into this cursed house."

Ophelia snuggled into his arm and grinned. "But cursed houses are our thing."

Fabian kissed her gently. Matt noticed Rachel using her book to hide a grimace and Samantha rolling her eyes. He had no idea what their problem was. Fabian and his new girlfriend seemed happy. Ophelia was lively, quite sexy, and she looked at Fabian like he was the saviour of the world.

At last, Jan and Lucille arrived in a minivan. Jan jumped out of the driver's seat and slammed the door behind him.

"Finally!" Fabian exclaimed. "Any longer and you'd have had a bunch more ice statues in the garden."

"I'd keep you warm," Ophelia suggested.

Rachel snorted, put her book away, and went to help Jan open the back of the van.

Meanwhile, Jan called them over. "Come on, you can help carry this. You'll be warm in no time. Lu bought out half the hardware store."

Lucille huffed with indignation. "Not true. I skipped the garden, plumbing, and lighting departments."

"Told you: half the store."

Matt grabbed a workbench and heaved it out of the van. "Where do we start?"

"Living room. I don't trust the kitchen."

When everyone had a load of wallpaper rolls, paint, glue and tools, Jan led them to the front door. But when he tried the key, the door wouldn't budge.

"It's frozen," he complained. "What's wrong with this house? What does it have against me?"

"It's winter," Samantha suggested. "And it's an old house. It probably just froze naturally."

From what Rachel had told them about Jonathan Blackstone's book, Matt doubted it was natural. "I could jump inside. Open it from the inside."

"Let me," Lucille said. She dropped her paint bucket on the step and held her hand over the doorknob. "Hiantes qetes mensura!" Heat wavered from her fingers, melting the ice in the keyhole. She took the key from Jan's hand and opened the door. "There you go."

Jan went first and immediately slid halfway across the room, landing on his butt. Panting, he turned to Samantha. "Don't tell me it's winter and the floors are old."

"The house has something against you," she replied dryly, much to Matt's amusement.

As if to confirm her statement, a gust of icy wind blew through the foyer, carrying snowflakes with it.

Cautiously, Jan rose to his feet and shook his hand at the house. "Whatever is in this house, show yourself! Immediately." Nothing happened, causing Jan to grumble, "As expected."

Lucille did her heat trick on the floor and the rest of them entered and made it to the living room without any further problems. There Lucille and Jan started a fire in the fireplace, while Matt set up the workbench, before grabbing a roll of foil and throwing it at Samantha. "Let's cover everything."

Fabian and Ophelia started attacking the old wallpaper with putty knives, while Rachel found an old armchair and sat down to continue reading.

"I made fire!" Jan shouted after a few minutes, pounding his chest for some reason.

Lucille patted him patronisingly on the head. "Yes, yes, you're a real man now."

The small flame burnt for a few seconds before a sudden snowfall extinguished it. Jan's shoulders slumped. "That's just mean."

"Let me do it." Lucille pointed her hand at the fireplace. "Globus Igneus!" Her fireball engulfed the wood, and a warm glow spread through the room.

Samantha sighed with relief. "So much better."

"Yeah, might have to take something off," Matt teased.

She huffed, then giggled. "Let's put on some protection first."

Now it was Matt's turn to gape. Was Samantha returning his flirtation? Or could she just not help her quick wit? Whatever it was, he was going to enjoy it while it lasted.

Together they began to cover the floor and the old table in the middle of the room, before approaching Rachel's armchair.

"Would you do us a favour and stand up?" Matt asked, amused that she was reading when they were all working.

Rachel jumped. "What?"

"Or, assuming you're part of the interior, we could cover you too," Samantha suggested, giving Matt a mischievous look.

Matt grinned. "Great idea."

He and Samantha moved towards the chair, pretending to wrap Rachel along with the furniture. Rachel fled with a little shriek, before bursting into giggles.

Across the room, Ophelia attacked the wallpaper as if it had offended her personally. "It's not coming off."

"You don't have to murder it," Fabian joked. "Just gently separate it from the wall."

Ophelia took another stab, showing him the tiniest patch of wallpaper. "What do you think I'm doing? This old wallpaper simply won't go, just like the ghost."

"It's all in the technique," Fabian said patiently. Then he put his hand on hers. "You have to do it with feeling." He moved her hand upwards in one smooth motion. A whole strip of wallpaper fell off.

Ophelia's frustration was gone in an instant. She turned to Fabian and beamed at him. "What would I do without you?" She dropped the putty knife and began to kiss him.

Jan picked up the dropped utensil and waved it in their faces. "Hey, you're supposed to be working, not kissing." Then he threw another at Rachel. "You, too. You can read later."

Rachel held up her book to protect herself. But then she put the book down on the mantelpiece, picked up the putty knife, and went to work on the opposite wall.

Meanwhile, Matt and Samantha had finished with the foil and were setting up the paint.

"Fabian's got game all of a sudden," Matt said quietly. "That's new."

Samantha rolled her eyes. "You mean Ophelia's got game and he's fallen hard for her."

"So, what's with all the drama?" He kept his voice low. "Why's everyone against it?"

"I'm not against it. It's just all very sudden. Lucille is all for it, because she feels guilty about falling out of love with him and getting involved with Philipp. And Rachel..." Samantha lowered her voice to a whisper. "I think she's still grappling with what the cult did to her. Hardly Ophelia's fault, but I get it. It's like a constant reminder. Especially since Ophelia still worships her goddess."

Samantha opened the lid on the paint and began to stir it with a long wooden stick. Slowly the oil and paint particles mixed until it became a smooth sky blue. "Looks good, doesn't it?"

"Me? Always."

Amused, Samantha gasped for breath, then dipped a finger into the paint and flicked it at Matt. It was so sudden he couldn't dodge it. It landed on his cheek with a cold splash. "True. Sky blue is your colour."

He began to grin. "Oh, you'll pay for that." He grabbed one of the brushes, dipped it in, and fired a whole salvo of paint at her.

Samantha shrieked as it hit her chin and hair, but then she picked up a brush as well, and the two of them started a proper fight.

"Hey guys!" Jan complained. "Not the good paint."

"At least they covered everything up before," Lucille commented as she collected the remains of the wallpaper into a bag. Just then a stray spray hit her. "Hey!"

She reached into the bag and threw a pile of wallpaper at Matt. Within minutes, they were all involved in a big paint battle, screaming and laughing.

The next morning in German class, Matt held the door open for the others. As they rushed in, Samantha made sure she was last. "How very gentlemanly of you."

"You know me." She was definitely flirting. Matt could hardly believe it. "You've still got some paint there." He held out his finger but didn't quite dare touch her.

Samantha lowered her eyes and hurried inside.

At her table, Lucille was unpacking her bag. "I think we did an excellent job and got a lot done yesterday."

"It's a big house, though," Rachel said.

Fabian shrugged. "We don't need all of it. Right now, it's enough to get one bedroom, the living room, the kitchen, and a bathroom into shape."

"And the garden," Samantha added. "It looks worse than ours and that's quite a feat. I could grow herbs there."

"Maybe you should ask Jan about that first," Lucille joked.

"As if Jan has any plans for the garden."

Just then Robert came in and sat down at their table. "Morning. I hear Jan's moved into a house? Anne told me."

Apparently, he was dating Jan's little sister now.

"Yes, the Blackstone House," Lucille announced proudly. "We're renovating at the moment."

"Really? That old thing?"

Fabian nodded darkly. "Yep."

"I couldn't do it." Robert shook his head. "Did you know Jonathan Blackstone killed himself?"

Everyone shared a worried look. *Was it the ghost of Jonathan Blackstone trying to drive them out of his old house?*

"No," Rachel said quietly. "How do you know?"

"I read his book. The Mask of Fire. Great read. I won't spoil it." Right now, Matt couldn't care less about spoilers. "After I finished, I did some research. Apparently, Blackstone threw himself off the Greenvalley Bridge and drowned in the freezing water."

That would explain the cold.

"The poor chap died without a penny to his name, ridiculed by the literary world," Robert went on. "And look what happened. They discover his books and they're bestsellers. How times change, eh?"

"Yeah," Matt said quietly. "Funny." Then he wrote a note on his pad and showed it to the others: *Do we need an exorcism?*

Rachel sighed deeply. "I'll look into it."

Jan

Caroline was gradually returning to the Magic Circle, allowing Jan time for renovations and eventually starting his training—if he got the job. The Blackstone House was within walking distance of the Magic Circle, making it easy to drop in. He arrived shortly after lunch to find sky blue letters scrawled across the foyer.

GO AWAY!

"Seriously?" He turned to the living room. All the foil had been torn to shreds and scraps of wallpaper were scattered around the room. It was a complete and utter mess.

He'd just about had it with this ghost. "Okay, listen up. I don't know who you are, but I bought this house and took out a pretty nerve-wracking loan. So, no, *no*, I'm not going anywhere."

He put his hands on his hips and looked around. As before, there was nothing to see, but the air grew colder until his breath rose in white clouds in front of his face. Worried, he took a step forward.

"This isn't going to work." He forced himself to hold out his hand, feeling a bit stupid. "I'm Jan. And you?" He swallowed, thinking about who might want him out of this house. "Is your name Jonathan?"

"Neve isn't Jonathan."

Startled, Jan looked up. At the top of the stairs stood a little girl of about five or six, with a pair of bushy white-blonde pigtails and ice-blue eyes.

"Oh!" Jan cocked his head to get a better look. "Hi... Neve? Is that your name?" She just glared at him. "I didn't know a little girl lived here." It was in keeping with the childishness of the pranks, but he'd expected something more frightening. Like another Egyptian sorcerer or worse.

Two razor-sharp ice crystals missed his face by a hair's breadth.

"Neve is not a little girl."

Knowing better than to argue, Jan raised his hands. "Sorry. I didn't mean to offend you." Especially not when she could turn ice into weapons. "So, Neve." He rubbed his neck before trying for a smile. "Nice to meet you. Looks like we're gonna be housemates from now on."

"No!" The little girl stamped her feet. "Jonathan and Neve live here. Not Jan!"

Suddenly the floor froze, and a gust of wind blew Jan straight out of the door. He stumbled over the step and landed on his bum in the snow. The door slammed shut. Ice covered it in seconds.

"Awesome," Jan groaned.

After an hour of trying to get into the house, Jan gave up and returned to the Magic Circle. His friends, including Ophelia and Philipp, had arrived and were sitting in the back room. Jan dropped into a chair.

"I give up. Can we sell the house?"

Lu gave him a pitiful look. "I'm afraid Mr Jensen doesn't want to see it again."

Jan groaned. "What am I supposed to do now? The house has locked me out and I owe the bank more money than I'll ever earn."

"Not true," Lu protested.

"If my parents get wind of this, I'm a dead man." The mere thought of having to explain to his father that he'd taken out a loan on a dilapidated building sent shivers down his spine.

"We'll find a way to make it work," Samantha promised. "Robert told us that Jonathan Blackstone committed suicide. He could be the one who's still in the house."

"Besides, you happen to know someone who knows a thing or two about ghosts," Rachel said. "I live with one."

"Not Jonathan, but Neve," Jan muttered. Maybe the girl could move in with Rachel, too.

"Snow?" Ophelia asked. When everyone looked at her in confusion, she said, "Neve is Spanish for snow."

It fit.

Lu turned to Jan. "Who's Neve?"

"A little girl who thinks the house is hers and Jonathan's. Oh, and she throws sharp ice crystals around, freezes the floor, and blew me out of the house." Even his poltergeist a year ago hadn't been that powerful.

Philipp cleared his throat. "Well, my article just got a lot more interesting."

"Article?"

"The *Greenvalley View* wants to do an article on the Blackstone House now that Jonathan Blackstone has become famous postmortem," Lu explained.

Philipp added, "If you don't mind, I'd like to take some pictures."

"Sure, just don't put me in them." The last thing he needed was to have his face in the *Greenvalley View* before he could confess his latest mess-up to his parents. "And bring a flamethrower."

"Have you tried talking to her?" Rachel asked.

Jan gave her a flat stare. "Guess what, I did! I was super polite. She didn't like it. But please, knock yourself out."

"Are you sure this isn't a prank?" Fabian asked. "Why is there a little girl in Jonathan Blackstone's house? He wasn't some kind of creep, was he?"

Gosh, please don't let there be a child skeleton in the closet. "She seemed quite fond of him." Jan clung to this fact as if his life depended on it. "They're supposed to be living together."

Matt snorted. "So, a flat share for ghosts?"

"I don't want to go back," Jan whined.

"Stop it!" Lu wagged her finger in front of his nose. "We bought the house, and we've started to renovate it, and *you're* going to live there. After all we've been through, we're not going to be scared off by a couple of ghosts."

"We aren't?" Fabian asked.

"No!" Lu snapped. "We're going to go over there now and talk to Neve and politely suggest an exorcism."

Jan sank deeper into his chair. "I'm sure she'll love that." He could only imagine her violent reaction.

Lucille

Lucille felt guilty for pushing this house on Jan. She'd only tried to help and had truly thought she'd found an amazing bargain. She should've known it was too good to be true. There was a lot of money at play and Lucille was going to do anything in her power to make it work. And if that meant fighting a ghost with the powers of snow, so be it!

She used her heat spell to get through the door, finding a sky-blue warning in the foyer. "Charming."

"I know," said Jan. "She's a real darling."

The living room was worse. All the work they'd done yesterday had been ruined. It looked like a battlefield, and not the fun one they'd ended up with after their paint fight.

"Hey, that's my book!" Rachel bent down and picked up scraps of paper with fine print. "I left it here yesterday."

The room got colder as it had done so many times before, but this time, a little girl entered from the shadows. Blue flames danced around her hands, throwing flickering shadows across her pale face.

"This is Jonathan's house!" she told them. "No one can steal it and put stupid foil over Jonathan's favourite armchair."

Rachel took a step towards the ghost. "But that doesn't mean you can destroy my book!"

The little girl—Neve—shook her head. "No one is ever allowed to read evil book. Jonathan forbade it."

Before they had time to process, Neve raised her little arms. The flames around her hands swirled faster and faster, until a storm of snow and ice was raging through the room. An ice crystal cut Rachel's cheek before Jan hauled her back and they all fled into the foyer.

Next to Lucille, Philipp carefully picked up his camera to take a picture of the girl and her snowstorm.

"When Jonathan comes home, he'll be very angry with burglars," Neve said, sending shivers down Lucille's spine.

What if there was, indeed, a second, more powerful ghost hanging around?

"I'm not a burglar. I *bought* the house," Jan said. "It's mine now."

"Liar!"

A sudden rumbling occurred. Confused, Lucille looked around. Suddenly, Samantha pointed up the stairs. "There!" A giant snowball was rolling down the stairs.

Quickly, Lucille jumped out of the way. The snowball crashed against the opposite wall and fell apart without crashing into anyone.

"Yikes." Matt stomped some snow under his shoe. "Guess she won't acknowledge your bill of sale."

"You think?" Jan sniped back.

Meanwhile, Fabian looked to Rachel. "You try talking to her. Ghosts are your strength."

Rachel had to duck out from under an icy sleet rain. "She's not a ghost."

"Not?"

The little girl huffed. "Neve is not ghost. Neve is snow witch, not boring ghost." Then she giggled, just as a little girl would do. "Jonathan lied to everyone. He said Neve is his daughter, so Neve could stay with him. Jonathan said others afraid of Neve if they know."

Lucille could imagine only too well why anyone would think so. At the moment, it was only snowing softly, but the very fact that it was happening indoors freaked her out.

"You really knew him!" Philipp exclaimed.

Lucille snorted. "I love the professional curiosity. But we don't exactly have time for an exclusive interview."

"But it's a golden opportunity to learn more about him. He was a huge recluse. According to the archives, he killed himself because the media tore him to pieces after his biggest opponents died in mysterious ways."

The snow started whirling around and the temperature dropped dramatically. Neve floated towards Philipp. "Jonathan isn't dead! Jonathan is taking a walk. He's gonna come home soon."

A terrible thought settled in Lucille. Keeping her voice as gentle as she possibly could, she said, "Jonathan Blackstone died over sixty years ago."

"No! Jonathan is coming back to Neve. Jonathan promised!"

Philipp shook his head. "He jumped off the Greenvalley Bridge in 1961 and froze to death. Jonathan Blackstone is dead."

Tears shimmered in Neve's ice blue eyes. "Jonathan promised Neve bonbons!"

Lucille's heart broke for the little snow witch. For sixty years, she'd waited for her adoptive father to return. She really seemed to have loved him.

"He broke his promise," Philipp said softly.

"Quiet!" Neve shouted. "Jonathan doesn't break promises."

She raised her hand and blew across it towards Philipp. He tried to back away, but it was too late. Within seconds, he'd been turned into an ice statue.

"Philipp!" Lucille shrieked.

"Go away!" Neve cried. "Neve doesn't want to see anyone. Neve hates you!" She disappeared straight back into the shadows.

"Did she just leave?" Fabian asked, outraged. "She can't leave Philipp like that."

"I don't think she cares much," Ophelia said softly.

"HIASTA QETES MENSURA!" Lucille pushed both her warm hands against Philipp, but apart from a few drops of condensation, nothing happened. "GLOBUS IGNEUS!"

"Lucille," Samantha warned.

Lucille wouldn't listen. She threw her fireball at Philipp and then another and another one. Neither could melt the ice. Sobbing, she collapsed on the floor. "The spell is too strong. I can't get through." She looked up at Samantha, "Can you do something?"

Samantha closed her eyes. For a minute, Lucille was hopeful, but then her friend shook her head. "It's beyond me."

Suddenly, a heat wave blasted through the room. Flames sizzled on the floor. The snow melted away, leaving nothing but Philipp's statue behind. In front of the stairs, a tall figure stepped out of the flames. Wearing a black and red robe, it looked like a man—or close enough to one. Fiery red hair shot up from his head as golden reptilian eyes scrutinised them. His thin lips were drawn back to reveal razor-sharp teeth.

"I can help you."

Lucille swallowed. "What?"

The demon, devil, or whatever it was smiled. "I grant wishes, I..."

Matt pulled Lucille back. "No, thanks. We're good."

"But he could free Philipp." The idea settled in her mind so suddenly, as if it'd been put there.

Rachel shook her head, alarmed. "He's the devil. Quirtubar. From the book."

If so, he'd already lost interest in them. Instead, he looked up the stairs. "Where is she? Where's my snow witch?" His split tongue flicked over his razor-sharp incisors.

"She's mine now," Jan suddenly declared. "I bought the house, with everything inside. If you want the snow witch, you'll have to go past me."

Horrified, Lucille stared at him. Had he gone mad? Why was he threatening this powerful entity for the life of the little witch who'd brought them nothing but trouble. She'd *frozen* Philipp!

"Did you forget how she attacked us?" Fabian asked, seeming equally weirded out.

"This one looks scarier." Samantha took a stand next to Jan.

The devil grinned at Jan. "I can get rid of the snow witch for you. Then the house would be all yours."

Jan gulped, but then the idiot shook his head. "Sorry, no can do."

Lucille couldn't believe it. They were wasting their only chance to get Philipp back alive. Was he still in there? Or did he die the moment Neve froze him?

"I'll get you the snow witch if you unfreeze my boyfriend here."

Alarmed, Rachel grabbed her arm. "Lucille, don't!"

Quirtubar turned to her. "You're interested in a deal."

Lucille wasn't that stupid, but if she wanted to make this work, she had to play her cards right. "Maybe, but not for that." Quickly, she ran through everything she knew. "The snow witch is already yours, isn't she?"

"She was promised to me."

That's what Lucille had thought. Slowly, everything was starting to make sense. "Well, I don't think you can handle her. She's very strong."

Flames erupted around Quirtubar. "The snow witch is nothing against me. I'm the mighty Quirtubar."

Lucille wet her heat-dried lips. "You can't even undo her ice spell."

Now, Matt warned her, "Lucille!"

"Clever try, human." Suddenly, the devil was right in front of her, wrapping his hand around her throat. Not only did her throat tighten, it also starting burning. "Did you really think I'd fall for that cheap trick? Where is she?"

"Go search for her yourself!" Lucille spat.

The fire spirit hissed and Lucille started screaming as the pain intensified tenfold. Just then, a jet stream of water pushed Quirtubar away and she fell to the ground, grabbing her own neck, as if that would protect it. Next to her, Matt had drawn his sword, but the fire spirit was now engulfed in flames. His robe wavered and his face was distorted by anger.

"Enough of this chit chat. Either you tell me where you hid her or you'll be nothing but mounds of ash when I'm through with you."

Jan sniffed and spat out. "We'll risk it. Fabian?"

The water mage pushed out his hands, directing more water at Quirtubar. This time, though, the water only superheated, turning the foyer to sauna-like conditions. Then Quirtubar began to pirouette, and the flames turned into a firestorm.

Matt picked Lucille up from the floor and fled with her into the living room. "Any plans?" he shouted at Samantha.

She already had her eyes closed. "Working on it. Distract him for me."

"Philipp!"

Too late, Lucille remembered about him. The firestorm had melted the ice at last, causing Philipp to collapse onto the floor. Matt took one look, before doing a quick jump there and back again, dropping Philipp in Lucille's arms. His eyelids fluttered and he felt terribly cold, but he was breathing.

While Fabian kept attacking the fire spirit with his water and Ophelia called on the shadows, the heat lowered again. Confused, Quirtubar spun around until his eyes fell on Samantha. He was just about to lunge at her when Matt jumped in between and shot energy at him. With a howl, the devil vanished in a fire column.

Sweat was running down Lucille's face and her neck hurt terribly, but for the moment, the danger seemed to have passed. Fabian extinguished some lingering flames, and the temperature returned to normal.

Ophelia fanned her face. "This guy's clearly too hot for us."

No one laughed. Instead, Jan dropped to his knees next to Lucille and healed her burn marks. "You were ready to strike a deal with the devil?"

"Of course not," Lucille said weakly. "I wanted to trick him. I mean, in the end it worked." She stroked Philipp's sweaty face. "How are you?"

His voice was a faint whisper. "Hot and cold at the same time?"

Jan moved to check up on him. "Seems like you got lucky. You're mostly fine. Like when I got turned to stone once. Your camera didn't make it, though."

The plastic had been reduced to a plastic blob, making Philipp whimper softly. "Just a few thousand Euros, you know."

"It's alright. The most important thing is that you're alive." Lucille kissed his forehead. She'd buy him three new cameras. The thought of losing him like this kept her heart racing. "Just don't annoy any elemental spirits anytime soon, okay?"

"So, what do we do now?" Fabian asked. "That one will be back." He faced Jan. "Your ghost flat share is getting creepier every day."

"Barking up the wrong tree, dude."

"Was that really *the* devil?" Samantha asked.

Matt shook his head. "No, that's just a title. I'm not a hundred per cent sure, but I believe it's only a fire devil, a mix of demon and elemental ghost. Third class demon, if you need to quantify it. He probably lives from making deals with elemental creatures. Fulfil a wish, get their magic."

"So, it *is* a deal with the devil," Ophelia said. "Just instead of your soul, you lose your magic. Man, Neve got herself into deep trouble."

"Not her!" Rachel snapped with unexpected ferocity. "Blackstone. He made the deal. It's all in the book."

"And now the fire devil demands his price: Neve," Samantha surmised.

Jan shot up, angry. "Blackstone promised his own daughter, or whatever Neve was to him, in exchange for some favour? How messed up is that?"

"But Jonathan's been dead for decades," Lucille pointed out. "Why is he only collecting his price now?"

"Because I bought the house?" Jan asked, full of doubt.

The timing was suspicious, but Rachel shook her head. "*The Mask of Fire*, the book. Blackstone died poor and with a ruined reputation. He was desperate for success, so he made a deal with the fire devil. But the price was too high."

Samantha picked up the thread with ease. "Neve said no one was supposed to read the evil book. But someone discovered and published it. After all these years, Jonathan got the success he'd always searched for."

Jan groaned and sat back down on the floor. "So, now the deal is up. What do we do? I don't want to pay the mortgage on a pile of ash."

Matt had put his sword away and was carefully scouting the foyer. "He's too strong to fight him directly. Probably devoured a lot of elemental creatures already."

"The book." Samantha turned to Rachel. "Rachel, you said the book felt autobiographical. How did it end?"

"No idea. I never got to finish it."

"I didn't expect to ever say this," Matt started, "but we need Robert's help. He finished it."

Samantha sighed. "It's worth a try. I'll ask him tomorrow morning in Chemistry."

Lucille looked up the stairs. A part of her wanted to protest and suggest leaving the two elemental spirits to it. Let there be a battle between ice and fire. After all, Neve had been nothing but hostile to them. She'd frozen Philipp in a childish tantrum, just because she couldn't believe her beloved Jonathan had died.

But then she imagined how she'd feel if her dad walked out one day, promising to return and never doing so. Only to realise he'd offered her soul to some devil. Jonathan might have killed himself to avoid the debt, but he'd only bought her more time, causing decades of abandonment.

"Let's hope the house is still here tomorrow."

Fabian

While the others returned home, Fabian and Ophelia walked back to the Magic Circle.

"I feel sorry for her," Ophelia said. "She's a little brat, but I would be too if the guy who pretended to be my father sold me out for fame and fortune, then lied to me so he could die of shame alone."

Fabian didn't know much about Jonathan Blackstone apart from what Rachel and Robert had told him, but he knew nothing was ever that simple. "I don't know what his relationship with Neve was like. But I imagine he suffered from depression. He probably thought she was better off without him."

"Well, she is."

"No, she's not. She misses him terribly. She was in that house all alone, waiting for him to come back." He hadn't felt much sympathy for the snow witch at first, but the more he thought about it, the more he felt sorry for her, too. No one had ever told Neve her father was dead. And now his sins were coming back to haunt her.

Ophelia shrugged. "It'll be better once she gets over him and embraces her new freedom. Assuming she doesn't get burnt to a crisp."

Fabian glanced sideways at her, suspecting she'd told him more about herself than Neve, but they'd arrived at the shop, and it was time to relieve his mother for the last two hours of the day.

Caroline sat behind the counter and looked up worriedly. "You're back... and you brought your new girlfriend."

"Ophelia will work in the café. She likes that. And I promise she won't be a distraction. The shop is safe in my hands."

Caroline chuckled. "I know that but thank you for filling my head with images I didn't want to see."

"Mum!" He didn't want her to see such images either.

She stood slowly, then looked at them both for a little too long. Finally, she sighed. "Very well. I'll see you for dinner." She took another deep breath before turning to face Ophelia. "Lia, have you got your dinner sorted?"

"Hm? Yes, of course."

Caroline looked relieved. "Good." She came over and patted Fabian's shoulder before leaving the shop.

Ophelia groaned. "Your mum hates me too."

"What? No! Why would you think that?"

"I don't know. Maybe because she looked annoyed when she saw me. Or maybe it was because the very thought of having me over for dinner seemed like such a chore." Ophelia clicked her tongue. "No reason, really." She entered the café and glared at the dirty dishes in the sink.

Fabian sighed. His mother *had* been uncharacteristically unwelcoming. At first, he'd thought of asking her if Ophelia could move in with them, but Caroline had made it clear it was out of the question before he'd even finished the thought.

"Look," he said, walking over, "my mum isn't feeling too well." He didn't quite want to tell Ophelia about his mother's mental health. She'd probably appreciate that, too, if he knew anything about her. "She's very stressed at the moment. There's a lot to do, so don't take it personally." He doubted his mother really didn't like Ophelia, but rather that the thought of hosting dinner was stressing her out.

"Don't take it personally?" She snorted and started to fill the sink. "And I *hate* working in the cafe."

"What? But you said—"

She threw a plate in the sink, then another. "I hate living in a flat full of morons and idiots, and I hate school." She quickly dropped all the other dishes, almost causing the sink to overflow. "I hate everything."

"Oh, Lia." Fabian hurried around the counter and threw his arms around her. "I'm sorry."

At first, she felt stiff against him, but then she slowly relaxed and sank into him. Something wet fell on his hand. Tears.

Fabian subtly reached past her to turn off the tap before the sink really overflowed and returned to hug her. "I'm sorry."

"You have nothing to be sorry for," she sobbed. "It's me. I'm the common denominator."

"Common denominator? In what?"

"In everything," she said with a heavy sigh. "No one likes me, except you." Ophelia turned in his arms and looked at him with big, teary eyes. "The people at school are awful. They all have their little cliques, and they don't like what I wear. The girls call me a slut and giggle."

Fabian winced. He'd hoped things had improved at school, but the truth was he'd just grown out of it. The younger teenagers were as bad as ever. "I'm sorry."

"It's the same in the flat share. They've already got their cliques, or they're weird loners, and I... I don't mind being alone, really, but—"

"Of course you do. Nobody wants to be alone."

She gave him a flat stare. "I'd rather be alone than the butt of every mean joke. I pretend I don't mind, but I see the way they look at me. Like the way your mother looks at me. Sure, she's stressed or whatever, but she hates seeing us together. Just like your friends hate me."

"No," Fabian had to take a stand. "I can assure you, they don't."

"They ignore me or snap at me. That Rachel girl hates my guts. I'm the intruder."

"You're the new girl." Fabian nudged her nose gently with his. "They just need some time to get to know you."

Ophelia huffed. "They didn't need time to accept Philipp into the group."

Fabian winced. Now that he thought about it, no one had batted an eyelid about the reporter hanging out with them. Meanwhile, Rachel *had* been quite hostile towards Ophelia. He pulled her closer and laid his forehead on hers. "It's because you were part of the cult."

"I don't belong here," Ophelia said quietly. "I don't belong anywhere now."

"No, no, no. Don't say that. You *do* belong here. It just takes time."

She started to cry again. "It's too hard."

He held her tighter, rocking her gently back and forth. "I know." He couldn't possibly imagine the adjustment Ophelia had to deal with.

Sure, her brother had been abusive, but the cult had been her whole life. She'd known all the rules and dynamics. Now everything was new and unfamiliar. And instead of welcoming her, everyone was judging her, either for her style or her past.

"I'll talk to Rachel," Fabian promised. "And the others. You're not alone in this. I'll be with you every step of the way."

Suddenly, she threw her arms around his neck and pulled him to her to kiss him. It was a kiss of passion and desperation, mixed with the salt of her tears. An intoxicating mixture that made it all too easy to be distracted.

The bell rang, startling Fabian. He looked over his shoulder, expecting a customer and found Samantha instead. His best friend cleared her throat and lowered her eyes. "Sorry, I didn't mean to interrupt. I can come back later."

Fabian let go of Ophelia with one arm, his body strangely undecided whether to go to Samantha or stay with Ophelia. "Sam, stay. Please."

"Um. I'm not voyeuristically inclined."

Ophelia slipped out from under his arm and started to wash the dishes. "You go talk."

"Lia..." With a sigh, Fabian walked over to Samantha. He couldn't help but be a little angry with her. She'd interrupted an important moment—before the kiss.

Her eyes widened as he approached. "Woah. What are you so mad about? I just came by to see how you felt about the whole Philipp situation, but I guess there's nothing to worry about."

"I don't care about Philipp." That wasn't quite true. It annoyed Fabian that Lucille had dumped him so easily. Sure, he'd moved on pretty quickly with Ophelia—and he really liked her—but... Fabian shook his head. "It's complicated."

"Honestly, it's a bit crazy," Samantha admitted. "First you two get together when no one's looking, and then you break up, only to date completely new people within weeks. Or in Lucille's case, hours."

"Well, she broke up with me."

Samantha cocked her head thoughtfully. "I know it irks me, too, believe me. So, as your best friend I have to ask: are you okay? You're not rushing into things just because Lucille thinks it's a great idea?"

"You think I'm only with Lia because of Lucille?"

"She wants you two together so she can stop feeling guilty about breaking your heart."

Fabian snorted. "My heart is fine. Thanks for your concern."

"Fabian." Samantha looked taken aback. "I'm just worried. You liked her, didn't you?"

He shrugged dejectedly. "Sure, but contrary to your opinion, I'm not an idiot." He earned himself an unimpressed look. "Don't you think by now I know when a girl doesn't want to be with me anymore? The relationship was over weeks ago. Lucille had already made her decision."

Samantha's face softened. "I'm sorry, Fabian." She reached out to caress his cheek, but he jerked his head back, not wanting her comfort. Not after her condescending interpretation of the matter at hand.

"I love you, Sam, but I'm not going to have this conversation. Not now, not when you think I deserve a pity fest. It may have come about a bit out of the blue, but I really like Lia, and it has nothing to do with Lucille."

"Are you sure? You always fall so hard."

"As people should." Now it was Fabian who studied her face. "Don't you think that's the whole point of it?"

To his surprise, she swallowed, then looked to the side. "Not all relationships are like that."

What was she talking about? He'd meant the way she was clearly developing feelings for Matt and how deeply he loved her, despite having so little hope for so long. Confused, Fabian suggested, "Then maybe you shouldn't talk me out of mine?"

Samantha's eyes widened. "I wasn't trying to. I just..." She clicked her tongue. "I wanted to make sure you were okay after the stunt Lucille pulled on you, and that you weren't rushing into anything."

"No rushing." He pressed his lips together. "Now, if you'll excuse me, I need to reassure my girlfriend that you don't all hate her."

Her eyes widened even more. "Fabian, I don't hate her!" With a huff, she pushed past him and set course for Ophelia. "Hey, Lia."

Ophelia turned to her like a deer caught in the headlights. Her eyes darted to Fabian and then back to Samantha. "Yes?"

Fabian felt a strong urge to grab Samantha by the jacket and throw her out of the shop when she started to apologise. "I'm so sorry if we made you feel anything less than welcome. We're always involved in so much monster drama that we haven't had the pleasure yet, but I like you and you seem to make my best friend very happy, so as long as that doesn't change, we're good. Just kidding—if he's an idiot, I promise I'll help you kick his ass."

Ophelia's mouth twitched and her eyes relaxed. A small chuckle escaped her lips, though she didn't seem to be able to trust it yet. "You'd kick his ass?"

"If he deserved it."

Fabian rolled his eyes. Usually, he didn't mind the joke on him, but today it hit differently.

"He doesn't," Ophelia said, surprisingly. "He's been nothing but good to me."

Samantha smiled. "Yes, he's one of the good ones. I'm actually quite proud of him the way he's looked after you."

That was new to Fabian. "How do you even know that?" They hadn't really discussed Ophelia until today.

"I talked to Caroline."

"She hates me," Ophelia muttered.

Samantha shook her head again. "No, she doesn't. Fabian's mother is incapable of hatred. She's one of the sweetest people in the world. She's just having a bit of a hard time. Both of our families are, but maybe that's something we can talk about another time."

Ophelia gave him a worried look and Fabian could only grimace. He didn't want to dump all his family's financial problems and Samantha's family's marital problems on Ophelia. Not when she had so much shit to deal with herself.

"And the others don't hate you either," Samantha continued. "Lucille would love for you two to be together, because then she can stop feeling guilty. Jan probably doesn't care, and Matt thinks you're good for Fabian. His standards are a bit low because we're still working on the whole 'what's love and what's lust' thing with him, but he definitely doesn't mind having you around."

This time Ophelia giggled for real. "I like hanging out with you guys. You're fun and you go monster hunting. But," she sobered up again, "you didn't mention Rachel."

Samantha sighed. "Rachel has her reservations. It's because—"

"Eresta wanted to sacrifice her, and I belonged to the same cult." Ophelia looked annoyed. "It wasn't my idea."

"I know. And she knows that, too. I'm sure she'll come around. But if you want, I'll talk to her."

Fabian put his hands on Samantha's shoulders, applying a bit of pressure to support his suggestion. "Why don't you do that now, while I take care of things here?" He added belatedly, "Thank you." As unwelcome as the interruption had been, it was nice of Samantha to reassure Ophelia.

She smiled softly, then threw up her hands in defeat and chuckled. "I'm going. Don't stay up too late, kids."

"Good night, Mum!" Fabian rolled his eyes. It wasn't even five o'clock yet. When the door was finally shut, he apologised to Ophelia. "Sorry, she's used to meddling in my affairs. We've known each other since we were babies, so she thinks she has to bring me up right."

Ophelia came over to him and tugged playfully at his shirt. "Well, if that's true, she did a great job." But then her face darkened. "So, what's this about Lucille feeling guilty?"

Fabian groaned. The whole situation was confusing enough as it was. Then again, he wanted to be honest with Ophelia, so he invited her over to the little sitting area and told her about his relationship with Lucille and how he'd been with her when he'd met Ophelia. And then he told her about his other failed relationships.

"Rachel, too?" Ophelia's eyes were wide.

"I know, I know. When you put it all together, it sounds ridiculous. Like I jump on anyone who gives me the time of day." Fabian shuddered. It sounded worse than it really had been. "Most of the time I just end up confused. Like with Sam. It's been years now, but it took me completely by surprise. I thought we were meant to be together or something ridiculous like that, but—"

"—she prefers half-demons?"

There it was again. Matt and Samantha. In his opinion, Matt still didn't deserve her and never would, but he'd be a hypocrite if he interfered in their relationship. "I suppose." With a heavy heart he added: "When I asked her *why* she'd broken up with me, she said it was because she knew me too well. That there was no mystery, no intrigue, just comfort. Personally, I don't know what's wrong with comfort, but it seems to be my thing. I'm comforting, boring. Rachel was supposedly so in love with me and then decided I wasn't as good as her dreams of me—she walks in dreams for real. And I was never good enough for Lucille. It just took her a longer time to realise it."

At first, it had been just a summer fling, but then it went on for another month, and another month, and before they knew it, they'd made it to half a year. The comfort zone.

"She was just playing with you," Ophelia said surprisingly viciously. "Just like she's fooling around with her photographer now. I bet in a few months she'll move on to the next one. And Rachel." She grunted in anger. "Sorry, but she seems so judgmental. Like she's holding you to some imaginary standard but won't tell you what it is. She could have confronted me a dozen times in the last few weeks, but she didn't. Just like she didn't tell you what was bothering her in the relationship. And as for Samantha—"

"Lia, please," Fabian laughed. "She's my best friend." He loved this fervour of Ophelia's. It gave him a little more trust in himself.

"Well, then she should have stayed your best friend," Ophelia said sullenly. "If she didn't really love you, what's the point of starting something?"

Fabian snorted quietly. "But that's the thing, isn't it? No one knows if they really love someone when they start something. Some people don't even care if they ever do. You have to trust the process." Although, if he was honest, he was starting to lose faith in the process. "Or maybe I'm just better at being a supportive friend than a romantic interest."

Ophelia shook her head. She got up from her seat to sit on his lap and throw her arms around his neck. "You're a great friend, I don't doubt that. But you're an even better boyfriend." She leant forward and her hot breath tickled his cheek as she moved her lips to his ears. "They're just blind." She pulled away slightly and gave him a wicked smile. "Their loss, because now you're mine and I won't let you get away like they did."

Samantha

Early next morning Samantha sat in her Chemistry class, going through experiments that might be part of the written exam. As usual, she was working with Cian and Robert, which gave her the perfect opportunity to ask Robert a question. "Didn't you read that popular book recently? *The Mask of Fire*?"

Robert's face lit up. "Yes, it was really good. Are you reading it, too?"

"I don't really have time to read for fun at the moment, what with all the exam preparations. But I'm curious. Would you mind telling me how it ends? Do they defeat the fire devil?" Despite all the studying, the occasional monster hunt, and the never-ending drama with her friends, Samantha still managed to read a handful of books a month. Not as many as before, but still more than the average person.

Robert squinted at her. "You want me to spoil it for you?"

Samantha nodded eagerly. "I love spoilers. They always make me more curious about a book or movie." Across from her, Cian raised an eyebrow. Probably because he'd introduced her to a lot of movies, but she'd never asked him to spoil any of them. "I just want to know how it ends before I decide to get it. I don't like it when the hero dies and the bad guy wins."

"Oh, don't worry," Robert said quickly. "It has a good ending. Not happy, but they manage to destroy the Mask of Fire before the deal is done, which defeats the devil."

If Rachel was right and the shard she'd found in front of Jonathan's fireplace belonged to the mask, then the end of the book seemed purely fictional. Hopefully there was something more to it. "But how?"

Robert seemed to find her question absolutely delightful. "Oh, it's really good. They manage to trick the fire devil into destroying it himself, because..." He raised his index finger and quoted, "'Only the fire that forged it can destroy it.'"

Breaking it into pieces certainly didn't help. "Mask, devil's fire. Fantastic."

"You should read it. It's amazing."

Samantha forced a smile. Inside she wanted to scream. Whoever had broken the mask had only made their mission more complex. Now they had to find all the pieces before tricking Quirtubar into destroying it. *If* the book wasn't pure fiction.

She got up with a sigh. "I'll wash the glasses."

The menial task helped her calm down and think a bit. She had a suspicion who'd tried to destroy the mask originally. Hopefully they could convince Neve to help them. If not, they'd have to search the entire house.

"Do you need help?" Cian had joined her at the sink.

"Cleaning up?" Samantha asked confused.

"No, with the mask. It's another monster, isn't it?"

Samantha studied his face, looking for any sign of eagerness. The memory of him falling into the snake pit at the mine was still fresh in her mind. "We have everything under control."

His lips curled bitterly. "Sure. You've got Matt."

Not this again. "Cian."

He shook his head. "What? I get it, I'm not as good with a sword that I can kill—I'm sorry." He let go of the sink and turned away.

Samantha grabbed his arm. "Cian, you know things between Matt and me are complicated. I didn't plan for us to—"

"Fall in love?" Cian suggested. While Samantha's eyes widened, he added: "Oh, well, it's Matt, isn't it? He's irresistible. Doesn't matter what you do when you're hot. I should know." He took a deep breath. "Well, I hope he doesn't drop you as quickly as all his previous conquests." It sounded surprisingly sincere.

Still, Samantha had to clear things up. "We're not dating. Matt and I," she clarified belatedly, "and I don't plan to." It didn't come out quite as certain as she wanted it to. But the fact was she couldn't trust

Matt. What she'd told Ophelia in jest was painfully true. Matt didn't understand love, not yet, maybe never. Then again, who did?

And now, looking at Cian—who she really liked and appreciated—she thought of her best friend. She still hadn't found the courage to tell Fabian about her friendship with benefits, and after yesterday she wasn't sure she ever would, but his words had gotten under her skin. Was it wrong to have what she had? What if she wasn't ready for deep, intense love beyond the point of no return like Fabian was?

Cian lowered his eyes, seemingly mulling over this new information. When he looked up again, there was a hurt in his eyes that hadn't been there before. "You know you're free, don't you? This thing between us... it's casual." Every word seemed to hurt him more.

"I know," she said, as gently as she could.

"Just..." His shoulders slumped. "Let me know when you want to stop."

This probably wasn't the right discussion for Chemistry class. Still, Samantha asked, "Do you want to stop?"

"I still want to be friends," Cian said hastily. "We are friends first, right?"

Samantha smiled. "Yes, nothing will ever change that."

He relaxed as well, unable to resist returning her smile. "Okay, well..." Then he craned his neck to look over her shoulder. "Robert. We shouldn't leave him alone for too long."

Alarmed, Samantha returned to their lab table with Cian. "Robert, your arm is on fire."

Confused, Robert looked down at his arm, which he'd somehow managed to set on fire. As he watched the hairs crinkle and burn, the chemical underneath was consumed, and the flames went out on their own.

Annoyed, Samantha fell back into her chair. "Seriously, Robert."

"Sorry."

For the supposedly cold season, there was far too much fire going around at the moment. There had been no more accidents after Robert's attempt at self-combustion, but now they were back at Blackstone House. With its black exterior, it was hard to tell if it had burnt out last night. Samantha hoped not. She liked the house quite a lot, despite the volatile squatters.

As before, the door was frozen, but Lucille had no trouble getting them in. Once they were all in the foyer, they decided to split into pairs. To no one's surprise, the couples stayed together, and then Jan asked Rachel if she'd like to search the basement with him, leaving Samantha alone with Matt.

"Um, I think it's the attic for us."

Matt smiled languidly before pointing up the stairs. "Ladies first."

Samantha was halfway up the stairs before a thought crossed her mind and she looked down. "You're not using this to stare at my butt, are you?" She was suddenly very self-conscious of her position.

Matt laughed. "What?"

"My butt. It's practically in your face."

"And it's a very nice butt," Matt said smoothly, "but no, I hadn't looked—until now."

Samantha's cheeks burnt. "You're impossible."

In a flash, Matt disappeared and reappeared higher up. He wiggled his ass provocatively before asking with a grin. "Is that better?"

The heat in her cheeks only intensified. With a groan, she fixed her gaze on the stairs. "Just go." As if she didn't know what a fine piece of ass he had.

Somehow, she made it to the attic without looking up, but now that he was helping her up, she couldn't help but be amazed. "It's huge."

The attic was bigger than the master bedroom and could easily have served as a mini apartment. It was also surprisingly bright, thanks to two large windows at either end. On the other side, she noticed a round structure and a door. "Is that the tower?"

"Let's find out, shall we?" Matt walked across the room, which was no dustier than the others, and opened the door.

It opened onto a winding staircase that led to a small round room with narrow windows. From here, one could see the forest behind the house, and the city spreading out along the Reese on the other side.

"If I were a Gothic writer, I would've made this my office."

"With all those stairs?"

"Makes it nice and quiet." She walked around the room in awe, taking in the view.

Matt came to stand beside her, his presence impossible to ignore. "If this was your house, this would be your witch room."

A witch room of her own. She could see it only too well: the shelves arranged around her, the cauldron by the window, the herbs from the garden hanging from the ceiling. It was almost too much with Matt by her side.

"But it's Jan's, and it won't be anybody's if we don't find the mask."

There were only two boxes up here, neither of which contained anything of use, let alone a mask. Matt checked the rafters in case Neve had hidden them up there but came back empty-handed.

They continued their search downstairs. Whoever had first taken care of the house after Jonathan's death had cleared out a lot. Unless Jonathan had never had a chance to fill his attic with anything, not even an ugly portrait. Instead, there was only an old wardrobe to explore and a few forgotten boxes in a dark corner. The former was empty, the latter contained books. Many books, all the same.

"*Under the Firs of Siberia* by Jonathan Blackstone." Samantha took out one of the books. The cover was plain, dark green with a stylised fir tree and snow. She turned it over to read the back cover.

"I take it this one wasn't a hit?" Matt said, after opening the fourth box with the same content.

"It doesn't look like it, but it sounds interesting. It's about an expedition gone wrong, and if I read this right"—she quoted—"'*the snow seems to be alive.*' It could be about Neve."

Matt snorted. "Did that man write about anything that wasn't part of his life?"

"If I went on an expedition to the North Pole or made a deal with the devil, I'd write about that, too." No one could say Jonathan hadn't lived an interesting life.

"A deal with the devil," Matt repeated in a sultry voice. "Would you make one?"

Samantha swallowed. She wanted to tell him to stop being silly, but the words that came out were, "What kind of deal?"

His eyes seemed to darken, or perhaps it was the fading light of the winter sun. "How about a date? The cinema. You and me, alone."

She took a sharp breath, her mind already jumping ahead. There was no way they were going to make it out of the cinema with full knowledge of the film they'd be seeing. It was... impossible.

"Stop," she begged. "I'm with Cian."

Immediately, Matt backed away. "I thought it wasn't that serious."

"It isn't. It's..." The fact was that it was getting serious. Not for her, but for Cian. "Complicated."

Matt laughed quietly. "Tell me about it. Everything about love is so complicated. I don't think I'll ever understand it."

"I suppose that's just human nature. We're all complicated." She laughed at herself. "Take me. I've always dreamt of great romantic love, and now I'm in a relationship that's all about sex and friendship. And you... it would be so much easier if I could hate you."

"Easier?"

"It would be normal, wouldn't it?" Samantha picked up one of the books and stood up. "You killed Daniel, and if I was a demon, I would've tried to kill you. And neither of us would have complicated feelings."

Matt stared at her, lost in thought. Then he swallowed. "Sam..."

"Matt," she repeated, holding her breath. It was the first time she'd let the complicated feelings inside her breathe.

They looked into each other's eyes, each waiting for the other to make a move. To say something.

Instead, someone screamed from the floor below. Matt and Samantha ran to the door and looked down just in time to see a flash of fire burning through the corridor. Quirtubar.

Rachel

Rachel was glad Jan had asked her to go with him before she was the last one left. It probably hadn't changed the constellation, but the timing alone made her feel better. Together they made their way downstairs to the basement.

"You know, there's one thing I don't understand," Jan said. "If Jonathan's been dead for so long, how come his book is a bestseller now?"

After Robert's comment and the destruction of her own copy, Rachel had done some research. "Last year they sold part of his estate and that's how they got hold of the manuscript. A publisher saw an opportunity and took it. Nowadays they call him the German Poe, but back then he had a collection of poems that made a bit of a splash, and then one flop after another."

"Poor guy."

"Yeah." If she was being completely honest, he reminded her a little of herself. Jonathan hadn't had many friends. His colleagues had seen him as a joke, and he'd lived here all alone with no one but a snow witch. No wonder he'd become bitter.

They reached a wall. "This is strange."

"What about it?"

"Well, that can't be it, can it?" Jan turned around. "This is smaller than the bathroom upstairs. Such a big house and—"

"Quiet."

As Jan closed his mouth, Rachel heard it again. A whimper behind the wall. "I think it's coming from here."

There was nothing but stone in front of them. Jan walked over to it, listened, and then started pushing stones around at random. To Rachel's surprise, one gave way and the wall swung inwards.

"Go away," a small voice said.

"You." Jan said to the snow witch. He took a step forward. "Is this your room?"

Rachel still struggled to see. "Jan, we don't have time for another blizzard."

Slowly, the room behind the wall came into focus. It was the only one that hadn't been cleared out. Instead, shelves full of books and random objects lined the wall. Rachel could see a mirror, a taxidermised fantasy creature, and an amulet. But there was more, much more. If the mask was here, it would take them hours to uncover it.

"What is this place?"

"Neve said go away." The little witch cowered behind a wine rack, crying.

Jan got down on one knee beside her. "We could really use your help."

"Neve doesn't want you here."

"I understand that. I'm not Jonathan and I'm an intruder to you, but this Quirtle-whatever is back, and he wants you."

Neve's whole body shook. "He wants to eat Neve. Wants to rip Neve's heart out."

Rachel realised Neve might be her only chance. "Listen! We're looking for the Mask of Fire. If we destroy it before he eats you, the deal is off."

"No one can destroy ugly mask. Neve tried. But it didn't work." She lowered her head.

Jan's eyes lit up. "So you know where it is?" She nodded stubbornly. "Can you show me?"

Neve shook her head and Rachel wanted to scream. "Neve not allowed in secret room. Jonathan forbade it."

"But you've tried to break the mask before, so you must've been there," Rachel pointed out.

"No, Neve is a good girl. Neve listens. Always. Jonathan had mask in office. Mask is evil and made Jonathan write, write, write. And devil said he eat Neve. So, Neve tried to destroy it, but it didn't work. Jonathan got angry." She began to tremble, as if the thought of her beloved Jonathan being angry with her held all power over her. "He took mask away and stored it in secret room."

Jan sighed in relief. "Neve, Jonathan won't be angry. He doesn't want anything to happen to you, that's why he tried to break the deal, but it didn't work. The only thing that works is the mask. Show us this secret room. Please."

Neve pointed to a door on the other side of the secret collection. Jan and Rachel hurried over.

It was a strange door, one foot above the floor and made of iron. Whatever room it led to had been added to the house as an afterthought. There was no keyhole, but when Jan pushed the handle down it appeared unlocked.

"It's heavy," Jan complained. It took quite some effort to keep it open. "You go in."

Rachel squeaked at first. Annoyed at herself for this cowardly reaction, she took out her phone and carefully stepped over the doorframe into the room behind. "Oh, I know what this is."

"What?"

"A photo development lab. When you close the door, it's completely dark." She leant forward to examine a light bulb. "And yes, there's a red light here." She looked around and found the switch. Red light softly filled the room, which wasn't much bigger than an old phone booth. But there was a chair and a custom-made desk. Rachel opened the drawers and hit gold.

"I found it."

By the time the three of them ran up the stairs with the mask, chaos had broken out. A red glow in the living room showed them where the action was. They slipped into the room and found Quirtubar in a rage.

The rest of her friends were scattered around him. Samantha was trying to weave, Fabian was shooting water, Matt was firing energy, and Ophelia was bringing the shadows closer, whatever good that might do. Meanwhile, Philipp and Lucille were filling buckets in the kitchen and throwing their water on the small fires Quirtubar had started.

"Where is it? Where is my prize?" Quirtubar swung his arm, hitting Matt and throwing him against the wall. Groaning, Matt collapsed.

"We need the mask," Fabian shouted.

"It's here!" Jan called. "We've got it."

"My prize!" Quirtubar roared.

To Rachel's surprise, Neve floated into the room. "Neve is here, too."

"Finally."

"What are you doing?" Rachel asked her, horrified. "Do you want to die?"

Stubborn as ever, Neve shook her head. "Neve does not want to die."

Quirtubar hissed. "The deal is done. His new book is a bestseller. Everyone is talking about him, and his adversaries are silent."

"You killed them," Neve revealed. "They died by fire. Your fire. You made Jonathan sad."

While Jonathan had surely despised his critics, he probably hadn't wanted them dead, Rachel thought. And yet it was his fault.

"I grant wishes," Quirtubar said. "Making people happy is not part of it."

What a terrible way to do business. What seemed like a dream could so easily turn into a nightmare. Rachel wondered what would've happened if she'd wished for better friends. Would she have condemned the ones she had to death? Would they have been replaced by attentive but terrible copies?

She shuddered and decided that making a deal with a devil was not in her future.

"The deal is done, little witch. Time for Jonathan to do his part."

Suddenly Jan jumped between the fire devil and the snow witch. "Over my dead body."

Silence fell over the room. Then Lucille cleared her throat. "Jan, if he eats her... he'll leave. The deal is done."

"She's been hostile to us from the start," Fabian added carefully.

"I don't care. That fire devil won't get her."

Quirtubar smiled, then suddenly disappeared and reappeared behind Jan. Before anyone could stop him, he'd grabbed Neve. Panic filled her small face as the air around her began to shift. He scratched Neve's face with one of his long, sharp fingernails and tasted her blood. "Delicious."

"Let's see how you like this." Jan threw the mask to the floor, but it just bounced off and stayed whole. "That would have been too easy."

"It can only be destroyed in his own fire!" Samantha shouted from across the room. She was still weaving intently.

Jan turned and held the mask into one of the small fires Quirtubar had started, but the flames were too weak.

Instead, an idea formed in Rachel's mind. "How about—?"

Suddenly, flames burst from the Quirtubar and shot in Samantha's direction. Just before they hit her, Matt was there, shielding Samantha with his back. Rachel could only imagine the pain he must be experiencing. Fortunately, Fabian's water interrupted the stream of fire.

"You again," Quirtubar hissed. He raised his hand in Fabian's direction.

Before he could unleash another firestorm, a blizzard blew up. Rachel stumbled back when she saw it was full of sharp ice crystals, all aimed at Quirtubar. Unfortunately, they melted before they reached his body.

Exhausted, Neve gave up. She lowered her arms and head, unable to fight him any longer. Horrified, Rachel watched as her light hair gradually turned black. Then she remembered her plan.

"Hey, why don't you try that on me?" She quickly opened her jacket and fumbled with the inner pocket.

"Have you gone mad?" Lucille screamed.

The fire devil's eyes met hers. "As you wish."

With a gruesome smile, he threw a ball of liquid fire at her. At the last second, Rachel managed to pull out her dreamweb and hold it in front of her. As with Malcolm, the dreamweb swallowed the attack, leaving a confused fire devil in its wake.

Rachel smiled. "Hey, Jan."

Jan, who'd been desperately trying to hold the mask in the various fires around them, looked up. Rachel released the energy and watched as a larger and more powerful version of Quirtubar's spell flew towards Jan.

Stunned, Jan waited and waited. Then, just before it was too late, he threw the mask at the fire and himself to the ground.

Fire and mask hit the fireplace. A bright light flashed. Then Quirtubar screamed. When the light faded, all that was left of him was the pile of ashes in the fireplace.

Neve, however, was still there. She was sitting on the floor, shaking and crying. Her hair was half black, half white, while her skin had darkened at least two shades. As Jan cautiously approached her, a small whirlwind of snowflakes erupted around her, taking her with it.

"Is it over?" Philipp asked, still holding a bucket.

"I think so," Samantha whispered. "Great idea, Rachel." She gave her a feeble smile before fussing over Matt. "You idiot."

Matt snorted, though it sounded painful. "You know I heal easily."

"Still."

Those two. Rachel rolled her eyes in amusement and looked around the room. Thanks to Fabian, the fires were out, but the damage was undeniable. All their work was destroyed. Several black spots remained.

Lucille sighed. "I guess we can start over with this room."

"Where did you find the mask?" Fabian asked.

"Neve led us to a hidden room in the basement," Rachel explained. "From the looks of it, Jonathan wasn't just a writer, he was a collector of all things occult. We should be very careful with the artefacts in that room. But he's got books, too."

As expected, Samantha's eyes lit up at the mention of this. "We found books, too, endless copies of one of his flops. I believe it tells Neve's story." She held up a book with a plain cover.

"Can I read it?" Jan asked.

"You want to read a book?" Lucille asked.

Jan shrugged. "If it holds information about my new roommate, sure."

Samantha handed him the book. "We can all have copies."

"No thanks," Fabian said. "I've had enough of the little terror." He sighed. "Let's hope she's grateful enough to let you live here now."

To Rachel's surprise, Jan had already started the book. "I'll find a way. Don't worry."

JANNA RUTH

To Rachel's surprise, Jan had already started the book. "I'll find a way. Don't worry."

Jan

Jan hadn't read the whole book, only skimmed through it. As interesting as Neve was, the way Jonathan wrote was as bad as any of the books Jan had read for school. It wasn't hard to imagine why no one had bought it. But there was a happy ending. After weeks of fighting the snow in Siberia, Jonathan's hero had made peace with it. He'd realised that the snow witch behind it all had just wanted to play, so he'd befriended her and taken her home to raise as his daughter.

This gave Jan an idea, but before he could put it into action, he received a call from Lu. "Hello?"

She giggled on the other line. "Oh Jan, Philipp has just found something amazing."

"Um, okay?" He said, not quite sure why he needed to know what her new boyfriend was up to. "So?"

"Gosh, Jan, it's about the house."

"What about the house?"

Lu took a deep breath to control her giddiness. "Philipp dug deep and managed to get access to Jonathan's will. He died poor, but he left everything to his daughter, including the rights to his books."

"Neve." Jan's mind was blank, too scared to pursue the thought.

"Nobody's been able to find her yet, but we have. And with a little help from my illusions, we can convince the lawyers of her legitimacy. With the new book selling like hotcakes, Neve will come into quite a bit of money from the royalties."

Jan let out the breath he'd been holding. "That's great for her."

"And for you!" Lu giggled again. "I bet she's grateful for how you protected her and that we saved her. What does she need money for? She's a snow witch."

Jan looked at his hand, weighing his small purchase for Neve.

"You could pay off a big chunk of the mortgage, Jan! Isn't that great?"

"Sure." Of course it was great, but the money wasn't really his. And as much as he needed it, it didn't feel right to bother Neve with it. Not now. "Well, let me know how you get on with securing it for her."

"Of course. Will you talk to her?" Lu asked eagerly.

"Yes." But not about this.

He said goodbye to Lu and descended the stairs to the basement and Jonathan's wondrous collection. Neve was crouched behind one of the shelves as before, crying her eyes out.

"How are you?" Jan asked.

Neve started and began to shake.

Jan felt so sorry for her. The traces of the fire devil's power were all burnt into her body. "It's just me, the annoying new owner of the house. Jan." She looked up at him. "Look, I'm sorry about Jonathan. I know he promised to come back, but he didn't. I'm not him, but I thought I could at least keep part of his promise." He handed her the small bag. "These are bonbons. I hope you like them. My sister eats them all the time."

Neve took the bag with big eyes. "Bonbons are for Neve?"

"That's what I said. I hope we can come to a truce. Bonbons for letting me stay? Because I really need a roof over my head."

To his surprise, Neve fell into his arms. "Neve likes Jan."

She snuggled into his lap and popped a bonbon into her mouth. Then she offered him the bag. "Jan likes bonbons too?"

Jan couldn't help smiling. "Of course he does."

As Jan chose a bonbon for himself, Neve cuddled up to him. It seemed that he hadn't just inherited Jonathan's house, but also his snow witch.

Part 5

Humans & Demons

Balthasar

Six times. Six times Balthasar had tried to kill Melaney in the last half hour of foreplay. And six times Melaney had redirected his attempts into lust, without even acknowledging. The seventh time, though, she'd had enough and brought him to his knees with the full force of her sin.

Balthasar's skin was flushed, and his breathing was short and uncomfortable. Meanwhile, his nether regions screamed in pain that only increased the longer she held his body immobile. To add salt to injury, Melaney's long fingernails raked his face before she dug into his hair and pulled his head back brutally.

"Do you really think I'd fall for that old trick?" She pushed him away from her, releasing the special hold she had on him. "Go away. You bore me."

Balthasar made sure he was well out of range before he said, "Do I now?" They'd been having fun until his murder attempts. "And you think he's better than me? This child?"

"Envy doesn't suit you," Melaney replied coldly, avoiding his question.

"He's too young for this."

Melaney's eyes shot daggers at him. "Not everyone needs a thousand years to take what they want. Now go, you've had your chance. Unless you want me to keep you under my control for longer? Until the morrow, perhaps?"

Balthasar gave her one last baleful look before he left. On his way to his own quarters, Melaney's companion Frennys crossed his path. He was a handsome man but useless for any ploy, for he was devoted to

Melaney beyond a shadow of doubt. A factor to consider in a coup, but nothing to worry about.

After Frennys had hurried into Melaney's rooms to finish what they'd started, Balthasar jumped into his quarters. As he often did, he found Chay in his study, poring over a pile of parchment.

"She used her power over me to keep me from taking what's mine," Balthasar began to rant before Chay could even look up. "She only wants *him.*"

"I know," Chay muttered, still too busy to face him.

Balthasar toyed with the idea of blasting him through the wall, but that was a Caspar move, unworthy of him. "You still won't tell me if she gets what she wants."

Despite his eyes fixed on the parchment, Chay said, "What we get is not always what we really want."

"I don't need a Chay wisdom." Balthasar scoffed. "Fine. You know what, let him have at it. Let him shoot his shot. She'll probably have to guide him to make sure his dagger actually finds its target, but that's not my problem."

Finally, Chay looked up. "And then?"

Balthasar smiled darkly. "Then I kill them." It was the perfect plan. Melaney would get what she wanted. Matt would actually prove himself to be useful, and Balthasar would end up exactly where he was supposed to.

Chay sighed heavily. "The path to Lust's power may lead through him, but not like this."

"I'm tired of waiting for him to make his move. Melaney is deluded if she thinks Matt will ever give her the time of day. He's too busy pretending to be in love." It was embarrassing to watch him flirt with that human girl when she barely acknowledged his affections. It was unworthy of someone who was considering deep diving into lust.

Chay nodded thoughtfully. "The path to Lust's power may lead through him, but the path to Matt is through Samantha."

Which meant only one thing: if he wanted to move things forward, he had to remove the Samantha factor. After his fight with Selima, Balthasar knew better than to try and kill Samantha. Matt would just get his boxers in a twist again.

He smiled darkly as the perfect idea came to him.

Samantha

Samantha was barely dressed and brushing her hair when she heard a loud crash downstairs. Startled, she stuck her head out of her room to find Meg had done the same. The two sisters exchanged a look that was interrupted when their father shouted, "Are you out of your mind, woman?"

Samantha tied up her hair and walked down the corridor to Meg's room. Meg had grabbed her school bag and announced, "I'm off."

"It's ten past seven. You're not even wearing make-up."

"Since when do you care about make-up?"

"I don't, but you do."

Meg scoffed, went to the bathroom and returned with her make-up bag. "Here it is. I'll put it on at school."

It said a lot about Meg and what she thought about what was going on downstairs that she was willing to be seen without make-up. With a sigh, Samantha followed her downstairs.

After some back and forth, her parents had fallen silent. Juliane was in the kitchen while Ben fixed his hair in the hall mirror. His face was a little redder than usual, the only trace of his outburst a few minutes earlier.

As Meg crept towards the door, Samantha tried a cheerful, "Good morning!"

Ben snorted. "Good morning indeed. Your mum is getting back together with her ex."

"I'm not!" Juliane shouted. She hurried out of the kitchen, still holding a towel.

Meg had her hand on the doorknob but was too curious to make her escape.

"You invited Max here."

"Max?" Meg asked. "Max Schönborn? The actor?"

"The actor?" Samantha had no idea who they were all talking about. If this Max was an actor, he wasn't one she'd seen much of. Then she remembered the TV doctor Meg and her mum had been fawning over a few weeks ago.

Ben pulled a face. "He is, but he's not just an actor, he's your mum's childhood sweetheart." His voice took on a nasty edge. "She wasn't interested all these years, but now that he's famous, all those feelings have come back."

Juliane crossed her arms. "Why don't you twist my words a bit more and claim we ran off together." She turned to Samantha and Meg and rolled her eyes. "I didn't have his number or address. Honestly, I'd mostly forgotten about him until he showed up on our TV. We were friends, nothing more."

"Sure."

Samantha was still confused as to what was going on. "And you invited him here?" If he was just someone her mother used to know, why would she invite him into her home and not a coffee shop?

Juliane groaned. "Is it really such a big deal?"

"Of course not," Ben said sarcastically. He put on his shoes and grabbed his jacket. "Why don't you ask him if he wants to move in? In the meantime, I'll be sleeping at the workshop."

"As if you don't hide there all the time anyway!" Juliane shot back.

Ben flung open the door. "Oh, shut up!"

Meg took her chance to slip out, too, before Ben slammed the door behind him, leaving Samantha alone with her mother.

Samantha couldn't help herself. She had to ask. "Why?"

"Why what?"

"Why did you invite him?" She closed her eyes and inhaled deeply. It seemed so unnecessarily insensitive, especially given the current tension. "I mean, couldn't you at least have asked Dad?"

Her mother snorted. "As if I have to ask my husband's permission to see another man."

Pained, Samantha made a face. "Mum." She was deathly afraid of this new development. Her parents should be coming together, facing the challenges of their family as a unit, not pushing each other further apart with each passing day. "Don't you love Dad anymore?"

She wished the words back as soon as she'd said them. It wasn't a thought she would tolerate. Her parents would be fine. They needed to fight like others needed air to breathe. Caroline had said so.

Juliane gave her a long look. "Go upstairs. I'll make your lunch." She hadn't prepared Samantha's lunch for years.

With a sigh, Samantha went back upstairs. Everything was coming apart, and the more she tried to hold on, the more the pieces cut into her skin.

Fabian

"If we do one more revision, I'll quit," Fabian complained as he and Rachel left English.

"Only one more month."

"Until the written exams, then we have to cram for the oral exam, and I still have to finish my project thesis." Why had he thought it was a good idea to sign up for a special project like Samantha? At the time it had seemed like a good idea to add a fifth component so that he could possibly make up for bad marks in the exams, especially Physics. But now it just felt like more work at an already stressful time.

Rachel, who'd made the wise decision not to bother with it, cocked her head. "What was your topic again?"

"Comparing five impressionist painters in technique and message." It was a cool project. He just wished he didn't have to write fifteen pages on it while studying for three four-hour exams.

They were walking down the corridor when they heard familiar voices. "As if it wasn't bad enough my parents are at each other's throats all the time, now we have to do a school project with *her*." Meg ranted at Anne.

The "her" in question was none other than Ophelia, who was just a metre away from the other two. "I can hear you, you know?"

"Then cover your ears!" Meg snapped.

"Meg!" Anne hissed, clearly uncomfortable with so much vitriol.

Ophelia clicked her tongue. "If it's such a nuisance, I can do it myself."

Anne shook her head. "No way, we'll all meet at my place this afternoon and do it together."

"No!" Meg cried. "Let her do it, if she's so keen. Little Miss Homeschool needs it more, anyway."

"Sure your parents weren't at *your* throat instead?" Ophelia shot back.

"You, nasty little—"

Ophelia ignored them and ran up to Fabian, her eyes sparkling with joy. "Hey!" She greeted him with an enthusiastic kiss.

As Meg and Anne walked past, Fabian heard Meg finish her snide remark. He gasped and started to speak, but Ophelia pinched his arm.

"Ignore her. She's just jealous and upset because her parents are fighting."

Although Fabian grumbled about letting Meg get away with her behaviour, he let Ophelia drag him along. On his other side, Rachel seemed to ignore them altogether as they entered the cafeteria. In the back, Lucille sat next to Samantha, her arm around her, while Matt stood in front of them, looking worried. As they approached the group, Samantha wiped her cheeks.

"Looks like Meg's not the only one upset today," Rachel said quietly.

Fabian was instantly overcome with concern. The last thing any of them needed right now was family drama.

As they came closer, he could see Samantha was on the verge of tears: "I just don't know how they're going to get through this. Sure, they fight a lot, but they haven't had a proper conversation since Christmas." She took a deep breath. "And now this Max thing? What am I supposed to think? What is that?"

Fabian desperately wanted to know who Max was, but Lucille already seemed on to it and he didn't want to interrupt her.

"Probably just what your mum says it is," Lucille said in a sympathetic and reassuring voice. "She's just catching up with an old acquaintance."

"An old acquaintance she had sex with." Samantha stifled a sob. "This is insane."

Lucille shook her head. "That was decades ago. Ancient history. I'm sure nothing will happen between them."

"And what if it does?" Matt shrugged. "Maybe a little sex will relax your mum, relieve some of the tension."

While Samantha gaped at him, Fabian quickly intervened, "Um, usually an affair is the last thing that relieves tension in a relationship." Meanwhile, he mouthed at Samantha, *Juliane is having an affair?*

But before his non-verbal communication could get through, Matt rolled his eyes. "Humans."

At last, he noticed Samantha and Lucille staring at him. "What? It's relaxing."

Fabian rubbed the bridge of his nose. It was like a car crash waiting to happen.

"And how *exactly*," Samantha said in a tight voice, "do you think it's going to help my parents' relationship if my mum cheats on my dad?"

"*He's* definitely not going to be relaxed afterwards," Lucille added.

"How does spending months screaming at each other help?" Matt retorted. "I really don't know what the problem is. They obviously hate each other, so—"

Fabian dug his elbow into Matt's back. "Stop talking, man. Stop talking."

"Why do two people who can't stand each other have to stay together?"

Lucille groaned in exasperation. "Because they made a promise when they got married."

"That just proves how useless those promises are."

"Sam," Rachel said quietly, drawing Fabian's attention to his best friend.

Unable to stand it any longer, Samantha began to pack her things. An angry tear ran down her cheek.

Meanwhile, Matt was still on a roll. "Are they supposed to be miserable together until they die? That doesn't make any sense."

Samantha's chair scraped across the floor as she stood up abruptly. She came face to face with Matt. "In my opinion, the fact that you don't understand what's going on is just further proof that you don't have even an ounce of humanity in you." Then she stormed off.

"Sam!" Fabian called after her. He turned to Matt, ready to give him a piece of his mind.

But the half-demon had visibly deflated. "On a scale of one to Daniel, how bad was I?"

Matt

Matt had a few hours to think about what had happened this morning. He still thought that the best thing Samantha's parents could do was break things off and move on to other people. Her mother seemed ready to do that, but apparently it was now the worst thing that could happen.

Lucille had tried to explain it to him, and it all came down to humans deciding at some random point that they wanted to spend the rest of their life with one person and one person only, not taking into account that their interests might change, that the world might change, or that they themselves might change. Matt had tried to comprehend the concept of marriage, but it made no sense to him. Even if it seemed romantic to promise eternity to a loved one when that so-called eternity would last half a century at most, it made no sense to force people together until everyone was miserable, much less, because of a decision made when everyone was so much younger.

Unable to reach a conclusion, he met up with Lucille, Rachel, and Fabian at the end of the day. Like so many times lately when Samantha wasn't around, they were talking about the surprise birthday party they were planning to throw at the Blackstone House.

"It's all arranged," Lucille said. "We're pretty much ready to go."

"Easy for you to say," Matt interjected, not knowing what exactly had been arranged. "I still don't have a present for her."

Fabian rolled his eyes. "You have another problem at the moment."

"Meaning?"

"This morning?" Fabian asked, sounding annoyed. "Samantha's not exactly your biggest fan at the moment."

Lucille nodded wisely. "Maybe you should think about a reconciliation gift instead."

Matt groaned. "Because things are going so well with the birthday present."

"I don't understand," Lucille complained. "This morning you talked yourself into an early grave without even taking a breath, but a simple birthday present has you scratching your head for weeks."

"I already missed her last birthday. This one has to be perfect." Last March, the two of them had been at odds. Matt hadn't even known it was Samantha's birthday until two days later, when Lucille had mentioned the little party they'd held. It was the first one he'd actually been allowed to celebrate.

"Let me put it this way," Fabian said darkly. "If you two don't make up quickly, you'll miss this one, too."

Matt had tried to catch Samantha, but she'd managed to avoid him all day. His apology would have to wait until tomorrow. In the meantime, he prowled the shelves at the Magic Circle, waiting for inspiration to strike.

He still felt his suggestion hadn't been completely unreasonable, but he understood Samantha didn't want her parents to split up and had taken it the wrong way. If an apology from him would make her feel better, he would give it to her. But that still didn't solve the problem of her birthday present.

Matt returned to the same shelf of potion bottles he'd visited twice before. At least half of them had been brewed by Samantha herself, but there were plenty of others that looked suitably witchy.

Lost in thought, he picked up a pink bottle with drips of wax around the neck. Sometimes it was hard to tell whether they were selling the contents or the vibe.

"Your problem must be worse than I thought."

Matt spun around, almost dropping the bottle when he heard Balthasar speak. "What are you talking about?"

His brother nodded at the bottle. "Do you need spells like that to get any action these days?"

Confused, Matt looked at the potion and realised what he'd taken. A *love* potion. Embarrassed, he put it back on the shelf. "It wasn't meant for me." He moved over to the bookshelf and looked provocatively at Balthasar. "What can I do for you this time? Lost any more demon spirits? Planning to create a new reality?"

"Interesting idea. I might try it some other time. But no." Balthasar leant against the other shelf with a lazy smile. "I want you to come back to Hescaryn with me. In short, I'm offering you a deal."

Matt frowned. "Only one can be the next archdemon."

"True, but if *I* become archdemon, I can get you a position in the Small Council. You could be one of Lust's representatives. Or whatever else you want to do with your long life."

"I just want to be left alone. Especially by you!"

Balthasar chuckled. "You know you'll never have peace as long as *she* lives."

Their mother wouldn't rest until the matter was resolved. But, at the moment, Matt couldn't care less. "Then maybe you should harass her instead of me." It suddenly struck him that, after all these months, Balthasar hadn't achieved that. "You can't kill her."

Balthasar rolled his eyes. "I'm not the one she wants."

It made no sense to Matt. His mother's wishes should have very little to do with the actual deed. "Melaney wants *me* to kill her?"

"You know exactly what she wants."

Matt swallowed. His mother wanted to have sex with him. Just the thought of it made him break out in hives. "I'm not interested. I—"

"You want Samantha, I know!" Balthasar groaned. "Have you been with her yet? Did you two have sex?"

Matt snapped out of his confused state and blurted out, "That's none of your business." It wasn't about the sex, Matt wanted to say, but he failed to remember what it was about. "Besides, she can't stand me right now." When Balthasar raised an eyebrow, looking slightly invested, Matt explained, "I said something stupid and accidentally hurt her."

Balthasar groaned impatiently. "Her parents fight all the time and I suggested they might be happier if they split up."

"*Why* would they want to stay together?"

"Exactly!" Matt cleared his throat, realising he'd gotten carried away in his enthusiasm. "I have no idea why I'm telling you this. As if you have a better understanding of the subject than I do." Balthasar was even more demon than he was. "I'll have to apologise to her again."

"So you can finally have sex with her?"

"No!" Matt scoffed. "Humans are more complicated. They want a relationship. Love. Feelings."

Balthasar looked at him doubtfully. "And why would *you* want that? Is it really worth it?"

"Because…" Matt shook his head. "You wouldn't understand." Turning to Balthasar for advice just showed how desperate he was. "Now go play with your little council."

Balthasar stepped away from the shelf. "Saying no to my deal is not a good move, Melchior. Here's a little tip. Stop all this nonsense."

"Nonsense?"

"You're a demon, Melchior. No relationships, no love, and no stupid feelings."

Matt's face darkened. "Half-demon. I'm a half-demon."

Balthasar pulled a face. "Makes no difference to the people here. Nor to me." The unspoken offer hung in the air as Balthasar vanished.

Frustrated, Matt slumped against the bookshelf. This morning at school he'd felt exactly as Balthasar had just said. His thoughts and feelings would never reflect those of his friends. They all somehow instinctively knew what to say when someone was upset about their parents fighting. Matt had thought he'd done a great job already, recognising that Samantha was upset about their parents' relationship, despite not being involved in it. In Hescaryn, he'd be more than confused if a demon was in tears over something that had happened between their progenitors.

But it hadn't been enough. Not even close.

After almost two years in Greenvalley, he still had so much to learn. Sometimes, like now, he found himself thinking the same thing as Balthasar. Was it really worth all the uncertainty and doubt?

Samantha

All day long, Samantha had been a mess. Every time she thought she'd pushed the thought of her parents to the back of her mind, Matt's words came to the fore.

Why do two people who can't stand each other have to stay together?

There were so many good answers. Because they'd made a promise to each other. Because they were her parents. Because they'd make it. Because you don't just throw away twenty years of marriage. But the question wouldn't stop sowing doubt.

Miserable, miserable, miserable.

It did her head in.

"Are you okay?"

Startled, Samantha wiped her cheeks and stared down at the chemistry book she'd been trying to read. She didn't know where she'd lost track of the text and looked up at Cian. "I'm fine."

He raised an eyebrow.

Samantha felt compelled to fill the void left by his lack of a question. "I'm just upset about Matt."

Immediately Cian's face changed. "Shit. What did he do?"

"Oh no. He didn't do anything," she said quickly before she sighed. "He was just being his usual unemotional Neanderthal self." Once the frustration was out, it was easy to fall into a tirade. "He thinks it'd be better if my parents split up. As if they haven't been married for twenty years, shared two daughters, and built a life together."

Somehow her voice took a dip towards the end. Cian dropped his bag, slid into the chair beside her, and pulled her into his arms. At first, Samantha refused to give in, but then the tears began to fall.

"Hey, guys," Robert's voice sounded.

She felt Cian shake his head, causing Robert's footsteps to recede hastily. Meanwhile, Cian stroked her back until she felt capable of speaking again. And this time, it was the bare truth. "I don't want my parents to split up."

"I know how you feel," Cian said quietly. "Does it help if I tell you it's not the end of the world?"

Samantha drew back a little to study his face.

Cian smiled weakly. "My parents divorced when I was fourteen. They fought a lot. Now I know they only stayed together as long as they did because of me. When it was finally official and my father moved out of the house, things got so much better. With both of them."

On an intellectual level, Samantha knew that a lot of people got divorced and that staying together for the children wasn't healthy for anyone. Cian was obviously fine. At least now.

"Was that when you started to take your frustrations out on other people?" Namely Fabian and the other boys he and Alan thought weren't cool enough.

Cian let go of her and shrugged. "Probably." He stroked her back once more before withdrawing completely. "But I got over it and so did my parents. They stayed apart, but we all get along now, which wasn't always the case, you know."

It made perfect sense, and yet it punched another hole in her heart. "Is it so unreasonable of me to want them to fight for their love?"

"As long as you don't go around forging love letters like I did."

It took Samantha a moment to realise what he'd said. When it finally clicked, a chuckle escaped her lips. Cian grinned. "Wasn't noticeable at all with my chicken scratch."

Samantha laughed. She could easily imagine the forged letters and how obvious it had been who'd written them. But then she thought about how painful the whole process must have been for Cian that he, a boy of fourteen, would write love letters for his parents. If his parents were decent—and she knew his mother was—they must've felt terrible too. And yet they'd split up. And it had been better for all of them.

She wasn't quite ready to give up on her parents yet, but she leant against his shoulder and whispered, "Thank you."

Cian put his arm around her and held her for as long as she needed.

At the end of the day, Fabian was waiting for her by the bikes.

"No Ophelia today?" she asked in surprise. Lately, his girlfriend was practically stitched to his side.

Fabian snorted. "She's at Anne's with Meg. The three of them have some kind of group project for History. *If* your sister doesn't get her claws out again. She was completely feral this morning."

Normally Samantha would scoff at Meg's bitchy tendencies, but today she had nothing but sympathy for her. "It's been a rough awakening."

"I know." Fabian helped her lift her bike off the stand and they rode home together. It was too early in March for the trees to bear leaves, but here and there snowdrops and crocuses peeked through the snow. Spring was on its way.

They talked about Meg and Ophelia. Apparently, Ophelia was still struggling to settle in, and Meg wasn't much help. Her sister was lashing out, but Ophelia wasn't letting her get away with it, so Samantha thought they'd both be fine.

As they crossed the bridge, Samantha got off her bike and started to push, dreading going home.

Fabian followed suit. "It'll get better. Remember when your dad lived in the workshop for three weeks?"

"Mum said he was just working late," Samantha remembered. "How long ago was that?"

"I think we were about ten or eleven. Anyway, after three weeks everything was fine again. And then the four of you went to Gran Canaria for the Easter holidays. I was so jealous."

Samantha had to smile. "The trip was wonderful. They danced every night." It had been such a whirlwind of a month; first the big fight, then the spontaneous family holiday. Samantha vividly remembered watching her parents dance and wishing for that kind of love.

"Deep down, they love each other," Fabian said. "And nothing will ever change that."

They'd reached the house and leant their bikes against the wall. With a sigh that was part hope and part exhaustion, Samantha opened the door.

A plate sailed past her and almost took Fabian's ear out. "I hate you!" her mother hollered at her father.

Ben's face was contorted with rage. "Don't you think I feel exactly the same?"

Samantha exchanged glances with Fabian. They'd just established her parents would always love each other and now they *hated* each other? She let the door slam behind her, drawing her parents' attention.

"We have a visitor."

Her father sneered at her. "What are you talking about? It's just Fabian."

Fabian was clearly uncomfortable with the thick tension in the room, but he tried to joke, "Just Fabian?"

"You got a problem with that?" Ben snapped.

The paper-thin amusement was wiped from Fabian's face. "No, of course not, I—"

Samantha felt her desperation rise again. If she didn't defuse the situation quickly she'd be in danger of bursting into tears. As if drowning, she clung to the happy memory Fabian had just reminded her of. "Fabian wanted to look at the pictures of Gran Canaria. Remember how beautiful it was?"

Remember! Remember, please, she silently shouted at her parents.

But her mother just looked at her coldly. "I burnt those."

Samantha swallowed hard. All the words left her, and her mind was blank.

In the meantime, Ben walked over to Fabian and grabbed his arm. "On second thought, I'm not in the mood for visitors." He opened the door and pushed Fabian out.

"Dad!" It was such confusing behaviour Samantha could only watch as Fabian stumbled down the step and looked at Ben with wide eyes.

"Go home, Fabian! Hold your mum's hand or whatever it is you do these days. You're not welcome here anymore."

He slammed the door in Fabian's face.

Shocked by her father's behaviour, Samantha struggled for words. "You're making fun of Caro's burnout?" Where were the Fantastic Four when you needed them?

"Did I ask for your opinion?" Ben snapped.

Samantha stumbled back, swallowing hard.

"Well, that's our Samantha," her mother said in a mocking voice. "Has to stick her nose in everybody's business to show us how great she is."

Tears welled up in Samantha's eyes. "What's wrong with you?" This wasn't normal anymore. In all the months they'd been fighting there might have been a curt word if you'd got in the way, but neither of them had ever taken their frustrations out on her or Meg.

"It's none of your business!" her father roared.

"Go to your room," her mother ordered. "And take care of your own shit."

Shocked, Samantha looked from one to the other, then turned and fled up the stairs. Before she reached her room, the fighting had resumed downstairs. By the sound of it, dishes were flying again.

Tears streamed down Samantha's face as she pushed through the door to her room. What should have been a safe haven was anything but.

The door scraped across shards of glass on the floor. Books and folders—and her meticulously written and sorted flashcards—were strewn across the floor. Her clothes were torn from her wardrobe and the lamp from her bedside table was smashed near the door.

Samantha walked around her room as if in a trance, being very careful of where she put her feet. She picked up some of the cards and folders and stacked them on the table. There, her eyes fell on a card that hadn't been there this morning.

She opened it and read the short message: *I'm sorry. Hope you like it. Matt.*

"Matt?"

When she didn't immediately see what he could be referring to, she took a step back and studied the desk closely. Something poked her toe, causing her to lower her gaze. Next to the desk was a pile of black pottery shards that she couldn't associate with any of her possessions.

Intrigued, she crouched down and picked a few up, as if they were part of a puzzle she needed to solve. The truth was that whatever present Matt had left in her room had been smashed in her parents' rampage.

With a sigh, Samantha continued to pick up the pieces when she noticed something else. Almost invisible against the grey carpet was something small and black. She pinched her fingers and picked it up to look at it in the light. It looked like some sort of fly.

She was about to ignore it when she noticed a whole handful of them. "What's going on?"

Jan

The interview process wasn't his first rodeo, but Jan's nerves were shot as he walked into the hospital and realised that he really wanted this job. Not just because it would mean having a proper plan for his future and employment, but because the more he thought about it, the more he could see himself in the position.

Contrary to his usual style, he was wearing a dress shirt and carrying a slender folder with his application materials under his arm. He'd spent every night last week preparing for all sorts of questions, even researching first-aid procedures in case there was a practical test. He was as ready as he would ever be, but as soon as he entered the hospital, doubt frayed his resolve.

He was a failure. A high school dropout. The interviewer would see through his sketchy track record and throw him out.

Jan tried to tell himself that they'd already seen his application and decided to invite him anyway, when he saw his mother at the reception talking to a doctor. The last thing he needed right now was her disappointment. It was almost enough to make him turn back, but instead his resolve hardened. He would show her that he was more than she ever thought he was.

He approached the reception desk with stiff legs. "Um... I'm here for an interview with EMT services."

"Jan?" His mother whirled around.

"Second floor, left corridor. Report to room 208," the receptionist said.

"Thank you." Jan was grateful for her quick information as it allowed him to ignore his mother. He walked away and headed for the elevator.

Behind him, he could hear his mother excusing herself. Then her footsteps followed. "Jan!"

She caught up with him at the elevator, panting slightly. Jan ignored her and pushed the button impatiently.

"What are you doing here? Did I hear that right? You're here for an interview?"

Annoyed, Jan turned away from the elevators and chose the stairs instead, taking two steps at a time to get away from his mother.

"I didn't know you were interested in a career in healthcare," his mother called after him. She tried to follow but was much slower. "Jan, please."

He didn't want to give in after she'd never reached out and begged him to return home. He wondered what it had been like to come home from a shift and find that one of your children had moved out. Had she just shrugged her shoulders and made dinner for three? Or had she sat in the room he'd left behind, wondering what had gone wrong? If so, putting things right hadn't been on her list of priorities.

"You never take my calls."

Jan hesitated, his hand curling around the railing. It wasn't true that she never rang. But every time he'd seen her name on his screen, the anger would rise again.

"We don't even know where you live."

It was the demanding tone, as if he owed them something, that got to Jan. "As if you cared," he said, and continued his climb.

His mother quickened her pace, hoping to catch up. "Of course I care. I'm worried about you."

He had more than enough of her so-called concern. "You don't need to. I've got a house, friends, and a job. And maybe an apprenticeship soon."

"A house?" And there it was, the ever-present doubt. "And you can afford that?"

"I inherited some money." Technically, Neve had inherited the money, but since the snow witch was incapable of financial responsibility—she would've just filled the house with sweets and wasn't exactly human—Jan had been named as the benefactor. Now the house really belonged to him, and they'd even been able to make some improvements. The ground floor and first floor were now quite habitable. In return, Neve reigned over the basement, where she built herself a winter wonderland. It saved him from having to buy a freezer.

His mother groaned. "Oh, Jan, please tell me you haven't broken the law."

Just a bit of magic-assisted fraud, where our current laws are inadequate. Technically, his mother was right, but it still grated on Jan. He stopped at the top of the second floor and turned to her. "That's all I am to you, isn't it? An idiot? A criminal."

His mother struggled to keep a straight face. "You're not exactly known for sticking to rules."

Jan couldn't believe it. "Do me a favour. If they ask you for a character reference, just tell them you don't know me."

"Jan!"

He spun round and opened the door.

"Jan, please. Let's talk about this. You could come for dinner. Lasagne?"

He hadn't had a home-cooked meal for weeks. "I'll see you at Christmas."

"That's ten months from now."

Jan opened the door. "Brilliant. That'll give me time to think about what I'm going to get you." Nothing at the moment. He'd rather eat sweets with Neve in the freezing cellar than see his parents again.

Despite the rough meeting with his mother, the interview had gone well enough to give Jan some hope. He returned home, immediately undid his top button and pulled his shirt out of his pants.

The pitter-patter of Neve's little feet greeted him. "How was Jan's chat?"

"Alright. I think."

"Matt is here." With the defeat of the fire devil, Neve had accepted not only Jan but all his friends, too.

Jan frowned. "What do you mean?"

"Matt is in the garden."

Confused, Jan left the house and walked around the back. Sure enough, Matt was there, picking up broken branches and rubbish. Jan rubbed his eyes, unable to believe what he was seeing, but his friend was still there.

Finally, Matt noticed him. "Hey."

"May I ask what you're doing?"

Matt dropped his branches into a corner. "I'm tidying up the garden. Adrianes is coming in three days to bring some plants."

It took Jan a moment to remember who Adrianes was. Then it hit him. Lucille and Fabian had told him of Balthasar's son who ran Hell's Gardens. "An unexpected honour."

"Not for you. Sam." Matt beamed at him. "I found it! My gift. She loves flowers and plants. She even works in a flower shop and wears the Flowers of Freya's Garden as her Emblem of Power. Your garden's a bit lacking, so I thought we could make it green."

"We could," Jan said slowly. "The garden was on my list."

"Well, it's on mine now." Matt didn't seem to see anything wrong with that.

Jan took a deep breath. "Because of Sam?"

"It's the perfect gift for her. She once mentioned how much she missed her old garden."

"And now you want her to have my garden?"

Matt shrugged. "Why not? It would do it some good."

"And then next year you're going to give her my house?"

The flaw in his plan finally dawned on Matt. "Possibly," he muttered.

"I don't think it's such a good idea." In fact, it was a stupid idea to give someone a garden. Especially a garden that belonged to someone else.

But behind Jan, Neve clapped her hands. "Neve likes idea. Neve loves garden parties."

"A garden party!" Matt exclaimed, his enthusiasm returning. "That's it. We'll have the surprise party here."

"In my garden?" Jan repeated helplessly.

Matt nodded eagerly. "Yes, and in your house. Otherwise it'll be too cold in the evening."

Jan ran his hands over his face. He had the feeling this conversation was getting away from him. Somehow, he had to keep Matt in check. "Okay, okay, slow down. Sam's birthday is in two weeks. In a fortnight, my garden might look a little cleaner, but it'll still be too cold for anything to grow."

"That's why I'm getting Adrianes. He'll turn it green in no time."

"With plants from Hell?"

"It'll be glorious."

A bell rang through the house, muffled by the walls. Jan threw his head over his shoulder and called, "Coming!" Then he turned back. "So, listen—"

Matt was gone.

"Great. Absolutely fantastic." Grumbling, he walked back around the house and found the woman of the hour standing outside his door. Her eyes were red and she was carrying a backpack, filled to the brim, which didn't bode well for Jan. "Are you okay?"

Samantha swayed slightly. "I want to use Jonathan's library."

Neve gasped with delight. "Neve will show Samantha library." She opened the door and they both disappeared inside.

Jan stared at the door, wondering what the hell had just happened. That backpack meant she was planning to stay longer. "Does anyone care that this is *my* house?"

Fabian

After being kicked out of the Kollmer House and helping his mother close the Magic Circle, Fabian made his way to the shared flat where Ophelia lived. One of her flatmates let him in and said *they* were in her room.

"Lia?" he called, knocking.

"One moment!" Ophelia called, her voice sounding strained.

Fabian waited patiently, but he couldn't help wonder what was going on. There was definitely someone else in there, a girl's voice that sounded vaguely familiar. They were doing something that required a lot of grunting and cursing.

"There!" Ophelia suddenly declared. Then her footsteps could be heard behind the door. A moment later it swung open. "Fabian!" She went straight for a kiss.

For a few precious moments, Fabian enjoyed the sweetness of her lips and the heat of her tongue.

"Ugh. There are minors present."

He *did* know that voice. "Meg?" Samantha's little sister had eschewed her usual stylish tops for Ophelia's darker palate. A black chiffon skirt covered her bare legs, while her breasts had been forced into a tight corset. "What are you doing here?"

"Nothing."

"Can't you see?" Ophelia asked, amused.

If he was honest, it surprised him to find the two girls in the same room after the catfight he'd witnessed this morning, let alone see them exchanging clothes. "Is that for Jan?"

"No, it's for me," Meg replied promptly.

"She needs a little distraction from all the drama at home," Ophelia quietly explained to Fabian.

He couldn't really blame her. "Speaking of drama, have your parents completely lost their minds?"

Meg crossed her arms and snorted. "Are you just noticing now?"

"Ben kicked me out. Apparently, I'm no longer welcome at your house."

Meg grimaced wildly. "Nonsense. You're the son he never had."

Beside him, Ophelia tried to keep up. "Does that make you siblings or something?"

"If you mean annoying little—" Fabian said at the same time as Meg complained, "Annoying big—" They both stopped, embarrassed.

Ophelia chuckled. "I see."

"Well..." Fabian rubbed his neck. "He was like a madman. I've never seen him like that."

"Welcome to my life." Meg dropped onto Ophelia's bed, then picked up a red-laced corsage. "Can I try this?"

Ophelia looked apologetically at Fabian. "Do you mind if I spend the rest of the afternoon with Meg? She needs it a bit more than you do."

Meg fiddled with the red ribbons. "Oh, don't mind me, if Fabian is needy."

As usual, Meg annoyed Fabian to no end, but after a non-verbal check-in with Ophelia, he was almost convinced it wouldn't end in a bloodbath if he left them alone. As usual, he just didn't understand girls.

To make a strange day stranger, Ben was at his house when Fabian finally made it home. He and Joachim were sitting on the couch in the living room, drinking beer, while his mother sat at the kitchen table, making little amulets. Still a little upset about his earlier treatment at Ben's hands, Fabian sat down next to his mother.

"When did he arrive?" he said, with a grim look towards Ben.

"With your dad. They're already on their second beer," Caroline said quietly.

Fabian shot another disapproving look at the two fathers. This time his eyes met Ben's. Anger gleamed in them.

Ben grunted. "Hey Caro, when are you going back full-time?"

"Hey," Joachim warned him as Caroline stiffened in her chair.

But that only spurred Ben on. "Oh, come on. This can't go on. I mean, sure, it's nice that the kids are helping out but that's not really their job, is it?"

"I work part-time," Caroline pressed between her lips.

With a glance at Ben, Fabian put his hand on his mother's back.

"It's been half a year," Ben pointed out.

"Ben," Joachim snapped. "I don't know what's got your knickers in a twist but leave Caro out of this. Or you and I will have a problem."

To Fabian's horror, Ben laughed coldly. "You want us to fight over this? Sure, if you need a punch in the face, I'm ready to oblige."

"Ben!" Caroline said, horrified.

Ben got up from the couch. "Don't worry. I'll see myself out." He was halfway out the room when his gaze met Fabian's again. "Tell your misbegotten son I don't want to see his face in my house again."

"Now you've gone too far!" Joachim jumped to his feet, angrier than Fabian had ever seen him.

His mother gave him a confused look. "What did you do?"

"I just can't stand his stupid face," Ben said, before Fabian had a chance to tell her he hadn't done anything.

Meanwhile, his father was clenching his fists. "Take that back."

Ben crossed his arms and smiled cruelly. "Or what?" Ice crept up Fabian's back. "Your son is a colossal failure, and your wife is losing her mind. What do you think that says about you, Jo?"

This time Fabian jumped up, too, shouting at Ben to take back his words, while his father had finally had enough and planted his fist into his best friend's face. "Get out of here!" Joachim shouted.

Blood dripped from Ben's nose. His eyes were almost black, threatening murder, but then some kind of sense seemed to come back to him, and he left it at, "You'll pay for this," before turning on his heel and marching out of the house. He slammed the door behind him so hard the frames in the kitchen shook.

Fuming, Fabian fell back into his chair. He had half a mind to follow Ben and drown him in ice-cold water. No one, not even an old family friend, was allowed to talk shit about his mother.

He looked to his side and all the anger left him. Caroline was staring straight ahead, tears streaming down her cheeks. Her whole body was shaking.

Fabian threw his arms around her and hugged her so tightly there was no room for trembling. "I'm sorry, Mum. I'm so sorry."

Joachim turned, his face full of despair. "I don't know what's gotten into him."

Juliane, Fabian thought darkly, although he knew it wasn't fair to blame Samantha's mother. At least she didn't go around lashing out at everyone.

And if she was... Suddenly, Matt's suggestion didn't seem as outlandish as it had this morning.

Rachel

Rachel knew she should be studying. There were only three weeks left before her big exams. But all the drama surrounding Samantha's family brought back memories she thought she'd long forgotten. Her parents had fought a lot, too, before they finally decided to divorce. Rachel knew exactly how Samantha felt right now, but there was no hope to be had. Parents who fought like that didn't magically get back together. They might make up and prolong the inevitable, but it was never going to be the same. Not if the trust had already been broken.

She sighed, having lost her place in the mock exam for the third time. Samantha's parents couldn't have picked a worse time to implode.

"What's wrong, Miss Rachel?"

Hugo hovered in a corner of her room. He'd kept his mouth shut for the last hour, but he obviously couldn't hold it any longer. "Is the maths hurting your brain?"

"A bit," Rachel admitted. She had to prove a theorem, but every time she thought she had an idea, her mind slipped to Samantha instead. "I can't seem to concentrate today."

"Is there a particular reason?"

Shrugging, Rachel told him everything she knew about Samantha's parents. She found it easy to talk to Hugo since he had no one else to spend his time with but her. "It's pretty clear they're heading for divorce, but gosh, it's ugly."

Hugo frowned. "Heading for divorce? Have they not consummated their marriage?"

"They have two daughters." Rachel was pretty sure you didn't get that without some consummation.

"Then what other grounds are there for divorce?"

Rachel sighed heavily. "Oh, Hugo. Times have changed. Marriage is no longer until the day you die."

Confused, he sat down on her desk. "So, what is promised these days? A decade?"

"Oh, you still…" Now that she thought about it, marriage was a pretty stupid concept. Or maybe divorce was. Then again, no one should be forced to stay together. "Let's just call it a long-term commitment. You go into it, hoping it will last a lifetime, but then life happens, people change. Or maybe you got married for all the wrong reasons."

"I don't understand."

Reluctantly, Rachel told him what she'd found out about her parents' relationship. "They only got married because she got pregnant."

"Your father did the honourable thing," Hugo said respectfully.

Rachel shook her head. "The honourable thing would have been to accept his part in the pregnancy and come up with a plan to support the children in the long term. Jumping into marriage was an immature fantasy. My parents didn't belong together. Because they forced each other to make it work, they caused each other and Nico and me all this pain."

"I see." Hugo didn't sound like he really understood what she was saying. "So, if the reason for the marriage wasn't real, then a mistake was made and should be corrected."

"I suppose you could say that."

"So then your friend's parents have made the same mistake?"

Rachel groaned. "No, they didn't. They've been together since high school or something. They really loved each other." That was the story, at least. A happy family, the dream of the picket fence. And now it was all falling apart.

"I give up," Hugo said, slightly deflated. "These two promised to take care of each other until the day they died because they loved each other, and yet they make each other's lives miserable, while your parents got divorced just to visit each other's beds anyway."

"My parents don't visit each other's beds," Rachel said, suddenly alarmed. "I'm just saying it would've been better if they'd been lovers for a while instead of having a shotgun marriage that was doomed from the start."

Hugo nodded thoughtfully. "Then they learnt their lesson. No more marriage, all intercourse."

"Hugo!" Rachel exclaimed. "You make it sound like my parents are having sex now."

"Oh no, I think they finished half an hour ago."

Rachel stared at him slack-jawed. Then she jumped out of her chair and dashed into the hallway. The sound of the toilet flushing alerted her to her right. The bathroom door opened and out stepped her father, wearing nothing but a pair of boxers.

Stunned, he swallowed before forcing a pained smile to his lips. "Hey, Bug."

"What are you doing?" Rachel asked mechanically. She hadn't even known he was visiting today.

"Um, I just went—"

"Never mind!" Rachel snapped. "Everyone seems to have lost their minds."

She hurried back into her room and leant against the door. Hugo hovered in front of her, looking worried. "I'm afraid you'll have to explain it to me again."

A mad burst of laughter escaped her. "Oh no, I give up, too." Nothing in the world made sense anymore.

Jan

Jan was about to make himself something to eat when the doorbell rang as if there was no tomorrow. He turned off the stove and walked over, wondering which of his friends was in trouble this time.

But it wasn't any of them. Meg was standing there in an outfit he'd normally have found extremely sexy, but which was marred by the fact that her eyes were red, and her make-up had left dark streaks on her cheeks. Without so much as a hello, he pulled her into his chest.

"My mum—" Meg sobbed, her words choked by tears and snot.

"Let's go inside first." He led her into the living room and sat down on the old couch he'd found in an outlet store.

As soon as her backside sank into the soft cushions, Meg burst into tears again. Jan pulled her close again and patted her back. "What happened?"

"She was horrible to me! She—" For a few minutes Meg could barely breathe as she gasped through her tears. Jan had never seen her so upset. "She slept with Max."

"Who's Max?"

"Max Schönborn, the actor."

Jan had no idea who that was. "An actor? How did your mum find an actor?"

"They've known each other from way back. Apparently, they promised each other to make it in the entertainment world." Bitterly, Meg added, "Well, she never did, so now she has to sleep her way in."

Jan was still playing catch-up. "Are you sure they had sex?" Meg was a trifle dramatic. She could have overheard something and run with it.

"I caught them on our couch."

"Shit!"

Meg nodded hastily, momentarily too angry to cry. "And do you know what she told me? I shouldn't make such a big deal out of it. Max was more bothered than she was." Her face dropped and her voice became whiny again. "And then she said I looked like a whore."

Jan couldn't help but glance at her revealing outfit. Her breasts were so tightly squeezed they almost spilt out of her corset.

"I borrowed clothes from Ophelia," Meg said flatly.

"That explains it." Not that he thought Ophelia looked like a whore, but she *did* like to flaunt her assets. He had no idea how Fabian had managed to pull someone like her.

Meg's eyes threatened to overflow again.

"Come here." Once more he pulled her close and stroked her back. "I'm so sorry, Meg."

Only now did her words really sink in. She'd caught her mother cheating—on the family couch. Shit, indeed.

It wasn't until he heard someone clear their throat that he remembered Samantha was still in the house. She was standing in the doorway, a small plastic box in her hand.

Meg whirled around. "What are you doing here? Are you two—"

"No!" Jan said quickly, remembering what he'd done under the influence of an evil spirit. "Sam was in the library doing research. I've barely even seen her."

"What happened?" Samantha asked her sister.

"I caught Mum cheating. She didn't even try to explain."

Samantha bit her lip. "Don't judge her too harshly."

Jan frowned. "Um..."

"It's not her fault. At least I don't think so."

Meg looked at Samantha as if her sister had turned into a blobfish. "That's pretty naïve, even for you. What do you mean, I shouldn't judge her too harshly? She seemed quite happy about the whole thing."

"Did she?"

"Yes!" Meg snapped.

Even Jan thought Samantha was acting strange. Why wasn't she more upset? And why was she apologising for her mother's terrible error in judgement?

"No, was she really happy? Or did she just not seem to care?"

Meg hesitated. "The latter. What's going on?"

Samantha breathed a sigh of relief. "She's been infected."

"Infected?" Jan asked.

Samantha stepped into the room and showed them the contents of her plastic box. Inside were a bunch of dead insects. Jan was no expert, but even he thought they looked a bit strange, with their shiny front legs and long snout. "What are they?"

"Soul parasites," Samantha said. "Minor swarm demons."

Meg groaned. "Not this nonsense again."

"It's not nonsense. Soul parasites infect a host and eat their soul. The host can no longer control their emotions, usually becoming cold and callous, sometimes violent. They won't stop until there's nothing left of the soul. The host will be an empty shell, kept alive by biology." Samantha shuddered. "They don't live long in our atmosphere. These didn't make it into their host in time. I found them in my room."

Meg looked at her with wide eyes. "These soul parasites have taken over Mum and Dad?"

"That would explain a few things."

Like why they were cheating all of a sudden. Jan rubbed his chin as a new question arose. "But how did the soul parasites get into your room in the first place? Did you grow them or—"

Samantha shook her head. "They were a *gift*." She didn't make it sound like a gift. "From someone who may mean well, but just ruins everything." She blinked away tears. "They came with a card from Matt."

Jan groaned. *What had that idiot done now?*

After Samantha left, Jan had comforted Meg, which had inevitably ended with the two of them in his new bed. That was one of the advantages of having his own place. No more annoying sisters or parents to worry about.

Unless... He checked his phone on the bedside table and almost fell out of his bed. "Shit! You should've been home ten minutes ago."

Meg stretched out in his bed and shrugged. "I don't think anyone cares."

"Your father's gonna light a fire under my ass!"

"My dad is probably passed out drunk in the workshop while my mum has her new boyfriend over." She laughed haughtily. "They don't care, remember?"

Jan handed her the phone. "Please, at least call them."

Meg pulled a face. "Ugh. You're so boring these days."

"Me? Boring?"

She gave him a racy smile. "Last year's Jan would've begged me to stay the night."

"Last year's Jan dropped out of school, got fired from his first real job, and was kicked out by his parents."

Meg rolled her eyes. "And now you own a house and are about to start an apprenticeship. No sense of adventure left in you."

Jan frowned at her harsh judgement. "Um, I still hunt monsters in my spare time." That was plenty of adventure.

Her eyes brightened and she sat up straight. "Let's go monster hunting."

"It's almost midnight!"

She fell back onto the bed with a groan. "Boring, just as I said."

Jan didn't like being called boring. It wasn't a word he'd ever associated with himself. Surely being sensible didn't make you a boring loser. "Fine. You can sleep here."

She was probably correct about her parents not caring right now. Couldn't, really. Still, he'd been living by her father's rules for over a year now. Meg wasn't supposed to sleep over at her boyfriend's house. She was only seventeen, after all.

Boy, he had turned boring. Frustrated, Jan rolled over and switched off the light. Behind him, Meg snorted and turned her back to him.

Matt

It was quite late by the time Matt sat down to study for PE. As he read all about muscle training, his mind seemed to be running on a parallel track. Again and again, he had to take a break from his studies to add something to the draft paper he'd started planning Samantha's garden on.

The shower stopped running in the bathroom, and a few minutes later, René stepped out in his pyjamas. He got himself a glass of water before looking at Matt's work. "Are you doing landscaping in Geography now?"

"What?" Matt dropped his pen. "Oh, no, it's a gift. I mean, it's for a gift. I want to make a garden for Samantha. Adrianes is going to help me."

His father whistled approvingly. "A garden. Not bad."

Matt was reminded of Jan's reaction and looked down in embarrassment. "Do you think it's too much?"

René chuckled. "I wouldn't say that. It just tells me a lot about you." When Matt frowned, he explained, "You're pretty serious about her, aren't you?"

"We're just friends," Matt said as he concentrated on the drawing.

"Just friends, I see." René sounded amused. The doorbell rang. "And what do you give your other friends?"

Matt rolled his eyes. He usually asked them what they wanted and bought it for them. "It doesn't mean anything."

When the doorbell rang a second time, René left him with a wink and walked over. A moment later Matt heard Samantha's voice. "Is he here?"

He hastily shoved the garden drawing under his PE studies and stood up, a smile slipping across his face as easily as if it had always lived there.

Samantha rushed into the room and slammed a plastic box with a greeting card on the table. "Is this your version of an apology?"

"Sorry?" The memories of this morning came back and he realised he hadn't apologised yet. Only, according to the card on the table, he had. "What's going on?"

Behind Samantha, René seemed unsure of whether to give them some space or stay before things got out of hand.

"You think my parents are better off splitting up. So you sent them soul parasites to get things moving?" Samantha's voice trembled and she looked like she was about to burst into tears.

"Soul parasites." Matt had heard of them. Every demon had, but fortunately he'd never come close to a swarm.

"Did you really think I'd be grateful for that?"

Matt swallowed. "Sam, I—"

"—destroy everything that's important to me." She sniffed, barely avoiding a sob. "I really thought you'd changed."

Before he could say anything, she'd left the apartment. Confused, Matt picked up the plastic box. Sure enough, there were a couple of dead soul parasites inside.

"Can you explain this, please?" René asked, the tension in his voice betraying his suspicion.

Matt shook the plastic box. "Soul parasites. But I didn't get them for her. I wouldn't even know how to get my hands on a swarm."

René took the card and read it. "What's this?"

"Not mine." The letters looked close enough to how he'd have written them, but he'd never held the pen. He knew better than to apologise with a secret message.

It suddenly hit him. "Oh, I'm going to kill him."

\#

Matt jumped straight into Hescaryn, dropping only a few metres from Balthasar's rooms. As expected, he found his brother there, sorting through important scrolls.

"I'm going to kill you!" Matt announced, barely resisting the urge to follow his words with a well-placed surge of energy.

Balthasar looked over his shoulder. "You're here. At last. You can do us both a favour and take your aggression out on Melaney. Come along."

To Matt's surprise, Balthasar started down the corridor that connected his rooms to the Residence of Lust. "Didn't you hear me?"

"You threatened to kill me. Caspar does it twice a day. When he's around." Balthasar smiled. "That means my plan worked. Samantha made it clear she didn't want you around and you're back where you belong."

"That was your plan?"

"Now you don't have to deal with all her complicated feelings, and you can finally sleep with Melaney."

"Compli—" Matt caught himself. "I'm not going to sleep with Melaney. She's my mother!"

"So?"

"I'm not going to sleep with my mother."

Balthasar sighed. "You're missing out here."

Matt couldn't believe what he was hearing. "Stop. Just stop." He took a few deep breaths to get back to his original problem. "You wanted the soul parasites to attack Samantha."

"Do I have to write down my plan?"

"Your bloody plan didn't work!" yelled Matt, his anger returning tenfold. He couldn't believe Balthasar would be so careless. Then again, nothing could make his demon brother care but his own damned ambition. "The soul parasites went after her parents. They're worse off now than before. And Samantha thinks it's my fault. She hates me!"

Balthasar shrugged. "Either way, you can finally leave her behind and return to lust."

"I. Can't!" Matt shouted.

"Melchior." Balthasar put a hand to his temple and sighed. "It's bad enough to have one half-brother serving the House of Wrath. I need you in the House of Lust. Sleep with Melaney so we can finally put an end to this mess."

Matt glared at him. "Never." He didn't care if his feelings were more wrath than lust. Instead, he drew his sword. "I'll kill you first."

Balthasar looked at the sword and then at Matt. Finally, he sighed. "That wouldn't fit in with my other plans. Fine. I'll help you."

"What?"

"Chay said you were the key to my success."

Matt narrowed his eyes. Since when did Chay and Balthasar work together? Surely his old friend hadn't betrayed him as well.

"Of course, he might be favouring you again, but I usually trust him."

That was definitely new to Matt. He fought the inevitable curiosity to find out more. Samantha needed his help, and Balthasar had just hinted that he could provide it. "You said something about helping?"

Balthasar walked past him and picked up a fat candle from a shelf. "I only have the one. The scent of it is attuned to this particular swarm of soul parasites. It lures them out of their host, and they usually don't return to the same body. All you have to do is get the parents near the candle and make sure there's no new host within reach. As they've only been infected recently, they should make a full recovery."

He placed the candle in Matt's hand, coming awfully close to the sword in his other hand. "Now, go. But remember. It doesn't make any difference to them. You're a demon and you belong here."

Matt still had the desire to kill him, but there were more important things to do. First, he had to fix Samantha's parents and explain the whole thing to her. And then, when all was well, he'd come back and kill Balthasar.

Lucille

Despite it being a school day, Lucille met up with the others at the Blackstone House. Only Samantha was missing. In her place was Meg, who looked as if she'd slept here. Lucille reserved her judgement on that, as there were more important things to discuss.

Apparently, Samantha's and Meg's parents had gone off the deep end and were behaving extremely erratically. Meg told them her mother had cheated on her father, and Fabian reported Ben had been a real ass to his whole family. Lucille didn't know Samantha's parents well enough to judge whether either reaction was in the realm of possibility, but she didn't have to.

Matt held up what looked like a fat candle with faint scratch marks. "Balthasar sent those parasites after Sam, but her parents got to them first. He says we can lure them out with this candle, but it only works once. That means we have to make sure Ben and Juliane are in the same place at the same time."

Meg held up her hand. "I can do that. I'll just tell them I want to talk to them."

It was a sound plan, but Matt flinched. "The problem is, you can't be around when the soul parasites leave their host. Otherwise, you'll be the next host, and there's no second candle."

"I'll be fine," Meg said confidently.

"Woah, wait," Jan complained. "Meg, this is dangerous."

From the way Meg turned up her nose, Lucille could tell they'd been arguing. "All I have to do is call my parents into the living room, light a candle, and leave them alone with it."

"I'll light the candle," Matt said firmly. "You call them."

"I can probably find a spell to light the candle from a distance," Lucille suggested. She was sure she'd read about one or two that could do that.

Matt nodded eagerly. "Perfect."

Meg pouted, causing Jan to put an arm around her shoulder. "What's wrong?"

She shook him off. "I'm tired of being treated like a child."

"Meg, I didn't mean it like that. I just don't want you to be the next victim of these soul parasites."

Meg huffed. "I can take care of myself.

"I know," Jan said, but then he added sarcastically, "no one is tougher than you."

"Well, I'm definitely tougher than you."

Lucille exchanged glances with Fabian and Rachel, feeling very uncomfortable about witnessing the lovers' argument.

Jan snorted. "I see." He was interrupted by his phone ringing. "Well, knock yourself out. I've got to take this." He went into the kitchen to answer the call.

"Are you sure you want to risk it?" Lucille asked. When Meg stormed off, she turned to Matt. "Where's Samantha? Doesn't she want to set her parents straight?"

"She hates me," Matt said, looking like a lost puppy. "She thinks I did it because of what I said at school. I don't know if she's gone back home or—" he swallowed. "Let's just get this over with so I can explain what happened."

Lucille's heart went out to Matt. He had acted like an idiot yesterday, but he didn't deserve to be made the scapegoat. Balthasar's plan was quite devious, blaming Matt like that.

"I'll check with Meg, see if she's up to the task." With both hands in his pockets, Matt left the room.

Rachel blew a few raspberries while he was gone. "You don't think there's such a thing as an opposite soul parasite, like one that brings people together?"

Lucille frowned. "As an alternative?" The candle sounded simple enough. If Meg didn't screw it up, her parents should be fine in no time.

"Oh, no, just because..." She sighed. "My parents started sleeping with each other again."

"What?" Fabian exclaimed. "How? Why?"

"See, it doesn't make any sense."

"Did you talk to them?" Lucille asked cautiously. Rachel had a tendency to forget that important step.

As expected, Rachel shuddered. "I came here before they woke up for breakfast." She grimaced. "But his shoes were still there. So, he definitely stayed the night."

"That's good, isn't it?" Fabian asked.

"Is it?" Rachel certainly didn't sound like that. "They only got married because she got pregnant. And then they fought and moved as far away from each other as humanly possible." She grimaced again. "Why would they suddenly be together?"

It was almost endearing how little Rachel understood about love. "Maybe they didn't get married for the wrong reasons."

"It was definitely because of the pregnancy."

"Sure, but your mother didn't get pregnant for no reason," Lucille suggested amusedly. "It may have been a bit hasty but they were obviously attracted to each other. Maybe they still are." There was another reason, but she didn't want to mention it.

Both parents had lost a child. As much as there was to separate them, they had that in common. Perhaps the loss of Nico had brought them together. "Would it be that bad?"

Rachel looked at her as if Lucille was suggesting that her parents would now be running around naked in her house all day. "Yes?"

Fabian chuckled. "I'm with Lucille on this one. I mean, they're adults after all, right? They're certainly not too young now. They know their issues and their challenges."

Rachel crossed her arms and looked at them glumly. "There's a reason they broke up."

"And there's at least one reason they got back together," Lucille whistled innocently, earning herself a dirty look.

Before they could continue, Matt returned with Meg. "You got your spell?"

Lucille pulled out her phone and quickly scanned the extensive note on it. "Yup."

"Then let's do Balthasar's dirty work."

Samantha

After confronting Matt, Samantha had spent the night with Cian. It hadn't been planned and she'd arrived quite late, but Cian had opened the door and offered nothing but comfort. Now she lay in his bed and thought about the damage that had been done to her family. The books she'd read said there was no cure. Soul parasites lived in a certain humid region of Hell and moved from one host to another, but only after they'd completely destroyed the host's soul. Not that there was much to destroy in Hell, Samantha thought. Most of the demons struck her as quite soulless.

Next to her, Cian stirred. "Good morning, beautiful." He leant over and kissed her gently on the temple.

Samantha wriggled a little deeper into the covers. She'd meant to stop this kind of booty call and yet she'd found her way back into his sheets. "Thanks for letting me stay tonight."

A lazy smile spread across Cian's lips. "Thank *you*."

"You know—"

"I don't have any false hopes. I know what I signed up for." Despite his words, a flicker of pain crossed his face. He didn't have to say it. It was clear he was completely smitten.

Samantha sighed. Cian was perfect in every way. He was kind and funny, charming and smart, and he came without any of the supernatural baggage she had to deal with. He deserved someone better than her.

A small voice told her that maybe *she* did deserve someone like him, but no matter how deep she searched, her feelings for Cian remained superficial. If he decided to break it off tomorrow, she wouldn't care. Instead, she had feelings for the worst person imaginable. The one who had swept into her life like a hurricane, leaving nothing but destruction and pain in his wake. He loved her too, but his efforts to help her were just as bad as when he expressed his feelings. Even an idiot could see he was no good for her. "I need to go." Samantha leant over her side of the bed to search for her clothes.

"What's your plan?" Cian asked, making no move to stop her.

She shrugged helplessly. "I'm going to go home, take a shower, get some new clothes." Just normal things. "And then I'll meet with the others to find a solution for my parents. Maybe all is not lost."

"Well, I hope they get well. If there's anything I can do you'll let me know, won't you?"

She finished dressing and leant over to kiss him on the forehead. "Thanks, Cian."

#

A few minutes later, Samantha stood outside her house and took a deep breath. If what she'd read about soul parasites and what Meg had said was true, her parents were being incredibly mean and hurtful. She couldn't let it get to her. It wasn't real.

She was just about to get her key out when Matt suddenly appeared in front of her, blocking her path.

Immediately her anger from last night returned. "Leave me alone, Matt. I'm not interested in your excuses."

"You can't go in there."

Was she imagining a hint of panic in his voice? Probably just the realisation of how much he'd messed up what they'd worked so hard to rebuild. "I live there."

"Yes, but your parents—"

"Are my responsibility. I don't want any more of your so-called help." She pushed past him and put her key in the lock. "You've caused more than enough damage."

"And I'll fix it. I promise, but—"

"Cian has already seen to that." It was a low blow, but one that gave Samantha the opportunity to open the door and enter her house.

As soon as she heard the sounds coming from the living room, she took off running. Her parents were *fighting*, physically fighting. Juliane smashed a flower vase over Ben's head, her hair dishevelled and her face a vicious snarl. Meanwhile, Ben swiped the vase away, grabbed Juliane by the throat and pushed her to the floor.

"Dad!" Samantha sprinted over and threw herself onto her father's back, trying to pull him away from her mother.

There was no hope. Her father's eyes turned black with unbridled rage, unconcerned that her mother was kicking him or that Samantha was clinging to his arm. A strangely pungent smell of sulphur crept into Samantha's nose and something like a dark cloud rose from her father's body.

Suddenly Matt was there. He wrapped his arms around her middle, lifted her with ease and threw her across the room. Samantha tumbled over the couch and crashed to the floor, her breath taken away by the impact and the shock to her system.

Assuring herself that she'd broken no bones and was reasonably well, she pulled herself up and looked over the sofa just in time to see two dark swarms swirling around Matt before entering his body. Not all the soul parasites made it into their new host, dropping dead on the floor instead.

As her parents stopped, almost flying apart, Samantha's eyes locked with Matt's. He'd known this would happen. That was why he'd thrown her across the room. To get her away from the emerging swarms. The swarms that were now inside him, eating away at his soul.

Matt swallowed and then vanished as fast as he could.

Samantha let out a shuddering breath. Her knees suddenly felt too weak to support her body. Matt was infected. Matt had sacrificed himself. For her—and her parents.

"Oh god, Juli," her father cried, his face a mask of horror. "I didn't mean to hurt you." He sat down in the shards of the vase, his hands over his mouth in shock.

"I didn't hold back either," Juliane replied, rubbing her bruised neck. True to her words, a thin trickle of blood ran down Ben's face.

"You're both blameless," Samantha forced herself to say, although an irrational voice screamed that none of this would have happened if her parents hadn't fought in the first place. Now, Matt... She swallowed. "You were infested by soul parasites."

Both her parents looked at her, as if they'd just realised she was there. "Soul parasites?" Ben repeated doubtfully.

Her mother laughed nervously. "Honey, what are you talking about?"

"They're a type of demonic insect. A swarm that will eat away at your soul until there's nothing left." And yet Matt had somehow managed to get them to leave her parents. Her eyes fell on a fat candle on the dining table, emitting thick grey smoke. It certainly hadn't been there before. "They're gone now," she said absentmindedly as she walked over to the table and picked up the candle. Sure enough, it smelt of sulphur.

Juliane cleared her voice. "This is a magic thing?"

"Sounds like it," Ben said cautiously. "I told you she hasn't lost her mind. This is real."

Samantha turned to her parents. "You were fighting over me?" She remembered the mess in her room. "You were in my room."

Her mother took a shuddering breath. "I'm sorry, darling. We shouldn't have done that. I just thought your father was out of his mind. Magic isn't real, is it?"

Without warning, Samantha drew the strands of magic in the room closer together and lit the candle, melting the wax until it was a smooth ball. "Is that real enough?"

Juliane swallowed. "I didn't know," she whispered.

"I tried to stop her," Ben said. "I'm sorry we made such a mess and broke the pot on your desk."

The pot? Samantha remembered the black shards she'd found. It must have contained the soul parasites. But if so... If the pot had been waiting for her and not her parents... That meant it couldn't have been Matt. Sure, there was the card, but why would he want to take away her feelings in such a cruel way?

Her legs felt like pudding again as she realised he'd been set up. And she'd *shouted* at him. Told him all those terrible things and ignored his warning. Her knees buckled as she realised it was all her fault he was now infected with soul parasites. That he would lose his soul.

A choked sob escaped her throat, and she sank to the floor.

"Hey, sweetheart," her father said gently. "This isn't your fault. I don't know how those soul parasites got here, but I know it has nothing to do with you being a witch."

It had everything to do with her being a witch, with her battling monsters and demons, with Matt.

Her mother hugged herself, looking like she was hanging on by a thread. "This infection... does that mean, none of what we did was real?"

"Oh, it was real," Samantha whispered. "You just can't be blamed for your lack of judgement."

Ben took a shuddering breath. "Does that mean...?"

"I really did sleep with Max," Juliane said, clapping her hand over her mouth. "I swear I didn't invite him here for that."

"Sure."

Juliane's eyes widened. "Ben, please! You heard Samantha. It's not my fault. I didn't want to sleep with Max."

"Well, part of you did," Ben muttered. "Why did you invite him over anyway?"

"To talk!"

"Because you can't do that in a coffee shop."

Juliane gasped.

"Dad, please." Samantha felt like she was losing her mind. Sure, the soul parasites had driven her parents to extremes, but their problems ran much deeper. "It's over," she said, tasting tears on her tongue. "You... you can recover from this." That might have been the wake-up call her parents needed. "Everything can be fine again."

"Samantha's right," Juliane said. "I'm tired of all the fighting."

Hope welled up in Samantha's heart.

"I want a divorce."

Fabian

Fabian waited with bated breath for Matt's return. Jan had left earlier to go to the hospital, leaving the rest of them at his house with Neve.

By this time, they were all late for school, but how could they go when the lives of Samantha's parents were hanging in the balance? Or if not their lives, then everything that made them who they were? He was still angry at Ben for what he'd said about his mother, but with any luck Ben would come to his senses and give her the apology she deserved. After all, it was thanks to his and Joachim's workshop she was in this predicament in the first place.

Matt appeared, causing both Meg and Fabian to jump to their feet. "And?" they asked as if from the same mouth.

"Your parents have been freed from the soul parasites. We ran into a little problem, but the result was the same. They can heal now. Samantha is over there explaining it to them."

"What was the little problem?" Fabian asked, knowing that there was no such thing as a little problem when it came to Greenvalley's monsters.

"Have you two been fighting again?" Lucille asked in dismay.

Matt shrugged. "A bit, but that's not the problem. I got too close to the swarm." He held up his hands to stifle their protests. "It's all good. It was my fault anyway and shouldn't make too much of a difference."

"It doesn't?" Fabian asked doubtfully. He didn't understand how Matt could be so blasé about being infected by those swarm demons.

"Demons aren't exactly known for having souls, are they?"

"Oh Matt," Rachel whispered.

Lucille shook her head. "That's rubbish and you know it. We will find a solution."

"There isn't one. One candle. One use only. The window of opportunity has closed," Matt said without so much as a twitch in his eye. "But it's time for school. So let's get on with it." He jumped away again.

Fabian sat down with a groan. Samantha's parents were safe, but the whole thing had just gone into round two. And despite Matt's confident attitude, Fabian knew he was wrong. Demons had souls, or if not demons, then half-demons. But if Matt lost all that now... "Who else is afraid there'll be a repeat of the Blood Night?"

Without a moment's hesitation, Lucille and Rachel raised their hands.

Despite their pending problem, the group made it to school after all. To Fabian's surprise, Meg and Ophelia seemed as tight as thieves as they walked to class together. Fabian and Rachel had to listen to one of Mr Herbert's tirades when they arrived twenty-five minutes late. The teacher was going on and on about how they weren't taking the exams seriously and how they should just give up, when Samantha arrived, looking like death twice over.

Before Mr Herbert could turn his wrath on her, she said in a toneless voice, "I had to deal with a family emergency."

The teacher frowned. "Is everything okay?"

"My parents are getting divorced."

That left Mr Herbert so perplexed he simply waved the three of them over to their seats. Fabian and Rachel made sure they took Samantha in the middle. "Divorced?" he whispered.

Samantha nodded. "The soul parasites only added to their problems. They're fine now, but they decided they'd be better off apart." She snorted quietly. "Really apart. Mum wants to move to Cologne."

"Are you okay?" Fabian asked, as Rachel took Samantha's hand and squeezed it tightly.

"I'll be fine. It's probably for the best." She smiled bitterly. "Matt was right."

"Matt..."

She looked over immediately. "Did you see him?"

Fabian winced. "He says he's fine, but... I'm worried."

"Hey," Mr Herbert called out, "it's bad enough you were late. No need to disrupt the class." His eyes fell on Samantha. "Hold the check-in until the break, will you?"

In response, Samantha pulled out her notepad. Fabian sat back with a sigh and did the same. Samantha's parents were getting a divorce and Juliane was moving away. After more than twenty years of domestic bliss, the Fantastic Four were irreparably broken.

They all sat in the cafeteria pretending to do their homework while Samantha explained what had happened to Meg. Her sister took it, predictably, with a good deal of vitriol. "This is all your fault."

As she stormed off, Samantha sighed heavily before making her way over to them. "That went well."

"Meg will be fine," Fabian said gently. She'd realise what an idiot she'd been soon enough and apologise. He couldn't even blame her. He'd probably lash out, too, if his parents got divorced after a battle with soul parasites.

Samantha slipped into a seat next to Matt, who'd been acting surprisingly normal so far. Lucille had tried to talk to him about it, but Matt had used study time as an excuse.

"How are you doing?" Samantha asked now.

"Shouldn't I be asking you that?"

Samantha gave him a helpless little shrug. "I'm miserable, but that's no secret." She gave him a little nudge on the shoulder. "You took the hit for me."

"Well, maybe this is my idea of an apology."

"Accepted," Samantha said with a gentle smile.

Matt finally looked up and for a moment Fabian was sure there was still vulnerability in him. "I'm fine, really. They have no effect on me. As you said the other day, I don't have an ounce of humanity in me."

Samantha's eyes widened in horror. "Matt, no—"

"There's Cian." Matt pointed ahead.

Fabian had no idea why that mattered, but Samantha looked anyway. A few tables over, Cian sat down between his friends Alan and Shayna. When he saw Samantha looking, he waved, and to Fabian's surprise, Samantha waved back.

He turned to ask, "What's going on?"

As Samantha blushed, Matt said, "When you said Cian had taken care of it, you were coming from him, right? You spent the night with him?"

"Did you?" Fabian asked. When had that happened?

"Did you sleep with him?" Matt asked, frankly as always. When Samantha lowered her eyes, he snorted. "I thought your little affair would be over by now."

There was a whole affair?

"It's not an affair," Samantha said. "We're friends... with benefits. One of those benefits was having someone to turn to for comfort."

"When you thought I'd ruined your life again," Matt mused coldly.

Samantha looked up, pained. "I'm sorry about that. I jumped to conclusions and... It was all too painful."

"I see."

Fabian didn't see anything. Especially not why she would seek comfort in Cian's arms when she had him. Well, obviously their friendship was without the benefits she suddenly longed for.

"I'm really sorry," Samantha repeated. "I should've known you'd never do something like this."

Matt brushed her off. "Don't worry about it. It wasn't far-fetched at all. Swarm demons show up and you're fighting with your demon friend. It fits."

"Half-demon," Samantha whispered.

"Whatever." Matt stood up. "Sorry your parents are still splitting up."

As soon as he was gone, Fabian slid over and put his arm around Samantha. Sure, he didn't have Cian's benefits, but he was able to comfort a friend. "Don't worry too much about him. He took the hit for you. I'm sure he'll forgive you in no time."

"His control is quite impressive," Lucille mused. "This whole Cian thing—"

"Or not," Rachel muttered as Matt walked past Cian, grabbed his head and slammed it into the table in front of him.

Immediately, Alan jumped up and shoved him. "Are you crazy?"

Cian stood up too, looking a bit dazed. "Yeah, what was that—?" He must have seen something in Matt's eyes that made him back away. "Matt."

"Hey, asshole."

Quickly, Fabian and his friends ran over to de-escalate the situation. With the soul parasites in Matt and Samantha sleeping with someone else, a repeat of the Blood Night was all too likely.

"Asshole?" Cian repeated, offended.

Alan, as always, had his back. "You're the one who attacked him for no reason."

"For no reason?" Matt asked coldly. Then he looked at Cian. "You're the one desperate enough to get laid by taking advantage of a vulnerable girl."

Samantha gasped as Cian turned bright red. "Matt!"

Meanwhile Alan was shoving Matt again. "Who's the asshole now?"

Matt's fierce eyes turned to Alan, the bloodlust in them undeniable. As he clenched his fist, Fabian took a quick step forward and grabbed his arm. "Let's take a walk, shall we?"

On Matt's other side, Lucille had linked arms with him. "Yeah, you need some fresh air, believe me."

Matt tore his arm away from Fabian. "Stay out of this."

"Please don't do this. Please!" Samantha pleaded, her eyes wide with panic.

"You need help, Matt," Fabian said, his water ready in case things got out of hand.

"Oh, he sure does," Alan grumbled.

Rachel stepped in front of Matt. "Let's go."

Though reluctantly, Matt allowed them to lead him away. Samantha stayed behind to apologise to a pale Cian before quickly following them.

Outside the cafeteria, Matt broke free again and grunted at them. "I wasn't going to kill him."

Lucille sighed. "Matt, I don't think these soul parasites are good for you."

"Of course they're not good for me," he snapped back.

"Maybe you should go into quarantine until this is all over," Fabian suggested.

"It won't be over. There was only one chance." Matt suddenly whirled around to face Samantha, who'd been hurrying after them. "And you blew it."

Stunned, Samantha stopped short.

"We'll find a solution," Fabian insisted.

"Great." Matt vanished, ignoring their public environment. Fortunately, there weren't too many students around and none of them had paid any attention to the group.

Samantha sniffled. When Fabian turned to her, tears were streaming down her cheeks. He walked over and put his arms around her. "We'll fix him, Sam."

Lucille also stroked her arm in sympathy. "Leave Matt to us."

Jan

Jan hadn't expected the hospital to be that quick with their decision. They'd accepted him! They'd actually accepted his application and signed him up for the EMT training programme. He was going back to school, but this time with a real purpose and lots of practical lessons to make up for the boredom of the theory. Hell, even the theory would probably be a lot less boring than hours of history or physics.

His exceptionally good mood took a nosedive when he ran into his mother again.

Her eyes widened. "You're here again? Does that mean...?"

"That I'm not a loser for once? Yes, I got the job."

"Oh, Jan, you're not a *loser.*"

Jan snorted. "Have you asked Dad about that?"

Ida grimaced, which told him all he needed to know. "Your father will be so proud when he hears about this."

"Of course he would." Jan shook his head. "I finally managed to live up to his standards. Woohoo. I think I'm gonna throw up." Just the thought of his father accepting him now made him want to barf. Most likely, Stefan would reserve his judgement until Jan actually had his diploma in hand before he risked his pride on him.

"Jan, you know I didn't mean it like that."

"Sure." He walked past her, feeling far too old to deal with this shit. He wasn't going to let his parents ruin it for him.

"Jan?" Ida called after him.

Jan turned with a groan. "What?"

His mother smiled softly. "Congratulations... colleague."

He found it hard not to smile in response. He'd got the job! No longer unemployed or doing odd jobs. He had a career ahead of him. One he was actually looking forward to.

With a sharp nod to his mother, he walked on, the smile now spreading across his lips. Last year's Jan was gone. This year belonged to the new and improved Jan, who wasn't boring, but actually got his shit sorted.

\#

His good mood had no chance when he arrived home to find Fabian, Lu, and Rachel waiting for him outside. "What are you doing back here?"

Lu quickly brought him up to speed, telling him all about the soul parasites, his girlfriend's parents getting divorced, and Matt going rogue again. "We need to summon Balthasar."

"Here?"

"If he attacks us, Neve could freeze him."

Jan shrugged. "Fair enough." He opened the door and let them into the foyer. "Thanks for your help with the application, by the way. I got a place on the programme."

Lu squealed and threw her arms around him. "Oh my god. I knew you would get in. We need a toast. I'll call for a round at the Maverick."

"How about we celebrate with a little demon summoning?" Fabian asked. "That seems more our style." He patted Jan on the shoulder. "That's great news, man."

"Demon summoning it is." Jan knocked on the door to the cellar. "Neve."

A flurry of snow announced the snow witch's appearance. "Jan called?"

"Yes, I need your ice on standby. My friends and I are going to summon a demon in the kitchen. I don't expect there to be a fight, but—"

"Neve will throw out demon if demon not behave," the little girl said darkly.

Jan stroked her hair lovingly. "That's my girl."

As they walked into the kitchen, Lu remarked, "You two are getting along much better now."

"Neve is cool. Literally."

Fabian went straight for the knife. "Let's get this over with."

"Someone's eager."

"It's Samantha," Rachel explained. "Besides, Fabian just found out he has some serious competition in the male-friend department."

Jan rubbed his chin as he watched Fabian cut his finger and draw a pentagram on the floor. "Ah, found out about the Cian thing, did he?"

Lu gasped beside him. "You knew?"

"It was so obvious," Rachel said with an eye-roll, causing Lu to huff with indignation. "They've been hooking up since last summer."

Any amusement at the situation left Jan as Fabian finished his pentagram and summoned Balthasar. The demon appeared and looked at them with disgust. "What do you want?"

"A cure for the soul parasites," Lucille said.

Balthasar frowned. "Didn't Matt give that to you?"

"He did," Fabian explained. "But they're in him now."

"Is that so?" Despite the intrigue in his words, Balthasar shrugged. "I warned him not to get too close."

"It was an accident," Rachel pointed out.

"Well, that's his problem. I don't have another candle."

Lu didn't give up so easily. "But you know where to get another one, don't you?"

"Each scent is perfectly matched to the swarm. No swarm, no candle." A wicked smile spread across Balthasar's lips. "Maybe he'll finally come home now."

As he disappeared, Jan looked at the others in horror. They all looked as helpless as he felt. "So, what now?"

Matt

As soon as he got home, Matt started packing. The incident at school had made one thing clear: he couldn't stay in Greenvalley. If he did, he'd only risk hurting someone he cared about—or *had* cared about. And that was the main problem. Now he still remembered those feelings, but soon they'd be gone. Just the thought of leaving Greenvalley, right in the middle of everything made him feel... nothing.

The door clicked open, and René came home from work. He frowned when he saw Matt with his backpack. "Are you going somewhere?"

"Back to Hell."

Something in Matt's voice must have alerted René, because his eyes suddenly widened. "Forever?"

"You have a problem with that?"

"Um, yes, of course I do." René dropped his bag on the table and came over to him. "This is all very sudden. Want to tell me why?"

"I've made my decision," Matt said without emotion. "I want the archdemon powers." Might as well get something out of it. "If it means sleeping with Melaney, then so be it." He really didn't care.

"You what?" René's eyes almost popped out of his head. "Matt, she's your mother!"

"Well, I'm certainly not the only son she's had sex with." Matt shrugged. "Or daughter." Come to think of it, he was probably the only one who hadn't.

For some reason, René's face darkened. "You're not like your brothers and sisters. You're my son. And my son certainly won't be sleeping with his mother."

Anger flared in Matt. He wasn't going to let anyone order him around, least of all an aging human. "Who do you think you are, telling me what to do and what not to do?"

René remained remarkably calm. "Your father." He shook his head with a sigh. "What about Samantha? You're in love with her. Yesterday, you wanted to give her a garden."

"And I told you yesterday: it's not what you think."

"Yes, it is, Matt. I know you. I've seen you grow and develop and… you love that girl more than anything."

The anger grew and Matt took a threatening step forward. "You claim to know me? For a year and a half? Love." He snorted. "I had sex before I was ten. I killed someone before that."

René's voice tightened. "I know your upbringing was different, but you changed. It changed you."

Matt bristled. "No, you just want to believe I've changed." His lips curled into a cruel smile. "Because if I loved Samantha, you could hold on to the desperate hope that Melaney could ever have loved you." His father paled. Score. Time to drive the point home. "You think I haven't noticed? You're not forty yet, René. Fairly good-looking for a human, and a pretty decent one at that. Don't tell me you've never had a mother flirt with you or the neighbour downstairs. And yet you're still single and have been for as long as you've known her. The mother of your son left you almost eighteen years ago and you're still wishing she'd come back."

"Are you finished?" René asked, deceptively calmly.

"With this town? Absolutely." Suddenly he couldn't get away fast enough.

"You had a fight, Matt," René said coldly. "Normally people talk things out and make up, especially if it was all a misunderstanding in the first place. Or you spend the rest of your life running away from your feelings."

Matt shouldered his backpack. "I don't have any feelings." At least not for long.

Before he left town, there was one last visit he had to make. Quietly, he jumped straight into a corner of Samantha's room. She was sitting at her desk, talking to her mother. Matt knew better than to interrupt such an important moment.

"You're leaving," Samantha said in a hoarse voice. She'd probably cried again.

Her mother stroked her cheek. "I'm not leaving you. And you're welcome to come with me. Meg's thinking about it."

Matt held his breath for a moment. Leaving?

"I can't."

Juliane took a step back. "Because of the monsters." Samantha nodded. Even now she was thinking of other people. "And because of Dad, of course." Juliane shrugged dejectedly, as if she didn't care. "I know you two are close."

"Mum."

Her mother walked backwards to the door. "Don't overthink it, Sammy. This has nothing to do with you. And look, you'll be leaving the nest soon anyway, won't you?" She paused at the door. "Just promise me you'll be careful, okay?"

Samantha nodded, but as soon as her mother had closed the door, she burst into tears.

Unable to bear the sound, Matt cleared his throat, making her jump. "Matt!"

"I'm going back to Hell."

Samantha blinked, hastily wiping away her tears. "Forever?"

"Look, what happened at school—"

She didn't even give him a chance to explain, instead jumping out of her chair. "Matt, you're not well. These parasites are eating away at your soul."

Anger flared up again, but Matt fought it back. She was just telling it like it was. "I know. That's why I wanted to come and see you before it all goes to waste." Her eyes filled with tears again on his behalf. "You should know I'm sorry. About Cian, but mostly about your parents. It's all my fault."

Samantha swallowed hard. "You didn't set those parasites free."

"But Balthasar only did it because of me. I could've just come to him when he'd called, accepted his stupid offer." Why hadn't he done that? It had been a surprisingly good one. "Anyway, I'm sorry."

Suddenly he couldn't help himself. It was as if his body had a mind of its own. He took a step forward and wiped a tear from her cheek with his thumb.

"You can get through this, Sam," he said gently. "You're strong. Maybe the strongest person I've ever known." He forced a smile to his lips he didn't feel. "You've already overcome so much." Most of it his fault. "You'll survive this, too."

He gave her cheek another light rub and stepped back, ready to leave.

Just as he was about to disappear, Samantha staggered forward and threw her arms around him. Tears streaming down her cheeks, she held him so tightly he could barely move. "It's all *my* fault," she sobbed. "I never should've said it."

Matt didn't know what to do. He couldn't space jump to Hell with Samantha attached. She'd get herself killed. "Sam."

"You *have* a soul, Matt. And you have way more than a shred of humanity."

He shook his head. "No, you were right. A half-demon isn't much different from a demon in that respect."

"Stop this nonsense! You're here. With me."

"To say goodbye."

"Because it's important to you. Because *I* matter to you," Samantha insisted. "Even when your soul is being eaten away, you still care about me." She turned her tear-streaked face to him. "Please don't let the demon in you win."

The demon in him. As if there were two parts to his soul. Melchior and Matt. Melchior didn't love Samantha. He wouldn't have minded killing her right then and there. Or maybe snap her mother's neck for hurting her.

No... that was Matt. That anger because someone else had hurt the girl he... the girl he *loved,* that was all Matt. Because there weren't really any halves, no two voices in his head caught in eternal conflict. There was just him, a half-demon. Raised by demons, changed by humans. Especially this human girl.

And how he loved her for it. He liked the person he'd become under her tutelage, through all the pain and all the doubt, the misunderstandings and the inevitable messes he'd made. It hurt to be human. Just as much as it hurt to be half-demon. This was what he was now. What he wanted to be.

His whole body began to itch, as if an army of hellworms were crawling under his skin. Matt shuddered at the thought, just as the first one burst out of him. Not a worm, but a tiny insect. A soul parasite.

One by one, they left his body and dropped dead to the ground.

Samantha let go of him and looked around in amazement. "You defeated them. All by yourself."

"By myself?" Matt whispered. "You were here the whole time." His hands trembled as he placed them on her face, in awe of this woman who wouldn't give up on him even when he was at his worst. Then his lips touched hers. Softly, like the beating of a butterfly's wing.

A sigh escaped Samantha's mouth, causing Matt to step back. "Thank you."

One day he might do more than that—if she let him. For now, there was something else to do.

Balthasar

Balthasar was enjoying the company of a woman when he noticed a shadow behind the sheer curtains. Moments later, a sword cut through them, lashing down. In a fraction of a second, he leapt out of the way, crashing into a bench as he reappeared a few feet behind the bed.

In front of him, Matt had brought his sword down, cutting off half of his partner's long hair and burying his sword deep in the mattress. The woman did the only sensible thing and fled. Balthasar shuddered at the thought he'd been in the sword's path only moments before.

Matt turned and came at Balthasar again, nothing but anger in his eyes. Balthasar shot energy at him, but the younger one just swatted it away, making Balthasar wonder if he even knew what he was doing. What he was capable of.

"You came." Diplomacy was of the order where brute force wouldn't get him anywhere.

Unfortunately, Matt was in full Caspar mode and kept coming. Balthasar had no choice but to jump away again, leaving the sword to destroy the exquisitely crafted bench instead. This time, though, he aimed his jump and reappeared right behind Matt.

The half-demon was faster. He caught Balthasar with his shoulder and pushed him into the wardrobe. Moments later, the edge of his sword was at Balthasar's throat.

But he stopped there. *Silly half-human*, Balthasar thought. Matt could have run him through, and yet he didn't.

Instead, there was a lot of glowering and smouldering as his younger brother leant in. "If you touch Samantha again, if you hurt so much as a hair on her head, I'll cut your balls off and shove them down your throat."

"Charming," Balthasar replied. He had no doubt whatsoever that Matt would be physically capable of overpowering him now, but the threat fell flat through sheer lack of urgency. Caspar would have just gone through with it.

Matt only grunted and disappeared.

As soon as he was gone, Balthasar straightened up and massaged his shoulder, which had suffered the unfortunate fate of being shoved into a drawer. When he wiped his throat, his fingers came away bloody.

"Your girl ran past me."

Balthasar looked up to see Melaney at the door. "You want to take her place?" He did not like being rudely interrupted.

She sauntered into the room, running her fingers over the broken bench before turning to the bed. Instead of beckoning him closer, though, she fingered the cut in the curtains.

"Who's Samantha?"

"Ah." He knew where this was going. "You met her at his birthday party."

Melaney narrowed her eyes and thought back. "The missing girl he was looking for. She called him a monster, said she hated him."

Balthasar snorted. Humans were notoriously fickle with such statements. "Apparently, they made up. He loves her." Surprisingly, not that fickle in that regard.

As expected, Melaney's fingers clenched around the curtain. "He loves her?"

"As long as she exists, he'll never find his way into your bed." Balthasar sneered. "Perhaps it's time to reconsider your choice."

Melaney squinted at him. Then, without warning, she ripped the curtains from the ceiling and shoved them down onto the bed. A wave of power hit Balthasar, reminding him of what he'd gifted her back then. He could taste the threat in the air. If Melaney chose to kill him, there was nothing he could do.

"I've made my choice." Of course she had. "This Samantha will have to go."

Poor Samantha, Balthasar thought. He rather liked her—for a human. Not that it mattered. With Melaney's attention on her, her fate was as good as sealed.

Dramatis Personae

Family de Cerque

Lucille – 18, one of the Six, a witch and illusionist
  Bastien – Lucille's absentee father, a busy man
  Linda – Lucille's stepmother, a designer
  Pascal – 10, Lucille's adoptive brother, a telekinetic
  Cecille – dead, Lucille's witch grandmother, killed by the Archdemon of Wrath
  Alena – dead, Lucille's mother, died in a car crash
  Albert – the de Cerque butler, a mind reader
  Tobias – the de Cerque chauffeur

Family Kollmer

Samantha – 18, one of the Six, a witch and potion maker
  Meg – 17, Samantha's little sister and Jan's girlfriend, best friend of Anne
  Ben – Samantha's father, runs a car workshop with Joachim Bendtfeld
  Juliane – Samantha's mother, an aspiring actor
  Elda – Samantha's grandmother, the Greenvalley Witch, lives in the forest
  Erich – dead, Samantha's grandfather, a demon hunter

Family Bendtfeld

Fabian – 18, one of the Six, a water elemental mage
 Joachim – Fabian's father, runs a car workshop with Ben Kollmer
 Caroline – Fabian's mother, runs the Magic Circle, a magic shop
 Merle – the family cat

Family Hadden

Rachel – 18, one of the Six, a dreamwalker
 Nico – dead, Rachel's twin brother, appears in her dreams
 Annette – Rachel's mother, a hair stylist with an alcohol problem
 Mick – Rachel's father, a Maths professor, lives in LA

Family Kerscher

Jan – 20, one of the Six, a healer, works at the youth hostel
 Anne – 16, Jan's little sister
 Stefan – Jan's father, a coal miner
 Ida – Jan's mother, a nurse

Family Traidous and Matt's demon relatives

Matt/Melchior – 18, one of the Six, a half-demon of the House of Lust
 René– Matt's father, a former demon hunter and elementary school teacher
 Crumbs – the family dog
 Melaney – Matt's mother, a demon, the Archdemon of Lust

Balthasar – Matt's oldest brother, a demon of the Houses of Lust and Greed, leader of the Small Council

Caspar – Matt's older brother, a demon of the Houses of Wrath and Lust, Menuha's twin brother, the general of the Black Guard

Menuha – Matt's older sister, a demon of the Houses of Wrath and Lust, Caspar's twin sister

School

Alan – 19, part of the Elite Clique, son of the local police chief

Ani – 18, part of the Elite Clique, Samantha's former friend

Björn – 18, part of the Elite Clique, Jennifer's boyfriend

Cheryl – 18, the Greenvalley High Queen Bee, leader of the Elite Clique

Cian – 18, part of the Elite Clique, in love with Samantha

Mr Herbert – teaches Physics, hates Fabian

Jennifer – 19, part of the Elite Clique, Björn's girlfriend

Ophelia de la Vega – 16, Fabian's girlfriend, can speak to snakes

Mrs Renner – the Greenvalley High headmaster

Robert – 18, a friendly guy who follows the Six around

Shayna – 18, part of the Elite Clique, parents own an inn

Mr Zobel – The Six's tutor teacher, teaches Politics and German

Demons

Chay – "The Seer" a half-demon, Matt's best friend, can see the future

Dorian – dead, Melaney's ex-lover, father of the twins

Frennys – Melaney's lover

Hel – the Archdemon of Pride

Iyaga – the new Archdemon of Greed

Malcolm – dead, Melaney's brother, the former Archdemon of Greed

Moloch – the Archdemon of Gluttony

Pyke – the Archdemon of Envy
Selima – dead, the previous Archdemon of Lust
Shenecra "Shenny" Delandeva – Stormbride, Caspar's second-in-command
Volac – the Archdemon of Wrath
Yash – the Archdemon Sloth

Others

Alecto – dead, an old mage and mentor of Caspar
Daniel – dead, Samantha's ex-boyfriend
Enrico de la Vega – 22, Ophelia's older brother, a cultist
Eresta – priestess of the Snakes of Ishtar
Herl Winter – dead, Jeyne's father, mayor
Hugo von Hohenstetten – an old-fashioned ghosts
Mr Jensen – a realtor
Jeyne Winter – a dead girl from another world
Jonathan Blackstone – dead, a writer, previous owner of the Blackstone House
Max Schönborn – a TV actor
Neve – a snow witch, occupies Blackstone House
Philipp Vendenberg – Lucille's boyfriend, a reporter for the Greenvalley View
Sokaris – dead, an Egyptian mage